ENCHANTMENT OF THORNS

SHANA J. CALDWELL

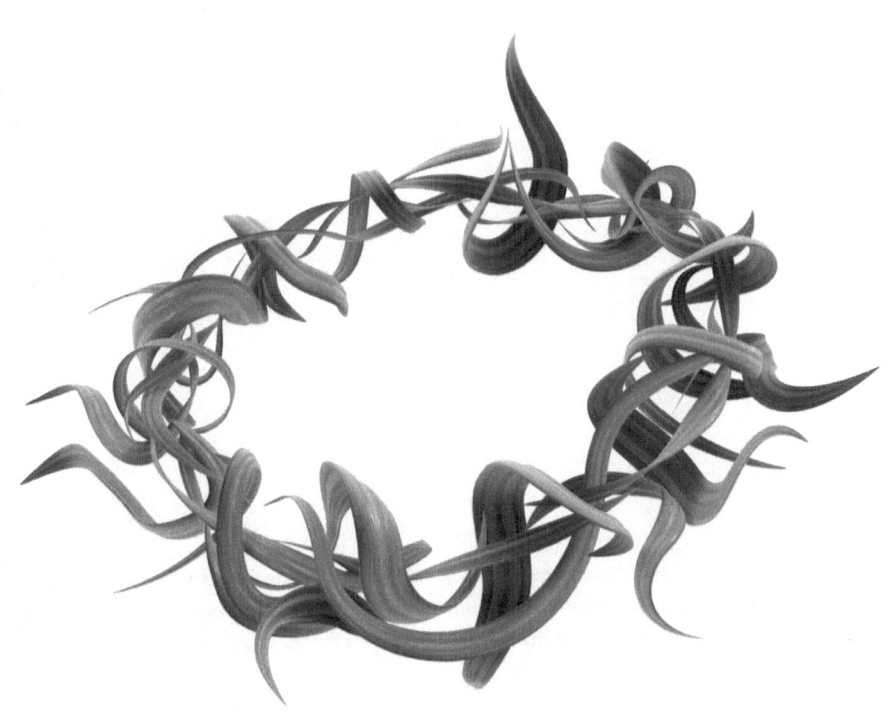

Cover Designer: coverdungeonrabbit (Frankziska Stern)
Interior Formatter: The Nutty Formatter
ISBN: 978-0-6455788-0-5

CHAPTER 1

Black and grey clouds begin to gather in the sky, their darkness leaking and spreading across the light blue as rain beings to gather in their depths. A cool breeze nips at my cheeks as I continue to stare, watching in awe as blue streaks of electricity light up the darkness. From the balcony of the castle, I can see the small village of Elderview nestled between the large sloping mountain walls on both sides which are coated in snow from the harrowing winter. I lean against the stone ledge and sigh, clasping my cheeks in both hands.

"Amaryllis, are you out on the balcony again?" A warm, soothing voice calls for me from inside. My mouth twitches into a smile at my mother's words. More often than not she found me on the balcony, lost in my own thoughts.

"I'll be inside soon," I call back with no real conviction, *soon* could be five minutes from now or five hours.

A delicate chuckle meets my ears. "Dinner will be ready in five minutes. Come in before it begins to rain, we don't want you catching a cold."

I can't help but smile now as her light footsteps retreat deeper into our home, no doubt going to find my father in the kitchen. I'd been blessed with the two best parents a girl could

1

ask for; an amazing mother who has been nurturing and caring from the moment I'd opened my eyes and my father, a protector and supporter in everything I do. Not once have I ever been met with resistance in anything I asked, or anything I did. If I wanted to go and spend time with my grandparents in Elderview they wouldn't bat an eye, just send me down with a basket of baked goods.

Thunder echoes in the mountain gully, a song to my ears. Wild droplets of rain begin to spatter on my arms, the wind grabs at my dress and hair demandingly. I sigh and push back from the railing, glancing once more to the sky before heading into my room. I shut the door firmly behind me, drowning out the sharp noises from the storm.

I lean against the door as I look around my bedroom, the white carpet is a nice contrast against the cobblestone walls and my large white duvet queen bed that sits against the wall to my right. I walk over to the vanity that sits across from my bed and take a seat, taking the golden hairbrush in my hand.

As I drag it through the knots that had gathered from the day, I cautiously I take a chance to look at my reflection in the three mirrors. It's almost like looking at a stranger as I sit here, brush paused mid-way down the dark raven locks that just reach my shoulders, clasped by a pale hand.

Round, doe eyes stare back at me; their violet depths turning a light lilac closest to the pupil. My father's eyes, if I'd been blessed with anything it had been his eyes. My heart shaped face is pale, save for the pink tinge to my cheeks and button nose from being in the cold weather. My pale red cupid bow lips are turned down at the corners, painting a picture of sadness.

I force myself to look away and hastily brush the rest of the knots out, I can't pinpoint the exact moment when I began to sour seeing what I did in the mirror. My mother and father always reassured me how beautiful I am, that I had nothing to be concerned about. But I *am*. I know that I'd been blessed with the features I have, but I could never say that. Admit to that out loud. There are things I would change in a heartbeat if I could, will them away and never think of them again. My appearance isn't the only distasteful thing about me.

I stand and sit the brush back down. I slide my hands into the hidden pockets of my pale blue dress as I leave my room and dark thoughts behind. Lanterns are lit in the large hallway, leaving no room for shadows as I head for the grand stairs that lead down to the main area of the castle.

I'd lived in here my entire life, save for the holidays at my grandparents. I know where every nook and cranny are, where the perfect hiding places are. My father had lived in this castle at some point in his life, I'd been told of the adventures he and my mother took before I'd come along. Even after years and years together, they still looked at each other with adoration in their eyes.

I doubt I'd ever find that.

I step into the large open expanse, wind and rain belt against the two large wooden front doors and glass windows. The lanterns flicker and dance but don't leave us in darkness. I follow the sounds of voices through the living room to my right and down another hall. When I enter the dining room, dinner has already been served, steam wafts off the roast chicken and vegetables that sit in the middle of the table as I take my seat.

"So, how is the storm?" Father asks, grinning around his glass of wine. His dark green tunic is creased from the long day he's had helping mother around the castle, unbuttoned and hanging slightly down his front. I smile before cutting into a piece of chicken.

"Very storm like, this is the first one all winter. I wanted to watch it approach." I say before filling my mouth with the warm meat.

Mother begins to cut up her own meal, "It's been a quiet winter, which is strange enough."

"When they hit, they hit hard," Father mutters, sitting his glass down and wiping the back of his hand over his lips.

"Do they all have blue lightning?" I ask. His hand falters on the glass and wine threatens to slosh over the rim as he looks up at me with widened eyes. Mother goes still beside me. I frown, confused at the tension gathering in the room, "What? Why are you looking at me like that?"

"This isn't good," Mother says urgently, looking to Father with *fear* in those steel grey eyes. He reaches out and takes her hand, squeezing reassuringly.

"It's gotten worse, but we can deal with it. There's nothing to fear Rav." He reaches out to tuck a strand of black hair behind her pointed ear.

"Can one of you explain what the hell this is about?" I demand, sitting my cutlery down. Mother turns her eyes to me and softens, reaching out for my own hand. I grasp it, surprised by her strength.

"There's been...a hiccup in Faerie. Your father's been dealing with it and working with the others to fix it. This storm just signifies it's getting stronger than we thought."

Her words are gibberish to my ears. They'd never taken me to Faerie, where father had been born and raised. My parents had been an odd couple; my mother was once human but risked her own life to defeat an evil that polluted Elderview with the help of my father long before my time. Her human soul had been intertwined with my father's faerie mother's soul and once she took the leap she returned as a faerie. She'd told me of brief visits there but had never elaborated. It had annoyed me at first, but once I realised they had no intention of taking me *home* I had pushed it aside and focused on better things.

"Your mother's right, I'll have to leave and meet with the others once the rain calms." Father closes his eyes and lets out a deep breath, massaging the bridge of his nose. I steady my breathing, feeling the anxiety wanting to claw its way up my throat. For months he'd been coming to and fro, sometimes taking mother with him and other times leaving her behind. He never told me what he'd been doing there, and tonight is the most truth I'd received from either of them.

"Can I help in some way? What's the problem?" I ask, looking between them. Mother frowns slightly, tugging her bottom lip between her teeth.

"Honey, it's more complicated than that. What your father does there takes a great amount of power and energy. It's not as simple as just going and solving it," Mother says softly, running her thumb over the top of my hand.

I stiffen in my seat, feeling my back straighten, "I would know more if you actually *told* me things."

"Ama you know we would tell you if we could," Father says, his pleading eyes begging me to understand. That sour feeling returns to my stomach for the second time tonight, I may be a lot of things but I'm no fool.

"Then why can't you?"

My question is greeted with heavy silence; I nod my head a few times and unclasp my hand from my mothers. The silence tells me everything I need to know. I rise from the table, clenching my jaw tight so I can't say anything I'll regret. I'm fed up with being left in the darkness, but I could never hurt my parents with my poisonous words or thoughts.

"With time I will tell you, but tonight is not the night. There's still too much danger and I will not put you in harm's way if I have a choice. I know you're not happy, but you will have to put up with it until then." His tone leaves no room for argument and as he stares up at me with unreadable eyes, I feel myself deflate.

"If you see anything abnormal or strange, please tell either of us." Mother says softly, still holding fathers' hand.

"Okay." I break eye contact and turn, leaving the room at a brisk pace. Thunder booms and lightning crackles reach my delicate ears as I move through the hallway. Most storms are violent, especially because we're high up in the gully but tonight the air feels...different. It hangs heavy with anticipation for *something*.

I round into the living room as a loud crack fills the space around me. I squeal and press my hands to my ears as I squeeze my eyes shut. My heart gallops in my chest, threatening to break its cage. The storm is close, too close. Fear ignites low in my stomach, I peel my eyes open and take hurried steps to the stairs; not liking the openness of the room anymore.

I'm one move away from reaching the first step when the front doors fly open inwards. I scream and stumble backwards, landing hard on my ass as my hand flies to my mouth. Rain and wind invade the open area as the lanterns flicker.

Three dark, tall figures step in from the storm and into the light. Their black hoods hide their faces, the one on the right and left turn and shut the doors against the battle of the storm. The middle one stays deathly still; the darkness of the hood is focused solely on me.

I press my hand to my heart, feeling it beating underneath the thin material of my dress. I am okay. I brush the stray strands of hair from my face, never taking my eyes from the hooded figures.

"What on earth is going on?" My father's voice fills the air around us as he and my mother enter the room. She looks as bewildered as I do.

The two hooded figures that closed the doors pull back their hoods, they're faeries. My father relaxes immediately, striding towards them. I watch as he and the hooded figure embrace, the cloak pulls back and reveals a hunting knife strapped to their muscular thigh.

"It's good to see you friend." The male's deep voice is as smooth as honey as he pulls away, holding my father at arms-length.

"As it is for me. What are you doing here this late?" my father asks.

"It's Faerie."

The room is thrown into silence as they all stand there, the other two males look to me expectantly. I scowl, pushing myself up from where I'd fallen. Of course, the *adults* can't talk while I'm in the room. Absolute nonsense.

"Gentleman, this is my daughter, Amaryllis," my father says, stepping out of the man's hands. They all look to me now where I stand on legs threatening to shake under the weight of their stares. I still can't see the face of the man that had embraced my father.

"Hi," I say through clenched teeth, my small smile is strained.

"I'm Hemlock," the blonde faerie says, his bright green eyes asses me for any threats. When he realises there's none, he breaks into an easy dazzling smile. His hair sits flat against his head and reaches the tips of his shoulders, drenched. He gestures to the other one who watches me carefully.

"I'm Odin," he says smoothly, his deep chocolate brown eyes trail over me once before looking towards my father, "the resemblance is uncanny." The deep brown locks of hair curl across his forehead, temples and base of his neck.

My father chuckles, "Yes, yes it is."

I look away from the two gorgeous males and stare at the hooded one. His broad shoulders are tense; the fabric of his cloak sits tightly against the weapons strapped underneath. He reaches up two scar covered hands and slowly lowers the hood as he watches me.

My heart stops and stutters in my chest as my breath is sucked from me. He's...the most beautiful male I'd ever laid my eyes on.

His honey golden eyes swirl with distaste as his eyes skim over my slender willowy figure, leaving me feeling stark naked in front of him and flushed from head to toe. Deep copper hair is pulled half up in a bun with long strands framing his high cheek bones and square face that's been freshly shaved. The rest is down and hanging limp over his muscular chest, reaching his waist. His olive skin is dark in the contrast of the lanterns.

"Eleazar."

I cross my arms over my chest, his eyes track every movement.

"Amaryllis."

"I know." His deep voice is rough as he copies my gesture, looking far more regal. I feel myself wanting to scowl, my cheeks flush with heat as we stare at each other. I refuse to cower under his gaze or feel embarrassed by repeating my name.

Mother's voice breaks the tension, "They're close friends of your father's."

Eleazar looks back to my father, dismissing me entirely. The...the *nerve*.

"There's been an incident with our...prisoner." His voice is all formality now, my father's eyes flicker to where I stand and back to him. He nods once in understanding. Frustrated, I turn and begin to stomp up the stairs, holding the skirts of my dress in both hands.

"It's fine, don't worry about your *vulnerable daughter* hearing any precious conversation." I throw the words over my shoulder as I disappear onto the second floor. I lean against the closest wall and will my heart to slow. That...that man is breathtaking. Why had my father never let me meet any of his friends before?

Most likely because I would have this reaction.

I strain my ears and listen as their footsteps head deeper into the castle, I'm tempted to follow but being stealthy is not my best skill set. Instead, I push from the wall and head into the safety of my room. I close the door behind me and walk over to where the balcony doors rattle. A small part of me wants to rebel.

I rest my hands on the metal handles, *feeling* the urgency and energy in the air. If only I could consume it, harness it to my will. I know I have magic; my mother is a seer and my father holds faerie magic. I'd never witnessed him use it, but I can sense it under his skin.

I let go with a sigh and decide to bathe instead, getting ready to sleep. *If* I happen to overhear anything on the way to the bathroom, well I guess I can't help that. I gather my deep blue silk nightgown and rush from my room; once I reach the bottom of the stairs, I ease myself into a light walk.

My ears pick up their soft voices coming from deep in the castle, no doubt my father's meeting room for formal events. A room I had never laid my eyes on in twenty-two years. The bathroom is still a stretch away from the large room, I gather my courage. I walk down the red-carpet hallway that leads straight to the room, it's a dead end. The room opens up and in front of me two large arched doors are sealed tightly. Two wolves are carved on both sides, rearing up on their back legs and their front paws meeting in the middle while flames flicker around them.

A lantern flickers off the wall on either side, throwing shadows around the circular room. I'd never before in my life felt the need to eavesdrop, but after the brief conversation tonight I am itching to know more. I make my steps light as I take small, calculated steps towards the door, they'd know I'm out here. No faerie would *not* hear me if I'm not careful.

I reach the stone wall beside the door and press myself into it, I lean my head towards the door as I strain my hearing. The voices are muffled. I hold in my frustration as I ease closer to the door until I'm pressed flush against the wood.

"...danger..."

"...reinforce the barrier..."

I'm only catching words, but I have to assure myself it's better than nothing.

"...powerless..."

"...the key..."

"...kill the c..."

All voices abruptly stop. I freeze, wide eyed. I don't have time to process what I'd overheard; if anyone opens this door, I am dead. No room for argument. I step back from the door, holding my breath. I turn and spider-walk to the hallway, once my bare feet reach the flush red carpet I hurry towards the bathroom; heart beating erratically in my chest.

I open the wooden door to the bathroom, thankful to find the lantern burning brightly. The white marble stone tub sits against the far wall in front of me, the golden shower head is angled directly above it. I don't hesitate as I rid myself of my dirty clothes and begin to run the hot water, I grab the wad of honey soap and slide into the tub, letting my hair hang over the edge as I stretch in the spray of the water.

I close my eyes as I begin to scrub my body gently,

breathing in the deep aroma of honey. My thoughts drift mindlessly as I relax, in these moments I have a scarce reprieve. No dark thoughts can find me here, corrupt me.

Once I've thoroughly washed every part of soft skin I rinse. What had they meant, the key, powerless? Whose power had they been talking about? Reinforcements? It all sounds like a riddle and I've never been good at solving them. I step out of the tub, leaving a puddle trail as I wrap a white wool towel around my body. The urge to sleep begins to claw at the edges of my mind, waiting to drag me under. I pull the silk gown over my head, throwing my dirty clothes and undergarments into the basket beside the door.

I open the door and yawn, shivering as a cool breeze bites at my bare legs. The gown cuts off mid-thigh, revealing my slender legs. It hugs my small waist and wide hips almost devilishly, although no one in the male species has ever seen me so bare.

I'm about to walk towards the front of the castle when suddenly a warm body encases me against the cold stone wall, the bite of a blade rests under my chin as an arm is leaning against the wall beside my head, trapping me. I draw in a breath as I arch my back from the cold, only to find myself pressing up against someone very warm, even with a blade pressed to my throat it ignites me. He smells of spiced rum and honey, it's mouth-watering.

"Why were you listening to a private conversation?" Eleazar's top lip is peeled back from his teeth, exposing his canines. I press my hands against the stone wall behind me to keep my balance, I lick my lips to talk but the blade stops me. I raise an eyebrow in annoyance.

He pulls it back an inch, giving me room to talk.

"Don't you think the knife is rather *dramatic*?" I grumble. His eyes dance with fire.

"Don't you think it's rather rude to invade other's privacy?" he snaps back.

I meet his eyes as I scowl, "Don't you think it's rather depressing to be kept in the dark from everything?"

"Your father means well. You shouldn't question the things he does."

I roll my eyes, letting out a huff, "Right, well try being in my shoes and then you can say that. I can't help growing restless and curious, it's in my nature."

"You'd make a terrible spy." He withdraws the blade and it disappears into the sleeve of his shirt, his eyes flicker over my face before realisation sets in at how close we are. His nostrils flare, his pupils dilate slightly. I raise my chin in defiance.

"You'd make a terrible murderer," I say back, feeling breathless. He steps away from me, practically landing on the other side of the hall. I push off from the wall and rub my arms, missing the warmth he'd been giving me. Goosebumps break out along my skin.

"If I wanted you dead, you wouldn't have even had a chance to blink."

"You're right, that small blade was so convincing." I let the sarcasm drip into every word as I look at him and level my eyes on his face.

"I have larger blades," he growls, leaning back against the wall as his arms cross over his chest. His hair had begun to dry now, curling slightly at the ends. He'd lost his coat, exposing the twin swords that peek over the back of his shoulders; the hunting knives strapped to both of his thighs. His chest is bare of any weapon, but from what I had felt moments ago he is a weapon in himself. I have no doubt in my mind he could do exactly what he's saying.

"I can see that, I do have two eyes," I state, flickering them to the handles above his shoulders.

"What are you doing this far into the castle, or were you truly trying to eavesdrop?" he asks, his voice slightly less menacing than before.

"I came and had a bath if you must know. I may have taken the wrong hallway briefly. But I realised my mistake and turned around." I gesture to my night attire; no doubt I look ready to crawl into bed and sleep. His eyes yet again make my skin seem to glow as he takes me in, lingering at the hem of the nightgown before snapping back to my face. There's that beautiful scowl again.

"I can see that, I do have two eyes." He mocks me, pushing off from the wall. I feel myself grow angry, though over what I'm not sure. I take a step forward.

"Then why ask you...you..." I struggle to find any form of insult, "you pointed ear buffoon."

I catch the hint of a smile grace his lips for a rare moment before it's gone again.

"What did you overhear?"

"That's none of your business," I snap, staring up at him in defiance as he takes another step forward. This close I can feel the heat radiate from him and a small part of me wants to cocoon myself to him.

"It was a conversation you shouldn't have heard at all. Nyx doesn't know that I've tracked you down to ask, but I assume they might question you tomorrow about it." His eyes stare daggers at me. I cross my arms over my chest.

"All I heard was words, something about danger, reinforcements, power." I rattle a few words off, looking at him pointedly. He nods a few times as I talk, eyes flickering over my face.

"Good. Nothing of importance." His eyes flicker down the hallway that leads deeper into the castle before focusing back on me. I hear the vague sound of footsteps approaching.

"Well, we wouldn't want them to catch you fraternizing

with me now, would we?" I tilt my head to the side slightly, my hair brushes over my shoulder at the movement. He steps back, putting a healthy expanse of air between us.

"If this is what you call fraternizing it's rather sad..." he looks down his nose at me, "you're not quite my type. Too snappy."

His words bite at me, ripping the small smile from my face. "Trust me, an arrogant fae male isn't *my type* either. I'd rather... I'd rather eat dirt than ever fraternize with the likes of you." Before he can reply and before my downright embarrassment and horror can set in that I'd just failed miserably to insult one of my father's friends, I tuck my hair behind my ears and turn sharply and begin to storm down the hall.

I don't bother looking over my shoulder, already knowing if I did I would find those guarded honey eyes trained on me.

CHAPTER 2

I'm on my balcony when my mother finds me the next morning, I sit on the ledge with my back pressed to the stone foundation and let my left leg dangle while I write in my notebook. Being the only child and only having the freedom to venture to Elderview, I had to find things to keep myself entertained. Writing wicked stories turned out to be my favourite pass time. I look up from where I sit and watch her walk to the ledge, she rests her hands on the edge and sighs.

My mother has always been soft, especially for me and my father. I'd never heard the details of how they met or what had happened. She studies the village below us as she gets lost in thought. I follow her line of concentration, the storm has no doubt left Elderview a muddy mess but the trees seem to be greener; the sky seems almost *too* blue.

"I want to apologise for last night," she finally says, keeping her eyes trained on the landscape. I feel my defence begin to come up again and try and battle it down, my mother hardly opened up to me about these things.

"It's okay. Nothing I'm not used to," I mumble, looking back down to my page of half scribble. I tap my pen against the paper, the story I'd been writing is temporarily lost on me.

"But that's the problem. You're used to it. When I was your

age or there about I hated being left in the dark. I hated being the last to know things so I took it into my own hands to change my fate." I feel her eyes on me now, no doubt seeing herself in me. I stay silent, letting her continue.

"Your father and I met under weird circumstances, but I wouldn't change it for the world. He wouldn't open up to me at the start, so I went and did my own hunting and research. I'm stubborn when I want to know something, and he eventually came around..." she pauses, I look up to see her lost in memory. "The night we defeated the Babunook I deceived him, like any human would for someone they loved. I trapped him in a faerie circle using his True name so he wouldn't be able to escape. I had what I needed to kill the creature, even though it meant giving my soul away for it."

I go still, my pen long forgotten. I'd never heard this. A breeze stirs my hair, tickling my cheek. My mother smiles softly before looking back out over the landscape. She grips the stone ledge with force, her knuckles turning white.

"Mother, if you don't want to talk about it..." I trail off, biting down on my bottom lip. She waves a delicate hand in the air, her golden wedding ring glints in the light.

"It was a long time ago now and I have nothing to regret. I'd been fighting the creature and it had me pinned to the ground, I could hear Nyx crying and screaming for me but he was powerless. I angled the stake and as the creature went for the killing blow, I did as well." She smiles softly. "My soul awoke on the edge of the clearing, I'd done it. The spell had been broken. The creature's body disappeared above me and your father came rushing over. Across the clearing the creature waited for me, there's only darkness and death where they go."

"*Mum—*"

"Nyx's mother's soul was intertwined with mine, she came and we spoke briefly and she took my place in death; sent my soul tumbling right back into my body and when I returned I was changed. A faerie. You can imagine how hard it was for me being human for so long, to being near immortal." She looks to me now; grey eyes fierce.

"Why are you telling me this?"

"Because there's a creature in Faerie that is destroying the land and killing the occupants. Your father and his men are trying their hardest to contain the problem but it's more difficult than they thought. They've contained the last one, but it's growing stronger and their containment is growing weaker."

"So, what are you saying?" I lean forward slightly, clutching my notebook in my hands.

"I'm saying I see myself in you, but I'm also saying you don't have the second chance of life hanging over you like I did." Her eyes soften now, "Your father wants to protect you from this because we may not be as lucky as I was. We love you more than anything in this world and beyond and it would destroy us if anything ever happened to you..." she trails off as she comes closer and holds one of my hands in her own.

"But I'm also saying that I trust you and have faith in you and I know you crave adventure. Your father's friends are still here and they will be for a few days while they plan their next course of action." My cheeks begin to heat at the mention of his friends. Mother smirks.

"They are rather nice looking, aren't they?" she muses.

"I don't know what you're talking about." I feel myself beginning to grin, unable to deceive her.

"I've known them for quite some time now and I swear Eleazar has always been a prickly pear." She chuckles to herself, shaking her head slightly. She'd pinned her long black hair back in waves using golden star clasps.

"I like him the..." I try to say least, but my mouth betrays me. I scowl, unable to say that I don't like him at all. In the slightest. Mother grins at me, winking.

"He has that effect on the females, I'd say it's the looks over his personality."

"Yes well he has the personality of a grizzly bear, complete and utter ass." I grin, hoping my words reach his ears. Mother lets go of my hands and steps back, she wears nice fitted deep brown pants matched with a loose fitted white long sleeve shirt. Only she could pull off such an outfit.

"He means well for most part. The other two are far warmer than him I assure you. How would you feel about heading into Elderview to see the family? I'm sure Kalin would value the company." She smiles softly, knowing I'd never say no to a visit. I sigh in defeat and hop down from the ledge.

"Have the baked goods ready, I need to change into something mud resistant." She follows me inside, humming to herself as she leaves my room. I rummage through the draws of my vanity and pull out an outfit near identical to my mother's. Black leather pants with a loose, pale green short sleeved shirt. I change quickly, pulling on my brown leather boots. I tuck the shirt in as I leave my room, feeling free to move with less grace than when I'm wearing a dress.

I reach the bottom of the stairs and wait patiently, picking at my nails. I look up to the sound of approaching footsteps and mother appears with no one other than Eleazar following behind her. He doesn't bother with any form of greeting, opting to step back with arms crossed over his chest. He keeps his eyes focused on anything but me.

I take the brown basket from mother, the aroma of cinnamon and apple reach my nose causing my stomach to grumble. "I hope you baked an extra one for my trip."

"You know I always do. Eleazar is going to accompany you," she smiles sweetly, clasping her hands in front of her. I nearly drop the basket, feeling my mouth fall open. She frowns, "Don't look so sullen, he's been a prickle in everyone's side this morning so the fresh air should be good for him."

"You speak of me as though I'm not standing four steps away," he grumbles, looking to my mother. She looks over her shoulder, raising an eyebrow at him; an open challenge to defy her. He sighs and finally looks at me.

"He won't be a problem, now go. Have fun, tell everyone I send my love." She waves her hands towards the door before turning and leaving the way she'd come. We stand there staring at each other, the silence thickens as I recall our conversation last night. I turn and head for the door before he can see my cheeks heat. I hold the basket in the crook of my elbow as I open the wooden doors, breathing in the fresh air.

Vines had weaved their way over the stone railing of the cobblestone porch over the years, small bright purple flowers now bloom from the recent rain. Early morning sun beats down on the forest surrounding the castle and the stone steps that descend. I pay Eleazar no mind as I begin to take the steps as fast as my feet allow without threatening to slip on the small puddles.

I hear him follow in silence, his steps as light as a feather.

Once I reach the ending of the stairs the once firm dirt is slick, I slow down as I begin to follow the path into the forest. The tall trees shelter most of the path from the sun, although a few streaks here and there keep it well lit. I hum a soft tune to myself as I reach into the basket, pulling out the promised muffin for the journey.

"So, what were you doing this morning to be punished with babysitting the child?" I ask before taking a bite of the muffin, not bothering to glance over my shoulder at him. I know he's heard me, I can hear the mud suctioning to his boots.

"I'm surprised you weren't listening to private conversations that don't concern you again."

"I had better things to do this morning. Clearly you weren't that important if you're with me right now and not back there." I shrug a shoulder, biting into the muffin again. The forest ahead clears and opens up to a large circle expanse of mud and dead grass. In the middle sits a forgotten throne chair, mud and leaves cover the stone surface. Before my time my grandfather would make the village people bring him offerings and this is where the ceremony would take place.

I walk around the chair and pick up speed, we're close to the village now.

We spend the rest of the walk in silence, every now and then I take a chance and look over my shoulder to Eleazar; he has a scowl permanently etched onto his face. I can almost see how the villagers are going to take his presence. I smile as chatter reaches our ears, we leave the forest and approach the middle of Elderview. Most children are in school and most adults are working hard, no doubt trying to fix any damage after last night's storm.

"Try not to scare the people here," I whisper as we reach the crowd, I slow down until we're walking in pace together. I don't look up to see if he'd followed my instruction, I nod politely to the people who do say hello. It was always a treat coming down and visiting everyone, I'd made a friend here and there.

"Princess! It's good to see you again," Colt's shout reaches my ear as he pushes his way through the crowd, he grins as it breaks apart. His black hair sits in waves around his face, curling at the ends. His blue eyes shine as he looks me over. "Looking as good as always."

"Princess?" Eleazar mutters, I look up to see him studying Colt; reminding me much of a wolf studying a lamb. I slap his arm lightly before smiling back to Colt. He finally comes to a stop in front of us, wiping his palms on his faded brown pants. His long sleeved shirt is rolled up to his elbows; the top three buttons are undone and show a glimpse of dark hair.

I'd met Colt when I'd been seven and he'd just turned six. Mother always arranged play dates for us when we were younger. As my visits became less frequent we fell out of touch, but for the last few years I'd made the effort to find him whenever I visited.

"Morning Colt, it's good to see you as well." I tuck a strand of hair behind my ear, smiling softly.

"What brings you down from the castle?" he asks, looking between me and Eleazar.

"Just visiting the family for the day, mother thought it was a brilliant idea to bring a body guard with me." I gesture to Eleazar before grabbing onto the basket again. Colt smiles as he offers him his hand.

I suck in my cheeks as Eleazar continues to look at him, not bothering with the handshake. I groan internally.

"Ah, nice to meet you then." Colt says, bringing his hand back to his side.

"Sorry but we best be off, if I see you on the way out I'll stop," I offer. He rubs the back of his neck but smiles softly at me.

"Of course, be safe princess." He winks before blending back into the crowd. I feel a small blush cover my cheeks, for a human he is rather attractive. I couldn't say if the attraction was mutual or not though. I continue walking through the crowd, paying attention to nothing.

We reach the slope at the edge of the village that takes us to my grandparent's home. I clasp the basket tightly in my hands as the ground turns uneven beneath my feet. Wind bites at my bare arms as we make the trip down, there's nothing to shield us from it. Once my grandparent's cream home comes into sight I jog the rest of the way, basket swinging madly.

I hop over the gate with ease and dash up the steps, I knock on the door a few times before scraping the mud from my boots with the stick they keep leaning against the wall. Eleazar opens the gate and strolls up, he takes the stick from me once I'm finished and joins me on the porch. He takes up most of the space as he leans over and scrapes his boots off. I fight off the urge to push him down the few stairs, knowing if I did he'd make revenge hell for me.

The door creaks open as my grandfather answers, white streaks his dull black hair as he pushes the screen door open for us. He smiles, the wrinkles on his forehead and around his eyes crinkle as he opens his arms for me.

"Hi pop," I mumble as I lean down and step into his embrace, careful not to knock him with the basket.

"I was wondering when you'd come back and visit, grandmas been nagging me for days now." He chuckles as he pulls back, his blue eyes shine with delight. I gesture to where Eleazar stands beside us.

"This is Eleazar, my personal escort for the day."

Pop reaches out a hand, to my shock Eleazar takes it and gives him a firm shake. "It's nice to see you again."

I look between the both of them with raises brows, "Wait, you know each other?"

"When Ravynne and Nyx brought us back from our adventures they'd always have a warm meal waiting for us," Eleazar says, letting go of Pop's hand. I lower my brows into a frown, feeling slightly jealous.

"Come now, Grandma's cooking some lunch up for us." Pop turns and walks into the house, I follow after and pull my boots off. The small house is warm from the crackling fire, I look into the lounge room to see my niece sleeping peacefully on the faded yellow couch.

I turn around to see Eleazar taking a seat at the table, Pop takes a seat beside him. I walk in and sit the basket in the middle of the table, grandma stirs something on the stove and hums softly to herself. I walk over and wrap my arms around her small waist; resting my head on her shoulder. I'm taller than all of my human family, taking after my father, so whenever I want to hug them I have to slightly bend down.

"Mmm what are you cooking?" I ask, breathing in the hearty aroma.

"Pumpkin soup, your favourite," Grandma says, resting her weathered cheek on my head.

"Where's Kalin?" I ask. "I see Emilia is asleep."

Grandma chuckles, shaking her head, "He's out the back doing the crops, she'd been helping him this morning but came inside for a nap. I think he works her too hard."

"Of course," I laugh lightly as I let her go. I reach up into the cupboard and pull down four white chipped mugs.

"How was the journey?" Grandma asks, looking over to where I make us all a cup of tea. I look to her and pause, her green eyes are dull today. I nibble my lip and look back to the cups, mother had told me many moons ago grandma was sick and that there wasn't anything we could do for her.

"It was fine, Mother sent down some muffins for you all and she sends her love." I pull the cup of cream from the cold box and put a dollop in each cup. I grab two and walk to the table, setting them down for Pop and Eleazar.

I keep my hand on his mug as he reaches for it, he looks up to me and arches a brow in annoyance as his eyes narrow.

"I made this one extra sweet, you could use some sweetening," I say smoothly as I let go.

"I'm refraining from replying because we're in good

company." He grabs the mug and takes a sip, staring at me the entire time. I roll my eyes at him and grab the basket from the table, I sit it beside the entryway and help grandma dish up the bowls of soup. I place the bowls down and help her sit, once she's seated I make quick work of putting the leftovers away and washing up the few dishes.

"Come girl, you must be hungry. You're skinner than the last time I saw you," Grandma scolds, looking over her shoulder at me. I smile apologetically, kissing her on the forehead before I sit down.

"Have they been feeding you in that castle or do you need some time down here to fatten you up?" Pop says, pumpkin soup leaks from his lips as he takes a mouthful. I hide my horror with an easy smile, brushing their comments aside.

"Nonsense, of course I'm well fed." I fill my mouth with soup, stopping the conversation. I feel Eleazar's eyes on me but pay him no attention, at this point I'd be more than welcoming if the earth could open up and swallow me whole.

"Are you just visiting for the day?" Grandma asks.

"Yeah I thought I'd come down and bring some baked goods and say hello to everyone." I say, swirling my spoon around the thick deep orange sludge.

"Make sure you see Kalin before you leave, he'll be disappointed if you don't," Pop says, scraping the remains of the soup into his mouth. Eleazar eats in silence, his large form takes up most of the table and I feel myself smile. It seems so normal to be here eating with my family even though he's here.

On cue the front door opens, I drop my spoon and stand. Kalin comes down the hall, running a hand through his black hair; wet with sweat. His green eyes find mine and widen in delight. He closes the distance between us and crushes me into a hug, I laugh as he swirls me around once.

"Stop it you buffoon, you stink!" I say once I've managed to stop laughing, he sits me down and grins.

"This is the stink of hard work, not that you'd know."

I slap his arm playfully, smiling wickedly at him, "For the record I've offered to come and help your crops on multiple occasions."

He throws his arm over my shoulder and pulls me down to his level as he ruffles my hair, "You know I don't want any boys in town to be perving on my niece, I have enough trouble keeping Colt away from you."

"Oh stop it, he means no harm." I grumble, feeling my cheeks heat. Eleazar watches the exchange, his lips twitch upwards into a smile.

"That's the problem, they're the ones you need to be extra careful of."

He lets me go and takes my seat at the table, leaving me standing there flustered with messy hair. I run my hands through it and shoot him daggers with my eyes. He shakes his head and leans back in his seat, crossing his arms over his chest. We'd come down a few months ago to celebrate his fortieth birthday with his wife and child, they'd moved in with my grandparents once they learnt grandma was sick. Martha, his wife, had taken over grandma's bakery in town to help support them.

"I can assure you he isn't a problem, there's nothing wrong with being friends with someone who isn't a female." I cross my arms over my chest as he looks up at me, his tan skin is covered in dirt and grime. His square jaw is covered in a rough gingering beard, his green eyes identical to his mother's.

"Yeah well I'm sure he's more than a pretty face."

"There's nothing wrong with that." I look to Eleazar, finding my eyes following the arch of his nose and down over the curve of his lips to run along his jaw. He'd worn his hair how he'd had it last night, the copper strands slightly wavy. He looks over to me and makes eye contact, his golden eyes swirl with annoyance at my open eye-ogling.

"Don't get any ideas with this one either," Kalin says, gesturing towards Eleazar, "he's far too pretty."

"I am not pretty," Eleazar grumbles, taking those intense eyes from me and focusing on Kalin.

"Yes you are big boy," Kalin says matter-of-fact.

"Well, we best be off." I interrupt before Eleazar can snap a reply. I have the feeling they've had this argument many times before. I walk over and give Pop a kiss on the cheek before going to give Grandma one as well.

"Thank you for lunch, I loved it," I whisper, burying my head into the crook of her neck. She pats my head and sighs.

"Thank you for coming down sweetheart." Her hair smells of lavender, reminding me of home. I squeeze her once more before wrapping my arms around Kalin's neck.

"I'm not giving you a kiss because you're all sweaty and gross." He chuckles but presses his cheek to mine.

"Yeah, yeah. Run along now, make sure this one behaves." We both look up to where Eleazar has risen, the handle of his swords shine in the sunlight that streams through the window. I bite my tongue and straighten, I was sure he'd never misbehaved in his life.

"Bye everyone, I love you!" I call as I leave the kitchen, I pull my boots on quickly as Eleazar approaches.

"I love you too." Their joint voice is a chorus that wraps around my heart, squeezing it painfully. I leave the house and jump down the stairs, waiting for Eleazar. We leave in silence and make our way across the road to the Densley's.

"You didn't finish your soup," he says mildly, surveying the house as we come to a stop at the base of the stairs.

"I wasn't too hungry." I shrug my shoulders as I walk up

the stairs and knock on the door. A moment later it's opened and Mike steps out. He's in his late fifties now, and the fact my mother should look similar to this...saddens me. I'd been blessed to have her as long as I do with nothing like health to put a stop to her life.

"Hi Mike, I was wondering if we could take two horses for a ride?" I ask, slipping four gold coins out of the secret pocket in my waistband. He shakes his head but smiles as he accepts the coins.

"Of course, you know you don't have to overcharge."

"I know," I grin, "I don't need the coins and they just lay around anyway. Plus I love the horses."

"Alright, I'll bring two around. The usual?"

"The usual." I can't wipe the smile from my face as I bounce down the steps. I walk to the front of the yard and step from foot to foot. Eleazar comes and stands beside me, frowning.

"You can ride a horse?"

"There are a lot of things I can do," I retort, looking up at him. He snorts but doesn't say a word as Mike leads out two horses. On his left is the large black stallion I always opt to ride, I'd named him Ash after our first ride. On his other side is a palomino mare, Butterscotch. Both horses are unsaddled, only wearing the bridle and reins.

Eleazar approaches Ash, I hide my smile behind my hand when Mike passes the reins of Butterscotch to him. The surprise on his face isn't hidden well as he looks over the mare who seems miniature in comparison to Ash.

"Thank you Mike, I'll return them before sundown," I say as I walk over, taking the reins for Ash. He snorts as he rubs his face along my shoulder. I run my free hand through his black and white streaked mane.

"Be safe," he waves as he heads back inside.

"Why do you get the stallion?" Eleazar asks sourly.

"He's my horse. Mother doesn't know that I own him," I say softly, giving Ash a kiss on the nose before throwing the reins over his head. In a quick movement I press both hands on his back and pull myself up, swinging my leg in time with the movement. I settle comfortably on his back, holding the reins in my hands. I look down to where Eleazar stands looking gobsmacked.

"If she finds out, it's your skin that's on the line," I warn. He shakes himself before hopping onto Butterscotch.

"A secret I'll keep to myself," he assures me, kicking Butterscotch into a trot. Ash is quick to catch up. We head down the rest of the slope and reach the river, the only water source for the village. Ash leaps over it with ease, breaking into a smooth canter once we reach the other side. I spur him on as we break from the dirt road and into the open expanse of green field that surrounds us.

Snow caps dot the mountains in the open valley, streaking down the sides as winter begins to draw to an end. I breathe in the cold air, letting it burn my lungs as the wind whips my hair to and fro. Out of the corner of my eye I see Butterscotch going her hardest to catch up. I pull the reins gently and click my tongue, drawing Ash back into a trot and then a walk. He snorts in annoyance but obeys, throwing his head back a few times to assure me he's grumpy.

"What's the plan?" Eleazar asks walking in stride with me.

"I don't really have a plan, I just ride and let Ash take me where he wants to go." I pat the stallion's neck in appreciation as I give him full control. I let the reins hang loosely in my hands, he heads towards the closest mountain with a large crack in the middle. We'd journeyed through the dense path once and had come across a small paddock and lagoon.

"We'll have to return before nightfall so I can be filled in with the plan Nyx has come up with," Eleazar says, idly looking around the land. I feel the prickle of annoyance stab me in the side.

"Wouldn't want you to miss your curfew." With that I squeeze my legs around Ash's large stomach and we burst into a gallop heading for the crack in the mountain.

CHAPTER 3

I slide from Ash's back and tie the reins close to the base of his neck, he licks my palm before trotting over to a green patch of grass and lowering his head. I brush my palm on my pants before patting down between my thighs to get rid of the horse hair that had stuck to me. I look over to see Butterscotch join Ash, my eyes trail to where she came from. Eleazar brushes off between his thighs, his copper hair catches the sunlight that streams through the canopy above us; casting it in golden and burning orange strands.

He looks up and catches me staring, I turn away before he can remark. I walk through the open grass paddock. Large trees have grown through the cracks in the side of the mountain, offering shade over the field. Ahead of me the crystal clear water shines in the small lagoon, I come to a stop at the bank and watch as small silver fish dart back and forth.

"You dragged me here to stare at the water?" I flinch at the nearness of his voice, I look to my right to find him standing beside me and watching the water. I look back to the water and sigh.

"Most days I swim while Ash picks at the grass," I lean down and untie my boots. I pull them off and sit them to the side while I roll my pants up my calves. I sit down and let my feet hang in the warm water, "Ash mostly comes here whenever I give him free rein."

"Do you know why that is?" he asks, still looming over me.

"Delicious grass?" I look up at him and shield my eyes against the sun. He shakes his head.

"They've really told you nothing, haven't they?"

"No?" I grimace, my answer more of a question. He rolls his eyes and takes his boots off before joining me. He leans back on his arms and closes his eyes as he basks in the sun. I lean forward and swirl my hand through the water.

"Okay to put it simple, have you ever used any of your magic?" he asks.

I feel my mood sour, "No."

"Nothing at all? You're what, twenty one? You're youngest years is when your magic is at its peak."

"I'm twenty two," I grit out, swirling my hand through the water more aggressively, "and no, I've never used magic. I've never been asked too. I can't even feel it inside me."

"Your stallion brings you here because this place holds magic."

I look at him, bewildered. "What?" I always thought this place was special in some type of way, but it never crossed my mind for there to be magic here. If there's magic here, why can't I *feel* it? Why am I closed off from it?

He opens his golden eyes and watches me carefully. "This lagoon is enchanted, hence why it's so peaceful and serene. I felt it the moment we walked through the enchantment that wards off unwanted visitors."

"I can't feel anything. Is there something wrong with me?" I ask, feeling the panic beginning to claw its way through my chest and up my throat. What if...what if I don't have any magic at all? What if I'm a fake, looking like a faerie but not one? Oh god, the thought makes me want to hurl up my lunch.

"If you tell either your mother or father that I've talked to you about magic it will be *your skin* on the line. Is that understood?" he asks sternly. I'm caught off guard for a moment, why would he want to tell me anything about magic?

"Yes."

"Right. The enchantment around the lagoon is Old magic, older than I. I'm suspecting whichever creature created this enchantment isn't of fae origin." He looks to the lagoon, seeing something my eyes cannot.

"Wait— old magic? I thought there was only one type of magic." I say.

"There's three type of magic, Old magic originates in the fae kind as well as other creatures that hail from Faerie. It's an ancient magic and only the elderly and a rare few others carry this magic. It's takes a lot of soul work and can be very dangerous if not harnessed correctly or controlled. The second type, Sacred magic, is the one every magical creature possesses. I have sacred magic, as well as your mother and father." He pauses, looking back to me now. His jaw tightens as he surveys me. I sit back and raise an eyebrow at him. He sighs, relenting, "the third is a mere whisper of a fairy tale now. After they were culled I have only ever met one creature who held this magic."

I lean closer to him, "What is it?"

"Fallen Magic."

Fallen magic.

The two words rattle around in my mind, the world around me seems to still. The heavy silence between us thickens as he watches me with a cautious expression, most likely waiting for me to break like my parents would. When would others learn I'm more capable than they assume?

"What happened to the creature?" I ask instead, leaning

away from him. I look out over the lagoon kicking my legs back and forth.

"It was killed. Fallen magic is unpredictable and extremely dangerous, although it's rare. I haven't met anyone else in centuries that held that sort of power." He leans forward, resting his elbows on his knees.

"What sort of magic is it?" I ask, my voice barely a whisper.

"I really shouldn't say." He pauses, "I shouldn't have mentioned anything about magic or enchantments. If your parents haven't told you there must be a reason they don't want you to know or they don't think you're ready to learn how to use your sacred magic."

I look away from him, studying the grass. Although I'm used to being disappointed, it's still utterly crushing. No one ever wants to tell me anything, enlighten me. I'm never able to be taken seriously no matter how hard I try. I shouldn't have expected anything more from Eleazar, he's one of my father's best friends.

"Don't worry about it then," I mumble. I shake my head as I rise from the water, I ignore his obvious staring as I grab my boots and walk over to where Ash eats grass. I sit down beside his large head and pull my boots on, I tie the laces tightly. Taking my frustration out on them. Ash nudges me with his nose, pulling his top lip back into a smile.

"Yes, I know the grass is good here boy," I say, giving his jaw a good scratch. I rise from the grass and untie his reins, Eleazar had followed my lead; his own boots now tied and Butterscotch's reins in hand.

"Let's go," I say bluntly, he opens his mouth for a moment before closing it. I jump up onto Ash's back and lead him towards the crack that leads us out. As we approach he comes to a stop, stamping his feet. I frown as I click my tongue, urging him forward. He lets out a low whinny before half rearing backwards.

"Woah boy, it's okay. You're alright." I feel my heart begin to pick up speed as he prances in the spot; refusing to go any closer to the opening.

"Don't get off," Eleazar says softly, "there's something waiting on the other side."

My stomach drops as I pull the reins back, getting Ash to retreat further into the paddock until we're beside Butterscotch and Eleazar. He dismounts without making a noise and unsheathes the twin swords he keeps strapped to his back. Their silver blades gleam in the light as he slowly begins to approach the large crack.

I strain my eyes, trying to see any signs of danger. All I see is the stone path, a few shrubs and the open field on the other side that leads us back to Elderview. Eleazar stops, tilting his head to the side.

"I can't see anything," I hiss. I slide down Ash's side, tying his reins close to the back of his head in case he needs to run and escape. I do the same with Butterscotch, never taking my eyes from Eleazar's still figure.

"Of course you can't, can you *feel* anything?"

I try my best. I really do, as I feel around inside of myself. Looking for something, anything really. I come up empty, as I always do when I try and find my connection to magic. I deflate, my disappointment sharp and painful.

"No."

"If Ash hadn't sensed it..." he swears under his breath, readying his blades.

"Maybe it's best if you let whatever it is take me. I'm as vulnerable as a new born, I can't feel any magic. I can't fight. I can't do anything."

"Now is not the time to feel sorry for yourself," he snaps

back.

"Right, die first and then feel sorry for myself later." Ever so slowly I begin to walk up behind him. If there's something waiting on the other side I want to see. The horses begin to whinny in distress the closer I move to the opening.

I stop behind Eleazar, close enough to breath in his scent. The wind blows his hair back, tickling my face. He smells of spiced rum and honey, a pleasant combination. I peer around his side, not tall enough to see over his shoulder.

Something scuttles up the stone wall path, loose rocks fall and clatter to the ground. His hands tighten on the handles, a wolf prepared to attack.

"Why isn't it attacking?" I whisper, breathless.

"What did I say about staying on your horse?" He hisses, baring his teeth as he looks down to see me. He'd been too focused in front of him to hear me coming up from behind. I shrug and offer an apologetic smile.

"I want to help."

"You'll be more of a hindrance than help." He growls, looking back to the opening. I can't see anything now.

"Why is it not coming in?" I ask, eyes searching every nook and cranny in the cracked stone walls.

"Because of the enchantment."

"What is it?"

"A wendigo."

"What's that?"

"*Enough questions.*" He snaps, I flinch at his tone and take a step back. I don't know what a *wendigo* is. Surely he can't expect me to know anything about the magical side of my life, does he not realise how sheltered I have been?

We stand there as time stretches on. I can't feel the creature or any form of magic, but every now and then I catch a glimpse of a clawed grey foot, see more pebbles fall to the path. It's waiting for us, just as we're waiting for it.

I take a few more steps back and steady myself, what I'm about to do is absolutely idiotic but there is no way we're waiting until nightfall for this creature to get us. I have a feeling it will wait as long as we're in here. To it we're easy picking. I step back on the balls of my feet and lean forward, ready to lunge.

It's now or never.

I burst forward, stepping under Eleazar's raised arm. He yells out for me as I close the distance with long strides to the path. I ignore all rational thought as the opening grows closer, I hear his heavy footfalls coming up fast behind me.

"Be ready!" I scream over my shoulder.

I burst into the opening and immediately feel the creature's eyes on me. Pebbles rain down around me as I run down the stone descent. My feet threaten to slip on the loose stones as I pick up speed. Above, a loud screech deafens me, I risk a glance up to see the horrid grey creature scaling down the wall; pale, depthless eyes solely focused on me.

The risk costs me.

I lose my footing and go sprawling forward with a yelp.

My pants rip at the knees, my palms are cut open as I try and stop myself from going head first down the rest of the path. I scream as two grey, clawed hands grip my shoulders. I'm thrown into the side of the stone wall, my whole body absorbs the shock as I fall back to the ground. I groan as I push myself into a sitting position.

Thin grey lips pull back into a vicious smile, revealing small, razor sharp teeth. They stand before me, looking far too human for my liking aside from the elongated nails on their hands and feet. Their dark brown hair is full of dirt and twigs, matted and hanging lifelessly around their face.

I grab the closest rock and peg it at the creature, it dodges it with ease as it begins to come closer to me.

I continue to try and hold it off with rocks, landing a few hits. Where the hell is Eleazar? Bastard. I'm running low on rocks to throw at this thing. Oh god, if I die here my parents are going to bring me back from the dead and kill me again. I watch stunned as the creature begins to sail towards me from where it had leapt.

An ear piercing roar breaks through the air.

A silver blade flies towards the creature, the motion of the blade spins in the air as it closes the distance. The wendigo only focuses on me, its next meal; too blind with hunger to see the blade that is now in line with it.

Red blood sprays me as the blade slices clean through the creature's neck. I scream as everything comes crashing back. Its head rolls down the stones as its body crumples to the ground; red blood courses from the clean stump.

I wipe at my face, my hands coming back red.

"What were you thinking!" the roar is now aimed at me and is as every bit terrifying as the wendigo had been. I stop screaming and look up to where Eleazar comes striding towards me, a nasty scowl covering his beautiful face. My fear turns into the sharp, bitter taste of anger.

My hands shake furiously as I push myself from the ground, I ignore the stinging in my knees and palms as I face him head on. He stops in front of me, looking about ready to throttle me.

"I was thinking I'd rather do something than wait in there until nightfall. We had to leave. We couldn't stay in there forever!" I exclaim as my hands fly into the air around me.

"You could have been killed!" He steps closer to me, practically breathing fire.

"Good riddance I say! I'm *sick* of being careful, I'm sick of being treated like I am fragile and will break. No one wants to enlighten me about anything! You weren't going to do anything but stand there and protect me, so I took it into my own hands. I gave you the opportunity to kill it while it was distracted."

"Don't you ever say that again." His voice is low, deadly. A warning to not push him any further.

But I do. I doubt he's met with resistance often.

"What? Good riddance to my existence?" I laugh bitterly, taking a step back from him, "you know nothing of my life. You don't get to decide how I choose to perceive it." His golden eyes swirl with anger, the flames I'd gladly burn in.

"You are a stupid, selfish child. Your parents do everything they can to protect you and give you the best life any daughter could ask for and this is how you thank them? By throwing yourself at a wendigo?"

"If I had come here alone I would be dead regardless, do you not get that!" My hands shake at my sides, "I don't *feel* my magic. I don't have *magic*! I only went out on a whim because I knew you were there and you'd be able to kill it."

He takes a step closer to me, looking down. If I took a deep breath my chest would brush against his, his warm breath hits my face, "And what if your whim had been wrong? What if I hadn't chased after you and killed it?"

I close the small distance, my chest presses into his own, "Then I'd be dead. It's that simple."

His jaw tightens as he looks away from me, eyes surveying the scene behind me. It all comes flooding back to me. I feel each drop of blood on my cheeks, nose, forehead, eyelids. I grimace and step back, wiping my bloody hands on my pants. My shirt is covered in blood splatter.

"Great. I can't go back home looking like this," I grumble, turning away from Eleazar. He says nothing as he walks past me and grabs his sword. I look up to see the two horses beginning to walk down the path, Ash in the lead. He relaxes when he sees me, nickering softly. I smile faintly, feeling drained.

"Here." Eleazar grunts, I look over my shoulder to see him now shirtless with his shirt balled in his hand. Extended for me. I look up to him in shock, mouth opening. His nostrils flare, "Your parents would kill me if I brought you back to them looking like that. I can handle their reprimand if you arrive in my shirt."

"You know what they're going to think, right? What everyone in Elderview is going to assume?" I ask hesitantly. He narrows his eyes at me, more than aware of what whispers will surround us when we enter Elderview and the reaction my parents will have when we return to the castle. I nod once. He turns away to give me privacy as I pull my shirt off.

"Wait here, I'm going back to the water." I hurry up the path and squeeze myself between the horses. I make quick work of scrubbing the blood from my face and hands. I wet my knees but I can't do much about the tear in the material. Once I'm certain there's no more traces of blood on me I return to where he still stands facing away from me. I drop my bloody shirt on the ground and hesitantly take his.

It swallows me, reaching down to my knees.

I clear my throat as I tuck the hem into my waistband, making it look somewhat presentable. I look up with burning cheeks as he turns towards me, the muscles in his shoulders and his toned stomach ripple with the movement. The dark brown band of his sword holder is a nice contrast against his caramel skin.

"Let's go." He says stiffly, mounting Butterscotch. I jump on Ash as we leave the decapitated wendigo behind, I avoid looking down at its dead eyes as Ash walks past it. Once we leave the narrow stone walls Ash breaks into a canter, eager to get as much distance between us and the fight as he can.

Eleazar's shirt suctions to my front while the back billows out. This man is *large*.

I savour his scent that clings to the smooth fabric, filling all of my senses. Damn him for smelling as good as he does. He doesn't seem phased by being shirtless as the cold wind bites at him, or when we reach the river and the inclined road that takes us to Elderview. My cheeks burn as we reach the Densley's and hand over the horses to Mike, he covers his shock with a cough before taking the horses away.

We walk in silence with a healthy amount of distance between us as we enter the small crowd as the late afternoon sun begins to cast orange and pink hues across the sky. The mud had dried up for the most part, making the ground uneven no matter where I place my feet.

"Amie!" Colt's voice catches my ears and I swear internally. I turn and force a smile as he approaches, he frowns as he looks to my overly large shirt that hangs off one shoulder and exposes my soft skin to the now shirtless Eleazar.

"Hi Colt." I rub my cheeks as he comes to a stop in front of us. Eleazar crosses his arms over his chest but doesn't budge from where he stands, surveying the area around us; no doubt looking for more danger.

"What... are you doing?" he asks, looking bewildered.

"We're just heading home. We've spent the afternoon riding and I took and nasty fall and my shirt was ruined. He," I jerk my thumb towards Eleazar, "was nice enough to offer me his shirt so I wouldn't have to go through town without."

"Ah...okay. That's fair enough." His blue eyes flicker with suspicion between us before settling back to me, "If you come into town tomorrow I'd love to catch up."

"Sure. I'll have to see what I'm doing," I shrug and offer a smile.

"Of course, the princess is always busy." He winks, grinning, "have a nice evening. I'll hopefully see you tomorrow."

"You too, Colt." I watch as he strides towards one of the buildings, smiling and greeting anyone who walks past him. Hmph. I turn away and begin to walk back towards the forest that now grows dark with shadows from the sinking sun.

"You do know he's trying to court you, right?" Eleazar breaks the thick silence between us as we enter the forest. I cross my arms over my chest and rub my hands down them, trying to keep the chill away.

"We're just friends. I doubt he'd be interested in me," I reply, avoiding looking at him.

"I don't think he believes you're just friends."

"Yes well if you haven't noticed I'm a faerie and he's human, not exactly compatible." I snort. Although he's handsome, I hadn't thought more of being anything more than his friend. I know mother was a human and father was a faerie, but they're completely different in comparison to Colt and I.

"What, not interested?" He asks casually.

"I don't need someone to love me and coddle me," I look sideways at him, "there's more to life than loving someone."

"I know there is. It's good to see you do have some knowledge in that big head of yours." The corner of his right lip twitches upwards and I nearly fall over my own feet, he's *smirking*.

"What can I say? I'm full of surprises," I hide my smile as I look away from him, we walk through the offering area and I catch the golden lights from the castle through the canopy of trees. Almost home, where I can put this day to an end.

"You're nothing like what your parents have told me about

you," he says quietly. I pause and look over my shoulder to him. He watches me now, carefully.

"What did they tell you?" I ask, going very still.

His eyes glow in the coming darkness. "It's not my place to say. You've simply surprised me."

"Right. Keep your riddles to yourself, I am not one for patience to solve them." I brush his comment off and continue through the path, relief flooding me as the rising steps come into view. We reach the bottom of them when his warm hand clasps my elbow gently.

I turn to him, almost encased in his frame. My right hand presses against his bare chest, my traitorous eyes trail over his well-defined stomach. A few white scars leave a story behind, only adding to his beauty. He looks down at me, jaw twitching.

"I'm going to have to tell your parents about the wendigo."

I open my mouth to protest, he holds up a hand to silence me.

"I will not mention what you did, but I will tell them about the attack. I'll tell them you stayed with the horses while I killed it. I'll drop the suggestion of them teaching you how to fight or use your magic. Do not say a word about it unless they bring it up. If they think you're over eager they might pull away from the idea." A muscle in his jaw twitches, "I don't like to keep secrets from them, but for your sake, just this once I will."

"Thank you," I say breathlessly, relaxing slightly. He releases my arm and we begin to walk the stairs together, I'm too tired to go through the notions of everything I've learnt today and how much Eleazar has showed me. It will be my job for tomorrow. We reach the top and I walk over to the closed door, I stop with my hand on the handle.

"I'll return your shirt after I bathe. I'll leave it on the couch in the living room," I say softly before opening the door. As he's shutting the door behind us, my mother, father and the two others enter the open area from the hallway beside the stairs. They stop mid conversation.

"I'm home," I wave sheepishly, cheeks burning.

Father looks as shocked as the other two males, while mother hides her grin behind her hand as she feigns shock. Her eyes sparkle with a million questions as she catches my eye.

"I can assure you, it's not what it looks like." Eleazar's deep voice rumbles behind me, sending warmth through me. I flee up the stairs before I'm hounded with questions I can't answer, finding myself secretly wishing, that just maybe, it had been what it looked like.

CHAPTER 4

I'm in the library studying the map of the continent when I feel someone approach, the skirts of my deep blue dress swish between my legs as I rise and turn to the light footfalls. I hide my surprise when Odin walks around the corner of one of the many towering bookcases, he stops and watches me. He's dressed in fine clothes today, a nice white fitted shirt with a deep purple vest embezzled with diamonds. He tucks his hands into his pant pockets. We stand staring at each other for a moment.

"Odin, may I help with anything?" I finally relent, tilting my head slightly in question. He walks up to the large, round mahogany oak table and takes a seat across from me. He looks over the scatter of maps I've spread out.

"Doing some light reading?" he asks. I narrow my eyes on him but take a seat, sitting my hands in my lap.

"I get rather bored in this castle with nothing but the dust bunnies to keep me company."

"Humour like your mother, good to see." He smiles as he looks back up to me.

"I don't mean to be rude, but what are you doing here?"

"I was tasked with teaching you what I can of sacred magic. Your father and I, as well as the other two, are leaving in the morning to return to Faerie. After the events of yesterday your parents both insist I teach you what I can with the minimal time we have." He sits back in his chair, waiting for a reaction.

"They're actually allowing that?" I ask, shocked. I must be mistaken, my parents wouldn't allow me to learn anything about magic willingly. He nods once. I frown now, crossing my arms over my chest, "What's the catch?"

"There's no catch."

"Sounds like something *someone* would say when there's a catch." I huff, leaning back into the plush chair. I watch him suspiciously, waiting for his reply. He sighs and shakes his head, rubbing the side of his face.

"Is she giving you trouble already?" Eleazar interrupts. I look up, startled, to find him leaning against the end of one of the bookshelves; watching us with an amused expression. A rare expression I doubt I'd ever see him make again.

"I thought she'd be more willing to learn," Odin drawls, looking to Eleazar, "she seems rather stubborn."

"I simply asked if there was a catch." I huff, looking away from them and down to the map I'd been studying. The human realms map, I marked out Elderview and Orrinshire, the only two places I'd visited. I had the map of Faerie around here somewhere, but I couldn't decipher the symbols and land marks.

"She gets that from her mother as well," Eleazar says smoothly as he approaches the table, stopping between Odin and I. I do my best not to squirm in my seat from his presence. I'd been true to my word, folding his shirt neatly and sitting it on the couch for him. We hadn't spoken since yesterday, but in fairness I've been trying my best to avoid him.

"You're more than welcome to stay and help me if you'd like, I fear this might be a two man job," Odin taps his long fingers rhythmically against the table in thought, the tune is somewhat familiar to my ears but I don't tell him that.

"I can assure you," I lean in slightly, brave enough to catch Odin's eye, "it would take more than two *men*."

His eyes widen ever so slightly, his pale cheeks turn a soft shade of pink as he looks to Eleazar in shock at what I'd suggested. I lean back in my seat, crossing my arms over my chest feeling rather pleased with myself. Eleazar sighs, pulling a seat out and lounging into it.

"Sharp tongue to her as well," is all he says, he finally looks to me now. I level my gaze at him, arching an eyebrow slightly. He looks extremely bored. It irks me more than I care to admit to myself.

"What are *you* doing here? Babysitting duties again?" I ask, tilting my head to the side slightly. I'd pinned my hair up into a neat bun today, letting two loose strands down to frame my cheeks. His eyes skim my bare throat before looking back to me.

"You're losing your edge."

"Something you could benefit from."

"Enough, the both of you," Odin snaps, drawing both of our attention to him. He smiles placidly as we sit quietly, he interlinks his fingers and takes a calming breath.

"Sacred magic is a magic all magical creatures and beings are born with. It's our base nature and very well intertwined into everything we are, every breath we take, everything we experience. All creatures from Faerie have Sacred magic, for example," he raises a calloused hand, palm facing towards the ceiling, "weather elements."

Slowly a blue and orange flame begins to flicker from his palm, forming a small burning fire. I open my mouth in awe, watching as the flame dances harmlessly over his skin. I turn to Eleazar.

"You're telling me you could have burnt the wendigo to a crisp, but yet you didn't?" I accuse, he scowls at me.

"When we use our Sacred magic for death, we experience what that pain is. We're taking, and to take we must also sacrifice. Taking a life using Sacred magic takes a toll on any magical being," he replies, as if I'm an idiot and should have known all of this.

"For displays like I'm currently doing, it's harmless." Odin draws my attention back to him. His fire dances a few more times before guttering out and disappearing, leaving the sickly scent of citrus in the air.

"We can use our magic to enhance food, drink, momentary enhancements to ourselves...amongst other things." Odin and Eleazar share a look, understanding passing between them.

"Intercourse?" I say bluntly, not sure where I've discovered this courage and sharp tongue. Before I'd met them I'd been a quiet, obedient girl.

"Yes," Eleazar grunts, looking heavenwards. Odin's lips twist in disapproval. Not that I'd ever been with a man, or knew anything about being intimate.

"That's getting off track." Odin glares at Eleazar, before looking to me apologetically, "your magic is a part of you. It's the blood in your veins, the bones in your body and the skin that protects you. Magic is a part of you in ways you may not currently understand. It's our essence. When we take too much and give double..."

"It has a cost." Eleazar finishes his sentence.

"Everything in this life has a cost," I reply nonchalantly, looking down to the map.

"When we give magic, we lose a part of it from our essence. It regenerates slowly, but if the ratio for taking and replenishing is unbalanced we can fall into...darkness," Odin continues solemnly.

"What does that entail exactly?"

"In most cases the occupant turns foul and corrupt, and the scales remain unbalanced. In rare cases the person or creature will die a rather cruel death. It's a horrid thing, rotting from the inside out." I look up to see Odin's expression sour.

"You've witnessed it?" I ask, slightly intrigued but horrified at the same time.

"We all have, it's definitely disheartening and enough of a reminder why we must always have balance in our lives with our magic. It's a terrible fate to lose yourself to something so completely you can't return from it."

"It sounds sad."

"It is. But alas, all good things must come to an end. Eventually we all stop and return to the dirt from which we came from." He sighs, seeming warmed by the fact. I, on the other hand, would rather steer clear from returning anywhere after my close call yesterday. I look to Eleazar to find him studying a dagger, he rests the tip against his leather pants as his fingers thoughtfully stroke the bone handle.

"That's a bit doom and gloom," I mutter, I force myself to look back to Odin, "how does your magic help in a fight?"

His eyes take on a shine as he leans forward and smiles, "Ah, this is the fun part. When we fight, magic can be harnessed however we wish to wield it—with limitations of course. Say you were fighting another wendigo, you could ask the ground beneath you to come to your aid or any of the elements. You can ask for aided strength and resilience, it's all personal preference really."

"Ah, okay. But how?"

"It's...very hard to explain," Odin frowns briefly, looking to Eleazar, "how would you describe it?"

"It's a deep knowing, like asking for water right now is as easy as breathing," Eleazar looks sideways at me, I feel the splat of a water droplet on my cheek. I frown at him as more droplets fall to my cheeks. I look above me to see a watery halo of sorts, the water bubbles and moves lazily in a circle, the occasional droplet falling loose.

"We only ever have to give magic if we take a magic life, doing these...party tricks is free of cost per say." Odin is amused as he watches the display.

"How would I unlock my magic though?" I barely hear my voice, unsure if I'd actually voiced it. Odin's eyes turn sympathetic as he looks at me, he smiles gently; as if not to startle the injured animal into biting. I'm grateful for this, I am. But yet I still find myself being sheltered.

Eleazar studies me for a moment, "It will come naturally to you, you're just a late bloomer."

Odin opens his mouth to say something but a fierce glance from Eleazar he shuts it just as quickly. I'm about to ask what that's about when the water halo comes crashing down, wetting my hair and my dress as water runs down my face and neck.

"You...you idiot!" I hiss, scowling at Eleazar. He grins lazily, openly waiting for me to challenge him back. I can't do magic, but even I have a few dirty, *human* tricks up my sleeve. Odin watches silently as my anger flares, he could have ruined my maps!

"I've been called much, much worse." He leans back, all arrogance. I suddenly stand, moving swiftly with confidence I'm not sure I even *have* as I yank out the small blade I'd stashed in my bra. In a blink I'm between his open legs, blade pressed to his throat as I lean in. His eyes widen in surprise as he intakes sharply. His breath hits my face but I'm too worked up to realise I may be a tad too close for comfort. We're in the same position, but roles reversed from our first confrontation.

"Dear lord..." Odin mutters, chair scraping.

"I can assure you, you've seen the least of what I can do and the insults that can come from my pretty little mouth." I smile sweetly at him as I stare him down, resting my other hand on his chest. His breathing is shallow as he watches me, his nostrils flare slightly as we stay like that. His eyes slip to my lips, wondering just what my mouth can be capable of. I wonder...what would those lips feel like pressed against my own?

The thought throws me off my high horse and with horror I realise the situation I'd gotten myself into. I can't imagine how this looks to Odin, his best friend's daughter leaning between this wicked man's legs with a blade to his throat.

He watches me with a hint of excitement, although the flare of it is dulled by complete and utter annoyance, "You may find I like the bite of a blade," he leans into the sharpened edge. I give in a moment later, shoving him as I straighten before slipping the small blade back into its hiding spot. I feel both of them watch me as I pat the skirts of my dress before wiping the rest of the droplets from my cheeks.

"Thank you for enlightening me about Sacred magic," I look to Odin and my cheeks blossom, "I do appreciate it. Truly, but I'm afraid I have other matters to tend to."

"Of course." Odin rises, holding his hand out for me. "Have a good day Amaryllis." I clasp it and shake once before withdrawing, well aware I'm still caged in Eleazar's legs. I don't look at him as I move from his legs, bumping them purposefully as I go. He grunts, the only goodbye I receive from him.

I move through the library quickly; hand pressed to my chest to my erratic, traitorous heart as I flee through the multiple rows of books. I leave through the propped open wooden doors and run for my room, suddenly feeling far too hot and needing to feel the cool breeze on my feverish skin.

I escape to my room without any interruptions. I pull open

the balcony doors and take a shaky breath. Fresh, cool air greets me like a lover, as I step onto the balcony. I try not to think about the chaotic mixture of feelings in my chest that seem to be a reoccurring nuisance whenever I've had an encounter with Eleazar, or have to be in his proximity in general.

He's so full of himself, so arrogant and annoying. He thinks he's so good because of what? He has magic and knows how to fight?

I pace the space of the balcony back and forth.

I stop myself from wanting to be curious about the scars on his hands and stomach. I know when to not let my curiosity get the best of me. One too many times I've landed myself in rather complex situations that I couldn't escape from, it's assured me that I've learnt my lesson well and truly.

Why must he push my buttons so? What does he get from being the thorn in my side? A large part of me is relieved to know they'll be leaving tomorrow, but the small part of me I don't wish to acknowledge is slightly disappointed that I may never see him again. It infuriates me even more.

A soft knock comes from my bedroom door. I go still, angling myself towards the room.

"Come in," I call, not having heard the footsteps. To my utter shock, Eleazar steps into my room. His eyes catch me immediately as he walks towards me, not bothering to take in my bare room. I take multiple steps back until I'm leaning against the stone ledge.

He pauses at the threshold of the door, looking annoyed.

"I've been asked to apologise," he grunts out, stepping onto the balcony. I go very still as he walks up beside me, a healthy distance away, as he looks down to Elderview. I keep my breathing even as I turn and look down at the village as well.

"That must get under your skin, which delights me." I look sideways at him, seeing a muscle in his jaw tick, "do continue."

"I'm only apologising for letting the water fall and almost getting onto the maps. I don't apologise for anything else that I've done or said that may have offended you."

"That doesn't sound very sincere."

He crosses his arms over his chest, looking down to me, "It isn't."

I nod once, "Good." It's actually a relief really, to have someone not walk on eggshells around me or watch everything they do and say. He may be a lot of things, but at least I know what I'm going to get from him. Unlike the rest. It dampens my anger I'd felt only moments ago.

"Good?" his voices echoes in question.

"Yes, good. Or are your fae ears not working today?" I lower my brows and look away from him, "I don't want you to apologise to me for anything."

"Well, with that in mind I can assure you I won't again."

"Oh is that a promise?" I ask, feeling a smile tug my lips. I feel his eyes watching me, I grip the ledge and squeeze the stone; not allowing myself to look at him. Far too easily he gets under my skin, it's dangerous.

"A vow. One I can stick too."

"You sound like you're in the business of disappointing others," I say idly, waving my hand in the air. He grunts and the sound almost reminds me of a rough laugh.

"It's my specialty really." Out of the corner of my eye he shrugs, finally looking back out over the landscape. I relax, it allows me to breathe easy once more when his observant eyes aren't studying me.

"One I'm sure you do all too well," I muse.

We stand there in silence, looking at everything else but

each other. I don't know what he's thinking but my thoughts are a one way ticket to Doomsville and although I find him so attractive that it hurts to look at him for too long, I know he can't think the same of me. The back and forth is fun and thrills me, but I know my limits. I know when to pull my reel back into my shell and hide. Not to mention he's my father's best friend.

Maybe him and the others leaving tomorrow will work well in my favour.

"We're leaving for Faerie in the morning," he breaks the silence, his voice bland of any form of emotion.

"Yes I know. Odin informed me earlier before you'd arrived," I say quietly, the pang of jealousy leaves a foul taste in my mouth. How I yearn to travel to Faerie to witness what I've been missing out on.

"Don't..." he trails off, pausing.

"What?" I ask, looking up to him. His eyes flicker to me before he frowns once more, an expression I'm more comfortable with.

"Forget it. Just behave for the sake of your parents until your father returns."

He looks down at me now, *really looks* as if he can see past the charade I do so well to perform. Past the barriers and walls I've built around myself in fear for my weak heart, leaving me feeling utterly bare before him.

"You know I can't promise that," I say softly, already an idea forms in the back of my mind. A rather dangerous, foolish idea that will no doubt land me knee deep in utter shit. An idea that may be dangerous, but will offer me a taste of freedom and adventure that I've hungered for, *starved* for. As if knowing this his frown turns into a scowl, letting me glimpse those sharp canines of his once more.

"Whatever foolish plan you're festering in that mind of

yours, I suggest you forget about it and carry on with your life. The path we walk is not one you must travel on."

I look away from him, hiding anything that may give me away, "I suppose I'll just have to forge my own."

"And if that doesn't work out for you?"

"I'm either dead or back to square one," I say bluntly, "I'd rather take a risk with my life rather than wasting it by not allowing myself to truly live."

He pushes off from the ledge, turning his back, "Then you're even more foolish than what I first assumed."

Oh how I haven't missed the sweet sound of disappointment that I seem to inflict in people. It only resolves my plan even more. If I must forge my own path then I will not falter to walk it alone.

CHAPTER 5

A knock stirs me from sleep, I'm bleary eyed and yawning as mother walks into the room. She smiles sweetly as she walks over and pulls back the dark red curtains, bright sunlight filters in. I flinch and cover my eyes, still trying to wake.

"They're leaving now but your father won't go until you come and see them off." She stops at the end of my bed, shaking my foot lightly under the blanket. I sit up and stretch.

"What time is it?" I ask, dropping my arms to my side.

"Mm about ten or so? A few hours from lunch. Hurry, they're waiting." She blows me a kiss before heading back down stairs, leaving my door wide open. I stumble out of bed, catching a glimpse of myself in the mirror. Good lord it looks like a bird has taken nest in my hair, sticking out at all angles.

I tug down my white silk pyjama shirt, the shorts hike up my thighs as I take the steps slowly. I ignore my horrendous state, father's seen me at much worse. I look up from the steps to see everyone standing in the foyer, both entry doors propped open. A cool, comforting breeze greets me as I reach the bottom. Father's dressed in his traveling clothes, deep brown leather pants and a short sleeved white shirt with his navy cloak clasped around his throat.

"Good morning sleepy head." He grins as I walk over, wrapping me in a warm hug. I lean into him and savour his warmth, I don't know when he'll return. It could be days or months, depending on how bad it is in Faerie.

"Morning," I murmur, holding him tightly. He strokes my hair, planting a kiss on the top of my head.

"I shouldn't be gone for too long, hopefully a few weeks at best. I'm sure your mother will enjoy the silence." I step back as he looks over to where she stands, grinning at him. She walks over, wrapping an arm around his waist.

"Enjoy indeed," she murmurs, leaning up to kiss him. I scrunch my nose up and look away, finding my eyes on Eleazar's. He watches me with no expression, arms crossed over his broad chest. I walk a few steps away from them, giving them a moment of privacy.

"How did you sleep?" Odin asks, his question takes me by surprise.

"Like the dead." I smile at him, he nods once before looking to Eleazar and Hemlock. Hemlock comes over, wrapping me in a hug. I startle before hugging him back, patting his back. He smells of freshly cut grass and lilies.

"I'm sorry we couldn't have had the pleasure of getting to know each other like you did with the other two, but I'll bring your father back in one piece." He grins as he steps back, tapping the tip of my nose gently. I can't help but smile up at him.

"There's always next time, I'm sure I can hold out for that long." I cross my arms loosely over my chest. I don't look to where Eleazar stands. I feel awkward as Hemlock steps back beside Odin. Father comes closer, picking up his travel bag and sliding it onto his back.

"I'll return, be safe and behave Ama," he looks down at me with love in his eyes. My heart expands in my chest.

"Always am, love you." I look to mother. She comes up beside me and wraps an arm around my shoulder.

"Love you too," she blows him a kiss, he catches it in the air and holds it to his chest. She laughs, shaking her head. He grins before looking to the men.

"Are we ready?" he asks. They all nod, walking out the door.

"Bye." I wave lamely as they leave, watching Eleazar's tense form disappear down the stairs. We stand like that for a moment, watching as they leave. Mother lets me go, still watching them.

"Any plans for the day?" she asks.

"Nope," I reply.

"Good, we're going to Elderview to visit the family. Go get dressed and brush that mess you call hair." She grins at me, "meet me down here in ten?"

"Okay, sounds good." I leave her at the bottom of the stairs and head back up into my room, I take a chance and rush out onto the balcony; grasping the ledge as I lean down and spot the four men moving towards the forest. My heart stumbles as a certain copper haired male pauses at the back of the group, glancing over his shoulder.

He stays like that for a moment, watching me, before turning and heading into the forest and out of sight. I let him take the crushing feeling in my chest with him, I'm rational enough to realise I'm most likely feeling these...emotions, because he's far too handsome. His personality certainly isn't my cup of tea in the morning.

I hurry back into the room, pushing him from my mind. I dress quickly, pulling on black leather tights. I go over to my vanity, opening up one of the draws I keep my plain shirts tucked into. My hand stills as I find a white shirt with a folded piece of brown paper sitting on top.

I open the letter to find delicate handwriting,

Amaryllis,

I'm going to assume you won't heed my advice, you're far too stubborn to listen for your own good. Even if it endangers your life, which I've come to realise you're not too fond of anyway.

I've left my shirt behind, the one you wore after the wendigo attack.

It's yours to keep, a reminder of what can happen while you can't use your magic, and, while I'm not around to play baby sitter.

Behave. I don't care to clean up your remains.

Eleazar.

I read the small note three times, unable to grasp why he'd do something so...kind for me. He certainly doesn't strike me as a man who would do something this caring, even if it's in his own sort of twisted way. I hide the paper underneath the other shirts at the bottom and take a hold of his, pulling it out. It smells just like him. I pull it on and tie the front into a knot to shorten it.

I pull my boots on and head down stairs, ignoring all my thoughts about Eleazar. I don't even really know him. I have to remind myself that he's still a stranger to me regardless of his connections to my father. I find mother at the bottom of the stairs, dressed in a simple pastel pink dress.

"Let's go." She links her arm with mine as we leave the castle, heading down the stairs and into the forest. The weather is slightly better than it was the day before, the sun warms my arms even though a chilly breeze has me holding on tighter to mother's arm. She hums to herself as we walk, looking up towards the canopy.

"So...when do you think they'll return?" I ask, peering up at her.

"You've never cared this much before when your father left, or is there someone else you're hoping will return with him?"

she muses, smiling down at me. My cheeks heat as I look forward.

"Nope. Just father," I clip, studying the trees to my left and finding them rather intriguing.

"I'm no fool darling, I know you're wearing his shirt." She pauses, "and there's nothing wrong with that. The fae males are rather impressive, your father's looks stunned me as well when I first met him."

"Yes but I don't... can't like him. I don't even know him." I sigh, shaking my head. She pats my hand.

"It still doesn't mean you can't appreciate beauty when you see it, he's always been on the harsh side with everyone he's ever met. It took him years to warm to me and I think that's only because of your father's persistence."

"Years?" I look up at her, mouth hanging open slightly. She laughs brightly, touching my cheek for a brief moment.

"Yes, years. I still don't know an awful lot about him, he likes to keep to himself but I trust him with my life. He's been my protector many times and his loyalty has never faltered from me and your father. He's a good man." She looks ahead, lips twisting, "his last partner was very similar to him, fiery piece of work she was."

"What was she like?" Curiosity and jealousy fight for the spotlight, Eleazar may very well have a women waiting at home for him to return...and I'm simply me. The thought is crushing and leaves me feeling foolish for wearing his shirt like some love sick teen.

"Annoying, I couldn't be around her for too long without wanting to pull my hair out." She chuckles, "I was quite happy when they separated, but they've remained very close friends... they'd been friends before taking it further."

"Is she helping with the mission in Faerie?" We walk through the offering clearing, moving without haste.

"I'm not sure, she may very well be." She shrugs her thin shoulders, giving my hand a squeeze.

"That's good." I feel myself frown, why would he leave me his shirt and that stupid note if he's still close with his ex-partner? I'm reading far too much into his actions. I should know I'll never get anything deeper with him; what's on the surface is what to expect.

"I'm going to sound very much like a mother right now, but be careful. I'd hate for him to break your heart."

"I can promise that you have nothing to worry about." It's my turn to pat her hand as we enter the village. Most people bow at the waist for my mother, her debt still on their shoulders when she sacrificed herself to save the village. I burn under their stares but keep my head held high, not focusing on anyone in particular.

"Princess!" Colt's shout reaches my ears. I pull mother to a stop and glance over my shoulder. He pushes through the crowd, grinning as he approaches, looking to my mother.

"Afternoon Colt," I say, wriggling my arm out from my mother's.

"Are you busy?" he asks. I look to mother, she rolls her eyes but smirks. I internally give her a shove, wanting to stop the conversation about me and men with my mother in general.

"No she's not at the moment," mother says smoothly, "Just make sure you return to your grandparents soon Ama. Your uncle wants to see you."

"Alright, I'll see you soon." I wave as she heads back through the crowd, her raven black hair a beacon in the sea of the shorter villagers. I turn to Colt and clasp my hands together. "What's the plan?"

"Walk?" he suggests, gesturing towards the river. We'd pass my grandparents on the way down. At least I'd be close.

"Alright, let's go."

We walk side by side in comfortable silence as we head down towards the river, out of the corner of my eye I really study Colt. After Eleazar had said he's trying to court me, I have to wonder how much truth there is to that statement.

He's slightly shorter than I am, slender with the hint of muscles. Very attractive for human standards, as all the village girls know. Over the years he's had three long term girlfriends, but he's been single for over a year now.

"How did your parents take you falling off the horse?" he asks, breaking the silence.

"What?" I blink in confusion, frowning. He looks at me, smiling hesitantly.

"Your fall? You had to wear that faerie's shirt." He tucks his hands into his pockets.

"Oh that! My apologies, clearly I have the memory of a goldfish. They took it fine, they were glad I'd come out with only a few scratches." I laugh lightly, feeling my smile strain. I didn't want to tell Colt about the wendigo, the humans don't need to be unnecessarily scared.

"Ah yes, lucky...what's his name?"

"Eleazar." I look away from him, biting my cheek.

"Ah, *Eleazar*."

"Why are you saying it like that?" I ask, raising an eyebrow at him. He grins, shrugging his shoulders. I push his arm lightly, feeling my smile widen, "Don't tell me you're jealous."

"Would it matter if I was?" he asks, sobering the light mood. He watches me carefully, a spark of hope in his eyes. My breath catches in my throat, Eleazar had been right. He is trying to court me. I must be quiet for too long because he clears his throat, I look away from him and find we'd made it to the river.

"How has your day been?" I ask instead, taking a seat at the bank. I pull my boots off and roll my leggings up before dipping my feet into the water. He sits down beside me, although he doesn't put his feet in the water like I have.

"It's been good, I helped mum at home with baking this morning." He lean back on his arms, shutting his eyes as his head hangs back. The sun shines down on him, complementing the angle. I look back towards the water, watching as the current bubbles and ripples.

"That sounds pleasant," I offer.

"Amaryllis...may I ask something?" His voice is hesitant. I look over my shoulder at him. He gulps, gathering his courage. I suddenly feel nervous, I don't know if I'm going to like where this conversation is heading.

"Sure."

"Eleazar...are you and him courting?" His neck begins to turn red as do his cheeks. I'm thrown off by the question. How am I meant to answer that? This is making me think about the feelings I'd had over the span of the last few days in a few seconds.

"I..." *No?* I grimace, not finishing my sentence. I owe Eleazar nothing, I know this. But...the small stubborn part of me wants to win him over somehow. Perhaps I need to hold off on the blades to the throat. Although he did say he liked them....

"Did you hear me?" Colt's voice crashed through my scandalous thoughts, I blush as I smile apologetically.

"Sorry. I wouldn't say we're courting, no. I only met him the other day, far too soon to start courting someone. Plus, he's a friend of my father's." I laugh, trying to lighten the mood. Colt looks away and sighs softly, I wouldn't have heard it if it wasn't for my fae ears.

"Okay, sorry for the brash question." He shakes his mood off, smiling back to me. "Did you want me to walk you back to your grandparents?"

"Yes, please." I stand, holding my boots in my hands as we begin to walk back. The dirt road is rough beneath my feet, but a welcoming feeling after the conversation I'd just been put through.

"Why don't you put your boots on?" Colt offers.

"No, it's okay. I like to feel the earth beneath my feet." I shrug, looking down at my now grimy feet. Very lady-like.

"Your choice." He looks straight ahead and I have the inkling feeling that it annoys him. The idea of me must be what entrances him, but the real me? I don't believe anyone would be able to hold onto these jagged edges for to long.

I stay silent as we continue the walk, Colt glances sideways at me occasionally but I avoid looking at him. If I were to try and...develop something between us, could I be happy with being a simple stay at home wife? A woman who sits back and wears the pretty dresses, says the appropriate things and doesn't get her hands muddy?

The idea makes my skin feel too tight, the air a little too harsh to breathe. A life with no adventure, I couldn't do. I've spent far too long sitting back and being the pretty porcelain statue everyone expects of me.

"I'll see you later," I say to Colt as we stop at the fence of my grandparent's home. I smile and wave before hurrying off, not giving him a chance to reply. The suns sits high in the sky, already noon. I open the doors and drop my boots as voices from the kitchen carry into the hallway.

"Ama's here!" Emilia's high pitched voice makes my ears throb, I look over in time to see her barrelling towards me at full speed. I laugh as she leaps onto me, grabbing at my shirt as I hoist her up onto my hip.

"Hello missy," I kiss her check before brushing the deep brown strands from her chubby, freckle covered cheeks. She'd received her mother's fair skin but had inherited the strong emerald eyes from her father. Her lashes brush her cheeks as she closes her eyes, leaning into me.

I carry her as we walk into the kitchen. Mother, Pop, Grandma, Kalin and Martha crowd in the confined space. Mother and I are the tallest, although Kalin comes close. Martha flitters about the room, her curvy figure admirable for such a short lady. Her pastel pink dress hugs her nicely, the white lace skirts reminding me of Aunty Mana.

Her bright blue eyes find mine and she smiles, her deep brown hair is curled nicely; resting against the top of her shoulders. "Hey Ama, it's lovely to see you again."

"As it is you," I lean down to give her a hug, breathing in the deep rose scent.

"Mama says daddy is going into Orrin today to get me a present!" Emilia trills, clutching her hands together as she looks down at her mother. Martha clicks her tongue, turning to where Kalin leans against the counter.

"I'm almost sure you have enough presents," she says, causing Kalin to grin. His deep green shirt is rolled at the sleeves, exposing his tanned arms and grime covered hands.

"You can never have enough presents, you use to love when I showered you in them," he winks at her, eyes sparkling. I watch the interaction amused. I'd always liked Martha with my uncle. They were like two piece's of a puzzle, fitting perfectly.

"Oh hush you," Martha chuckles, coming over to the sink. Mother helps Pop with the plates for lunch while Grandma sits at the table, she wipes her forehead with the back of her hand. Her pale skin is shadowed today, casting hollows under her eyes.

"I'm going to sit with granny, okay? Go play in the living room." I help Emilia to the ground, she beams up at me before running away. I shake my head as I take a seat across from

Grandma. I reach out my hands, taking her wrinkled one in my own.

"How are you feeling?" I ask, rubbing my thumbs over the back of her hand. The blue veins are visible through the frail skin, something I shall never experience. She looks at me with dull green eyes, sheltered by her reading glasses.

"I've felt better, but I've felt worse. Just another day under the weather," she gives my hands a soft squeeze. Mother comes to the table, placing the plates down. I catch the worried look that takes over her face when she looks at grandma.

"We're going to have some leek and potato soup, your favourite," Mother says sweetly, plastering a smile to hide the worry. Pop brings over the large black cauldron and sits it in the middle of the table, I let go of grandma's hand as I sit back. Kalin and Martha take the seats beside me while Pop and Mother sit next to Grandma. Martha scoops out the thick white soup and takes a plate into the living room for Emilia.

"So, Amaryllis, how do you feel about adventuring to the big city?" Kalin asks, nudging me with his elbow. I almost drop my spoon.

"To Orrinshire?!" I ask, looking wide eyed between him and Mother. She chuckles, shaking her head.

"Of course," he laughs, "I thought it'd do you some good to get out of that castle."

"Will we be riding or taking the cart?" I ask, already over-whelmed with excitement. Father and the others had left this morning and most likely had to go through Orrinshire...I am determined to not be left behind this time. I'm taking my life into my own hands and forging my own path through the long grass and thorns.

Even if it means going alone.

Although one may argue I am an adult and can do as I

please, with over protective parents like my own, this will definitely be running away.

"We'll ride, should do the horses good to get some decent exercise." He grins. Kalin had been there when I'd purchased Ash and he couldn't have been more proud of me if he tried. I doubt Mother would care, but I liked to have a sliver of life outside the castle walls.

"Oh Mother please, please you have to let me go," I look across the table to her, propping out my lower lip. She sighs, rolling her eyes.

"I suppose the time away will do you well," she softens as she looks between her parents, "I'll spend the time with Ma and Pa while you're gone."

"When do we leave?"

"After lunch," Kalin goes back to eating.

"Oh! I have to pack a bag," I say, quickly filling my mouth with soup. I'd need to hurry. Orrinshire is a two day journey away. I couldn't miss picking up the trail my father and the others might leave behind.

Kalin laughs, causing the others to chuckle, "Well you best hurry then."

I drop my spoon and jump from the table, "I love you!" I shout over my shoulder before fleeing down the steps. Their laughter reaches my ears as I head into the village. This is my perfect opening, a light in the dark. Father thinks he can shelter me from life forever; that he has to protect me. I will show him I'm no feeble woman. I am his child after all.

CHAPTER 6

The two day journey to Orrinshire passes with ease, anticipation is thick on my tongue as the road around us begins to thrive with other travellers. I receive curious glances for the most part, my faerie heritage on display for anyone and everyone to see. Kalin doesn't seem to notice the glares as much as I do. We're currently waiting on the outskirts of the city on the main road. Someone's cart has toppled over ahead and caused a blockage.

I tell myself I don't mind the wait, but I do. I have to track down Eleazar the moment I'm free. I haven't told Kalin of my plan, he's as protective as mother, if not more.

"What's got you jumping in your seat?" His voice breaks my train of thought, I pull my wide straw hat down and shade myself from the noon sun as I look sideways at him. He leans back on his mare, her white hair a pale shade of brown from the dust.

"It's been some time since I've visited the city. I'm excited." I comb my fingers through Ash's mane as I smile, hoping the deception isn't written on my face. He narrows his eyes for a moment before he relents, he wipes his forehead with the back of his hand and blows out a breath.

"Your mother likes to keep you locked up in that castle, that's for sure."

"I know. It drives me mad most days," I murmur, looking back to the front of the line. Ever so slowly horses begin to trod forward, cart wheels creaking as they go. The murmur of the crowd picks up again as everyone begins to move. I urge Ash on, clicking my tongue.

"She does it because she loves you," he offers, walking in step beside me.

"How can you love something so much and yet still keep it confined in a cage of your liking? How is that love?" I ask, casting my eyes anywhere that isn't Kalin. No one truly understands the toll it takes to be on watch all of the time. To have secrets upon secrets mounted around them. If it wasn't for Eleazar I'd still know nothing, but, if it wasn't for Eleazar I'd be wendigo dinner.

Bastard.

"She has her reasons. Before I was born your mother—*we* —had a sister. Cecilia. She drowned in the river one day when your mother and Mike were down there swimming. I wasn't born then but I know she still carries the burden of her death like a second skin." Kalin looks over to me, offering a sad smile, "she truly means well. She just can't lose you either."

"She won't lose me if she gives me the freedom I desperately crave. I'd always come home...I just need to live my life outside of the castle built on secrets. It's tiring." I shake my head looking back to the road. My chest aches for my mother. I had never known she'd had a sister. Even as my mother there's still so much I don't know about her past and how she came to be the woman she is today.

"I'm sure she'll come around one day."

A loud bang echoes behind us. Ash startles, darting

forward and knocking into the man that walks in front of us. His basket of linen falls to the dirt, the colour patch sheets hit the ground with a thud. He snarls as he turns to look up at me. My eyes widen at the anger.

"Stupid faerie bitch," he growls, leaning down to scoop up the sheets.

"Don't you dare speak to my niece like that," Kalin swoops down from his mare, reins in hand and looking very much like an avenging angel. The man looks up from where he leans over, spitting in the dirt in front of Kalin's boots.

Other travellers are beginning to look towards us now, up ahead the guards begin to turn to us. The toppled cart has been righted and the contents in check, the line begins to move around us again.

"I'll speak to her however I want to, faeries are good for nothing and should be wiped from our country. Go back to where you came from." Kalin's neck begins to burn bright red as it creeps up his throat. I jump down from Ash, wanting to diffuse the situation.

"Look I'm so sorry, something spooked my horse and I couldn't control it. I'm sorry." I come up behind him, wanting to help. He turns and shoves me backwards, his large meaty hands seem to burn through the material on my shirt as I fall hard on my ass.

People shout and the thud of flesh being hit reaches my ears. I groan as I stand, no one offering to help. I look up to see the man wiping blood from his nose, Kalin fumes in front of him; knuckles split. I'm terrified to walk around the man to Kalin so I do the next best option; I leap onto Ash.

"Please Kalin, let's go. He's done." I plead, looking down to where he stands. He takes a moment before he comes back to reality. He shakes his shoulders out.

"If you ever touch her again, the least of your worries will be a broken nose." He snarls before jumping onto his mare. We weave around the man before heading forward, leaving the man and his fallen sheets behind.

"Are you okay?" Kalin asks, reaching out for my hand. I give it a quick squeeze, feeling guilty at the broken skin. He pulls back, wiping his knuckles against his shirt.

"I am. I'm sorry I didn't see—"

"You do not apologise to me for the likes of people like him. You couldn't help it. No man ever lays a finger on you in harm under my watch, or your consent. I could go back and give him another piece of my mind," he spits on the ground away from us, earning glares from those closest. I slump down in the saddle, wanting their prying eyes to find something else more entertaining.

"I know, but your knuckle," I whisper. My eyes begin to burn, a dam of tears threatening to spill over.

"My knuckle is fine. I'd do it again if meant protecting you. Are you okay? He shoved you fairly hard."

"I'm fine, just a little sore. Nothing a warm bath won't fix." I look up as we pass through the guards and into the large city. Today they celebrate the life of Sheeba, goddess of sun and life, one of their human gods. Kids and people stream through the crowd, painted in bright yellows and oranges. Market stalls are set up, the beating of drums reaches me as we skirt around the outside.

"Where are we staying?" I ask, almost shouting over the noise of the crowd.

"I wrote to Matt last week about staying, he fixed up his old home for us. It's on the other side of the river." Kalin takes the lead, weaving us down a few side streets until we come out to a large expanse of bare ground by the river. He gestures to the empty space, "This is where they usually have the farmer's market where I get the seeds."

"Nice." I nod a few times before following him over the large bridge, water rushes underneath, gurgling and bubbling from the force. We begin to ascend up the road until finally Kalin comes to a stop outside of a vine covered fence. He swings down and opens the gate, leading his mare through. I stay on Ash as I follow, looking over the home.

It's small, definitely homey. Vines and flowers of pink and yellow cover the front of the house, birds flutter from the rafters as Kalin heads around the side of the house.

"When was the last time someone stayed here?" I call. A paddock overflowing with grass sits at the back of the property. A small trail leads through to a water trough, Matt must have known we'd bring the horses.

"A long time ago. Matt usually lets our family stay here if we're in passing. He's a good fella." Kalin unsaddles his mare, taking her bridle from her. She snorts as she walks into the paddock, immediately leaning down to eat the grass. I slide from Ash's side, following Kalin's lead. I throw the saddle over the fence with his bridle. He nudges me with his nose softly before he walks into the paddock, tail flicking as he goes to the water trough.

"You and that horse have a connection I can't work out," Kalin murmurs, rubbing his face in amazement. I shrug although a smile tugs at my lips.

"I know. I can't describe it either."

He chuckles as he grabs his bags, I follow his lead and we head into the house through the back door. Thankfully Matt has cleaned up inside, the air is slightly stale but a hint of mint mingles with it. I walk down the small hallway, peering into the bedroom and tiny bathroom as I pass.

"It's...simple," I comment, walking into the largest part of the house. I drop my bags down beside the quilt covered couch, staring at the fireplace. Fresh wood is stacked beside the mantle for us. Kalin rummages around in the kitchen.

"It was good for when he first lived here. I don't think he thought he'd ever fall in love and start a family of his own," Kalin calls over the counter. I move around the couch and take a seat. My ass aches from where I'd fallen but I hide the pain from Kalin. Less of a reason for him to go and murder the man.

I'm accustomed to the snide comments of being a faerie. Kalin is not.

"I'll have to meet him one day. How does mother know him?" I ask, looking over my shoulder. He takes a greedy bite into a green apple, the juice running down his chin. He chews and swallows before answering.

"I do believe he was trying to court her and then Nyx came along and swept her off her feet before Matt got the chance. They've remained good friends though, he's been awfully helpful to us."

"Speaking of...I think Colt may be trying to court me as well..." I trail off, wringing my hands together as my cheeks begin to burn. I could talk to Kalin about this with more reasoning than mother. She'd swoon.

He snorts, raising an eyebrow at me. "He's been trying to court you for years. I can't believe it's taken you that long to work out."

"I only noticed because Eleazar told me." I huff, turning back to the unlit fire and sinking into the chair.

"Why would he tell you that?" he asks, coming around to the front of the couch. He puffs his chest out, "Do I need to have a few words with him as well?"

"God, no," I drag my hands over my face, "when we were returning to the castle the other day Colt came up to talk to us and on the walk back Eleazar said he was trying to court me.

He just likes to annoy me and get under my skin, you have nothing to worry about."

"Okay, okay, I'm just making sure. Especially because his ex is still in the picture and not exactly as just friends." He twists his lips, realising what he's implying, "I didn't—"

I wave my hand at him, "I know. Don't worry. I'm more than capable of handling a grumpy faerie."

"Okay. Good." He turns and begins to chuck logs onto the fire. I stifle a yawn as I get comfortable, willing myself to not ask more questions regarding Eleazar or his ex-lover. I have a lot of work to do once Kalin goes to wherever he needs to go, the last thing I can afford to do is be distracted. I had to dig the map of Akrania out of my bag and find someone who could point me in the right direction, wishful thinking I know.

"What do you have planned for the rest of the day?" he asks, lighting a match and waiting for the crumpled piece of paper to catch.

"I could really do with a cat nap. What are your plans?"

"I'm thinking of going to the markets, did you want to come?" The logs catch and burn softly. He throws the match in and stands, wiping his hands over the back of his pants. I sigh, deflating.

"Alright I'll come, let me wash my face and I'll meet you out the front."

I pull myself up from the couch with more energy than I care to admit and trudge into the bathroom. I scrub my face with water, washing away the grime of the morning. I stare at myself in the small cracked mirror. I readjust the hat, tucking my pointed ears in. My eyes seem to twirl with life, I sigh and leave the bathroom.

I meet Kalin out the front, he takes my hand under his arm as we begin to walk back down to the bridge. I breathe in the fresh, cool air, taking my time to look over the flourishing trees and flowers.

"So...Eleazar's ex..." I venture, unable to stop myself.

"What would you like to know? I shouldn't say anything. He'd skin me alive. It's really not my business to tell you."

"I just want to know more about her. What's her name?" I look sideways at him, hopeful. He sighs, relenting.

"Her name is Helena, that's what we call her anyway. I don't know what they call her." I taste her name on my tongue, fairly common for a faerie. I'd expect a human to carry that name.

"Mother says she's a warrior." I sigh as we hit the bridge. People don't stare for long once they catch my sharp gaze, I doubt there's other faeries in the city. I'd never seen any live here. I can't imagine they'd like to. There're too many people and not enough *life*.

"She is. As hard as Eleazar, which is why they went together so well. I think it was their ultimate downfall in the end, she's not the type of woman who needs protecting. She has been hardened over the many years. Stunning, as all faerie's are." He smiles politely at passing strangers, still on alert in case another human starts on me again no doubt.

I feel myself crumble, I'm no warrior. I know the basics of using a blade, I can't even use magic. Utterly embarrassing to believe Eleazar would even want to take an interest in me.

"She sounds like a dream," I say dryly, knowing she'd chew me up and spit my out if our paths ever crossed. She's the lion and I'm the lamb. He pats my arm reassuringly.

"You don't need a man in your life to complete it Amaryllis. If love is to find you it will, no matter who you are or where you are."

"How do you know when you're in love?" I ask softly, not wanting everyone else to overhear me. We're in the city now, moving towards the markets we'd skirted around earlier. He grins at me, a dimple forming on each cheek. I'd never been in love, or had anything close to it.

"A lot of people believe it's similar to fear, it's utterly consuming whenever you're around the person. We must remember we must fall in order to fly."

"Riddles and more riddles." I slap his arm softly smiling. He laughs, the sound deep and warm.

"Oh sweet girl, you'll know when you're in love. It'll hit you like a horse on fire."

I laugh at his phrasing, the sound bursting from me. It's light and full of warmth, surprising me. Kalin begins to whistle a tune, looking around at the market tents. I wipe my eyes as I look around, itching to blend in with the crowd to see if I can find my father and his friends. I can only pray they're still in the city.

"Kal, I'm going to go look around at the stalls, I'll meet you on the outskirts in an hour?" I ask, wiggling my hand from his arm.

"Alright, we meet back on the edge of the markets from where we come in. If you're not there I'm going to tell your mother," he says, pointing back towards the opening between buildings. I see the bridge in the distance.

"Okay, see you soon!" I peck his cheek before blending in with the crowd, losing sight of him immediately. I keep my head down but ears open as I move like liquid, I can make myself almost non-existent when the time calls for it.

I'm reaching the far left side of the market, closest to the taverns and bars when I feel *someone* watching me. Their eyes burn into my back and as I turn towards the flames, I stop as I look over the occupants out of the tavern and bar but see no one familiar. I frown and set off forward once more, going into the closest tent.

I walk up to the woman behind the front desk, it's a stall for travel bags.

"Excuse me, I'm looking for a group of the fae that have travelled in. Do you know where I'd be able to find them or hear anything regarding them? I'm awfully lost." I widen my eyes and feign innocence, clasping my hands in front of me. Her dull mud coloured eyes flicker behind me in annoyance, I'm no doubt holding her line up.

"I've heard they're staying at one of the inns closest to the front of the city." She grunts, extending her palm.

"Thank you, thank you!" I dig out a gold coin, dropping it into her palm, "it would be awfully generous if this conversation stays between us."

She grunts as response, shooing me away. I'm pleased with myself, now all I must do is find exactly where they're staying. My plan is coming together but I'm going to get stuck on the next part. Breaking into their room and hoping they have a map that's got Faerie marked out. If not, then I'll have to find a way to follow them without getting caught. Father would flay me alive.

I leave the tent, relieved to find no more burning eyes on me. I stick to the outskirts of the markets as I travel towards the front of the city, keeping my eyes open and peeled for men who are a good foot taller than the humans here.

I reach the front of the city, trapped down a small alley as a horse and cart slowly walk past. The wheels creak, threatening to break under the weight of whatever is stashed as cargo. I keep my breathing easy, I'd need to be heading back to the bridge soon to meet Kalin. I have to find their inn first.

The cart moves from my vision and I slide back into the street, rounding the corner of the building. I stop short when I see two men heading down a set of tall stairs, coming from one of the inns that are on the second level.

Hemlock laughs, slapping his hand against Odin's arm at something they've said. Odin grins, breaking the mask of being serious all the time. I gawk, standing there, unable to move. They stop and look back up the steps, my father comes down with Eleazar in tow behind him, a scowl plastered on his face.

I'm momentarily star struck as I watch him take the stairs, his auburn hair flowing freely around him. Its copper shine is gold and orange in the sun, the strands looking soft as silk. His white shirt hugs him, complimenting him in every way.

His golden eyes begin to drag themselves upwards, away from my father. I beg to see them, *need* to see them. My right foot shuffles forward against my will, drawn to him.

"Let's enjoy the markets, we set off tomorrow morning so let us make the most of tonight." My father's voice reaches my ears, spurring me into movement and breaking whatever spell had been cast over me. I spin and hurtle back down the street, slipping as I go down the alley. I thump against the wall as I press myself there. I breathe deeply, willing my heart to slow.

I'd found where they're staying and from the sounds of it they won't be back until later tonight. I can return at sun down and make the most of the few hours I have. I wait five more moments before mingling back in with the crowd, heading straight for the bridge. My heart is a galloping horse in my chest, my eyes continuously sweep my surroundings; afraid one of them are going to spot me.

Relief flushes through me when I find Kalin standing on the outskirts, two kebabs in his hands. I smile in greeting as I come up.

"You're late." He frowns, passing me the kebab.

"I'm sorry I got caught up, did you find a present for Emilia?" I ask before taking a bite of the kebab. We begin to walk back to the home we're staying at, Kalin takes the distraction I place in front of us and begins to tell me about the trouble he had finding her a gift. I stay interested, avoiding the urge to look over my shoulder every two seconds.

Tonight I'd make my life my own, a plan begins to unravel in my mind as the sun begins to sink low in the sky. My nerves calm instantly, I have found a purpose to focus on. I'm going to prove my father and mother wrong, I'm more than capable.

CHAPTER 7

I finish writing the letter, double checking to make sure I've noted down everything that is of importance. Kalin will show my mother this letter without a doubt, so I need her to known I'm safe as well. The sun had set hours ago and Kalin had gone to bed not long after, shutting the door to his room. The dim light of my candle is all I have to work with as I sit the note under the pen, signing it with love.

Before I can think more I grab my bag from the couch and slide it over my shoulders. I blow out the candle and place it back onto the kitchen counter, letting my eyes adjust a moment. Moonlight spills in through the open windows, lighting up the hall.

I keep my steps soft as I creep down the hallway, holding my breath as I flick the lock and peel the door inwards. The gods must be on my side because it doesn't make a noise as I shut it behind me. I don't relax just yet, still keeping my steps soft and slow as I head to the paddock. Ash knickers softly and comes up to the gate, he flicks his head as I grab his bridle.

I open the gate and let him slip past, his belly swaying and almost hitting me as he walks out. I swat his butt gently, earning a flick of his tail to my arm. I hiss at the burst of sharp pain from the lashing, who knew a horse could have such a sassy attitude.

He stays quiet and still as I put his bridle and saddle on before I hoist myself up. I lead him to the furthest side of the yard and head to the front gate. My heart is beating so fast I fear it might just stop. I can't be caught doing this or I'll be locked in that castle forever.

Ash jumps over the gate with ease, his hooves thudding on the dirt as he begins to walk down the road. A grin takes over my face, I look up to the stars and crescent moon. I'd done it. I could scream with happiness. It threatens to burst out of my chest and cover Ash with its warmth. He must feel my excitement as he breaks into a canter, carrying us over the bridge as quick as lightning. We're a mere shadow moving through the city, he navigates with ease and a confidence no horse should have.

I slow him to a walk as we head through the abandoned tents, everyone has packed up for the day, no doubt at the taverns to celebrate and do it all over again tomorrow. The chatter and music from the taverns and bars reach my sensitive ears, Ash snorts as a drunk couple stumbles past us. I'd dressed accordingly for the night, black leather pants with a black long sleeved shirt. My black cloak floats around me, concealing everything save for my hands on the reins and my head.

My hair stirs in the breeze, I'd left it down to help hide my face.

We reach the alleyway I'd come across earlier, I dismount Ash and back him in. He snorts in annoyance but does as I say, stopping once he's fully hidden in the darkness. I kiss his nose, scratching under his chin.

"I'll be back soon. I need to get a map before we can head off for our own adventure. If you hear my low whistle come running. I'll be at the front of the building. If I don't whistle wait here and I'll find you soon. Okay?" I whisper, stroking his large cheeks. He knickers and nudges my chin with his nose. I grin at him, his chestnut eyes hidden in the darkness. I never questioned the bond I shared with him, I just know that deep down there's more to it than just a woman who loves her horse. Or maybe there isn't.

I give him one last stroke before heading along the side of the building. I peer around the corner. My eyes trail the wooden stairs that climb up the front of the building, a steel railing the only protection from falling to the ground. A lantern blazes against the night, lighting the way. No one is out. I gather my courage and head for the stairs, holding my head high and shoulders back. I tuck my hair behind my ears, letting the pointed ends show.

I take the stairs two at a time, ignoring my sweaty palms as my nerves begin to come back. If I'm caught in their room...hell I can't even think about it. Not when I'm a few steps away from the small balcony that takes me inside.

I open the wooden door and walk in with purpose, the interior of the inn is simple. To my left is a desk with an open archway that leads to a back room. The red velvet carpet runs from the incredibly small lobby and down the hallway. The man behind the desk shoots up in his chair as I close the door behind me.

"Good evening, what brings you to my inn this late?" his deep voice raises the hair on my arms as he looks over me, lips puckering. I smile brightly at him, relaxing my body as I walk over to the desk with confidence.

"Good evening! My friends checked in earlier and I only just arrived, I was caught on the road getting to town. They're at the tavern down the road at the moment but I thought I'd check in and freshen up before re-joining them to celebrate."

His eyes narrow on me before he looks down at the book in front of him, dragging his finger down the names listed. I lean over, "It'll be under Nyx."

"Ah yes. Nyx with four occupants. They never mentioned there was a fifth." He looks back up to me now, raising a grey eyebrow in question. His grey, curly hair is thin but fluffy against his head. In the dim light he looks far older than what he must be.

"I was originally going to book another inn but they insisted I stay with them. Nyx is my brother." I drop the smile slightly, urging myself to believe my lie as he watches me with precision. *I am Nyx's sister. The resemblance is uncanny. I am his sister.*

"Hmph, I suppose I can write you in. Name?" he grunts, grabbing a pencil.

"Allison." I blurt the first name that comes to mind, he scribbles the name down beside the notation and passes me a key. I smile brightly as I take it.

"Room four, on your right." He looks back down to the book, dismissing me. I hurry down the door, unlocking the fourth. I slip into the dark room, turning the gas on to the closest lantern. It splutters to life.

I lean against the closed door, my palms stick to the wood.

Two single beds press against the right side of the room while two others mirror them on the left. Each bed has the person's bag on it, I spot Eleazar's twin swords on the left bed closest to the other wall. I move quickly, running to his bed. My hands shake as I look down at his two large, brown leather travel bags.

Oh my god, am I really doing this?

Yes.

I unlock the buckle and pull back the top. Clothes are packed neatly inside, a few devices I don't recognise sit down the sides. I grab a small knife that's been tucked down between shirts, the scent of rum and honey and *Eleazar* hits me like a horse, full speed and unrelenting. Goodness I could stand here all night smelling his clothes alone.

The wooden handle is warm in my hand as I look over the gold blade, words of a language I don't understand are carved in both sides. No doubt a faerie blade for magical creatures, I scowl and shove it back in between shirts. I buckle the bag back up and hover over the second, smaller one. I don't know why I'm snooping through his bags, why would he carry a map on him?

I peer into the smaller one, finding a small red leather journal, bound shut by a piece of black rope. I itch to open it and read his thoughts, not believing he'd be one to journal. I just can't picture him sitting down after a long day and divulging his thoughts.

I sift through the papers in there as well, a lot of them I don't understand. Words I can't translate, symbols I don't understand. It frustrates me more than ever, how did I let myself become so sheltered? It spurs me on even more.

I buckle his bag again and sit them together, hoping he won't know I've touched them. I walk to the bed beside his, a single brown cotton bag sits on the deep red quilt. I unbutton the two buttons and look inside, relieved to find papers I understand. Maps I can read.

I flick through them, finding a map that has our continent, split down the middle to show Akrania and Faerie. In the bottom right corner of Akrania, over a river and hidden in the forest is a small cross. Scribble beside it is one word that has my heart soaring, *Faerie*.

I pull my own map out from my shirt, grabbing a loose pencil and lining my map up next to this one. I quickly scribble down the mark, as well as the lagoon for Dead Man's

Hollow. I don't know what's there but it's a half way point between Orrinshire and the entrance to Faerie. I slide my map back into my waistband under my shirt before dropping the pen back into the bag. I fold the map and replace it where I found it.

I close the bag and make quick work of the buttons. I need to leave, now. I've already wasted time going through Eleazar's bags. I give the two beds I've touched one last look, hoping it's exactly how they left them. I blow out the lantern and leave the room.

I walk to the desk, the casual movement spurs my anxiety. They could walk in any minute. The man looks up, eyes guarded. I drop the key back down.

"Thanks but I might change my mind about the room. Staying with four of them would be torture, I'm sure you understand," I say apologetically, batting my lashes at him. He sighs, scribbling the fake name out.

"Nothing but trouble," he mumbles under his breath. I turn and leave, pulling my cloak around my body tightly as I fly down the stairs. I can't focus on anything but getting back to Ash. I either camp out until they leave, or I leave now and hope to arrive before them. I glance out at the darkness of the bare land, mountains and forest rise in the distance but there's no chance of coverage. I'll have to leave first.

The map seers the skin of my hip as I slip down the side of the building, I relax slightly as I creep down towards the alley. I'd packed accordingly and had packed enough fruit and dry meat to last me a few days. I could leave tonight, letting Ash carry me to my next adventure.

My heart stutters as I pause. What am I going to do once I reach the entrance? Can Ash come through or will I have to leave him behind? I hadn't thought that through. Maybe I can leave him at Dead Man's Hollow if there's a stable. I have more than enough gold on me to cover the costs. He'll be okay. I can't think or believe anything other than that.

"Well, I wasn't expecting to find you out here but damn you've just turned my night around," a man's voice rumbles from behind me. I freeze, recognising the scorn and hatred behind his words. It's the man from this morning, the one who had shoved me.

"I don't want trouble," I say softly, raising both hands in the air so he knows I'm not armed.

"You don't, but I do." His voice is closer now. I spin on my heels and come face to face with him. His eyes are glassy, whiskey fills the air with each breath out. It doesn't help I have to look down at him, he pulls his top lip back; exposing yellowing teeth I hadn't noticed at our first encounter. Moonlight hits each inch of his face, he is enraged.

Simply because I'm a faerie.

"If you want gold I can give it to you." My voice is a squeak as I take a step back. I may be taller but he's far wider. His meaty hands fist together as his eyes narrow in on me.

"I don't want your stupid fucking faerie money!" He yells. Spittle flies from his mouth. I stumble backwards again, heart erratic. What a good way to start my journey of freedom. I'm face to face with a faerie hating human. I lower my hands, knowing I've got a small blade tucked away into my bra. If I could find a moment to retrieve it I might have a chance of walking away without too many injuries.

"It's normal money..." I trail off, my words only enraging him more.

He moves fast for a large man, so fast I don't see his hands coming for me until it's too late.

I hit the dirt ground hard, the breath whooshing out of me. I gasp, terrified as I scramble to sit up. He towers over me now, staring down at me with that snarl. A snarl that suits Eleazar so much it makes me swoon, but this man, this man terrifies me.

The heart of a human man is horrid, so full of hatred they refuse to see anything else.

"You stupid smart ass bitch, no one is here to save you now." He spits down at me, stalking closer. My heartbeat is a drum in my ears, I can barely make out his words as I sit there. Like an idiot, completely terrified to move.

I can't—

I can't move.

I have never felt terror like this.

I cry out as his boot connects with my calf, it drags me from the depths I'd found myself trapped in. I move too slow. His boots kick at whatever part of me he can touch, I curl in on myself. My back explodes with pain, my legs. I protect the back of my head and face, tears stream down my cheeks and dirt sticks to them.

I can't breathe.

My lungs deflate in my chest, the urgency to breath has me squeezing my eyes shut. I open my mouth but I can't draw in a breath.

There's so much pain.

I can't—

I don't notice when he stops kicking me, the pain consumes me. I hear the buckle of a belt and the zip of a fly, a struggle with clothes. I'm dragged by my feet towards him, I cry out now as I struggle against his hold.

He uses his weight to his advantage as he flips me over in the dirt.

I get a mouthful of dirt as my face slams into the ground, more tears stream down as my face aches. I taste blood.

A rough hand pulls me back over, a warm, large body is pressed against me. Whiskey breath hits my face.

"Ain't so tough now are ya?" he spits, hand grabbing my delicate throat.

Now I truly can't breathe. I claw at his hand, nails ripping away flesh as my eyes begin to bulge. Black stars begin to spot the corners of my vision, I struggle to stay conscious as I gasp for air, anything to stop the explosive pain in my chest from consuming me.

His large hand releases me before the darkness consumes me. Oh dear *god* I've never been more happy to breath in my life.

The relief is short lived as he struggles to pull my pants off. Now I do fight back, I slap at his chest and face, pulling his hair and trying to get my fingers into his eyes.

It's no use.

My breaths come in gasps as I struggle to stay in the present. This can't be happening.

I scramble for the blade in my bra, he's too busy struggling to get his underwear down to notice I've gone utterly still.

My mind clears as he lowers himself above me, shoving my legs apart.

Something breaks inside of my soul.

Darkness comes rushing to the surface, curling my fingers around the blade. I snarl in *fury* as he looks back up to me, startled.

"What the fuck is going on—"

My arm moves on its own as I take a backseat in my mind. Whatever has been let out of the broken piece of my soul is starving. It hungers for death. The destruction.

Slicing the blade through his throat is as easy as breathing.

He splutters as both hands rise to the gaping gash. There's a pause before blood gushes out of the wound, I shove him sideways before wrenching my pants back up and securing them. I leap on top of him and drive the blade into his chest, over and over.

I don't stop even after he's taken his last breath, until his chest is a mess of flesh.

I look down at my blood covered hands. I feel the droplets slide down my face; in my hair. My entire body trembles as I realise what I've done.

I've killed a man.

No one would believe me if I claimed self-defence...with his chest in ribbons and head barely attached to his neck.

Something nudges at me inside, urging me to reach forwards with that darkness once more. I'm too weak to resist, too emotional wrecked to fight it. My lips part as my body takes a deep breath, my chest rattles as I see *his soul* begin to leak from his lips. The white smokes curls and dances towards me, his desperate screams echo softly as the smoke is sucked in through my lips.

Once the last drop is gone my shoulders slump.

I blink as if in a daze as I stand, my legs threaten to buckle but I force myself forward. I find Ash and hoist myself up, he knickers in distress, head tossing. I feel the map in my waistband, I pocket the knife in one of Ash's saddle bags. I urge him forward, heading for the entrance of the city. I don't dare glance down at the body we leave behind in the shadows.

Ash's warmth underneath me is the only thing that grounds me, the only thing that stops me from breaking into a million pieces.

Something has awoken inside of me and it is starving.

CHAPTER 8

I'm utterly lost. Ash doesn't relent from galloping until we reach the cover of the closest forest, only then does he slow from a gallop to a walk. He heaves each breath, rivers of sweat run down his neck and belly. We'd ridden most of the night, the distance to the forest from Orrinshire is extremely misleading. As if it's a mirage.

I try not to think about the blood that coats my hands and face, dried in my shirt and pants.

I try not to think about the feeling of *something* inside of me, dormant until now it's had its first taste of death.

All I can see in my mind is the small knife coming down on his chest. His throat cut and those lifeless eyes staring up at me; frozen in fear. I can't think about what he would have done. I'm thankful for whatever came to light in that moment, but now it's here, what if it wants to stay? I shake my head, taking deep breaths to calm my thoughts before they race away on me.

The sky brightens gradually, melting into soft hues of gold and blue. I look over my shoulder to find forest behind me. There's no city in sight. I pull Ash to a stop and climb from him, guilt gnaws at me as I follow droplets of sweat.

"I'm sorry boy," I sob, bringing my face to his. I press my

forehead to the skin between his eyes, stroking both of his large cheeks with my hands. He nudges me, leaning into my touch. A few tears escape my eyes, falling into his hair. "Come on, let's find a place to rest."

I hold his reins tightly in my hands as we begin to walk deeper into the forest, with the dawn breaking I can finally make out our surroundings. Wildlife begins to wake with the rising sun, birds begin to chatter sweet tunes while small rodents scurry through the underbrush.

Elm and birch trees make up a majority of the forest, leaving enough space between each trunk to move freely through with Ash. Orange and gold leaves scatter the forest floor from the passing winter, crunching under each step I take. In the distance I hear the trickle of water, it perks me up slightly.

I lead Ash towards the noise, putting the low shrubs out of the way as I walk. Wherever we've ridden in has no path whatsoever. The thought scares me, if I'm lost in this forest...my mother and father's wrath will be the least of my worries.

Ahead the trees break, green grass sprouts a few metres before turning to small black stones as it reaches the river. I halt Ash, undoing his saddle and resting it on a low branch of an elm tree. I unclip his bridle, hanging it on the saddle. He immediately heads for the river, his heavy hooves splash in as he paws at the water; it just reaches his large stomach.

I manage a smile. It cracks at the blood on my face.

I strip down to my bra and underwear, digging out a new shirt and pants to wear after washing off the dry blood. I pull out the small cloth I'd brought, it'll help dry me. I walk on the stones and crouch down once the water reaches my calves. I sit back, gasping at the chill. Ash whinnies and paws at the water before getting down to his knees and sitting on his side. He drinks heavily before throwing his head back and smiling.

I roll my eyes at him, getting to work on my blood covered hands.

I scrub relentlessly until the skin on my hands are raw and pink, I scrape under my nails with a piece of bark that had been floating past; desperate to not leave a trace. If I can't see the blood I can almost fool myself into thinking it didn't happen, that it was just a horrible dream that I couldn't wake up from.

I wash my face next, dipping my head down and splashing the water up. I rub viciously until my cheeks are smooth and there're no bumps of dried blood. I sink lower into the water, lying back so the morning sun can bask down on my bare skin.

I close my eyes as the water fans out around me. I grip the rocks underneath to stop myself from floating down the river. It's peaceful, every noise is dulled; the only thing I can hear is the water moving.

I sit up and open my eyes, Ash still sits on his side watching me with those intense chestnut eyes. I drag myself from the water, shivering at the breeze that caresses my skin like a lover. I hurry to drag the small cloth over myself, drying as best as I can.

I change into the new set of clothes before pulling my cloak and boots back on, I pull my hair back into a high messy bun. The water splashes behind me, I look over to see Ash striding up the bank. He stops before gracefully dropping and rolling, grass and dirt sticking to his hair as he rolls.

"What's the point of having a bath if you're just going to roll and get dirty again?" I sigh, grabbing his bridle as I walk over to where he stands and shakes. He doesn't resist as I slide the bit in his mouth, clasping it in place. I lead him back to the tree, tying the reins close to the base of his throat.

"You're too wet for the saddle just yet, we'll rest here and you can eat the grass and keep guard. I might take a small nap." I pat his neck, he snorts before walking a few feet away and lowering his head. I grab the saddle and prop it on the ground as a makeshift pillow before lying down.

It takes me a few moments to get comfortable but when I do, I try my best to relax. My mind is fried, my thoughts quiet for once and leave me utterly alone. I feel safe in this small slice of paradise, with Ash on guard I can grab a few moments of shut eye before figuring out the rest.

I need a good nap to chip away at the iceberg.

I GROAN AS I STIR, blinking as I come to. My neck aches from the odd angle I'd slept on. I wipe my eyes as I sit up, yawning. I look around the dim clearing, Ash raises his head from where he drinks at the river. I look around, shadows grow and begin to darken the clearing and the thick forest beyond it. I grimace as I stand, rubbing my back.

Everything aches.

I walk to the edge of the clearing and begin to gather small broken branches. I'd have to try my hand at a fire. Ash wanders over to where I begin to stack the sticks, I go back and forth until the pile is knee high. I shuffle through the saddle bags, desperately searching for anything that could help start a fire.

Ash nudges my back. I reach behind and push his head away, "Boy not now I'm trying to start this fire." I grumble, eyes straining against the darkness. I don't have much longer until I'll be blind.

He nudges me harder, I tumble forward. I groan as my back explodes with sharp pain, hands splayed in front of me, "Ash, I love you but if you do that again I swear to god I'm never taking you to that enchanted paddock back home again."

"Need a light?" A deep, rumbling voice says from behind me. I freeze, struck with fear. Ash whinnies softly, pawing at the ground. I suck in a large breath as I slowly turn around, still crouched down. Ash towers above me, protecting me from wherever that voice came from.

A golden flare erupts from the other side of the river, I peer under Ash's large belly. Midnight black legs stand on the other side of the clearing, their bare feet sink into the grass. A circle of blood red and black thorns encase them. The breeze stirs their black silk leg slip, exposing the skin up to their knee.

My heart jackhammers in my chest as I reach up and grasp my small knife, my hands shake violently as I stand. I step around Ash but still stay close, his ears flatten against his head as he snorts. I can't say the thing standing on the other side of the bank is human, or faerie. Their black skin is covered in whirls of gold, twining from their hands to the base of their neck.

Depthless black eyes stare at me, not blinking as they watch.

Darkness swims around them like a second skin, the night is nothing compared to this thing. Flat, white hair sits against their shoulders. The wind doesn't stir it. I look back down to their open palm where the golden flame burns brightly.

"What are you?" I whisper, utterly terrified.

"I am not of this world." His deep voice rumbles in his chest, he's tall and muscular, that much is evident under the thin material of his clothes.

"What...what are you doing here?" I try and find my courage but it's left me behind, hightailing the moment he spoke. He smirks, exposing white teeth.

"You have something that I lay claim to. You are in debt to me."

My breathing picks up as I begin to feel myself panic, "I don't know what you're talking about."

He tilts his head slowly, like an owl "Your soul belongs to me."

"I belong to no one but myself," I feel myself bristle, "I don't know what you think you're doing here but you aren't welcome."

"Is that any way to speak to a God?"

Suddenly we're surrounded by darkness, its inky caress makes my skin crawl as it paws at my ankles and calves. Ash rears up, whining in distress. I press into his neck, comforting him as best as I can. The man begins to walk slowly towards me, nothing but a predatory gaze in his eyes.

"You—you're a God?" I whisper, my eyes bulge as he walks on top of the water. He smiles cruelly as he makes it to the other side, power radiates of him in waves. Dark and hungry and *awful*.

"I am the most feared god of all in Faerie." He declares, stopping mere metres away from me. I have to tilt my head back to keep eye contact. I'm too afraid to look anywhere else.

"I don't know about the god's in Faerie," I say slowly, completely struck dumb. He blinks, in shock or surprise I'm unsure.

"You're a faerie are you not?"

"Of course I am. I've lived a sheltered life."

He sucks at his teeth, those emotionless eyes survey me; stripping me of any guard or comfort and leaving me feeling utterly naked before him. "I am Salis, god of death. I am the creator of Fallen magic."

Fallen magic.

As if those two words have shouted a call, the darkness inside me begins to stir to answer. I struggle to push it down, hide it, anything that will make me less of a target for him. I'm unlucky as I feel it run through my legs and to my arms; all the way up my face.

"Ah, there it is." He growls with satisfaction, watching me with hungry eyes now.

I'm frozen in place, caught in his eyes. The darkness warms in recognition at his voice, bringing up memories I don't want to remember.

I blink and look down, the mutilated corpse of the man is underneath me; blood coats my hands as the blade catches the light of the moon.

"No," I whisper, my breath fogs in front of me.

I scramble backwards, "No, no, no—"

My stomach clenches as I feel the urge to be sick. This isn't real. I can't be here, I killed him.

"Now do you see?" his voice comes from nowhere but everywhere in the darkness around me. I look around frantically, my hair whipping at my face. Tears begin to spill over my cheeks as the panic begins to build in my chest.

"You belong to me, you have no choice. Once the hunter comes for you, your soul will be mine." Laughter rings in my ears, "he's already looking for the creature that used fallen magic. I'm thrilled to see how long it takes him to realise it is you he's after."

I can't talk as I'm trapped in place, the scene around me begins to melt and change until I'm standing alone in a barren field. Broken trees claw at the air, towards a deep red sky. Groans and moans reach my ears as my eyes look around. A cold wind bites at me, tearing at my shirt.

Arms begin to break through the hard, charred ground around me. My breath comes in sharp bursts as faeries begin to climb out of the ground. Their white, milky eyes all swivel to me, their hands clawing at the ground towards me.

"This is the fate that awaits you." Salis's voice whispers in my ear.

Faeries begin to walk towards me now, their outstretched hands guiding them straight to me. My nostrils flare as they gather around, they all freeze and stare. I can't see anything other than the faeries, all of them have milky white, dead eyes.

"These are the souls of fallen magic that I collect, this is where you return to."

Salis appears before me, grasping my chin between his fingers. His cold breath hits my cheek, his black eyes glow as he forces me to stare at him, I struggle against his hold "I suggest you learn what you can about fallen magic before your time is up. Just know I'll be waiting, your soul..." he inhales, something tugs out of my chest and slips through my lips; light blue smoke stretches towards him and disappears into his mouth. "Your soul is divine."

I relax as my body explodes with euphoria, sagging against Salis. Another arm snakes out, holding me in place. My eyes flutter closed, I want to give him whatever he's taking. I've never felt this good in my life.

"I'll be waiting Amaryllis. Until we meet again."

I'm thrown back into reality, gasping for breath where I lay face down in the grass. Ash knickers frantically, tossing his large head at me before prancing around in alarm. I cough and splutter as I roll onto my side, my eyes are dry as I peel them open to see my fire blazing with golden flames.

I hadn't been dreaming.

The God of Death is waiting for me, a debt I never want to repay but have no choice.

CHAPTER 9

After the visit from Salis I can't shake the feeling of being watched, my every move seems to be tracked. My skin crawls constantly as the hours turn to days, Ash doesn't complain when we ride through the day and rest for a few hours at night. Whatever is making my skin crawl must be making his as well.

I had met Salis, the God of Death. The creator of fallen magic.

I have fallen magic.

Once I'd found myself at the fire the darkness inside of me had receded, dormant now that its master had left. I'd thrown up until I was gagging, nothing left to expel in my stomach. I can vaguely recall what Eleazar had told me, that the fallen are doomed. There's no way someone with fallen magic can be left to live and if they are the magic is going to consume them anyway.

I can't win.

I push the thoughts from my mind and my cloak billows out around me as Ash gallops through the forest. I let the midday sun warm my skin as I tilt my face towards the blue sky. I haven't bothered to look at the map, I can't bring myself to think about why we'd come here in such a hurry. The map is useless to me for the moment.

Up ahead the trees begin to thin, I slow Ash until we're walking. Small cottages come into view, a few people mill about. Heads turn towards the noise of a traveller. The ground beneath Ash turns to a dirt road, leading to the small village and heading straight through it.

I tense as we come closer, everyone here is human from what I can see so far.

I pull Ash to a stop, climbing down to lead him. Everyone in the village dresses the same, men wearing brown pants and white shirts with overalls for the small farms behind the cottages while the women wear simple dresses with white aprons over the front.

I scan the crowd, looking for a tavern of some sort. A place to rest for a night that isn't under the stars. I stop as we reach the middle of the village, the space around us opens up to reveal a well in the middle of the road.

"What brings you to these parts?" A strong, female voice says to my side. I look over to where she stands, hands planted on her hips as she stares down at me from the patio of her home. Her dull brown hair is pulled back into a low bun, exposing her sharp features.

"I'm passing through. I was wondering if you had a tavern with a stable that I could rent for the night." I say smoothly, smiling lightly. Her eyes narrow as she comes down the steps, gathering the skirts of her dress in her hands as she walks across the dirt.

"For three gold we might." She comes to a stop, eyes dragging over my figure. My shirt's crumpled, my pants are stained. My hair is a greasy mess and I'm no doubt covered in bruises she can't see. Three gold is nothing to me. I turn and dig into the closest saddle bag. I pull out the velvet money purse I carry.

"Four gold if my horse is tended to." I state, looking back to her. Her green eyes trail over Ash and even though she may not like me I see the adoration in her eyes for the stallion. He snorts as if he knows it.

"Deal. Follow me." She spins and takes a road to the left from the large intersection. I walk a few paces behind her, glancing at the wooden homes and small shops.

"So, what is this place?" I ask, looking back to her thin form.

"This is Elk, we're between the great river and Dead Man's Hollow." She looks over her shoulder at me, "where are you from?"

"I'm from Elderview but I've travelled from Orrinshire." I shove the money purse into my pant pocket and pull my map out, opening it with both hands. I trust Ash to walk along with us and not run off. "Would you be able to show me on my map where exactly we are? I'm actually lost."

She stops in front of me, I pause and open the map for us both to look at. Her finger runs along the great river that stems from the one that protects Elderview. She taps a spot in the middle, just pass the trees but before the mountains.

"This is it, where is your destination?" she watches me warily now. I fold the map and shove it back into my pockets.

"I was heading to Dead Man's Hollow." Truth enough.

"Hmp."

We reach the end of the dirt road as it breaks into a large corn field. She stops, gesturing to the tavern to our left. Its deep brown wood is weathered from the sun, two stories with four windows on the second floor that I can see. I walk over and tie Ash's reins to the wood post near a water trough. I pat his neck.

She walks up the stairs, gesturing for me to follow. I give Ash one last look before following her up, the two doors are propped open with large rocks. There's few people in here, they all stop talking and eating as they look up at us. It's dim in here but cool.

"We have a traveller, she's needing a room for the night and a stable for her horse." The girl says, stopping at the bar. A middle aged woman peers around her to where I stand just inside the doors. Grey streaks her sandy blonde hair, she adjusts her glasses.

"One night?" she asks, her voice deep.

"Yes please. I'm sorry it's on short notice." I pull out the money purse, ready to pay whatever the cost. I need a bath desperately and a warm bed without the fear of something coming for me through the night.

"No need for apologies," she waves her hand, smiling at me, "come closer girl."

I do as she says, smiling sheepishly as I stop beside the girl.

"What's your name?"

"Ama," she nods a few times, up close she looks older than I first picked her for. Smile lines crease the skin around her mouth and corners of her eyes.

"I'm Magda, this is Poppy." She gestures to the girl who led me here, she huffs.

"It's nice to meet you Ama." Poppy says, picking at a loose thread in her pale blue dress.

"Is four gold enough?" I ask, pulling out four coins. A few occupants gasp, I raise an eyebrow in question. Poppy chuckles, smirking at me. I look to Magda, dropping them into her extended hand.

"Gold is rare in Elk, we don't see it often." Her fingers close over the coins as she opens a draw behind the bar. She passes me a wooden cube, attached to a piece of rope that attaches to a key. "Your room is upstairs, number two. Grab your things and Poppy will take your steed to the stables. You'll see the barn from the porch, past the field."

I close my hand over the wood, nodding my thanks. I follow Poppy out and grab my two saddle bags from Ash's saddle.

"He's stunning," Poppy sighs, rubbing a pale hand down his nose.

"He knows it as well," I mumble. He knickers, turning his head to me. "What? You do." I say to him, rolling my eyes.

"It's like he understands you," she says, undoing his reins.

"Some days I think he does." I throw a bag over my shoulder, holding the other in my hand. "Where are the stables?"

"Over there," I turn to where she points, behind the corn field is a large red barn. There's a path that runs down the middle of the field to the barn. I nod a few times, it's close enough that I can escape if anything goes wrong.

"Okay. Thank you." She smiles as she leads Ash away, he walks alongside her more than eager. He'd be starving for a good feed that isn't just grass. I walk back into the tavern, keeping my eyes down as I find the stairs in the back right corner. I walk up them, my feet half dragging.

The small hallway opens up before me, at the end there's a vase of red roses on a small wooden table. I head to the second door, unlocking it before pushing in. I sit the key on the desk as I walk in and shut the door behind me.

A single bed and a cupboard is all the room consists of. I dump my bags on the ground and walk over to the window, looking out at the street. I can see the stables from here. I turn back and sit on the bed, tugging my boots off. I run a hand through my hair, tugging out the knots.

I need a bath.

I gather my energy and grab the bag that has my clothes, I

grab the key and leave the room; making sure to lock it behind me. I walk down the stairs and head to the bar, Magda stops the conversation with another worker and smiles over at me.

"Any problems?" she asks as I come over.

"No, it's great, thank you. I was wondering if you had a bathroom?"

She points to the other side of the room, "Just over through that door." I look over and see a door. I smile in thanks and quickly walk over to it, avoiding the stares of the other people here still. The bathroom is small but clean. I lock the door behind me and make quick work of pumping water into the metal tub, it's not luxurious but I'm too exhausted to care. I'd been bathing in a river, anything is an upgrade from that. I strip down, looking in the mirror that hangs above the sink.

I turn slowly, looking over my shoulder.

My back is covered in purpling bruises, a clear boot mark stretches from the top of my right shoulder and meets at my spine. I'd got the shit absolutely kicked out of me. I have a few bruises on my thighs, but my back is the worst.

I climb into the tub and lower myself into the water, grabbing the bar of soap that sits on the edge of the tub. The water's warm. I scrub at every surface, ducking under to scrub my hair. I only stop once every bit of skin is rubbed raw and my hair is clean. I climb from the tub and grab a towel, drying quickly before dressing in my last clean outfit. It's a pale green dress that swims around my legs. I leave the bathroom, hair dripping, as I head back to the bar.

"Would I be able to get something to eat?" I ask, drawing Magda's attention.

"Of course love! Go upstairs and put your things away, if you have dirty clothes just bring them back down and I'll get them washed for you." She smiles at me, unafraid.

"Thank you." I do as she says, dumping the bag on the bed

with my dirty clothes gathered in my arms. I'd slipped my boots back on, I'd go and check Ash is settled in once I've eaten. I take a seat on the cushioned seat at the bar. I pass another worker my clothes as they come over with a wooden basket.

"So what brings you to these parts?" Magda asks, sitting a bowl of soup in front of me. I take the spoon and have a mouthful before answering, shutting my eyes at the hearty taste of meat and vegetables.

"I was travelling to Dead Man's Hollow but got lost. I'm not the best at reading maps," I say, looking back to her. She wipes down the bar, placing a glass of water down for me.

"It's easy to get lost in this forest, wicked thing it is. We rarely get travellers though, it's nice to see a fresh face for once."

"You...you don't care that I'm a faerie?" I ask, tilting my head as I watch her. She barks out a laugh, shaking her head.

"Of course not girl, we've had all types of creatures, human and other, pass through. Business is business here, doesn't matter who it comes from. We simply ask you pay and make no trouble while you stay." She grins, the lines of her mouth creasing, "it's quiet obvious you're no human."

I blush, looking back down to the bowl of soup, "I know. I just know it makes some humans...uncomfortable."

"You have nothing to worry about here. The villagers are cautious but nice." She leans back, throwing the rag over her left shoulder, "so what's your story?"

"My story?"

"Yes, your story. Why are you heading to Dead Man's by yourself? It's rare for a woman to travel alone."

"Well...I'm looking for an adventure. I grew tired of staying in Elderview and decided I wanted to travel, find more places to add to my map. Make friends along the road." I shrug my shoulders. I couldn't tell her I'm heading to Faerie and tracking my father and his friends. I finish the soup and sit back with a sigh of relief.

"An adventure I'm sure you'll find. Dead Man's is definitely worth the travel, the folk are nice for the most part but you seem smart enough to steer clear of trouble when it arises."

"Have…any other faerie's passed through?" I ask, looking up to her.

"Not yet. We get them from time to time." She raises an eyebrow, "Why? Are you expecting some to come through?"

"I don't know yet," I suck at my teeth, thinking, "a group of my friends are heading through Dead Man's and I was hoping to catch them and travel with them."

"I can let you know if any arrive?" she offers.

"Yes please," I stand from the bar, belly full, "thank you for the meal. I'm going to check on Ash and then I might catch a nap. I'll see you later."

"Anytime Ama." She watches me leave, smiling warmly. It's a nice feeling, not being judged simply because I'm not human. I head into the sun, it warms the top of my head as I walk through the corn field, the large stalks are taller than I am; their crop ripe and ready to be harvested.

The town is simple…but eerily quiet.

All I can hear is the chatter of birds, the murmur of crops. The folk are quiet, peaceful. Nothing like the bustling streets of Orrinshire of the chatter of Elderview. Flowers spot the grass around me as the crops abruptly end and open up to the large dirt path. Red wooden doors are held open, exposing a hay floor and rows of wooden stable gates.

I walk in and find a few other horses in their stables, they watch me with large unreadable eyes as I head to where Ash has his head sticking out over the gate. He whinnies as I approach, pulling his lip back in a smile as I come to stop in front of his stall.

Poppy had unsaddled him, taken his bridle off and given him a good brush down. She'd sat his things on the wooden pole in front of his stall. I lean over the gate, he'd eaten through a fresh square of green hay. In the corner a small cement water trough sits, full to the brim.

"I'm glad she looked after you," I say softly, resting my forehead against his. I rub my hands over his cheeks, scratching under his chin. He calms me as I breathe in, the reality of our situation setting in. I have to find a way to think about the events that have led up to this point without breaking down, without breaking entirely. I'd barely kept myself together the last few days, hanging onto a thin thread tethering me to the present.

I'd have to accept what I'd done sooner or later, but for the afternoon and tonight I'm going to focus on just being present and enjoying the comforts of a warm dinner and a comfortable bed.

CHAPTER
10

I count to ten as I toss and turn under the covers, music and laughter reaches me through the wooden doors. I'd left Ash and had something to eat and I've been in my room ever since. No one had mentioned that the tavern beneath me would be holding a celebration, a part of me is thankful for the constant noise. It drowns out my own thoughts.

I relent, climbing from the bed. My washed clothes had been sitting outside my door in a cloth bag once I'd finished dinner and I'd been able to wear my pale blue nightgown that reaches down to my ankles. I pull on my cloak and head out of the room, I won't be sleeping anytime soon so I may as well make the most of it.

I pause on the last step as I look around, the tavern is packed with people. In the right corner of the room, beside the bar, a small band is set up. They start up a new song, the banjo plucks like mad as one of the others plays a tune on a flute. The chatter and laughter and singing reach my ears, there are no thoughts of my own that I can hear.

"Ama, what're you doing down here?" Poppy asks, appearing in front of me. Her hair is down in loose waves, her dress a deep ruby that clinches at her waist before cascading into skirts. She holds a glass in her hand.

"I couldn't sleep." I look back over the crowd, my eyes zone out as the room blurs.

"You could have worn something that isn't pjs." She takes my hand, drawing my attention back to her. She tugs, throwing her head towards the bar, "Come on, let's get you a drink."

I don't argue as we walk through the crowd, she sits me down before sliding into the stool beside mine. Magda smiles as she comes over, radiating with joy. I feel myself shrivel, slumping my shoulders and dipping my chin down.

"I was wondering when you'd come down." Magda says.

"I couldn't sleep," I look back up to her, "I don't mind it though."

"It's like this at the tavern every night," Poppy chirps, "has been from the moment I was old enough to walk."

Magda laughs, "Oh please girl, it was like this long before you came along."

"We never have nights like this in Elderview," I say, drawing both of their attention to me. Poppy raises an eyebrow, sipping her drink.

"I've been there a handful of times, it's rather dull." Magda sighs, shaking her head.

"What's it like?" Poppy asks.

I shrug my shoulders as I draw circles on the bar, "It's small. Probably smaller than Elk. I live with my mother and father in the faerie castle above the village in the forest but I have family down there. It's in a mountain gulley protected by a river. I don't think many people know it's even there."

"What do you do for fun?" Poppy leans in, puzzled. It startles a laugh from me.

"I spend time with my grandparents or I spend the days riding Ash."

Magda pushes a glass towards me, I peer down at the dark contents and look back up to her.

"It's wine, home made from my very own grape vine." She smiles, proud at herself. I lift the glass to my lips, taking a small sip. I scrunch my nose up at the sudden sour taste that melts to bittersweet. Poppy laughs, slapping her hand against the bar.

"It's not...horrid?" I take another sip. It's definitely a taste one would have to grow accustomed too.

"It isn't for everyone, but at least you can say you've tried it." Magda smiles, "I have to go serve but I hope you girls have a good night." She turns away, quickly turning back a moment later.

"What?" I ask, frowning slightly at the look of shock on her face.

"There's another faerie in town. He's staying at the smaller tavern down the road, I thought he might be one of your friends. Have a good night!" She turns back and walks down to the opposite end of the bar. My heart slams in my chest, adrenaline coursing through me. My hand tightens on the glass.

"You look like you've seen a ghost," Poppy says, prodding my shoulder. I look to her, shaking myself. It's no use. The unease has already set in. Who could it be? It may not even be one of the men with my father.

Oh god what if it's my father. I don't know which option is worse.

"Where's the small tavern?" I ask instead, her eyes narrow.

"It's towards the front of town, it has a water trough out the front. It's the only other tavern in town." Poppy takes my glass. I open my mouth to argue. She shrugs and cuts me off,

"What? You look about ready to flee. We don't want to waste the wine."

She holds both glasses up to her face, grinning.

"Fine. I'll be back soon." I rise from the chair and slip through the crowd. It takes all my patience not to burst out of the tavern and run towards Ash. Now that I knew where I was and had marked it on my map I could leave and get to Faerie by myself. I don't need to follow the others there.

I leave the tavern, the dirt soft underneath my bare feet.

I run through the corn field, moving like a wraith through the night. The barn doors have been closed for the night. I come to a stop and pull the doors apart enough so that I can slip through. Moonlight spills in through the high windows, basking a few of the horses in silver light. I walk down to Ash's stable. He turns from where he'd been standing facing the wall, no doubt sleeping. His dark ears flicker as I open the gate and slip into his stall.

I crouch down and lean back against one of the wooden sides. My nails dig into the skin of my knees as I keep myself together. Ash nudges me with his nose before playing with my hair.

"I just need to think," I whisper to him, pulling my hair from his lips.

I have two options. I stay the night and leave early morning and hope I don't run into whichever faerie is in Elk or, I go back to the tavern and pack my things and leave now. Leaving in the daylight would be more ideal as I can't read a map at night time but leaving in daylight might let the other faerie find me if they're looking for me. Either way I'm screwed.

I chew my bottom lip anxiously coming to a decision.

"Tonight we leave," I whisper to Ash, rising from the stall. I give his neck a quick scratch before leaving the stable again, his saddle and bridle still sit on the pole in front of his stall. I begin to head for the front of the barn, nerves nearly fried. In ten minutes I'd be leaving, heading god knows where.

I slip from the barn doors.

I'm slammed against the barn wall by a warm body; the air is sucked out of me as my back explodes with pain. I whimper as involuntary tears stream down my cheeks. My whole body locks up, every bruised muscle in my back throbs like a heartbeat.

"What have you done?" Eleazar snarls, his hot breath hits my face. I open my eyes to find both of his hands placed beside my head, caging me to the wall with his body. My legs shake as I feel the pressure building behind my eyes. I am going to cry even more.

"I—"

"I warned you of the things that can happen when I'm not around to save you. I thought for once you might actually listen to someone other than yourself," he snaps, his top lip peeling back to expose his teeth and canines.

"I know," I whisper, my shoulders slump. Tears still stream down my cheeks from hitting the barn so hard, his eyes track the movement and regret flashes across his features. It's gone in a split second, his guard going back up in place.

"I smelt you after we'd returned to the room. You'd been through my things. You're an absolute idiot." His words are like a slap to the face, I lean further into the wall. My back screams in pain but I do my best to hide it. "Why couldn't you have stayed home?"

"I was sick of being left behind and having everyone treat me like a child." I keep my tone even, knowing if I want a fight I'm going to find it.

"They do it because they care about you and love you. Your mother is no doubt worried sick and your father is beyond livid. He would do anything in this world to protect you."

"Love me? They keep me locked in that castle like I'm some sort of rare bird. It's a cage and it drives me mad being in there all the time. I can't do anything but go to the village, I'm a faerie and have not once stepped foot in the land which I come from." My anger spikes as I shove him, he doesn't budge so I do it again. He's a firm wall of muscle and warmth.

"You wouldn't be able to step foot in Faerie without being a target," he snaps.

"Why not?"

"Because you don't have magic. You'd be a weak picking for all of those creatures."

I slap at his chest now, the hits half-hearted as I take my frustration out on him. He doesn't stop me, just watches intently as each hit is replaced by another. I don't think I'll ever stop hitting him, it won't solve anything but god it's good to let the anger out on someone who can handle it.

I don't know when I start crying, really crying.

Warm hands press over my own, holding my hands to his chest. I blink through the tears and up at him, feeling myself beginning to calm. Touching him grounds me, brings me back to earth. I draw in deep breaths, not taking my eyes from his golden ones.

"Your father sent me to retrieve you and then return to them, you'll be coming with us to Faerie. I guess your wish for adventure has been granted." He says softly.

"I didn't know what else to do. Why didn't he come and get me himself?" I ask.

"There was...a murder in Orrinshire. A man." He surveys my expression and I shiver. Images of him laying splayed out like a cushion pin covered in blood surface, my bloody hands and blood splattered face. I stay silent, letting him continue.

"We don't know who killed the man or what, but it's shrouded in fallen magic. It's all we could detect from the area.

We don't know if the fallen wielder killed him or was drawn to his dead body." He lets my hands go, taking a step back. "That is why your father was worried. He thought whatever killed the man had gotten you too."

The breath leaves my lungs, my heart squeezing, "I'm sorry." For worrying him. For scaring my father. For killing that hateful man.

"You have nothing to apologise for. It's not your fault. I'm going to hunt whoever this fallen magic wielder is and put an end to their lives." Eleazar mistakes my look of horror. "You're safe. I'll protect you and so will the others and your father."

I nod once, tramping down the horror. Eleazar is the hunter Salis had mentioned to me, the one who would be coming for me. If he hasn't figured out that *I'm* the fallen magic wielder, it's only a matter of time until he does. He can't protect me from himself.

"Come, I'll walk you back to your room. We leave early morning." I start walking, wincing with each step. Eleazar walks beside me, keeping his steps slow as we walk through the cornfield. The noise from the tavern already reaches my ears and I sigh, I'd never get any sleep tonight.

"What is it?" he asks, looking down to me.

"I'll never get any sleep tonight, they're drinking and enjoying themselves. Who knows how long the noise will go on for." I watch as a few people stagger from the tavern, talking loudly and singing as they walk down the dark street. Eleazar stops us at the edge of the path, watching the commotion. He sighs.

"Come. You can stay in my room tonight." He gently grabs my elbow, guiding me.

"What? No—" I start to protest, my mind going to thoughts of us sleeping in the same room. Together.

"You said it yourself. You'll never get any sleep tonight and

I don't wish to deal with a grumpy Amaryllis tomorrow for our journey," he says calmly. I blush deeply, of course that's what he'd been meaning. I'd be foolish to think otherwise, he'll always see me as his best friend's daughter.

We reach the start of Elk, a small lantern burns on a small tavern. Eleazar lets me go and strides forwards, walking up the steps and opening the door for me. I trudge after him, holding my cloak around myself tightly. I pause inside the dimly lit room as the door shuts behind me.

"This way," he murmurs, heading to the left side. There's a small desk sitting in the middle at the back of the room, keys hang on hooks behind it. Eleazar opens up the first door and walks in, holding it for me.

I slide past him, warmth radiates from him as my shoulder brushes his chest. I try to ignore the sizzle of electricity at our touch, the urge to lean in closer and drown myself in him. The room is simple, a double bed sits against the wall in front of me. A lantern burns on the wall to my right. Eleazar's two bags sit on top of the light brown dresser along with his two long swords.

Nothing looks more comforting than the deep red quilt covered bed.

"Where will you sleep?" I ask, looking over my shoulder to where he stands. His shoulders are tense as he watches me with those golden eyes, he watches me as if I'm a puzzle he can't quiet figure out.

"I will take the floor."

I gasp, "No you will not. This is your room. I should be taking the floor." I object, crossing my arms over my chest. He sighs, rubbing his face.

"I've slept in worse places. I'm sure offering my bed to a pretty woman and sleeping on the floor is something you should be thanking me for."

As soon as he's said it, his eyes widen. We both stand there, staring at each other. He'd called me pretty. My heart beats wildly in my chest. How am I meant to sleep now?

"Come on. I won't bite. I can't have a guilty conscience knowing you'd slept on the floor because of me." I turn and hide my burning cheeks. I unclasp my cloak and fold it before walking over to the dresser and sitting it on top of his bag. I avoid looking at where he still stands as I pull the sheets back, the white pillows look like heaven.

I sit down and tuck my legs under the blanket. I look up at him, he still hasn't moved. I'd almost go as far as saying he hasn't breathed. He keeps his eyes on me as he pulls his boots off, he takes cautious steps as he comes to his side of the bed.

My heart warms as he pauses. He's giving me time to change my mind.

I roll my eyes at him, giving him an easy smile, "Hurry up. It's like you don't want to sleep at all."

"Of course I want to sleep." He grunts as he lays down, he slides his legs under the blankets and tucks an arm under his head. "I hope you don't mind the lantern being left on."

"Afraid of the dark?" I ask, lying down beside him. I tuck my hands under the pillow as I lay on my side, facing him. He tilts his head and looks down at me, his expression void of any emotion. Our bodies are close, if I stretch out a leg even an inch it will collide with his.

"Yes." I almost miss his reply.

"Okay. It doesn't bother me." My eyes flutter shut, unable to continue to meet his gaze. My heart is chaotic in my chest. I've never laid next to a man before. Especially not one that I find painfully attractive, "Sweet dreams, Eleazar."

"Sweet dreams, Amaryllis."

As soon as I fall asleep, the darkness finds me.

CHAPTER 11

"**A**ma! *Wake up!*" A strong hand shakes my shoulder, drawing me out of the nightmare that had consumed me. I gasp as my scream is cut off. Tears stream down my face as I blink into the dim light of the room, Eleazar is leaning over me; worry etched on every beautiful feature.

"I'm sorry—" I take a sobbing breath, "nightmare."

"Are you okay?" He asks, gripping my chin gently.

"Yes. I'm fine. I'm sorry," I whisper, shutting my eyes as I lean back into the pillow and out of his touch. The last tendrils of the nightmare leave me but I know what I'd dreamed of. I'd been killing that man in the street but he had been replaced with Eleazar and the darkness hungered for his soul. It feels too real, clinging to me like a second skin.

"Do you want to talk about it?" His voice is soft, the softest I've ever heard it.

"No. I'm so sorry for waking you up." I open my eyes again, reaching up to wipe the last few tears from my eyes. As I lower my hands I realise how close we are, his lower half presses to my side from where he'd lowered himself on his right arm after I'd woken.

"You don't have anything to apologise for." He looks me

over once more before moving to lie down on his back beside me. I stare at the ceiling as my heart slows, my sweaty palms dry and the anxiety I'd felt clawing at my throat recedes.

"Come here," he grunts. I look at him in confusion. To my surprise he has opened his arm for me; giving me a space to cuddle up to his side.

"You want...to cuddle?" I ask, puzzled. He narrows his eyes at me, arm still extended in offer.

"I want to sleep, this may keep the nightmares away, which lets you sleep." His jaw twitches as he looks away briefly, "don't think anything more of it."

I ignore my heart crushing at his words and I hesitate a moment before I move into his arm, resting my cheek on his chest. He lowers his arm again, resting it over my waist.

Sleep beckons for me again.

"Sleep," he murmurs, his own drowsiness dragging him under. It doesn't take me long to follow suit. His warmth calms me, makes me feel safe. Nothing has ever made me feel so calm, as if I'm floating on a cloud.

I rest my hand over his chest, pulling my leg over his as I cuddle into his side and get comfortable. He grunts once, his only sign of what I can assume is annoyance. I may never get this chance again, so while I can I'm going to savour it as much as he'll allow. I cuddle into his side, pressing my entire body to him. His arm tightens, keeping me in place.

I've never slept so peacefully.

I WAKE TO A COLD BED. I lay there for a moment longer before relenting and opening my eyes. It takes me a moment to realise I'm not in my own room, my eyes flitter over to where my cloak is folded on top of the now empty dresser. I climb out of the bed, throwing my cloak on before slipping from the room. I close the door softly behind me, my cheeks burn when I make eye contact with the worker behind the desk. I look away first and hurry from the inn. I'm assaulted by the bright early morning sun. I throw my hand up and squint. A few of the villagers whisper to each other as they look at me. I ignore their stares and hurry back down the street and head for my tavern.

Anger and shame are bitter on the back of my tongue.

Eleazar had left.

Eleazar had left *me*.

I try not to let the thought hurt, but god it does. He'd held me, comforted me from a nightmare I'd woken him from. I assumed I'd wake up with him warming the bed beside me. I scowl, of course he wouldn't. I'd been a fool to think he would stay, that maybe I'd meant something to him.

Why would he say he'd protect me? Why would he say those other things last night when he'd cornered me outside of the barn, the words someone would say when they cared? It only angers me more. I'm a walking ball of anger and shame as I storm up the steps of the tavern.

I hurry up the stairs and slam the door behind me. I pull on my black leather pants and Eleazar's white shirt he'd left with me. I tie the bottom into a knot, making it reach my belly button. I pull my boots on before I pack the rest of my bags, stuffing my cloak in. I grab an extra gold coin before hoisting the bags over my shoulder. I leave the room and head down to the bar. Magda watches me sympathetically as I approach.

"Mornin' sweetheart. How are you feeling?" she asks, leaning against the bar. I sigh, sitting the key and gold coin down on the bar. Her eyes widen at the extra coin.

"I'm ready to see where my next adventure takes me. I'm thankful for your service and the extra gold is for looking after Ash as best as you could. I'll be sure to visit again." I summon a tight smile, my shoulders tense. To hell with Eleazar, I can head to Faerie without him.

"Be safe on the road dear, stay with that fae male. Seems like a good protector."

I turn away, studying the wooden floorboards. "He's already left."

I don't wait for her reply, heading quickly out of the tavern and going straight through the corn field. Once Ash is saddled I'll be hightailing it out of here, I can't stand the embarrassment of facing Eleazar again. My emotions are too chaotic for me to discern.

I walk into the open barn doors and go to Ash. He knickers and throws his head up as I approach. A real smile settles on my face as I stop in front of his stall, unlatch the gate and let him out. His hooves *clop* on the dirt as he walks out, sniffing at his saddle.

"I hope you had your fill of feed this morning, you won't get another good meal like that until we reach Dead Man's Hollow," I say to him. I manoeuvre the saddle onto his back; throwing the saddle bags over and clipping them into place. I place his bridle on him next before I climb up, settling in for the long journey ahead.

He walks out of the barn, tail swishing happily back and forth. He grows restless in confined spaces, much like his owner. The other horses knicker as they watch him pass and I can imagine they're saying goodbye.

I'd definitely return to Elk, if only for another day or two. It's a cute little village, unbiased to fae kind. I'm sure Pop and Grandma would love the sound of peace here, not having to hike to get fresh water and having to live around small-minded villagers.

I'm looking over the corn field to my left when Ash comes to a sudden stop, jolting me violently in my seat. The horn of the saddle digs painfully into my stomach from the force.

"Bloody hell, Ash what on earth are you doing?" I groan, looking down to what's stopped him. Eleazar stands there, arms crossed over his chest as he looks up at me with disapproval. I straighten immediately, resting my hand on my stomach. His eyebrows furrow.

"Where do you think you're going?" he asks calmly. I snort, why would he care?

"I'm leaving, as you can see." I reply with just as much calm.

"I told you last night we'd both be heading to Faerie together or to your father and the others, whichever comes first." He says it slowly, as if I'm too small brained to understand the meaning of his words. It makes me bristle.

"I assumed after I woke to an empty room I'd be on my own. I'm familiar to the feeling of people leaving me behind. You're no different," I snap, digging my heels into Ash's belly. He snorts as he walks forward, ears flat against his head. Eleazar holds up a hand, forcing Ash to stop. It annoys me, why is Ash listening to him? I'm the one he listens to.

"I had to ready my own horse and you'd been asleep. I didn't want to wake you after you'd only managed to get a few hours of decent sleep last night." His voice is quiet as he watches me with that same guarded expression. I think over his words. I blink. *Oh*. That's why he'd left. He hadn't been leaving me behind at all. My stomach bottoms out as I realise how stupid I'd been. His eyes gleam at my change of expression.

"I'm glad that's apparent. Let's go," he walks over to Ash's left side.

"What're you—" I squeak as he jumps up behind the saddle, his thighs press flush to my own as he sits behind me.

His hands rest on the horn of the saddle loosely, careful not to touch my waist. Ash stamps in annoyance, looking back at both of us. Eleazar grunts. I urge Ash forward, sitting stiff as a board in the saddle. In the darkness being this close to Eleazar had felt different, almost surreal. It had felt so familiar sliding into his arms and cuddling him.

In the daylight? I couldn't be more awkward about the entire thing.

It's clear I've thought deeper into it than what it actually was; Eleazar comforting his best friend's scared, sad daughter from a nightmare. But the cuddle? His arm tightening against me? Maybe I had just imagined it. It would definitely make more sense than him actually wanting to cuddle me back. He did say not to think more into it and here I am doing exactly that.

I pull Ash to a stop as a chestnut horse comes into view, a man holds the horse patiently; smiling hesitantly as Eleazar slides from Ash and strides over to them. He squeaks as he passes Eleazar the reins, making a hasty exit.

"You don't have to scare every living creature whenever you get the chance to," I grumble, eyes trailing the street where the man had retreated.

"Where's the fun in that?" Eleazar says, drawing my attention back to him. He slides smoothly into the saddle, urging his horse away from the village and towards the forest. I click my tongue, allowing Ash full steering as we follow Eleazar. His blades are clasped to his back while his bags had been clipped onto this saddle.

"What's your horse's name?" I ask, walking in stride beside him. His horse is the same height as Ash, with a white strip running down its light chocolate face.

"Oak, he's from Orrinshire." He pats the stallion's neck, combing his fingers through the white and brown flecked mane. Oak nods his head a few times before looking at Ash briefly. Ash flicks his head, ears flattening as he walks a few paces ahead of Oak. I smirk, holding onto the saddle horn. It appears Oak may be more like Eleazar and Ash more like me than I thought.

"Where are we heading?" I look over the forest as we grow closer, birds fly from the canopy; their long feathered wings throwing shadows across the deep green shrubbery that blooms around the wide dirt path.

"To Dead Man's Hollow." Eleazar's words are more of a grunt.

"Why?"

"To drop the horses off."

I look over my shoulder to him, raising an eyebrow, "Then how are we getting to Faerie?"

His eyes narrow on me, those golden depths flaring slightly. His lips are pulled back between a snarl and a scowl. "By foot."

"It's good to see you back to your insufferable self," I clip, turning back in my seat and facing forward. We reach the forest. He doesn't reply, a heavy silence settling over us. I try not to dwell on it, how we'd fallen back into the bickering as if it was the wendigo afternoon all over again. He's only bringing me along because of father and is only going to protect me because that's what father has asked of him. He doesn't seem to care about me outside of that.

If that's the case, I can act just as cold towards him.

I refuse to speak. He doesn't utter a single word either.

As the day drags on ever so slow I try to find small things to keep my mind occupied, anything that stops me focusing on the broody fae male ahead of me or the fact my hands are now stained red. I keep the darker thoughts at bay, not allowing myself to focus on the man I'd met in the woods or the power I have. I study Eleazar's broad shoulders, each step the horse takes has him moving smoothly in his seat.

Two twin swords are strapped criss-crossed over his back, in their pale brown leather sheaths. At least one of us is armed. I'd left my own small knife in the saddle bag. Mother had said he's good to his word and if he's said he's going to protect me, he is.

I shouldn't be so trusting, after what the last week has put me through. Watching his cooper hair swirl in the wind and cascade down his back has me wanting to put my life in his hands. It's dangerous, the feelings he's conjuring up whenever I'm around him. As if feeling my thoughts he looks slightly over his shoulder at me.

"What is it?" he asks.

I shake my head, "Nothing."

"We're still a decent trek away from Dead Man's Hollow and the sun is beginning to set. Would you like to set up camp for the night soon?" He slows down Oak until we're beside each other. He faces forward, eyes scanning the area around us. I stroke Ash's neck absently.

"Yeah, we can set up camp. Is there a river near here?" I ask.

"There's a stream, we should reach it before sundown if we hurry." He clicks his tongue. Oak bursts forward into a gallop, leaves scatter under his hooves as he flies forward. I whistle as Ash breaks into a gallop after him. I lean forward in the seat, urging Ash to go faster.

We gain on Oak easily, his brown rump growing closer and closer with each stride of Ash's long legs. He loves to run whenever I give him enough free rein to.

Ash flanks Oak as we rush through the forest, all I hear is the roar of wind as my hair lashes against my cheeks and back. I glance to Eleazar. He's smiling as he focuses ahead of us, leading us effortlessly through the shrubs. My heart squeezes in my chest.

The sun touches the top of the canopy as we come to a stop, the horses breathe heavily beneath us; both coated in a layer of sweat. Oak walks forward between two large berry bushes, Ash follows. Ahead of us a small stream bubbles, the area on both sides of the stream is enough for us to set up camp for the night.

I pull Ash to a stop and slide down, my legs shake and my back aches as I stretch my arms above my head. I quickly unsaddle Ash, letting him have his freedom. He walks over to the stream, lowering his head. I look around and survey the area. The trees in this part of the forest have thick trunks and high branches. I wouldn't be able to hang his saddle.

I walk over to the largest trunk and lean the saddle against it, lowering the bridle over it as well. I turn to see Eleazar doing the same to a trunk a few metres to my right. Oak walks over to Ash, dropping his head beside him.

The stream is larger than I imagined, a few metres across. It would most likely just reach above my waist. I sit down and rummage through my saddle bag, pulling out a nightgown. I unclasp my cloak and sit it over the saddle, draping my night-gown over my arm.

"I'm going to find firewood. Will you be okay here?" Eleazar asks, drawing my attention from the horses to him. His swords are still strapped to his back, the wind pulls at his white shirt and hair; the sun casting a golden glow around his head.

"Yes, I'm going to bathe." I sigh as I stand. I pull my boots off as I listen to him head into the forest. Once I can't hear his footsteps anymore I make quick work of getting out of my clothes. I leave the nightgown in a pile on the ground before I quickly walk over to the stream. I cover my chest with my arms as I walk into the water, it's cold and bites at my skin. I'm covered in goosebumps from toe to head but at least I'll be cleaner.

The water just reaches my bellybutton, I lower myself until my chin touches the water. I scrub every part of me with my bare hands, the rocks are smooth and sturdy beneath my feet. Looking down into the water I can see the bottom of the stream, small fish swim past me. I straighten, my back facing our camp.

Sun light hits me from the right side as it begins to sink and the moon begins to rise to my left. I swirl my hands through the water, the water numbs all my aches and pains. I wiggle my toes, seeing them move but not feeling them. I shake my head in amusement.

A sharp intake of breath comes from behind me.

I go rigid in the water, my hands freeze.

I hadn't heard Eleazar return.

Oh god oh god oh god.

My entire body locks up in horror, not only has no man ever seen me this bare; my back is a black and blue mess. I hadn't intended for him to return so soon. I didn't want him to see me in this state. Dread curls in my stomach as tears threaten to fall. I can practically feel my skin burning as his eyes sweep over my back, again and again.

"What happened?" I barely catch his words they're that quiet.

I take a shuddering breath, "I was in a...fight."

"What the fuck happened, Amaryllis?" His steps are heavy as he begins to walk closer to the water. I'd almost forgotten I'm standing here naked. This water hides nothing. My cheeks burn in embarrassment now.

"I don't want to talk about it." I cover my chest as I slowly turn around, I look at his feet; unable to meet his eyes. He stands just shy of the water, close enough that I can hear his ragged breathing. I brace myself as I look up to his face.

Golden eyes swirl with *fury* and the promise of death.

"Who did this to you?"

My bottom lip quivers. "It doesn't matter," I mutter.

"Yes it does. You're going to tell me who the fuck did that to you and then I am going to hunt them down and make them regret even looking at you." His voice is low and deep, his eyes are solely focused on my face. I shake my head, my heart aches. I begin to walk out of the water, he'd seen the worst of me. My cheeks burn with shame.

I walk past him, almost touching his shoulder. I reach down and grab my nightgown, pulling it on over my head. It sticks to my wet body but it's better than being naked. I walk over to where he'd dropped the sticks. I gather them in my shaking hands.

"Who is it?" he demands, coming closer. He takes the sticks from my hands, they groan under the weight of his grip as he looks down at me.

"It. Doesn't. Matter." I say between clenched teeth. I can't remember what I'd done. Not tonight. Not with him.

"You're going to tell me." He drops the sticks to our right, the scatter as they hit the ground. His hands ball at his sides. I cross my arms over my chest as I look up at him, tipping my head back slightly.

"No. I'm not. I've dealt with it and there's nothing you can do about it. I don't want to talk about it."

"What do you mean you've dealt with it? You're pow—" he stops himself, snarling down at me.

"Say it," I demand.

"No." The snarl is wiped from his face.

"Say it!" I yell. My hands dig painfully into the flesh of my arms.

"You're powerless." A statement. A fact. His eyes stay on mine, his lips form a thin line.

I suck on my bottom lip, my lashes wet with tears. I take a step back, away from him. He has no idea what I'm capable of. He doesn't know the monster that prowls beneath my skin. If he knew, he wouldn't hesitate to drive a sword through my black, stained heart. It hurts.

"And you're an absolute asshole," tears do fall now, sliding painfully slow down my cheeks, "I may seem weak to you, but I wasn't, when being strong was all I had left."

"Am—"

"Start the fire. This conversation is over." I turn and walk over to my saddle. I grab the cloak and clasp it over my shoulders. I sit down and huddle in my cloak, it's cold tonight and that argument has left me feeling hollow.

Eleazar makes it obvious he's angry at me, at what has happened to me. He makes the fire closest to me, the flames flicker to life before burning brightly. It warms my face pleasantly. I reach my hands out and hold them out to warm. Ash comes closer, standing near me as he picks at the grass.

I watch as Eleazar unsheathes his swords before pulling his shirt over his head. The flames cast shadows over his back, the sight is almost enough to make me forgive him for what he'd said earlier. I've come to the conclusion he's used to getting what he wants without a fight, without resistance. I doubt many people in his life would ever defy him or outright tell him no.

Lucky for him, I'm not like the others.

He walks towards the stream, out of the sight of the fire. I hear the rustle of clothing hitting the ground before the splash of water. I look back to the orange and gold flames.

The moon hangs high in the sky tonight. Stars are scattered

and bright against the black canvas. It's beautiful, being this close to nature.

Eleazar appears on the other side of the fire, he pulls a black long sleeved shirt on over his wet chest. He's wearing darker long pants. He takes a seat on the other side of the fire, staring intently at the flame.

His eyes meet mine.

I look down at my hands, lowering them on my lap. I have no appetite for dinner.

I just want to sleep.

I move back until I'm curled in my saddle, I use a saddle bag as a pillow as I lay on my side and get as comfortable as the hard ground will allow me to.

I don't bother with a goodnight. I close my eyes and hope the darkness can erase this afternoon.

CHAPTER 12

M y eyes open involuntarily, tearing me from the dream I'd been having. I look over to the fire, the embers are orange but the flames of warmth are long gone. I yawn and stretch, reaching my hands above my head. It's still dark but the morning sun is almost ready to crest the horizon. I snuggle into my cloak, warm against the cold morning air.

I take a deep breath as my eyes flutter shut. Spiced rum and honey—

My eyes shoot open.

I grab the cloak on top of me, shocked to find I have my own underneath me and still clasped around my shoulders and one on top of me. The large one draped over me covers my entire body, keeping out the cold air.

I rub the thick fabric through my fingers, his scent envelopes me. I look over to where he lies on his side, facing the fire. He hadn't moved from his original spot where he'd been sitting last night. His face is relaxed in sleep, it's the most peaceful I've ever seen him.

I stand on stiff legs, gathering his cloak in my arms. From here I can see the shiver in his shoulders. He'd be freezing. How long did he go without his cloak for? I shake my head as I walk over to him. If this is his form of apology...a smile twitches my lips.

I gently open the cloak and fluff it out before gently draping it over him, making sure he's covered. He'd be no use to us if he's frozen once he wakes. He needs to be the fighting power of our two man band. I walk back to my saddle and sit down, watching him sleep.

I tug my cloak tight around me, already missing the warmth of his.

I lean my head back against the trunk and look through the canopy, I listen as the animals of the forest begin to stir. Ash and Oak are on the other side of the stream, standing side by side as they rest. I shut my eyes, I might be able to grab a few more moments of rest.

My moment of rest doesn't last long. Eleazar stirs, yawning and drawing my entire awareness to him. I hear his cloak rustle, I can almost picture the frown he'd be wearing when he realises his own cloak is draped over him.

Do I feign sleep? Or open my eyes as well?

It doesn't take me long to choose as his light footsteps make their way towards me. I hear the rustle of his cloak as his presence nears me. My eyes fly open, locking on his. He freezes, arms up and cloak ready to be draped over me.

"Oh—you're awake." He swiftly throws his cloak over his shoulder, clasping it at the base of his throat. I look away from him as I stand. Early morning light breaks up the dark sky, catching the thin layer of dew on the stalks of grass.

"When are we leaving?" I ask, staring intently at the grass that's in the light. Just because I'm talking to him and have slightly softened over the cloak he'd given me during the night, I am still hurt. All he sees when he looks at me is this weak, small girl with no magic.

"Now, let's get the horses ready and go. We've got a solid

day of riding ahead of us. We won't stop until we reach Dead Man's. We've already fallen behind by staying last night." He walks over to his saddle, copper hair fanning around his face as he bends down to grab it.

"Oh, so it's my fault?" I ask, crossing my arms over my chest.

"I didn't say that."

"You didn't have to." I whistle to Ash. He startles before looking up at me. I smile as he trots over to me, splashing through the stream as his tail swishes happily behind him. Oak follows behind, heading over to me as well.

"Good morning boys," I kiss Ash on his nose before kissing Oak as well. I stroke his cheeks and look into his caramel eyes. He nudges me, top lip pulling back in a smile as he throws his head back. I laugh, rolling my eyes at him. "A kiss from a girl is all it takes to make you smile?"

Oak snorts, pawing at the ground.

"I'll keep that in mind," Eleazar grunts as he walks over. He places Oak's saddle on him and gets him ready. He's so close to me I could reach out and touch him if I wanted to.

Or stab him.

I hurry as I get Ash ready for the day ahead of us, Eleazar waits on top of Oak while I fiddle about. Once I'm astride of Ash he sets out into the forest. I quickly follow after him, Ash thunders through the underbrush to catch up with them.

"So what's the plan?" I ask as Ash canters in stride with Oak.

"The plan is to get to Faerie as fast as we can. I've already wasted enough time."

"Okay..." I hesitate, "what's the plan with the creature with fallen magic?"

His sharp eyes dart to me, I shrug innocently. He looks back towards the path ahead, a muscle along his jaw twitches and I know I've irritated him. Good. Back and forth is what we're best at, not being nice to each other.

Definitely not that.

"Once the creature in Faerie has been dealt with I will go hunting for the fallen, which is why I'm impatient. Containing the creature in Faerie isn't easy but with the fallen on the loose I don't know what havoc it's reaping." He shakes his head, truly disgusted talking about the fallen. If only he knew.

"Can you tell me more about the both of them?"

"No. Absolutely not. You've gotten me into enough trouble and it only started after I told you about magic," he snaps.

"Do I not have the right to know? I am a faerie as well." My irritation rises, from the start he'd been the most lenient when it came to telling me things I deserved to know. He'd talked about magic with me in the enchanted paddock before the wendigo attack. Why couldn't he talk to me now?

"Just because you're a faerie doesn't mean I'm the one to educate you."

"Who else will? We've already come this far, I do believe it's only fair you tell me something. I want to know about the creature that's wrecking-havoc in Faerie. I want to know about the creature with fallen magic. I want to *know* things." I feel his patience thinning.

"You don't need to know anything other than the fact we're going to Faerie and once we get there you'll be staying in Oakwood until your father retrieves you."

"Like hell I will be," I snap. "If you honestly think locking me away in some faerie house is going to stop me then you have another thing coming. I will not lie down and be obedient just because you say so."

"Have fun telling your father that."

"I will fight tooth and nail against him." I look towards Eleazar, "I am his daughter."

"Trust me. I'm more than aware of that." He catches my eye, displeasure is evident on his face as his eyes do a quick sweep over me before he urges Oak to go faster. I fight the urge to make Ash go faster and catch up. He is insufferable. One moment he's holding me from a nightmare and the next he's looking at me as if it's my fault I'm his best friend's daughter. As if I'm not worth looking at.

I keep my mouth shut after that. As we ride I stew over his act of kindness last night, after his rude statement and now the look of distaste as he'd gazed at me. He's so hot and cold and I'm getting fed up with it. On one hand it's like I'm drawn to him in ways I can't explain, when he's around I find myself gravitating towards him as if I'm the earth and he's the sun. On the other he fights me on almost everything, knocks me down whenever he can and is quick to remind me I'm magicless.

Well, he thinks I'm magicless.

If that's the case he's not a very good hunter. His fallen magic wielder is riding on the horse behind him heading to Faerie, oh the havoc I'm reaping. Put me down before I do more damage of riding my horse to find adventure.

I get fed up with his brooding silence as Ash trots in time with Oak. Eleazar refuses to look my way and instead scans the area around us. His ears twitch slightly, he'd pulled his hair back into a high sweeping ponytail. It showcases his sharp jaw and thick neck.

"Can you at least tell me something about the creature in Faerie? We both know I'll be coming along regardless, if you lock me in a room I'll only find a way out of it. Wouldn't you rather I know at least something when I decide to track you all down alone?" I ask over the sound of the rhythmic sound of the horse's hooves. The forest had grown sparse the deeper we'd travelled. I'd almost guess we're near a cross over that will lead us to Dead Man's Hollow.

"You'd be stupid to do that."

"Do you really think I wouldn't?" I wave my hand around us, "look where *we* are right now."

"You shouldn't know," he states, hands tightening on the reins.

"I don't really care if I shouldn't know. I want to know. What is this creature doing that is putting Faerie in danger? I was on the balcony that night of the storm, I saw the blue lightning."

"If I tell you and your father finds out what I've disclosed, we will both suffer the consequences. He loves you more than you know and if he realises I've been feeding you information I'm just as good as dead." He slows Oak to a walk, I feel his eyes burn into the side of my face. I tuck my hair behind my pointed ears and keep my eyes focused ahead.

"I know what the consequences are."

"You still haven't received the consequence of leaving Kalin and running away," he points out.

My stomach turns, "Here I thought having you chaperone me was punishment enough."

A surprised laugh breaks the tense silence between us. I look at him bewildered to see a smile on his face. He shakes his head, the smile still in place. A small dimple forms in his cheek. I'm in shock as I stare at him, mouth slightly parted. He looks to me and the smile is gone in an instant. He clears his throat.

"Heedless to say if he knows I've told you about the creature it'll be much worse than my company I can assure you."

"If I can survive travelling with you I'm quite certain I can very well survive anything," I point out, raising an eyebrow at him. He huffs and looks back towards the path. He shakes his shoulders out. I wait patiently.

"The creature is called a bulburoos. Many centuries ago they roamed all over Faerie, for most part they were harmless. All magical creatures in Faerie worship our gods, apart from Salis. The bulburoos were worshippers of Nula, the goddess of night. They were creatures of the night, only emerging when the earth was cast in darkness." He pauses, looking over to me.

"I don't know about your gods," I say impishly. He sighs, rubbing a hand over his face.

"We have four gods. Ma'an, goddess of day. Du'ur, goddess of life. Nula, goddess of night and Salis, the god of death. We have the three types of magic which you know of. Old magic was blessed from the gods to certain creatures. Bulburoos were in that category and were favoured by the gods." He stops, "are you keeping up?"

"Yes." I nod, hands straining on the reins. I'd met Salis the other night and he is frightening.

"The legend goes Ma'an decided to source her magic as sacred magic so all creatures born in Faerie could have basic magic. Du'ur and Nula agreed with Ma'an and together they created sacred magic. Salis had other plans and created his own magic, fallen magic. The three other gods siphoned out their magic without a price while Salis demanded to be repaid.

"You know carriers of fallen magic were hunted, if the hunters didn't get to them first their magic did. It's like an infection, corrupting the wielder from the inside out. While performing any sort of magic has a price, fallen magic has a steep repayment. When a fallen uses their magic, it draws from the living and dead creatures that hold magic.

"Sacred and old magic returns to the land once the host dies and their soul is either reborn or becomes one with the gods again...from what I've learnt, those who have fallen magic are in debt to Salis. Once death claims them their souls return to the underworld and are trapped in his cage while he receives his piece of power he'd given out. In a way I pity the fallen, they don't ask to be monsters. They just are."

My skin goes clammy as we walk along, he makes it sound terrifying, but he's telling me the truth. That human—I'd taken his soul. Even though he wasn't a magic carrier, the power inside of me still wanted to take and steal.

"Sacred magic wielders can kill other sacred wielders without harm if they don't use their magic to go through with the act but the gods decided if we chose to use our magic against others like ourselves to kill, we would also experience the pain of their death. It keeps us accountable for the actions we decide to take, I've heard when a fallen would kill a magical creature they'd experience euphoria and hunger for more."

"That's very morbid," I mutter.

"It's not pleasant. Anyway I've got off track. Bulburoos. Over time their population has dwindled and there's only a few hundred left roaming Faerie. Lately they've begun to change, act abnormal. We haven't found any signs of poisoning but one bulburoos has been fighting against the doses we've been giving it."

"What do you mean they're acting abnormal?" I ask.

"We've found a handful roaming in the daylight, eating meat, even their magic has been random. They're herbivores, harmless creatures of the night. So far we've found ten infected and we've managed to treat nine and put them under quarantine. The tenth..." he shake his head, voice full of frustration. It's a lot to process but I'm keeping up. I'm terrified of the fallen magic inside of me but maybe I can help the bulburoos. Maybe I'll be able to discover a connection they've missed.

"The tenth hasn't responded to any treatment. It's constantly breaking through the barriers that are keeping it confined in the cave in darkness. It won't eat the grain we've tried feeding it and we've had to resort to delivering dead cattle. We can't have it starve. It's one of the oldest of its kind. Whatever has a hold of it has its claws in deep."

We're silent for a moment as I make connections he hasn't yet. Whatever has a seed planted in this bulburoos is clearly something deep inside that's tampered with its magic. How he's described it to me sounds similar to that of a fallen magic wielder.

"To me it sounds as if its magic has been changed. Tainted," I offer, shrugging my shoulders.

"What do you mean?"

"Well, you say it's acting out of character. To me, coming from what you've told me, it's corrupting from something internally. Not physically. It's either a magic corruption or a mental one although a magical corruption could lead to the downfall of its mental state. Making it act out and do things it wouldn't normally do." I look at him to find him already staring at me, as if he's seeing me for the first time. My cheeks begin to burn, "what?"

"You're suggesting that the gods are tainting the bulburoos?"

"Not all of them. Salis. He's the god of death right? What if, metaphorically speaking, he wants his revenge after you'd wiped his magic from Faerie? What if this is his way of punishing the other god's creations?"

"Why would he want that?" he asks, brows furrowed slightly. I shrug.

"I don't know. It just seems like these creatures are now harbouring a touch of fallen magic and it's killing them. Can magical beings have more than one magic?"

"Not that I know of, no." He shakes his head, looking forward again. I feel determined now. More interested in this adventure than I had been when I'd first fled into the forest on a whim. If I can find a way to rid the bulburoos of the fallen magic, if it is fallen magic, then maybe I can use the same technique on myself.

"That's my theory anyway."

Eleazar doesn't say another word on the matter and neither do I. I itch to learn more, to know more, but I fear he'll take my interest in fallen magic the wrong way and begin to suspect me. I can't have that, so I keep my mouth shut.

He'd only confirmed my fears. Once I'm dead my soul will be chained to the underworld with the other lost souls. Salis hadn't been lying, he's waiting for the moment he can snatch my soul with his greedy hands and drag me down with him.

I keep my eyes focused on the path ahead of me, pushing all thoughts of fallen magic from my mind. I can worry about my inevitable ending once I've reached it. For now my focus is on helping rid the bulburoos of whatever is corrupting it. My eyes trail to Eleazar, he'd broken Oak into a canter and Ash had followed willingly. He rides ahead of me, the sun high in the sky and basking down on us.

If Eleazar learns that I'm the magic wielder, will he hesitate to drive that blade through my heart?

If he does—

What does that mean for me?

CHAPTER 13

We arrive on the outskirts of Dead Man's Hollow as the sun sinks below the earth, casting pink and orange hues across the darkening blue sky. I tip my head back and watch as stars begin to flicker into existence, their bright white sparkles are enchanting against the open sky.

"Come on," Eleazar grunts, dragging my attention back to earth. I follow as he walks through the last of the forest, the horses trod along the wide red dirt path. Ahead I can see the lights of a village beginning to come to life.

"Have you been here before?" I ask.

"Multiple times."

"What's it like?"

"If you wait five seconds you'll find out," he snaps, urging Oak faster. I poke my tongue out at him as he walks ahead of me, holding my hands at the side of my face. God, he is such a grumpy man when he chooses to be.

"Very mature, Amaryllis," he calls over his shoulder. I drop my hands and pull my tongue back into my mouth. I scowl, annoyed at him for knowing somehow what I'd been doing behind his back. The smugness in his silence doesn't go unnoticed.

A large lagoon comes into view on our left, the dark water still. Dark green lily pads sit in a tight circle in the middle, a few are nearly in bloom. The dirt path crests the lagoon in a curve, leading us straight into the middle of the large village. People watch as we approach, murmuring to one another as we come to a stop just before entering the village. I slide from Ash and hold his reins in my hand as I look around.

Each wooden building is strung with a small string of lights, they line the gutter of each building; connecting across to the other buildings. Above the path through the buildings is a ceiling of light. It's magical looking at it, the atmosphere is a different contrast to the name it's been given. This place screams out life and enjoyment.

"Come. We're going to find a tavern for the night." Eleazar walks down and heads into the village, I follow behind but keep my steps slow. Lanterns have been lit on the posts of the railing that surrounds most buildings. Music drifts towards me with the twang of a banjo and the beat of drums.

Eleazar turns down a side street to our left and I hurry to catch up. Each street looks the same to me, the lights dazzle me and have me stopping to admire them more times than not. Eleazar lets out an impatient sigh when he turns to find me standing there, looking up at the string of lights above.

"Amaryllis, tonight if you don't mind. Let's check in and then you can explore. The horses most likely want to rest. I know I do," he calls out. I startle and look towards him. He'd reached the curve of another street. I hastily catch up, cloak billowing out behind me. We walk down the long street; a large red barn sits at the end. The red doors are propped open to display stables, light streams out into the night and guide us. The windows above the stables are alight, I sees shadows moving back and forth.

"What's above it?" I ask.

"It's a stable and inn. We'll spend the night here," Eleazar says. We fall back into silence as we reach the barn. A man dressed in black greets us, smiling ear to ear. His light blue eyes look over me slowly, his smile stretching.

"Good evening folk, looking for a room?" he asks, eyes flickering between the two of us.

"Yes, just for the night. How much for two rooms?" Eleazar crosses his arms over his chest.

"Seven gold."

I gawk at that, mouth dropping. Seven gold for two rooms? What on earth does he take us for? Eleazar must have the same thought as I do, he glances over his shoulder; eyes flickering over my face. He sighs.

"What's the price of one room?"

"Four gold. That includes the care of both horses." The man clasps his hands behind his back, still smiling. Four gold is far more reasonable, it just means Eleazar and I will once again be sharing a room. A bed.

No. No way. I'll opt to sleep on the couch if there is one.

"How does that sound Am?" Eleazar asks. I blink at the use of my nickname. He's asking me?

"Uh, it's fine. I don't mind," I say politely. His shoulders tense slightly.

"One room it is. I want both horses cared for immediately, we've had a long journey." He walks to his saddle bag, pulling out four gold coins. He hands them over to the man silently. The man grins, sliding the coins into his pocket.

"Of course. They'll be looked after immediately. Sean! Sean, we've got two horses." He calls over his shoulder into the bustling barn. A scraggly teen appears, dressed in brown pants and a dirt stained white shirt. His brown curled hair hangs over his eyes.

I grab my saddle bags, draping them over my arms as he

takes Ash. Eleazar follows my train of thought as he takes Oak from him a moment later. I watch as he leads them into the large barn, turning and disappearing with them.

"Right this way please," the man says, turning on heel and heading into the barn. I follow beside Eleazar, hesitant. As we enter, the scent of horse and leather is overwhelming, it invades my senses as he takes a sharp left and heads up wide wooden steps. Eleazar lets me go first, I hold onto the rail as I follow the man up. The wooden steps have been worn over time. The man opens a door inwards and holds it open for us.

We enter a hallway that runs to our right. I can barely hear the commotion of workers underneath us in the stables, it's eerily quiet above the barn. I study a vase of flowers as the man slips through a small doorway. Eleazar closes the stairwell door as he enters.

"This way please," the man remerges, a black skeleton key hangs from a cord of brown leather between his hands. He walks down the hall. "There is a bathroom built into the room. If you need assistance, do call out. If you're hungry, Old Mal's is the best burger place in the village. It's just down the end of the road, you'll be able to see the sign though."

We come to a stop at the last door on our left, the man unlocks the door and pushes it inwards. He leaves the key hanging in place. I peer in; the room is cast in shadows. Eleazar walks in first, a moment later light flares.

"Thanks." I nod once to the man before walking in, I grab the key from the lock and shut the door behind me. I wait for his footsteps to retreat before heading deeper into the room. I walk around to find a large double bed sitting against the back wall, the pastel pink quilt is dotted with green flowers. Eleazar has dumped his bags on the round wooden table that sits to my left, between the bed and the table is an open arch-way. He shrugs out of his twin swords, I place my bags down against the wall and dig out a clean pair of underwear and a dress.

I'm tired but I want to explore what I can of the village, while I can. If I know anything about Eleazar by now, it's that he has the patience of a small human child.

"I'm going to shower and head back into the village, grab something to eat," I say over my shoulder as I walk past him and into the bathroom. It's simple but clean. A white sink sits facing the open room while the shower curtain is clasped against the wooden wall, the white bathtub sits away from the eyes of the room to my right. I place my clothes on the sink and turn the black handle. Pipes groan as water splutters from the bronze shower head.

I hum to myself as I plug the bottom of the bath, a fresh yellow block of soap sits on the side of the tub. It's going to be a good night being squeaky clean.

"Would you like company?" Eleazar's voice reaches me. I shrug out of my shirt, pulling my boots off next. I begin to unbutton my pants even though my heart stutters in my chest at his question.

"I can assure you I'm quite capable of bathing myself," I call back.

"I meant in the village, not your bath."

Oh. Of course he'd meant that. My neck burns as I pull my pants off and toss them to the side. I quickly hop into the tub, lowering myself down to find it toasty. I pull the shower curtain across as the spray of water hits my chest and face, I let my arms rest on the side of the tub as I close my eyes.

"Of course you meant that. It's your choice," I say back.

"I know a place we can eat that's better than the one our...*attendant* offered." He makes his displeasure well known. I chuckle.

"Yes, he was definitely something."

"He couldn't take his eyes off you," Eleazar spits. I hear the rustle of clothes and footsteps. Suddenly his shadow falls over the shower curtain. I freeze as the water to the sink runs.

"I think you're being dramatic, I would have noticed," I retort as I will my heart to calm. He's already seen me stark naked once before so why am I reacting like this now to him being this close? Nothing has changed between us. I can't let my heart forget that, or his true intentions.

"You were too busy being dazzled by everything," he snorts.

"Why do you care anyway?" I ask as I grab the soap and begin to wash myself.

"Men who look at a woman like she is an object of their pleasure and taking, disgust me. There's no respect or honour in the way his eyes devoured you," he says softly, the honest response startles me. I grab the edge of the shower curtain and peer around to look up at him. He leans against the sink, arms crossed over his chest. He looks sideways at me, his golden eyes flaring slightly.

"Well... I don't know what to say to that."

"Have I, Eleazar the ass, left you speechless?" He mocks, lips tilting upwards ever so slightly. I feel myself grin; he had heard me that day on the balcony when I'd confided in mother. Good. He should know.

"Unfortunately you have, it's hard to believe under that cold stone exterior that there's a warm, beating heart." I say.

He laughs; the sound flowing freely through his lips. It's a heavenly sound, for a moment I'm awestruck as I watch him. His smile shines, lighting up his entire face while his laugh shakes his chest. I wish he would laugh more.

"You, Amaryllis, are sometimes like a breath of fresh air." He stops laughing but the *smile* stays on his face as he looks at me.

"You mustn't leave the house much," I snort back, rolling my eyes even though my heart skips a beat at his compliment.

"I'm away from home more than I'm there I'm afraid. You might have to accept the fact that sometimes," he pauses, "*sometimes* I don't mind your company. It helps when you don't ask a million and one questions. Which by the look on your face means there's another coming."

"What look on my face?"

"That one," he leans forward, staring at me intently, "the small crease between your eyebrows when you're thinking, the slight narrow in your eyes. Your lips do this twist that I don't think you're even aware of."

I open my mouth to reply but no sentence can form. He'd taken that much notice of me?

"Twice in a night? I must be in a good mood." He shakes his head, leaning back. I let the curtain go and lean back in the water, washing the last of the soap from my body before I stand. I turn the handle and shut the water off.

A white towel is held out for me, just inside the bath. I take it from him and wrap it around myself before stepping onto the bathmat. I tuck the wet strands of hair behind my ears as I look at him, he watches me; head titled slightly to the side, lips parted.

"I know I'm a horrendous sight to look at," I huff.

"You don't really believe that, do you?" he asks, suddenly serious. I shrug, keeping my lips sealed. I reach beside him and grab my clean dress, I breathe in his rum and honey scent and the musk of him from a hard day of riding. It goes straight to my head, making me feel as if I weigh no more than a feather.

"I'll shower and then we can go," he says. I nod and step back, he turns and faces the small square mirror on the wall as he pulls his shirt over his head. I'm stuck in the archway, my eyes rake over his bare back.

He grips the sink basin but I'm too busy admiring the view, his shoulders are tense and strain. Up this close I can see thin white scars that scatter across his back, a map with a story I'd die to hear. I have the urge to move closer, so I do. I don't know where I find the courage.

Whatever line we walk along, the sides are beginning to blur.

I stand directly behind him. I reach up and trace a white scar that runs down his right shoulder blade, it curves with the muscle before ending. I trace another and another, I don't stop until I've traced every scar on his back. Twenty three. He is utterly still underneath my touch.

I lean in, my lips gently brushing over the first scar I'd traced. "You are the one who is a breath of fresh air, Eleazar." I murmur against his skin, "I see you and I'm unafraid." He truly has no idea how magnificent he is, even if he is an ass sometimes.

I take a few steps back, utterly shocked at what I'd just done. I look up and meet his eyes in the mirror. The golden depths are a raging inferno and are utterly captivating as we stand there, never looking away.

He won't be looking at you like that once he realises you are fallen.

I turn quickly, striding as far away from the bathroom as I can get. That one thought pulls me away from him, away from the wanting that comes whenever I look at him. That evil voice is right of course, if I slip up he won't hesitate to end me.

I look back to the archway, would he hesitate?

I shake the thoughts from my head as I get dressed. I feel refreshed and clean, slightly mortified with what I'd done and said only moments ago. I tie the ribbons around my waist, adjusting the bow at the front. The dress is simple, a pale purple that clinches at my waist before flowing like water around my legs. I let my hair hang down, it brushes past my shoulders and over the thin straps of the dress.

I walk into view of the mirror and turn around, I pull my hair out of the way as I try to catch a glimpse of my back. The colouring has gone down, now only yellowing bruises remain. I sigh with relief, soon that night would be a mere memory I can force myself to forget.

I sit on the bed and wait for Eleazar.

He walks out of the bathroom, towel wrapped low on his waist. Droplets of water slide down his chest from his wet hair, they paint a map as they travel over the planes of his chest and through his defined abdomen. I drag my eyes away as the water droplet disappears into the dark hair that trails from his bellybutton to underneath the towel.

I feel my cheeks burn as I get up hastily, I walk past him and into the bathroom. I pull on my boots and take a moment for myself. I breathe through the fire that has ignited in my veins at the sight of him, at the thought of those scarred tan hands against my white skin.

Stop it Amaryllis, this thinking will only lead you to heartbreak.

"Are you ready? I'm hungry," he calls, bringing me back to the present. I walk out of the bathroom, tucking my hands into the skirt of my dress. I pause as I look over him, he'd dressed down. His dark pants flare around his legs but clinch at his ankles, his boots hold the material in place. His white shirt is rolled up to his elbows; the front crests down in a V and shows off the peaks of his chest. He'd thrown his hair back into a messy bun, a few wild strands stick to his throat and sides of his face. He raises an eyebrow in question.

"I'm just making sure you're presentable." I tsk at him. I walk over to my saddle bag and pull out my coin purse, the velvet soft between my fingers. I look down to see the small knife I usually carry sticking slightly out of the pocket. Since

Eleazar had found me I hadn't bothered with a weapon, he made me feel safe.

It's dangerous being so soft around him.

"Maybe I'd be better off without the shirt," he says, my head snaps up to him. His eyes flicker between my tightened fist on the coin purse and the knife. I stare at him for a moment before I find my thoughts, the knife slips through my fingers.

"I mean, if you want someone to warm your bed tonight I'm sure that's the right way to go about it." I sniff, relaxing my grip on the coin purse. I walk past him after I grab the key, he follows behind with ease.

"You wouldn't mind, would you?" he taunts behind me. I lock the door behind us before I reply.

"Of course not, up until this point I thought it impossible for you to let your guard down enough to allow a woman that close," I reply. I slip the key into the pocket of my skirt with my coin purse as we walk side by side down the hall.

"Not every encounter in my bed with a woman means letting my guard down, sex doesn't always have to mean something." He shrugs, tucking his hands into his pockets. Of course it wouldn't mean anything to him. I can't imagine how many girls have warmed his bed and even the thought of another woman indulging in his body makes my stomach twist violently.

Am I *jealous?*

"So you'll defend my honour to my face when another man eye's rove over me, but you'll have sex with another woman for your own pleasure?" I ask.

"I can assure you, it's never for my own pleasure. The women are yet to complain." He looks down at me, an eyebrow raised. I scowl at him, stomping ahead. I open the door and head down the stairs. I don't want to hear about him pleasuring another woman. God, not after I'd just traced the scars on his back and kissed them. Not when I'd just touched him.

He's quick to catch up, "Am...have you ever been with a man before?"

"Now that is none of your business," I snap at him, my legs stride faster trying to carry me away from his conversation.

"It's not something to be ashamed about," he says softly, slight confusion in his voice. It causes my cheeks to burn, I seal my lips. I am not talking to him about this.

He walks in step with me. Out of the safety of the room his entire body is on alert even though to others he'd just look like a man enjoying the night. My eyes widen as I look away from him, I'd been paying as much attention to him as he had been with me. Gods damn it.

We walk out into the night, I shiver slightly against the cool breeze. I'd forgotten to grab my cloak, my steps jolt for a moment before I find my footing. Eleazar shoots me a questioning look; I shake my head and focus on the village. I can't hide my bruises from their prying eyes.

"Where are we going?" I ask as we turn left, heading down another busy street. The village people talk and laugh with one another, most of the buildings doors are propped open with light flooding out into the street. It's alive here, there's no trace of darkness.

"A small eatery, it's just up ahead." Eleazar gently grasps my right elbow as he guides us down a small street, hardly any people mill about. Ahead there's a door propped open, dim light filters into the street.

"Is that it?" I ask, pointing to the door. He nods once, letting my elbow go. I walk a step behind until we reach the door. I reach out and grab his arm, he stops and looks back at me with an eyebrow raised in question. "I'm sorry. Can you—

can you please walk behind me? I didn't bring my cloak," I whisper. Shame burns in my chest as I let go of his arm.

"Of course." He steps aside to let me step past him, "wait,"

I pause in front of him, he steps close. His scent wafts on the breeze.

"May I touch you?" he asks softly.

I swallow, "Yes."

Slowly, his hands come around my waist and rests on the curve of my hips. He cages me in as I stand there, his chin rests against the side of my head as he leans down, his breath tickles my ear and entices a shiver from me. It has nothing to do with the cold.

"We'll look like two lovers out for dinner. No one will see your back," he whispers, "now walk."

I move ahead slowly, he walks easily behind me even though I'm almost plastered to his chest like a decoration. The eatery is small, dim lanterns hang off the wall every few metres. Most of the seats are occupied by other couples, a few glance as we make our way through the round tables and to the main desk. A woman with bright red hair looks up from the till and smiles when she sees us approach.

"A table for two?" she asks.

"Yes please, at the back preferably," Eleazar says, straightening slightly but still holding onto me.

"Of course. What will you have?" she looks from him to me, a patient smile.

"I'll just get whatever the special is with a glass of water please," I say. Eleazar's thumbs begin to brush against my hip as we stand there. I lean back into him until my back is flush against his warm chest.

"I'll have the venison steak with vegetables and water as well, please." His chest rumbles with his words as his thumbs continue to move. It's a comforting touch, warming. It makes me feel safe and at the same time it begins to make me burn.

"This way." She gestures for us to follow her. I walk ahead, careful not to lean into him again. We walk down the left side until we come to a private table in the back corner. She nods and smiles before disappearing back to the front. I slide out of Eleazar's arms and slip into the cushioned seat that's attached to the back wall. He takes the wooden seat in front of me, resting his elbows on the table.

"This place is nice," I offer. The dim lighting gives each couple their privacy, from where we sit I can't really see what the couple at the table to my right are doing.

"It's definitely a hidden gem in the village. It's more... romantic than the other places you can eat at." He rests his chin on his palm, sighing, "there's that look again."

"The look of a question?" I ask. I lean back into my seat and fight a smile.

"Precisely."

"Just one?" I ask. I fiddle with my bow as I keep my eyes on his. He rolls his eyes but there's no malice behind the action.

"Fine. One question and then no more for the night."

"Okay. Deal. You said earlier you're away more than you are at home. Where is home for you? Is it in Faerie somewhere or in Akrania?" I ask, resting my head against the wall.

"It's in Faerie. I live with Hemlock and Odin in a manor on the outskirts of Oakwood, it's far enough away to have no prying eyes but close enough in case I'm called for duty."

"Do you three always stay together?"

"Most times. I'd be with them in Faerie now if you hadn't decided to embark on your own journey," he remarks, raising an eyebrow. I cross my arms over my chest, as if this mess is my fault. I was getting by without his babysitting.

"Back to babysitting?" I retort.

He smiles slowly, showing teeth, "I'm certain that's three questions."

"It's good to see you can count."

"I wasn't born yesterday. I can do a lot of things you wouldn't know about. Now it's my turn for a question." I still, a slice of fear cutting through me. What sort of question will he ask?

"What could you possibly want to know about boring old me?" I drawl.

A waitress brings us two glasses and a jug of water, she smiles apologetically; eyeing Eleazar up before slipping back away. I stare after her, annoyed she'd ogled at him. He clears his throat, I look back to see he'd poured both of us a glass. I take it and bring the rim to my lips.

"Once you return home, do you plan on courting Colt?"

I spray water across the table at his question, he wipes a hand down his face and looks from his palm to me. "No, I do not plan on courting Colt. What sort of absurd question is that? I'm a faerie and he's a human." I laugh, completely shocked. I thought he'd ask me a question I couldn't answer. I wipe the few droplets of water from my chin.

"I think spitting your water was a tad dramatic," he grumbles as he fights a smile.

"I think that question was a tad dramatic. If I was going to court Colt, do you really believe I'd be here right now...with you?" I ask, I lean forward and rest my elbows on the table as I look at him. "Do you really believe I would have run off if I was so happy?"

"No, but I'm coming to the conclusion that you're full of surprises." He takes a sip of his water before placing the glass down. I tap my nails against mine, watching him.

"Why ask me that question? Do you really care if I'm single or taken? I thought you'd been doing all of this," I wave my hand in the air between us, "because it's what my father has asked of you. You made it that clear when you first found me and shoved me against the barn."

"I apologise for that. I didn't know about your back, it must have hurt." He leans back, crossing his arms over his chest.

"You didn't answer the question. Would you care if I was taken by another?" My heart beat is in my ears as I wait for his lips to open, his next words will either allow me to continue in the illusion there might be something between us, or utterly shatter me. My palms are clammy. I set the glass down and wipe them against my dress.

"Would it change things if I did?" I look up from my dress, startled. I'd barely caught his words, I didn't think he would have replied. If he did I was ready for a snarky reply. He stays still as I process what he'd said, his eyes studying me.

"It would change everything," I whisper, heart clenching in my chest.

There's a warm feeling spreading from my heart to every other cell in my body as I watch him. He watches me just as intently back and for the first time it's like we're really taking the other in. My eyes trail of the hardened planes of his face, the light stubble along his jaw and slightly down his throat.

"Here's your meal, enjoy," the bubbly waitress chirps, sitting down Eleazar's slab of meat and my chicken and salad combination. I smile in thanks as I pick up the fork and knife with shaky hands. I fill my mouth with food to avoid saying anything foolish.

As the night begins to grow late we finish our meal and drinks, we'd spent the rest of the evening talking about nonsense. It was far easier than talking about the very real tension that hangs between us like a heavy cloak now. Eleazar walks behind me like he had earlier as we go to pay, I dig out two gold coins and we leave the eatery.

"It's a bit cold tonight," I murmur. I hold my hand over my mouth as I yawn. Eleazar lets me go but walks close enough that our shoulders brush together with each step we take. He leads us back towards the barn.

"I'm definitely ready for bed," he murmurs, voice deep.

"That makes two of us." We walk around the curve into the main street, my eyelids grow heavy under the sparkle of lights above us. I shiver again and I rub my hands against my arms to try and keep the chill away.

Eleazar wraps an arm around my shoulder, curing me into the warmth of his body. I don't protest as I lean into him, resting my head on the side of his chest as I slide my arm around his waist. He radiates warmth and it only works to make me feel even drowsier. We walk like that for the rest of the short trek, all too soon the barn comes into view.

He lets me go once we reach the stairs. I walk ahead and open the door to the hall. My body is exhausted from the last two days and the night spent on hard ground. I get to our room and unlock the door, I toss him the key over my shoulder as I head straight to the bed. I get out of my boots, I grab one of his shirts from his bag and quickly strip from the dress and pull it over my head. It swallows me, reaching mid-thigh.

I pull down the sheets and climb into bed, sprawling on my back as my eyes drift shut. I hear Eleazar chuckle as the door locks, clothes rustle before the lantern is dimmed.

"Are you going to hog the entire bed? You've already taken claim to my clothes." His voice is deep. I half-heartedly roll on my side, allowing him enough room to lie down. Once he's settled I drape my arm and leg back over him, he chuckles. The noise vibrates against me.

"Comfy?" he whispers.

"Mmm. Very much so," I murmur. He sighs before rolling me on my side, he gently curls himself around me. His legs nestle against my own as an arm gently rests over my waist. I'm too tired to think more of it. I nestle back into him. He buries his face into the back of my neck and takes a deep breath.

"Sweet dreams, Am."

I begin to drift into sleep, warm and safe in his arms with that same warm feeling from earlier, spreading through my body. I realise what it is moments before I lose the battle to sleep.

He's given me hope.

CHAPTER 14

I brush Ash down, starting from his neck and making my way to his tail. Sweat beads roll down the sides of my face and back of my neck, soaking into the bottom of the pale blue shirt I'd dug out of my bag. The black leather pants stick to me uncomfortably, rising up to my bellybutton. I'd cut the end of my shirt off earlier that morning, it'd been far too hot so now it rests just below my breasts; allowing the soft breeze to cool me somewhat.

"So we'd gone out for dinner and it was lovely Ash, I don't know what to think of it. The way he looked at me, touched me. It's everything a girl like me could dream of," I say softly as I stroke him, pulling black hair from the brush every now and then. I'd been talking to Ash about Eleazar. I had to talk to someone who would listen, if only to get it off my mind so I can think more clearly about it.

"Then we'd fallen asleep together, cuddling. I've never slept that well in my life before and you'll never guess what happened next!" I lean into his face, whispering into his ear, "He'd been in bed this morning with me when I'd woken. He'd been leaning on one arm, watching me."

Ash knickers, bringing those large deep chocolate eyes to look at me. I pat his nose, shaking my head.

"I'm screwed Ash, totally and royally done for."

"Why are you screwed?" Eleazar's voice startles me. I spin to see him leaning on the gate to Ash's stall watching me, a slight smile on his face. His copper hair is half up half down today, his face clear of any stubble.

"Because this walk to Faerie is going to kill me," I sniff. I give Ash a kiss on his nose before walking over to the gate. I pause in front of it, swinging the brush from my hand as I look at him. I wasn't lying; this walk is going to kill me.

"I'm sure if your feet get sore *princess,* I can easily carry you."

My cheeks heats, "You know I'd never let you do that. What happened to the Eleazar that would make me walk a million miles, only telling me to keep up?" I smirk. I hang the brush up on the railing of the door. Eleazar steps back as I slide out of the stall. I clasp the gate behind me as Ash comes over, watching us.

"He must be hiding behind that stone wall you mentioned last night," he retorts, coming to stand beside me. We watch Ash in silence for a moment. I run the back of my hand across my forehead. I'd had a shower when I'd woken and already I feel the urge for another.

"When do we leave?" I ask.

"Now, it's why I'm here. It's almost lunch. I just stocked up our bags with dry fruits and meat for the journey with a flask of water each. I've paid the gold coins for them to look after the horses until we return. According to the map it's a two days journey, so most likely three for us," Eleazar says. He places his hands in the pocket of his pants. I sigh and walk closer to Ash, I hug his large head.

"I'll be back before you know it boy. I promise. Behave without me. I love you," I whisper to him. He knickers softly, leaning into my touch. I'd given the owner of the barn the last twelve golds I'd had to ensure Ash was especially taken care of. He assured me that Ash would still be here waiting for my return, Eleazar had promised nothing good would come from it if we were to return with our horses gone.

I kiss his nose before turning back to Eleazar, my eyes brim slightly with tears. My heart tugs in my chest as we begin to walk towards the front of the barn. Eleazar had brought our bags down, he'd clasped his two swords to his back again. I pick up my two bags and hang them over my shoulder in the most comfortable position I can find. I follow Eleazar out of the barn and into the burning light.

"So what's the plan?" I ask, catching up to walk by his side. His eyes take in everything around us, always on alert. Last night had been the first time he'd let his guard down for me, he'd let me in, in a way I never thought possible. Once he finds out I've lied to him about my magic...I'm going to betray the trust we're building.

"We walk until sundown or if you need to rest, we'll set up camp to rest for an hour or two but if we feel fine we'll carry on. The faster we get to Faerie the better, your father probably thinks the worst right now." Eleazar guides us through the streets, more people move about; most of them carrying sacks of grain. Most are farmers trying to make a living. At least this village is larger than Elk.

"Okay, I'm sure I can withstand that. What could my father possibly be thinking?" I snort, tucking my hands under the straps over my chest. Eleazar looks sideways at me, arching a brow. I look up at him in confusion, "What?"

"We've been gone longer than necessary. If I'd been more adamant about returning at my pace we'd be arriving in Faerie tomorrow night. The others are most likely waiting at my estate for our return before we head into the Covnos mountains to deal with the bulburoos."

"So...what would he be thinking?" I urge, leaning forward slightly.

"He'd be thinking I'm softening towards you," Eleazar huffs, looking away from me as we reach the edge of the village. Eleazar doesn't hesitate as he strides into the thick forest, I scramble to catch up to him; not wanting to get lost so soon on my own.

"He wouldn't be wrong, would he?" I catch up to him, slightly breathless from running with the bags on my back. Already sweat runs down my spine and between my breasts. It's going to be a long walk.

"No, but that's a conversation I want to have privately with him." He looks over his shoulder at me, "with no little mouse eavesdropping."

"It was only once," I grumble. He chuckles as he faces forward again. He moves the shrubs out of the way as we walks, kicking sticks and debris to create a clear path for me as I trail behind him. Would it be like this all the time if we'd pursued this?

"Yes. I remember the encounter quite clearly."

"When you think about it, we haven't actually known each other for that long. Maybe two weeks?" I muse.

"Two weeks and you're a thorn in my side already," he calls over his shoulder.

"You told me you like sharp things," I sing sweetly back. He relaxes slightly. We continue to walk in silence, Eleazar stops occasionally to redirect us or to double check the map as we walk. I don't complain about the sweat that pools in my boots or the blisters that are already beginning to form on my ankles. I've suffered worse and survived.

The canopy above us does its best to bring shade, but the

sun is unrelenting as it basks down on us. If Salis isn't going to kill me, this walk certainly might. The thought of his name is like a poisoned kiss to my soul. Everything Eleazar had told me had been truth, Salis will be coming for my soul one way or another and taking it to the Underworld with him.

What would kill me first, Eleazar or my own magic?

Over the last few days I haven't felt the dark power swimming beneath my skin and pumping through my traitorous heart. After Salis visited me in the clearing it had been quiet, as if it's waiting like a coiled snake to strike. But strike at what? Or better yet, who? I would take the blade to my own heart before I drove it through anyone that I cared for.

"When we reach Faerie, what happens to your magic?" I ask suddenly.

"I'll change in appearance. You'll see me in my true form, as I'll see the real you. Since you can't glamour your appearance, your mother does yours as well as her own."

"What do you mean glamour?"

He slows until we're walking side by side, I look up to see sweat running down his throat, "It's a form of magic we can perform. It dulls our appearance so the humans aren't scared of us. Faerie is magic, it strips away any glamour we have in place so we can be our true self."

"Oh..." I hardly liked what I saw in the mirror now. Being told I'm going to see my true self? It makes me quiver.

"You're beautiful Amaryllis, don't ever doubt that," Eleazar says softly. He looks ahead of us as if he hadn't just given me a compliment that has my cheeks heating.

"You're quite handsome yourself," I respond, looking ahead as well. "What does being in Faerie do to your magic? Is it stronger?"

"Yes, it's more...chaotic in a sense. It's heightened because there's so much magic in Faerie. You have nothing to worry about, I told you I would protect you and I will. Your visit to Faerie may even unlock your magic," he offers gently.

My stomach drops, being in Faerie is going to heighten my magic. What if I can't conceal it from him or the others? I'm sure he's not the only faerie who would hunt down a creature that has fallen magic in their veins. Would I be able to confide in my father? Would he protect me? I'm not evil. The worst I'd done is kill that man in self-defence or even I might not be walking and breathing right now. His hatred for my kind was like a rot inside his soul, if it wasn't me it would have been another defenceless faerie female.

"What if...what if I don't have sacred magic?" I whisper, utterly terrified to admit the thought out loud to him. Eleazar looks down to me, studying me.

"Is that what you're worried about?"

"Yes." I breathe out, feeling faint. I wipe my forehead.

He's silent for a moment. "You come from a family of sacred magic, it'd be almost impossible for you to inherit any other magic. If it was possible, you'd know by now. Don't worry, I'm sure you're stressing for nothing. We'll deal with it when the time comes."

"Okay. Okay. I can do that." I smile up at him, wincing at the same time.

"Can I ask how you got those bruises on your back?"

I trip over my feet. Eleazar's hand shoots out and grips my elbow as he steadies me. I feel my hands shake, if I told him the complete truth I don't know what would happen. He'd felt fallen magic at the murder scene. I don't want to deceive him either.

"It's not a pleasant memory, so if I share it with you, it goes no further than between us. My father doesn't need to know, or anyone in my family. It was my own stupid fault in the first place." I look up to him, he still grips my elbow. He takes my right shaking hand gently in his, grounding me to this moment. He intertwines our fingers.

"I promise it won't go further than between us," he assures me, voice serious. I take a deep breath. I am going to do it. I am going to remember that horrible night that I'd spent the journey supressing and trying to forget.

"It was the night I went through your things to find a map that would lead me to Faerie. That day when Kalin and I had arrived, while we were in line Ash had startled, knocking into a man and causing him to drop his basket of cloths. I'd gotten off to help and apologised but he'd shoved me and I'd fallen, Kalin had punched him and I had to de-escalate the situation before it got out of hand," I say. The memory is clear in my mind as if it was yesterday. I still remember the thud of Kalin's fist as it connected with the man's face. The hatred he had for me.

"He hated faeries, even though I'd never done anything to him. I get it a lot when I travel to Orrinshire so it's nothing new to me. After that I'd forgot about the encounter with him. That night when I'd decided to leave I'd tricked the man at the desk of your inn and I'd gone through your things and the others to find a map that could help me." I smile sheepishly up at him, "sorry about that."

"I'm sure I can forgive you." He squeezes my hand. It's so small in his calloused palm, delicate.

"I'd left your room and I let my guard slip, I was so excited to finally be taking my life into my own hands. I didn't hear the man coming up behind me. He'd said something and got my attention. I'd turned around and it was the man from that morning." My voice goes quiet.

"If you want to stop, you can," Eleazar says, noting the change in my voice. I shake my head, it might be good for me to talk about it with someone. Even if it is him.

"No. I need to get it off my chest. I replied to him, unable to help my stupid smart mouth. He shoved me to the ground and started kicking the life out of me. I couldn't move. There was so much pain. His foot just wouldn't stop." I feel detached from my body as I walk along and recall that night, silent tears slip down my cheeks. "When it finally did I was so caught up in the pain I didn't have time to register what was going on, when I heard his pants come undone—" I choke on a sob as my free hand comes to my mouth.

Eleazar envelopes me in his arm, holding me tightly to him. I wrap my arms around his waist and begin to cry into his chest. One hand cradles the back of my head to him while his other rubs my back up and down.

"You're safe now," he whispers.

"He—he pulled my pants down. I was frozen, I couldn't move. When he put his large body against mine I fought and fought, I was clawing and hitting him but he wouldn't stop. I had a single second of freedom." I stop as I lose control of my tears. I bury my face into his warm chest and hold onto him like he is the very air that keeps me alive. My anchor. Eleazar stays silent but continue to rubs my back.

"I grabbed the knife from my bra and I slit his throat. There was so much blood and the force of my swing cut through everything. I pushed him off me but I couldn't stop as I continued to stab him. I couldn't stop feeling the terror in that moment."

"You were the one who murdered that man?" he whispers.

"Yes. I'm sorry I know I shouldn't have—"

Eleazar pulls my head back, tipping my face towards his. I meet his fierce eyes, my heart raw in my chest and utterly his for the taking in the moment if he so chooses.

"Don't you ever apologise for protecting yourself, if you hadn't I would have been returning and doing far worse than what you did." He cups my cheek, stroking his thumb through my tears, "I am so terribly glad you found the strength to draw that blade. I don't know what I would have done to that filth if he'd managed..." his face contorts in pain as he rests his forehead on my own.

"I know. He didn't. I just wish...I just wish I had been stronger earlier."

"You are strong, so incredibly brave and strong," Eleazar whispers, his breath hits my lips. Our chests are pressed together, I can feel his heart beating wildly in his chest; matching my own. He opens his eyes and stares down at me. "I see you and I am unafraid."

"Stealing my lines I see," I say weakly, he smiles gently.

"As long as you're around I will steal them as I please." He draws back and presses his damp lips to my forehead, kissing it fiercely. I relax in his embrace, feeling the corners of my own lips turn upwards. I had told him as much as I could and in doing so I had strengthened the bridge between us.

Oh, how I'm going to break our hearts when the truth of what I am comes out.

"Are you okay?" he asks, leaning back to watch me. His golden eyes are chaotic with his emotions.

"I'll be okay...one day at a time," I assure him, squeezing his back.

"One day at a time," he echoes. "The fallen wielder must have been drawn to the essence of his death."

"I'm assuming so." I look away from him, unable to meet his eyes. "Let's continue walking, hopefully we can find a stream at sundown so we can bathe. I feel like a pig rolling in the mud." I step out of his arms; he catches my hand in his and intertwines our fingers. We walk together in comfortable silence, my hand warm in his. Even though our palms are slick he doesn't let me go.

As the sun begins to descend in the sky, I find my eyes

trailing back to Eleazar. He catches me staring a few times and offers me a rare smile, squeezing my hand before focusing on the path ahead of us. Each step we take brings us closer to Faerie, closer to my unravelling.

I can only hope he will still be there to catch me after I fall.

CHAPTER 15

"Is that a river I hear?" I gasp, untangling my hand from his to burst through the shrubs in front of us. Eleazar's laugh reaches my ears as I struggle through the underbrush, branches snag at my clothes and nick my skin but the sting is nothing compared to the relief I feel when I see the deep blue bubbling water. I reach the clearing, black and grey pebbles are firm under my feet and spread to the other side of the wide river. I catch a glimpse of a red and black fish, scales shimmering in the dying sun.

I shrug out of my bag. I pull my shirt off effortlessly. It drops to the ground with a wet thud, drenched with sweat. A cool breeze pebbles my bare chest as I lean down and untie my boots. I gingerly pull my feet from their confines and sigh as I see the angry red blisters covering the backs of my ankles.

"I'm undressing," I call over my shoulder, untying the black ribbon to the front of my pants.

"Is that an invitation?" Eleazar calls back, his voice close. A smile twitches my lips as I undo my hair. It fans out around me, clumping in places. I look over my shoulder as I hear the shrubs crack. Eleazar appears, scowling at the branch that tugs at his shirt. He rips it; the small tear leaves behind a piece of fabric. His eyes trail towards me. He stops and my chest tightens.

"It's nothing you haven't seen before," I say sheepishly, facing forward again. My heart threatens to burst in my chest as I begin to pull my pants down, I leave my underwear on.

"Still as beautiful as the first time," he says gently. His bag thuds to the ground before I hear his swords being unclasped. I wade into the water. Warm water welcomes me as I walk deeper, until the water just reaches my chest. I pull my hair forward, keeping my hands in my armpits crossed over my chest.

I watch as he begins to set up a small camp, he's quick to fetch sticks to create a small fire. He uses his magic to light the twigs, his palms burning a deep blue with an orange flame surrounding it. The twigs catch easily, crackling and popping as they burn brightly into the darkening night.

"My...invitation still stands," I call softly, cheeks burning. Eleazar stiffens where he crouches over the fire, the flames on his palms gutter out as he slowly turns his head to the side to look at me. His golden eyes swirl with...with *hunger*.

"Are you sure you want to share the water with a brute like me?" he asks as he slowly rises to his feet. He takes a few steps forward, the late afternoon sun catches his copper hair in one last embrace before disappearing behind the thick shrubs that surround this little alcove.

"I'm sure I can make room." I take a few steps back until the water laps at my collarbones, I swish my hands nervously under the water as I keep my eyes trained on him. He slowly pulls his shirt over his head, his muscles rippling with the movement. My legs go weak as my breath is torn from me.

Something deep inside my chest stirs, warming at the sight of him. It catches me off guard, the tug that I feel towards him. I've always felt some sort of softness towards him, but now it feels physical. As if my hands can't wait a second longer to touch him.

He pulls his boots off next, his pants following to expose thick thighs and defined calves. This man is a warrior in every form. He leaves his undergarment on, the thin cream material ends just before his knee. He strides towards the water as my eyes take in the sight of him.

He is *beautiful.*

He pauses as his toes reach the water, "Are you sure you want my company?"

"Goodness how many times must I ask?" I huff, raising a brow at him.

"As many times until I know you're comfortable this close to me," he answers, taking a step into the water. It laps at his ankles now, enticing him as much as it had with me.

"I've been closer than this before, if you can't recall last night?" I take a step towards him, the water now just reaching the top of my breasts. I am as nervous as anything for him to see me now and be *close* to me like this. After last night, something has shifted between us. Something I wished to explore if he wishes to as well.

"I recall it perfectly." He takes another step, the water reaching his calves. He takes another until it laps at the back of his knees. I find my courage as the softness in his eyes strengthens me. I take another step forward, the water now resting against my navel. He sucks in a sharp breath but never takes his eyes from my own.

"But something...something's different now. Isn't it?" I whisper, struggling to keep my breathing in check. Mother warned me to be careful with my heart, warned me of the consequences of giving it to him. What if his heart still belonged to his last lover? Mother said they were still close. What would become of my heart?

"Yes." He strides deeper into the water, meeting me in the middle. The water laps at my waist as we stand in front of each other. I tip my face up to look at him, burying my fears and doubts. In this moment, all I have is him and I. It is enough for me.

"I don't know how to do this," I gesture between us, resting my hand on his chest where his heart beats like a galloping stallion. "I've never felt something so strongly for another before, this is all new to me."

His hands rest on my hips and drag me closer to him, they splay against my back; his thumbs stroking over the dimples beside my spine on either side "This feeling is new to me as well. I've had my share of lovers and courtships but I've never felt that insistent tug in my chest when I look at you. I felt it the moment I walked through your father's doors and saw you on the stairs."

"The moment you walked in I was done for," I reach up and rest my other hand on his other breast, stroking my fingers over the muscle. "When we reach Faerie, what will happen?"

"I will need to talk to your father and explain. He isn't only your father but he is my best friend. I've known him for many centuries, I know how much he cares for you and how deep his love runs for you and your mother." His eyes search mine. As the sun casts the world into darkness the full moon bathes us with silver rays of light. His golden eyes glow, enchanting me.

"You're afraid he won't approve?"

He nods once, lips twisting. "I can't go against his word. If he sees me unfit for his daughter it is a request I must respect."

"Let's hope the gods are on our side." I slip from his arms, catching his hand as I lead us deeper into the water. My body is alight with flames, his simple touch igniting me in ways I can't fathom. I stop once the water sits below my chest, turning to face him again. I reach up on my toes and undo the leather band from his hair, I slide the band on my wrist before combing my hands gently through the knots. Eleazar is still, barely breathing. His hands sit on my waist, anchoring him to this moment.

Once the knots are out I lean back, tucking a loose strand behind his pointed ear.

"I am no warrior or fighter. I am a dreamer with a light heart that carries me on swift wings." I whisper, running my fingers down his smooth cheek, "If what you want is a warrior who matches you in every aspect you won't find her in me." My mind flashes to his last lover, mother had said they'd been so similar. Equals.

"I don't want a warrior to match me. As selfish as it is, I want someone who I can protect. Someone I can fight for and know they will fight for me back in their own way," one of his hands leave my waist, cupping my cheek. I tilt my face into his touch as I watch him, hanging on his every word.

"You're the first person in centuries to stand up to me with your sharp tongue and quick wit, you've never cowered from me. You've never been afraid of who I am. You threw yourself into danger with that wendigo because you knew it would give me a chance to kill it."

"Yes, well you thought me rather foolish in the moment," I smile, covering his hand with one of my own.

"How could I not? You'd thought of a plan to distract the creature so I could have an opening, as terrifying and foolish as that plan was, it worked. From that moment, I saw you. Who you were underneath the mask you would wear." He pulls me closer to him, sliding his hand around to cup the back of my head. My chest presses to his, the rest of my body plastered to his own as if we can't get close enough.

"Who you are, is who I want. I couldn't care if you were a warrior or knew nothing about holding a sword in your hand. I couldn't care if you were the best cook in both worlds or if you struggled to make stew. Who you are is who I've come to want," he says softly, eyes burning into my own.

"I feel this is too good to be true," I whisper, eyes beginning to fill with tears. I know it's too good to be true. I know this moment won't last and I may never get a chance like this with him again, so close and vulnerable before me. "I want you for all you are, the whole and the broken pieces of your heart. You've made a home under my skin and no matter how much I bath, you refuse to budge."

"I have indulged in everything this life has offered me," he pauses, those golden eyes holding me in place, "yet you make me lust for *more*." His rasped words wrap around my heart, squeezing it painfully. I reach my hands out and wrap my arms around his neck, I lean up on my tip toes; my body sliding against his own with the simple movement. My legs quiver as each nerve stands on end, the effect he has on me in catastrophic.

I tilt my face towards his as he leans down, closing the distance between us.

His lips are a gentle caress at first, soft and warm as they skim over my own. His arm slides and tightens around my waist, leaving no room of air between us. His fist gently wraps in my hair, tilting my face towards his even more.

"Amaryllis, you have undone me," his words are thick with emotion. I lick my lips.

"You were always going to be my undoing," I whisper back, showing him the truth of my words in my eyes. From the moment he pulled his hood back I knew I was doomed, my heart had already wandered out of my chest and planted itself at his feet for the taking. Every touch, conversation and argument after that only worked to strengthen the roots. My emotions blossomed for him before I acknowledged them, resting and waiting for the moment I would.

Here in his arms, I bare my soul to him.

I could deal with the consequences of my magic once I came to that bridge and if I must set it on fire to keep him and the others I love safe? Then so be it. I refuse to give myself over to the darkness that swims through my veins, I refuse to be the evil occupant Salis desires me to be. I refuse to be another weapon for someone to wield. This is my life and I chose how I weave my path, I choose my happiness. My love. No one, no god or faerie will ever take that from me.

Do you hear that Salis? I will fight you with every morsel in my body. I refuse the fate you have given me. I refuse the life you wish for me to have. I am the only one who controls my life and I refuse to die for you or your magic. I refuse your debt and I will spend each second I am breathing, fighting you.

Eleazar kisses me, his lips gentle and warm. He is a breath of fresh air and tastes just as sweet. I kiss him back, not hesitating as my lips claim his. It ignites a fire so deep in my soul the skin that doesn't touch his, aches.

He hoists me in the air, I wrap my legs around his waist as I lower my head to meet his again while his large hands rest on my rear and hold me into place. My hair fans around us as I grasp his cheeks in my hands, our kisses desperate with longing and building with each touch.

I feel something hardening underneath me and my thoughts are lost to him. He pulls back from my lips at the same moment, my breathing is just as ragged as his. His eyes burn as they focus on me, we're silent for a moment; caught in the moment as our breathing fills the air between us.

"I want you in every form you will give me, but not here like this," he manages to say, resting his forehead against my own. I struggle to breath regularly, it is impossible being this close and having my skin ignite under his touch. If I am death, he is my destruction.

"This is enough for now," I rasp, curling my hands behind his head into his hair.

"Come, let's finish bathing and we'll rest for a few hours. Would I be able to braid your hair?" he asks, still holding me close. I smile, kissing the tip of his nose.

"Of course you can." He lets me slide down his body until I find my feet, my legs are quaking underneath me. He laughs as he helps me stand. I narrow my eyes at him even though my lips betray me with a smile.

I slip from his hands and duck under the water, my hair fans out ghostly around me as I scrub my fingers through it. I gasp for breath as I break the surface. Eleazar lowers himself into the water as well, running his hands through his hair and scrubbing at every inch of skin he can reach. Before long we're both clean, he takes my hand as he leads me towards the fire.

I wring my hair out as I stand there dripping, beginning to shiver. A white towel is wrapped around my shoulders, I laugh as I look over my shoulder at him. Another towel is tightened around his waist.

"Did you steal these?" I say between laughing, he smirks and shrugs his shoulders.

"I prefer the term, borrowing." He comes closer to the fire, holding his hands out for the warm flame. I shake my head, grateful for the towel. I quickly dry before pulling on a clean pair of brown pants and the white shirt Eleazar had given me, I clasp my cloak over my shoulders. I hang the towel over a low hanging tree branch before taking a seat in front of the fire. Eleazar dresses quickly, he sits beside me and stretches his long legs away from the fire.

"So once we return to Faerie and go to your estate, will we

be heading directly to the mountains that cage the bulburoos?" I ask, resting my elbows on my knees as I watch the fire.

"That's the plan. The others will have everything ready for our arrival. I know you won't be staying at my estate, even though every fibre in my body wants you to." He sighs, leaning back on his arms.

"Where's the fun in that? I might surprise everyone and be able to help. If I'm right about Salis tainting the magic in the bulburoos..." I might be able to somehow use my own power to rid the creature of his magic until only sacred magic swims through its veins. I can't voice that.

"Then we're in more trouble than we thought." I look to Eleazar, his jaw twitches as he thinks.

"Do any of you have anything to stop it if I'm right?" I ask.

He shakes his head, his wet hair swinging with the movement, "No, not that I can think of. If the creature is tainted with fallen magic the best thing we can do for it is to end its life."

"Why would you kill it?"

"I've told you before that fallen magic is unable to be tamed and controlled. It eventually takes over the host and kills them in a slow, painful death. It's the only blessing we can give the creature." He looks at me, "I was the lead hunter when it was declared fallen magic wielders were to be slain. Once we've dealt with the bulburoos I am oath bound to hunt down the wielder of fallen magic that has shown itself in Orrinshire."

My body freezes, but I keep my expression carefully blank as I stare at him.

"Has it ever been heard of someone controlling the magic and not turning evil?"

"No, it hasn't. If there has been I wouldn't know. They've most likely gone into hiding and then Salis has claimed them."

"Have you ever...witnessed someone with fallen magic

going up against Salis?" I ask softly. He arches an eyebrow in question, his eyes blazing with curiosity.

"No, I haven't. Either they chose not to or their soul had already been claimed by Salis and his magic ravished them. I mean, technically it would be possible if they chose too." He sits up and leans close to me, his breath hitting my face. "Why are you asking these types of questions?"

Now is the perfect opportunity if I wish to tell him the truth, to divulge the heavy secret I've been keeping from him. Looking into his golden depths, I can't do it. I can't disappoint him like that and sever the connection we have.

"I'm just curious. Everyone knows the legends of what happens with sacred magic, it's hardly ever heard of what happens to those with fallen magic."

He reaches out and tucks a strand of raven hair behind my ear. "That's because it's forbidden in Faerie, anything related to fallen magic has been wiped from the books. No one in in Faerie wishes to acknowledge fallen magic considering it only brought death and destruction to our land and our people."

I take his hand in my own, intertwining our fingers together. He pulls me to him, I slide onto his lap and rest my back against his chest. He wraps his arm around my waist, resting his chin on my head. I place my hands over his own, cuddling deeply into him.

"If someone with fallen magic could be good and not hurt others...would you still kill them?" I ask, already knowing the answer I'm going to receive. He kisses the top of my head, squeezing me to him for a moment. He begins to braid my hair, his fingers moving swiftly. He reaches for the leather band on my wrist before tying the braid off. It runs from the top of my head and down my shoulders.

"I would still have an oath to fulfil. If the fallen could prove they aren't their magic and could control it...I'm not sure. I've never considered the possibility of someone with that type of magic being good. Don't worry Am, you're safe with me," he assures, taking my tense shoulders the wrong way. I hide my worry and tilt my head towards his, brushing my lips along his jaw.

His lips meet mine, fitting perfectly. His arms tighten as he holds me to him, I sit up in his lap to allow myself better access to him. He may protect, but can he protect himself from me?

Can I save his heart, even if it means breaking my own?

CHAPTER 16

I notice the shift in the air around us before I see the large fallen tree, its trunk so thick is stands taller than Eleazar. Bright green grass sways softly under our feet, with each step I take the grass recorrects itself back to its original position.

"The entrance is on the other side," Eleazar says, walking a few steps in front of me. We'd managed to reach the entrance to Faerie just after the sun had hit the middle of the sky. I wipe sweat from my forehead, looking over the tree. Its thick dark brown bark has rivets that cover it, the perfect foot holds to climb over.

"Alright, well how do we get over there? Climb?" I walk past him and press my palm against the trunk, its rough texture biting at my skin. He chuckles, I look over my shoulder at him. His twin swords are strapped to his back, he'd pulled his hair back into a high bun today. He looks every inch the warrior I know he is.

"I'll help you up." He comes closer and laces his hands together, I put my foot in his hand and grab onto the bark. "One, two, three." He pushes me into the air. I scramble to get a hold as I'm launched into the air. I hook my fingers into a gap at the top of the trunk, my arms strain as I pull myself up. I straddle the top and look down to Eleazar, he smiles up at me.

"It's high." I say, peering over the other side. The clearing on the other side of the fallen tree only holds green grass and a faerie circle, red and white dotted mushrooms form a tight ring. The grass inside the ring is shorter than the grass that sways on the outside.

"I'm coming up," Eleazar calls. Moments later he appears in front of me, he smirks before leaping from the trunk. I gasp as he lands on his feet, he looks back up at me.

"If you think I'm doing that you have another thing coming," I call down. My hands tighten on the bark I'd found.

"Come on, I'll catch you if you fall."

Oh bloody hell. I turn and slowly begin to lower myself down, the front of my shirt catches on the bark as I struggle to find foot holes as I begin to go down. My hands find holes to grab easily. My right foot slips from its hold and I pivot backwards.

I open my mouth to scream as the ground rushes up towards me, only to collide with a hard warm body. Eleazar huffs as I knock the breath from him. He helps me stand on both legs and leans over to catch his breath.

"I'm sorry I didn't mean to lose my footing." I say, wincing as he narrows his eyes at me.

"It's alright, are you ready to finally go to Faerie?" he asks, straightening. I look around him to the mushrooms.

"That's the doorway isn't it?"

"Yes it is. When we reach Faerie I will...change. I have a reputation there of being a formidable warrior, weakness is a target in Faerie and if any creature suspects either of us is weak they will pounce. If you have to meet the Queen remember to bow and use your manners."

"I use my manners all the time, thank you very much." I cross my arms over my chest and stare up at him.

"My appearance is going to change, as will yours. Once we arrive I can show you what you really look like." He reaches out a hand for me, wiggling his fingers. I push my hesitation down and slide my hand into his. He leads us into the ring of mushrooms. He pulls me to his chest, resting his hands on my lower back. "Don't take your eyes from me until we're there."

That's the only warning I'm given until the world around us begins to break into pieces and fall away. I keep my eyes on Eleazar's golden ones, out of my peripheral vision the blue sky and forest around us disappears. My breath is sucked from me as our hair begins to rise, as if we're falling.

Blue, green and pink fractured light surrounds us, lit up with multiple bright white and silver stars. It's beautiful and breathtaking and begs for me to turn towards it. I grasp my hands in his shirt, not wanting to get lost in the unknown.

Suddenly the colours of a sunset are plunged into darkness, so black that it seems to breathe life. My body goes rigid as my breathing comes in sharp bursts. The inky substance seems to move around the ring, trying to break in to smother us.

"Look who it is...she's returned at last."

"We will chew her up and spit her out."

"Salis is going to be pleased to know she's here."

The voices are made up of thousands, like a snake hissing a thousand harmonies at once. If Eleazar can also hear what I'm hearing, he is going to ask questions about why Salis wants me here. From the look on his face, he's hearing and maybe seeing something completely different to what I am.

"The dark one has returned. She will be their reckoning or ruin."

"She's bedding the great golden wolf. We will be there to feast on her soul once he cuts her down."

"Salis said she tastes sweet."

I block the voices out, pure terror rushes through me as they all begin to chant faster about my demise until they're screaming, their thousand voices threatening to pierce my eardrums. We plummet down, moving faster but standing stock still. I ignore the urge to let Eleazar go and join them, that darkness inside of me awakens.

We've reached Faerie.

Before my eyes, Eleazar changes.

I thought he was beautiful before, but now? Now he's the equivalent to a god. He grows taller, his ears sharpening. Those sharp, cunning eyes become like blades of flame. The gold swirls with milky white as he stares down at me, still holding me to him. He keeps his muscular build even though his face sharpens.

I feel myself beginning to grow slightly, just stopping as my nose meets his chin. My black raven hair fans around my face, the black locks shining in the light that now surrounds us. I can't seem to look away from him, even though we've reached Faerie. Noise reaches my ears and it so crisp and clear, I take a deep stuttering breath. Fresh air fills my lungs with the slight tang of blackcurrant.

"Blackcurrant?" I ask, breaking our silence. My voice is like nectar to my ears, oozing with richness. Eleazar grins, exposing those two sharp elongated canines.

"It's the magic. Welcome to Faerie, Amaryllis." Eleazar's deep voice sets me off instantly, making my toes curl in my boots. His eyes flicker to my lips, his hands tightening against me. As if he knows exactly what his voice alone does to me.

"Do I look...different?" I whisper as I splay my hands against his chest. I look down at my long, pale fingers. I drum them along his chest, dumbfounded. He chuckles, shaking his head.

"Come, I'll show you." He lets me go and steps out of the circle. I follow after him; stumbling over my long legs. I look down at myself, the change has made me leaner. All angles as sharp as a knife. I look around us. Mountains litter the edge of the bright blue sky that surrounds us. In front of us is a thick forest, sheltering a large white castle. Creatures fly in and out of the forest, a large river runs down from the mountain to our left and disappears into the forest.

Grass tickles my ankles as we walk towards the castle, Eleazar's shoulders tense with each step he takes towards the darkening forest. I look towards my right, in the distance thick black clouds have gathered in the sky over large mountain peaks. Bright blue electric lightning streaks their dark depths. That must be where the bulburoos is being kept.

Eleazar slows down a fraction until we're walking side by side. Our shoulders brush but neither of us dare touch more than that. I don't want to be seen as weak to the other faerie's here. We reach the forest and begin to walk down a white cracked cobblestone path, it's littered with black roses still on their branches. I reach down and pluck one from the ground, my thumb catches on a thorn. I suck the small bubble of blood into my mouth.

If I leave any blood behind, would they be able to scent the fallen magic in it?

The forest breaks apart as we walk through a stone arch way, green goblins look towards us. Their gnarled noses and yellow, sharpened teeth crunch as they shrink away from Eleazar. I marvel at how he carries himself. In this place he is nothing *but* a warrior, from the swords strapped to his back down to his very teeth.

I hold myself as best as I can, extremely aware of the very bland outfit I wear. Not to mention I most likely smell like a salt bath, I'd sweat so much on the adventure here. I look towards the goblins and small pixies, they flitter about; darting closer before darting away. Over the stone courtyard wall to my right a large tree has grown, its mottled brown and green leaves hang slightly over the edge.

I look to Eleazar, he pauses before drawing himself down on one knee. He bows his head, his eyes catch mine underneath his arm. I quickly follow suit, unsure if I'm even meant to bow like him. My cheeks burn furiously, I should have asked before we'd arrived.

"Well. I never thought I'd see the day the golden wolf brings a brittle lamb to me," a sweet, female voice says. Each word drips with charm, "you both may rise."

I do as she says, immediately looking to her. She's draped across the white stone throne like a decoration, her vibrant red hair is curled around her; bright dandelions have been weaved into the curls. Her pale skin glows ever so slightly, radiating magic.

"And who might you be?" she asks, narrowing those white eyes on me.

"Amaryllis, daughter of Ravynne and Nyx," I say with a sliver of confidence. Her eyes flare with recognition as she rises from the throne. Her white silk dress parts down each thigh as she walks down the steps towards me. I don't cower under her piercing stare. The skirts of her dress flutter in a soft breeze as she stops in front of me.

"I thought those lilac eyes looked familiar." She reaches out and strokes a hand down my cheek, tilting my face to each side as she observes me. "You look so much like your mother."

"Thank you."

"It's not a compliment." She lets my face go. Her eyes rake over me and leave me feeling bare before her. This must be the queen. The other faeries go quiet at her insult, all listening and watching intently to see what I will do. This must be the part where I'm meant to keep my mouth shut, like Eleazar had suggested earlier.

"I can see why she never wanted me to visit before. I wouldn't want to be in your company either," I say coolly, narrowing my eyes at her. Her red lips pull back in a snarl as gasps echo around us. Insult me all you like, no one insults my family.

"You will respect me. I am the queen and I rule over your very existence," she hisses. Her bright red nails elongate with her anger while her milky white eyes burn brightly. If I wasn't angry, I'd definitely be terrified of her.

"I don't know you from a grain of salt. You don't earn my respect by insulting my family," I say back, fisting my hands at my side as I meet her eyes. "You don't rule over me in any aspect. This is my first time stepping foot in Faerie."

"Eleazar, why on earth would you bring this parasite into my home?" She turns those burning eyes to Eleazar and he stiffens beside me. We're all silent for a moment, my heart thunders in my chest. My magic stirs, pushing against my skin as it senses the magic she wields. A deep hunger awakens, yawning in the depths of my soul. I struggle to compose myself as my stomach cramps, desperate for a taste.

"On Nyx's request I had to retrieve her," he says slowly. I look to him and try to focus on his voice rather than the dark one that now swims around my mind. It peers out through my own eyes, racking its starved gaze over every creature here. It'd have a field day if I let it take control of me again like it had when I'd killed that man.

"You tell him once that bulburoos is taken care of, that she is never permitted to these lands again until the moment I'm off this throne," she spits. She turns to me, "it would do you well to hold that tongue of yours. Next time you snap back, I will cut it out."

She spins on her heels and stalks back to her throne, once more draping herself over it. She flicks a wrist and the spell held over the court is broken. Eleazar looks down at me and narrows his eyes; anger burns in those depths. I stare back at him with just as much venom.

"Eleazar! It's been so long!" A sweet female voice interrupts our silent argument. We both turn from the throne to see a gorgeous faerie approaching us. Her milky pale blue skin is adorned with golden jewellery. Her deep sapphire hair swims around her, a small creature appears from the depths of its curls; wide yellow eyes stare at us as she approaches.

"Kay, it's lovely to see you again." He greets her, nodding as she stops in front of us. Her cheeks flush a deep blue, her bright blue eyes light up with joy. She's stunning in every way. Her seashell dress hugs her curvy figure tightly, water leaks from the cracks in the shell and pools at her feet. She turns her eyes towards me.

"You are either extremely foolish or have more courage than all of us combined," she laughs, the sound reminding me of waves lapping against the shore. She holds a hand out for me, I take it.

"I'm Amaryllis, it's nice to meet you." I smile.

"I'd say she's foolish," Eleazar grunts. Kay lets go of my hand and smiles at him, waving her hand in the air.

"How was the journey? Helena mentioned you'd be coming back. She didn't mention you'd be bringing Nyx's daughter though," Kay says, eyes flickering to me quickly in question. Eleazar tenses beside me. I look between them...could Helena be his ex? I can't grasp her name for the life of me. I swore mother had told me.

"It wasn't planned. She's a bit of a run away and her father wanted her safe, even if it meant bringing her to Faerie."

"Ah I can't wait to see his surprise when he hears about

this little encounter with the queen," Kay muses, smiling at me.

"No one insults my mother," I state, looking around the crowd. Many of the faeries here have coloured skin, their features matching their skin colour. A female with golden skins sways past us, her bright yellow hair is a tangled bird nest on her head; a black raven nests on the top and keeps watch as she walks along.

A male with deep green skin talks with a goblin, his fingers are the shade of the deep brown as he uses his hands to express his conversation. There's others that are like Eleazar and I, more typically normal looking. I look back to Kay, she looks like she's freshly stepped out of the oceans depths.

"Are you heading to your estate now?" she asks.

"Yes, we'll be off. Nyx is probably worried she won't be returned in one piece," Eleazar looks down to me, narrowing his eyes. I huff and look away from him. I'd be getting a mouthful once we were out of hearing range of the others.

"Alright, Helena said that you won't be leaving until tomorrow morning. There's a feast tonight that you'll all have to attend. I'll see you both there," Kay beams at us both before moving like liquid as she heads back to a group of female faeries that are perched on a large, blooming pink and white frangipani. Eleazar strides back the way we came, shoulders coiled. He snarls at any who dares to look at us now, they shrink away from us as we head through the archway.

He storms through the forest, mumbling and cursing under his breath. I hurry to keep up with him, stumbling over broken branches and slipping on fallen leaves. We break free from the forest and take a left, walking along the edge of it.

"Are you positive you have a brain in that head of yours?" he barks over his shoulder. I flinch at the tone of his voice, wanting to avoid the blade of his words.

"Of course I do. I told you before, no one insults my mother. I don't care who you are or your importance." I snap back, feeling my anger flare. The darkness fuels my anger, begging me to rile him up more.

"We are in Faerie Amaryllis, she is the queen of all magic creatures that reside in this section. You can't just bite back when she entices you. She would not have a problem following through with her threats and Nyx and I would have our hands tied."

"Oh so you'd be on her side if it meant cutting my tongue out?" I clench my fists, imaging a thousand daggers raining down and embedding into his back. He stops and turns towards me, he grabs me and pushes me against the trunk of a tree. "Let me go." I struggle against him, he pushes himself against me harder. He cages me against the tree, his hot breath hits my own as he stares down at me.

"I would never let it come to that, and neither would your father. You need to think smarter while you are here. The creatures here are not humans, they are cunning and cruel." His anger burns to an ember, a small kernel of what it was only moments ago. I push my hands against his chest, digging my nails into his shirt.

"I'm not like you or the others here," I say. My jaw tightens as the reality of my words cement around us. "I will never be like you or the others. Ever. I am more human than I am fae."

"Did I ask you to be like the others here? No."

"You don't have to ask! Already I'm in trouble because I let my tongue slip."

He cups my face, running his thumb over my bottom lip, "It is because I care about you and don't wish for you to find trouble while we are here."

"You seem to forget, trouble is all I find." I sigh, feeling my anger beginning to dissolve. The darkness growls as it shrinks, moping inside of me as I push the hunger down. It's like a dog that I need to keep on a tight leash.

"Lucky I'm able to deal with trouble." Eleazar leans forward, kissing me sweetly. I melt into him instantly, wrapping my arms around his neck as I pull him towards me. A new hunger awakes that has nothing to do with the darkness. His canines nip at my bottom lip, causing me to groan low in my throat. He pulls back, our breaths mingling.

"If this is the punishment I receive for running my tongue, I'm going to be a very naughty girl," I say, catching my breath. He smiles slowly, kissing my nose gently. He steps back, helping me stand on both legs. They quiver, but I do my best to hide it. He holds his palm in between us, the air on it quivers.

"What are you doing?" I ask.

"Showing you how beautiful you are," he says. The air solidifies as a mirror forms, the size of a dinner plate. He holds it up for me until my reflection comes into view. I gasp as I look at myself. My lilac eyes swirl with deep streaks of violet, my heart shaped face is slightly more angled; my high cheeks complimenting my now sharpened ears. I reach up and run my fingers over my lips.

"You are even more beautiful Amaryllis, can you see it?" His voice is soft. Warm.

"I..." I shake my head slowly, unable to answer. I don't *hate* what I see as I look at my reflection, at the sharpness of my gaze. My lips are slightly swollen from the kiss we'd shared, a small cut stings on my bottom lip. I run my tongue over it. Eleazar had done that.

My blood runs cold.

Does he taste the fallen magic in me?

"Come, let's go meet with the others. We both need to bathe and eat." The mirror fades, leaving Elazar staring at me. I struggle to smile, he watches me for one more moment before taking my hand in his own. He pulls me along the forest, not giving me a chance to change my mind.

We reach the descent of a hill, in the distance sitting in front of another thick forest that spreads left and right is a small manor. From the distance I can faintly make out the cream exterior and five large rabbits the size of horses wandering out the front.

"What the hell are they?" I ask, pointing towards them.

"They're rabbits, but some faeries use them to ride on their travels. We'll be using them to head to the Covnos mountains."

"I've never ridden a rabbit before." We walk down the hill before we crest another smaller hill. Far sooner than I'd like we reach flat ground that is only a few metres from his manor. It's only one floor, with two windows on each side of the front door. The rabbits all turn to look at us as we approach, their large noses twitching.

"I'm nervous," I whisper, stopping us shy of the steps that lead us up to the door. The others hadn't heard us approach. Eleazar slips his hand from mine, brushing my hair behind my ear as I turn to look up at him. Not only am I going to get an earful from father, but I fear Eleazar's ex-lover will be inside.

"Don't be. Your father won't be too mad," he says softly.

"Eleazar...who is Helena?"

He sighs, scrubbing a hand down his face before meeting my eyes again. "She's my last lover. I can assure you, you have nothing to worry about. Do you trust me?"

"Yes, I trust you." I begin to frown, dread nags at me deep within. He gently presses a kiss to my forehead, running a hand through my hair.

"Thank you."

The door swings open, startling us both. I step away from Eleazar, cheeks on fire. A woman steps out, her emerald eyes finding Eleazar immediately. They warm when they meet his, her whole demeanour softens. Her blonde hair is pulled back into a high ponytail, her tan skin peppered with white scars that are similar to his. She's armed to the teeth with blades over her skin tight black leather outfit. She's stunning, radiating power and confidence. Her eyes sharpen as she looks down at me, they fiery depths turn ice cold as her lips tighten with disdain.

I deflate. This is Helena.

CHAPTER 17

Helena's stare doesn't waver as she stands there, hands casually resting on the two knives that are strapped to her side. Eleazar is tense beside me, most likely reading the tension that hangs between the two of us.

"They're here." She calls over her shoulder, her voice is soft. Feminine. I was expecting it to sound like sharpened steel, not like the soft caress of a lover. She sniffs once before stepping to the side, closest to Eleazar.

My father appears moments later, the tension and worry is hidden with relief when he sees me. Those violet eyes swirl with gold as he closes the distance between us and wraps me into a crushing hug. I wrap my arms around him, my seams threaten to come loose in his arms. I want to tell him everything, this burden is beginning to become too heavy for me to carry alone.

"Thank god you're okay, I was so worried something horrible had happened." He breaths me in, nestling his head on top of mine. I lean my head on his chest and relax.

"I'm sorry. I was sick of being left behind." I whisper, only wanting him to hear it.

"I know petal. You're here now so let's just focus on that.

We can talk about…the rest, once we return home. I'll send word to your mother so she doesn't worry." He steps back, eyes assessing me for any injury. My back twinges in phantom pain, I stuff it down and smile up at him.

"Alright, come inside. You two must be starved." Father keeps an arm around my shoulders as he guides me inside. My boots slap against polished wooden floors as we enter a large, empty room. We go left and enter a living room, Hemlock and Odin look up from the card game they play on the coffee table. A white couch sits to our left, a deer pelt is draped over one arm. A white marble fire place sits to our right, fresh wood is stacked inside. Paintings of landscapes decorate the white walls, at the end of the room is a large elk head, its black horns spiral down to its white skull.

"It's good to see you again Ama," Hemlock grins. Odin tilts his head in acknowledgment but stays quiet.

"It's nice to see you both again too," I say, smiling. Eleazar and Helena talk in hushed tones behind us, their voices too low for anyone to hear. My heart twinges but I push my fears aside, I trust him. I have to trust him.

"This is the living room." Father lets me go and heads towards the back of the room, I keep up with ease as we head through an archway. We enter a large kitchen, vines hang from the ceiling, holding pots and pans above a black marble island. "Kitchen."

"Where are the bedrooms?" I ask, running my hand along the smooth counter as I walk past. It's definitely a home for royalty or for people of importance.

"This way." Father walks to the end of the room, the archway is made of twining brown vines, exposing another hallway. I slip in behind him as we head deeper into the house.

He rounds the corner and we come to a more secluded hall-way. We reach the end and he opens a cream door, letting me walk in first. I walk in and look around. The white plush bed sits against the back wall, a tapestry of a copper fox sits still above the bed and covers the entire wall. It's stunning, it's golden eyes seem to focus on me as I stand awestruck by it. I dump my bags against the end of the bed, looking over to the grey loveseat that is pressed against the right wall, beside light oak drawers.

"The bathroom is in there," Father walks in and opens another door, I look in to see a white marble bathroom.

"Thank you," I say, walking back to the bed.

"Ama...we will need to talk. I know it may seem that I've been lenient from the moment you decided to run away, but I expected better from you." His voice is tinged with disappointment.

"I know. I just...I couldn't do it anymore. I couldn't keep being left behind. This place is my home just as much as it is yours." I grab my bag and pull out a clean dress, the white material is thin and light. I look over my shoulder to where my father stands, arms crossed over his chest as he watches me. His violet eyes hide little, causing me to shrink under his gaze.

"When we picked up the trace of fallen magic...I was afraid whoever wields it had gotten you as well."

"Eleazar mentioned that." I hate lying to him, of all people my father deserved the truth. I could tell him, divulge all my secrets to him and hope he can protect me when they finally bubble over and explode from me.

"Once you shower, meet us back in the living room. I'll be cooking something up." He walks past, shutting the door behind him as he leaves. I don't hesitate to pull my boots off. I walk into the marble bathroom and turn the golden handle for the shower. I pull my shirt and pants off before looking in the mirror.

I lean in and watch as the colour in my eyes dance and swirl, it's magical.

Hot water sprays to my right, steam slowly begins to fill the room. I hop under the spray and pull the green leaf shower curtain against the other wall. I grab the bar of purple soap, scrubbing every inch of skin.

I sit at the bottom of the shower and let the water spray the back of my neck as I watch the water trickle down the golden drain in front of me.

With Helena here...I don't think Eleazar is going to have that conversation with my father about whatever has unfolded between us. The moment I laid my eyes on her, I could see exactly why he had fallen for her. She is his equal from what I could see and sense. She's hardened, a warrior who only seemed to soften for him.

What could he possibly see in me? Or have the last few weeks only been entertainment to him? I can't think like that, but the doubt is trickling in. He assured me I had nothing to worry about and I've never questioned him before.

Not to mention, I can feel the fallen magic swimming actively inside of me. I'd have to keep my guard constantly up if I'm going to survive my stay here. One misstep and I don't think *someone* would hesitate to drive one of those shiny blades through my heart.

I look down at my pale hands. I call the darkness to me, wanting to experiment with how much control I have over it. Slowly the tips of my fingers begin to darken, spreading the inky darkness down through my hands and swirling at my wrists. I turn my hands over and marvel at them. The power....the power I have shouldn't be possible. I shove the darkness back, watching as my hands return to their pale colour.

I get out of the shower after that, drying quickly and slipping the dress over my head. I adjust the thin straps before tying a large bow at my back with the silk belt. It's a simple dress, the front covered in lace as it clinches at the middle of my waist and cascades down to two layers of thin white material. It's as if I wear nothing.

My hair hangs wet around me as I head back down the hallway, I tuck my hands in the pocket of the dress and round the corner. I head through the vine archway and quickly skirt around the island in the kitchen, walking into the living room to find Hemlock, Odin and my father sitting down at the coffee table, all playing cards. Eleazar and Helena are nowhere to be found.

"How are you feeling?" Hemlock asks, drawing my anxious eyes down to his.

"Clean." I smile. He laughs, picking a card up from the deck.

"Are you hungry?" father asks, looking up from his cards.

"Not yet, I might go out and pat the rabbits." I walk past them, keeping my steps light. I head out the open front door to find the five dappled brown and white rabbits still picking at the grass. I go to the closest one. I rip a clump of grass from the ground and offer it to the rabbit. Its yellow eyes swivel towards me as its nose twitches.

Its soft mouth plucks the grass from my hand, chewing.

I stand closer, rubbing a hand through its soft fur. I reach up behind its large ear and scratch gently, one of its back legs thumps at the ground as it turns its head into my hand. I smile, thinking of Ash. He'd love it here, love meeting these large rabbits.

I stroke my hand down its back as it continues to pick at the grass. I pull tufts of soft fur from my hand as I continue to comb my fingers through.

"I thought I'd find you out here," a warm, male voice says

from behind me. I continue stroking the rabbit, not bothering to look behind my shoulder. Eleazar will be standing there, watching me.

"Not much else to do," I say, sliding behind the rabbit to stand on its other side. Its large head turns and sniffs me before it chews at the ground again. I catch a glimpse of copper hair over the rabbit as Eleazar approaches.

"How was your shower?"

"Wouldn't have been better than yours," I mutter. I kick myself for the lack of trust, but where was she? Was she with him? Did she follow him into his room?

My stomach twists and my body flushes. I need to stop my thoughts from running away from me before it comes back to bite me on the behind.

"What is that supposed to mean?" Eleazar asks, stalking around the rabbit. I back up a few steps as he approaches me, staring at me with that same guarded expression up. I see nothing under the cracks of the man I'd softened for in our travels.

"Take it how you will." I stare up at him defiantly, still stroking one hand down the rabbit's side.

"I can promise you," he stops in front of me, leaning in until his cheek brushes past mine. My breath stutters at the closeness, his hot breath tickles my ear "*my shower* would have been much better if you had joined me."

"Wouldn't want the others to get the wrong idea," I say back, breathless. Somehow still able to find a bite to my words although I'm flushed head to toe from his suggestion.

"And what idea is that Amaryllis?" My name is a blessing coming from his lips. He still leans close, his breath tickling my cheek as I'm frozen in place.

"The idea that you have softened towards me." I step back

slightly and tilt my head and meet his eyes. He's silent for a moment as he studies me.

Would it be best I push him away now, cut the head of the snake off before it can bite me?

"Do you care if they know?"

"Of course not." I step backwards, putting of air between us, "but I fear you do."

He straightens, tilting his head as he looks down at me. "My fears are larger than what my fellow brothers will think of the woman I've chosen to court."

"Trust me, mine are as well." I huff and look away from him, unable to meet the intensity in his gaze. Warm fingers grip my chin, bringing my face back towards his. He steps close, my chest brushes his.

"What are you hiding from me?" he asks softly, stroking his thumb over my bottom lip. My tongue darts out as I swallow. I search his eyes, wanting desperately to tell him. But he is the wolf and I am a lamb.

"Nothing of concern." I cover his hand with my own, kissing the pad of his thumb.

"But there is something?" He tilts his head down, nose brushing my own. I close my eyes and lean into him, breathing his scent in.

"Let's strike a bargain," I whisper, "I will tell you what is haunting me if we cure the bulburoos. The moment the bulburoos is cured, I will take you aside and tell you of the ghost."

"Deal. Not one minute after, the moment the bulburoos is cured you will tell me."

I open my eyes, meeting his. "Deal."

He studies me for one more moment before bringing his lips to mine, I melt into him like warm butter left in the sun. His hand cups my cheek as his lips claim my own. I get drunk off him, everything else dissolves in this moment. There's only him and I. I break from the kiss first, a question nags at me.

"Have you spoken to my father?" I ask.

"Not yet. I was going to pull him aside after we'd eaten something...I'm not sure how he's going to take it." He sighs, stroking my cheek.

"There's only one way to find out, you being out here with me for this long is probably going to be an indication." I smirk before I nip at his fingers, he smiles down at me. So soft and full of warmth, trust. Will he still look at me once I tell him of my magic?

"It's best I tell him now, otherwise how else will I be able to keep you by my side from prying hands at the feast tonight?" he muses.

"If you're lucky I might stay by your side willingly." I dance out of his arms, the skirts of my dress fanning around my legs. I grin at him. He smiles like a predator as he stalks towards me. I laugh as I twirl out of his reach.

His hands wrap around my waist as he spins me around, we're both laughing. He lowers me flush against him.

"I hope the gods are on my side. I'd rather not scowl from a distance," he says, kissing my forehead.

"If it makes you feel better, you still look as handsome as ever, even with a scowl painting those pretty lips of yours," I whisper, leaning up to a steal a kiss from him. "Come on, we best head inside. I'm sure father wants to know my idea of what might be wrong with the bulburoos."

"The others will be intrigued as well," Eleazar agrees. I slip from his arms and begin to walk towards the front door, he walks close behind me. I feel his eyes trace my back and head lower. My cheeks are flushed, my lips wet. We walk into the living room to see the three men still playing cards, Helena sits perched on the couch arm, glass of wine in her hand. Her eyes narrow as Eleazar stops just behind me, his shoulder touching mine.

"How do you find the rabbits?" Hemlock asks, flickering his eyes up to me before looking back to the six cards in his deck.

"They're gorgeous," I say simply, my eyes stay focused on Hemlock. I don't want to meet Helena's stare.

"Am has an idea of what might be going on with the bulburoos." *Am.* The little nickname he's given me makes my hear stutter. Eleazar draws everyone's attention towards us. My cheeks heat under their stares. Odin's eyes flicker between Eleazar and I, noticing how close we stand.

"Why would you tell her?" Helena asks, narrowing her eyes on me.

"She has a point," my father sighs, "I didn't want Amaryllis knowing the business we're doing here."

"You don't have to talk about me like I'm not standing right here." I look to my father, defiance in my eyes. He looks up at me with the same fire burning. It's good to see the apple didn't fall far from the tree.

"I told her because she asked to know. She insisted she was coming with us and as you sent me to protect her, I promised I would do just that once we were here. Would you rather have her with us or in this house on her own?" Eleazar asks, crossing his arms over his chest.

"So instead of focusing on the mission you'll be torn between wanting to do your duty and protect the child?" Helena asks. I bristle.

"I can do both," he grits out. She scowls at him.

"Going to the bulburoos is dangerous. It's not for those who can't fight," Father says, staring at me. I feel myself anger at his words. If it wasn't for him, I would have learnt how to fight.

"She is more than capable," Eleazar says. My heart warms at his words, his willingness to protect me.

"My attention will be divided if she is with us. I'll be torn between focusing on the task at hand and checking on her every other second to make sure nothing is happening to her." Father places his cards down, the glint in his eyes means we're nearing his level of patience.

"I said I would protect her and I will. I have never let you down before and I'm not about to start, Eleazar states, chest rumbling. I do my best not to shrink under Helena's piercing eyes.

"I think we should hear her out," Odin interrupts, taking us all by surprise.

"I do as well. Ama, what do you think?" Hemlock urges, ignoring my father. Odin watches me as well, curious. Eleazar brushes his shoulder against my own, reassuring me.

"From what Eleazar has told me, with how the creature is acting I've come to believe that maybe Salis has tainted the sacred magic that runs through its veins. To me it seems like something is eating the creature from the inside out and from the legends, that is what fallen magic does." My voice wavers as my father's eyes narrow on me. He had no idea I knew so much about the magic we have or how it works, even the forbidden magic.

"How do you know about fallen magic?" Father stands, staring down at me.

"I am not the only one that carries secrets, *Father*." I hold my chin high even though I want to cower under the look he's giving me. I've never openly defied him before.

"Say you're right," he strides towards me. Eleazar steps closer to me, as if to jump in and guard me if it comes to that. Father notices the small movement as well. He stops, eyes a violet thunderstorm as he looks at Eleazar.

"Say I'm right. The way to cure the creature is to somehow kill or take the fallen magic and leave the sacred magic alone," I say desperately, not liking the stare off between the two of them. I step in between them, my back almost flush with Eleazar's chest.

"She...she has a point." Odin's words are a dull blade between the thick tension that hangs heavy in the air. Father looks down to where Odin sits. A muscle in his jaw twitches.

"Carry on."

"If Salis has poisoned the creature all we need to do is kill the fallen magic that's festering in its soul. It won't be easy, but if it works accordingly then the creature might be cured." Odin looks to me, his brown eyes gentle, "that is if the problem is fallen magic. If not, our best course of action is ending the creature."

"How would you do that?" I demand.

"The only way now is with magic, it's festered for too long," Helena says, her voice sharp.

"The only way to kill a magical creature with magic is to experience the death, offering your essence and tipping your internal scales." I say, shocked. I look to my father. "Who would do that? Who the hell here is going to be that sacrifice and hope they can rebalance the scales? From what I'm assuming this creature is powerful, even now I can see the storm thickening in the sky."

My father's eyes trail to Eleazar. I turn and look up at him, shocked and full of disbelief. He can't be the one doing this. He looks down at me, jaw set. His golden eyes offer an apology, one he can't voice.

"You..." I whisper, trailing off.

"It was decided before we left your castle," he murmurs. He runs his tongue along his teeth.

"But..." I turn and look at my father, desperate for some

sort of solution. I come up empty from the look on his face. I turn back to Eleazar, "What if you can't rebalance the scales? What if you don't come back?" My voice is full of fear.

"I'll be fine," he says, looking over my head to my father. My heart constricts painfully in my chest. If my fallen magic doesn't rip us apart, it might just be this. I turn to my father.

"That bulburoos is far too strong."

"Eleazar is aware of the consequences," he says slowly, shoulders slightly deflating. Odin watches me with soft eyes. Hemlock looks away with a sigh. Helena sits rigid on the couch, her hands trembling.

"You can't," I whisper. My hand rests against the base of my throat as I see the finality in my father's eyes.

"I can and we will. This is not up for discussion, Amaryllis. Some sacrifices must be made, no matter how much we wish not to make them." His words cement in the air around us.

I open my mouth to argue, to demand they find another way. Eleazar's warm hand clasps my elbow gently, I look over my shoulder at him. He shakes his head, eyes hard as he looks to my father. I clamp my lips shut, tears stinging my eyes. I don't want to cry in front of everyone.

"We need to talk," father says, pinning those violet eyes on Eleazar.

Eleazar watches me for one more moment, so many emotions swirl in his eyes before his wall goes up. His guard is back in place, shielding him. He lets me go and steps back, "That we do."

I look between them before fleeing from the room. I rush out the front door and run to the forest behind the house. I need a moment to clear my head, to clear my heart. If the balance in Eleazar remains tipped, he won't be coming back.

Fallen magic is going to be the last of my worries when Eleazar's life may be ripped from him.

CHAPTER 18

I look up from the large boulder I'm perched on, my hand stills with the small branch clasped in my grip. I'd been scratching my initials onto the boulder, passing anxious time. I hadn't gone far into the forest, knowing I'd get lost if I did. The shrubs in front of me sway and snap, the darkness rises in defence as my heart anxiously waits to see what will emerge from the other side. To my relief Hemlock appears, his blonde hair has snagged a small stick and a few green leaves. He shakes himself before looking up at me, smiling brightly.

"They said I'd find you out here somewhere." He comes closer to the boulder, leaning his back against the space beside where my legs dangle.

"If I went further I would have gotten lost," I shrug, going back to scratching at the boulder with my stick.

"Your idea about the bulburoos is brilliant, even Odin agrees with me. It's just hard for your father to grasp at the moment, especially with the vision your mother sent him," Hemlock says, tipping his head to look at me. I frown.

"What was the vision?"

"She sent a slip of paper with it scrawled out, it terrified him. Having you here and knowing about fallen magic has put him on alert."

"Can you tell me the vision?" I insist.

"I only briefly skimmed my eyes over it when he passed the message around hoping to get our opinion on it." He looks forward again. "It mentioned darkness, with an army of ghosts rising from the earth, blue electricity striking the ground and it mentioned someone wouldn't be walking away from this. It wasn't specified but your mother wrote down a colour that's an indication."

"What was the colour?" I whisper, dread curling my stomach. The army of ghosts would have to be the souls Salis has stolen but if father has already pieced that together no wonder he's on alert. Mother's vision might be more accurate than ever, but who would be the one controlling the ghosts? Salis?

"Red. A deep maroon red." Hemlock looks back up to me, "I know your mother's vision are more than accurate and I can see why your father wants you to stay here. If anything was to happen to you I don't think he'd ever forgive himself."

"I can't just let Eleazar offer up his sanity on a silver platter." I look down at my hands, sighing.

"He offered you know, that morning before we'd left and discussed the plan of action. It was the morning after he'd accompanied you into the village for the day, before he and Odin found you in the library." Hemlock straightens, turning and watching me.

"And?" I whisper.

"As a warrior at heart, his only wish of death would be to go out honourable. He's strong and his essence of magic is full, he's been reserving everything he can to make sure he can bring himself back to us."

That was why he hadn't killed the wendigo with magic, because deep down he knew he'd be the one taking the chance. How long had he known he was doomed? Has the bond between us been a desperate bid at love before he completely turns?

"It's not fair." I slide from the boulder, landing softly. I run my hands down the skirts of my dress as I look at Hemlock. He smiles sadly before offering me his elbow for the journey back to the manor. I take it, leaning my head on his shoulder as we begin to walk.

"I know it's not fair, hardly anything in this life is fair. I have to believe he is strong enough to balance his internal scales once the creature is killed, if it can't be cured. That's another problem, if the bulburoos is infested with fallen magic..." he trails off.

"Only someone with fallen magic can eradicate it," I finish for him.

"Exactly and that's were our shortcomings begin."

I stay quiet for the rest of the short walk, mulling over everything he'd said. If I reveal that I have fallen magic once we get to the infected bulburoos, maybe they'll let me live long enough to retract the magic from the creature before cutting me down. If I can save Eleazar from taking the risk, I will do it. Even if it costs me my life.

We pause just short of the manor, the sky has darkened; bright silver and gold stars flicker across the expanse. From here I can see a plume of smoke rising from inside the court-yard walls, hear the soft beat of drums that lure magical crea-tures in. That's where we'd all be heading soon.

"Tonight will be new for you, don't get distracted by the parlour tricks the other fae will play on you. If you get lost just look for one of us, enjoy the wine that'll be served and please stay away from the queen." He smirks as he releases my arm, "I heard about the small encounter this morning."

"I'd do it again," I murmur, turning back towards the

manor. Hemlock chuckles, following me as we walk up the steps.

"I can only hope I'm there the second time."

I roll my eyes at him as we enter the house, a hearty thick scent fills the air. My mouth waters as my feet lead me into the kitchen with Hemlock close behind. We walk in to find father and Odin both standing over a pot on the stove, steam wafts from the contents. Helena and Eleazar aren't in the room.

"That smells absolutely delicious." Hemlock practically drools where he stands, leaning against the kitchen island.

"Deer and vegetable soup, nothing fancy," Odin says, throwing in a small handful of dried green leaves.

"It's almost done," father says, smiling over his shoulder at us. His eyes soften when he sees me, I raise an eyebrow. Still annoyed.

"Why are we eating if there's a feast tonight?" I ask, tapping my nails against the marble counter top.

"We're not eating this for dinner. This is for the journey to the mountains." Odin offers me a rare ghost of a smile over his shoulder before turning his attention back to the pot. Hemlock sulks, crossing his arms over his chest.

"This isn't fair. You should at least let me indulge on one bowl to assure the quality is good enough for everyone," he argues.

I sigh, turning away from them. "I'm going to change," I call over my shoulder.

I walk through the archway and head down the hall and take the curve that leads me to my room at the end. There's another three doors closed along the wall to my right. I keep my steps feather soft as I lean my ear to the closest door. Silence greets me. I move slowly to the next, anxious I'm going to get caught eavesdropping.

Anxious I might hear something that will break my heart.

The second door is in silence so I head to the third door, only a handful of steps away from the room I've been given. I lean my ear against the door and hold my breath. Silence...until I hear a very familiar grunt.

Eleazar is in this room.

I'm frozen in place as my heart is doused in ice water. "Eleazar...why are you doing this?" Helena's hushed voice says.

"It's more complicated than what you may be thinking," he says back.

"How is it complicated? Once you returned I assumed we'd be picking up where we left off." She sniffs, there's a rustle of clothes.

"Helena..." his voice is pained, sorrowful, "I need time. I've spent the last week with her by my side, I swore I would protect her."

"Why would you need time? What could you hope to get from her?" Helena's voice sharpens.

"You wouldn't understand."

"Do you like her?" she asks.

He's silent.

"I'll take your silence as a no," she says. A bed groans. "I know there's still something between us."

His silence kills me.

"You know I love you, but you shouldn't be in here. You need to leave," he finally relents.

"You haven't kicked me out yet," she says softly.

I straighten and hurry to my room, my eyes sting with tears as I slam the door behind me. I flip the lock, leaning against the wood as I slide to the floor. Of course he doesn't like me. I'd been a fool to think otherwise. *Of course I'd be thrown to the side once we returned.* What was I hoping for? That we'd get here and everything would stay the same?

He'd told me to trust him and I had.

Look where that has gotten me.

I cry into my arms, bringing my knees up to my chest as it cracks open. It hurts, god it hurts. I now understand why mother warned me. I now know why she'd told me to be careful of him, I should have listened to her. I should have listened to my brain over my stupid, love sick heart.

I wipe my eyes, the tears soaking into my dress.

I love him and the realisation threatens to make me drown myself in tears again. He's my first love...my first everything. I press the heel of my palms into my hands and take deep, stuttering breaths. It wasn't going to last regardless if he didn't feel the same towards me, he is the wolf. I am the lamb that's almost ready to be slaughtered.

"Ah, it's such a pity when your heart is broken." That terrifying male voice that plagues my nightmares fills my ears. I look up to find Salis standing in the middle of my room, running a night sky hand over the white quilt, his black eyes flick to me. Darkness encases him, sucking the light from the room.

"What are you doing here?" I say weakly. I should be alarmed the God of Death is in my room but I can't find the will to care. He smiles, all sharp teeth.

"I could hear your heart breaking from the Underworld. I was coming to inspect the collateral damage." He's in front of me in the blink of an eye, grabbing my chin in his hand. The gold markings on his arm glow at the touch, my own darkness rises and begins to stain my hands and arms.

"My pretty little broken prodigy," he clicks his tongue, his white hair fans his face as his eyes dissect me. I don't have the will power to pull away or demand he leave, in this moment I am utterly raw and terrified.

"What do you want?" I manage to whisper.

"A taste again." He leans in, eyes hungry and depthless as

they flicker to my lips. I struggle against his hand, his fingers tighten firmly and keep me in place. "One kiss, one taste."

"What do I get out of it?"

"What do you want?" he muses, a smile stretching his lips.

"I don't want to see you again until one of two options, your magic overtakes me and claims me or someone kills me," I say through my muddled thoughts, faintly remembering the euphoria I'd felt when he'd tasted a hint of my soul. He thinks about this, watching me with calculating eyes.

"I can agree to that," he purrs. He lets go of my face as he takes my hands, pulling me up. His dark hands brush the last tears from my cheeks as he stares down at me, my back is flush with my door. He steps closer, leaning one hand against the wood beside my head.

"Be fast about it."

His lips close the distance without hesitation, immediately I'm filled with that warm feeling and find myself kissing him back. I slide my hands around his head as I press my body against the hard planes of his, he's a drug and I'm an addict.

He lets out an otherworldly groan as one arm slips around my waist, his other hand burying into my hair. I feel his lips part. I slacken against him as he pulls his lips back, my eyes flutter closed as that familiar blue smoke passes from my lips to his own.

My thoughts cloud over as my body begins to numb. If this is dying...it's not as scary as I first thought. It's painless, almost intoxicating.

A hard bang comes from the door behind us, my eyes struggle to open. Salis stares down at me, greed and hunger in his eyes. He breaths blue smoke back into my mouth, I begin to feel my body again as my mind clears. He snaps his lips closed, stepping away from me. His black eyes glow a subtle blue as he watches me with a malicious smile.

"Until we meet again, Amaryllis." He disappears as quickly as he'd appeared. I stumble forward, wiping my mouth furiously as the knock comes from my door again. I sit on the bed, trying to gather my bearings.

"One second," I croak, my voice feels like sandpaper in my throat.

"Amaryllis, we need to talk," Eleazar says, tapping at the wood again. The earlier heartbreak threatens to consume me once more at the sound of his voice. I rise from the bed once I feel more on balance and unlock the door. I walk into the bathroom as the door opens and he walks into the room.

"What do you wish to talk about?" I ask over my shoulder. I cough into my sleeve. I splash my face with cold water before taking a few gulps, I grip the edge of the sink and stare up at myself. My cheeks are tinged pink, my eyes glassy and bloodshot. The only indication Salis had been here, tasting my soul. If it means not seeing him again until my time is up, I can live with that.

He'll be taking my soul anyway.

"Can you come sit down?" his voice is soft. I move stiffly towards the bed, avoiding his eyes as I take a seat. He sits beside me, taking a limp hand between both of his large warm ones.

"I spoke with your father." I continue to stare down at my hand that's encased in his.

"If you're here to break my heart, don't bother," I murmur, his conversation with Helena replaying in my mind. His silence, reluctance. I'd been foolish.

"What makes you assume what I have to say will break your heart?" I laugh bitterly, the sound broken.

"If having Helena in your room is any indication, I can only imagine how this conversation will end." I tear my hand from both of his and stand, unable to be near him. I walk to the wall in front of the bed and stand facing him. I finally look at him, his golden eyes hold me in place and make my heart scream.

"I can explain." He stands, arms hanging by his side.

My eyes well with tears again. I have to cut the head off the snake before someone gets bitten. I am the snake, I need to use my fangs.

"I don't want an explanation. I should have known how this was going to end the moment we stepped into Faerie. I was naïve and foolish for believing your care for me ran deeper than an order from my father." I cross my arms over my chest, grasping at my dress so he can't see my hands shaking.

"It does run deeper than an order, if you'd just listen—"

"How do you think it looks to me, having her in your room? Disappearing with her at any moment I'm otherwise occupied? You told me to trust you and I *did*. I trusted you and then I hear —" I choke as tears begin to fall, "I hear her in your room. I hear your silence. I hear you tell her you love her."

"Am—" his eyes are a wild fire of emotions. I refuse to burn in the blaze this time.

"If you love her why would you make me fall *in love* with *you*?" I cry, covering my eyes with my hands. The darkness is threatening to consume me, it wants to *take and take and take*.

"It's not like that." The desperation in his voice hurts me even more.

"It is! You love her and I can't fault you for it. I was warned about her and you, the bond you'd shared. I gave you my heart willingly in the stupid hope you might actually give me yours in return." I choke on a broken laugh, wiping at my eyes as I stare at him through the watery haze.

"I've known her most of my life Am, of course a part of me loves her."

"You need to get the fuck out of my room!" I shout, pointing towards the door. The darkness is a starved dog, biting at my heels as I stand there. If he doesn't leave I'm going to break, I'm going to shatter like a vase and the darkness will be unleashed. Upon him. He needs to leave. Now.

"I'm not leaving you!" his voice rises as he takes a step towards me.

"You weren't here with me to begin with, so go! Walk away! It's nothing I'm not accustomed to." I desperately grasp at the cage I've kept the darkness in. It hurts, god it hurts. I'm spiralling, my broken heart and weakened soul aren't strong enough to keep the darkness at bay for much longer.

I understand why they say fallen magic is uncontrollable and chaotic.

"I'm not walking away from you! I will *never* walk away from you!" He closes the distance between us and wraps his arms around me. I squeeze my eyes shut as my breathing comes in gasps, the darkness grins. Eleazar is a beacon of flame I try to claw towards, desperately wanting to push the darkness back.

"You need—" my voice is rasping, changing, "to leave. Now."

"Amaryllis, I will not leave you. I can explain everything." He whispers into my hair, burying his face into my shoulder. I'm a string pulled tight, about to snap in half.

"I—I can't explain. I'm sorry—" my breathing stutters as I peel my eyes open. My fisted hands on his chest are black, the darkness begins to swirl down my wrist and towards my elbow. Panic so hard and sharp slices through me, the need to protect him overcomes the pain of my broken heart.

I push away from him, hiding my arms desperately behind my back.

"Am," He reaches for me, begging me. My bottom lip trembles. "Please."

A broken plea.

"Go." The only word I can form.

"I won't give up on you this easily. I will give you tonight to think, but you will hear me out. I want this Am. I want you and everything you have to offer me." He stays there for a moment, eyes desperately flickering over my face. "you aren't the only one who has fallen." He walks to the door, hand pausing on the knob. My eyes follow his each step.

"Tomorrow we will talk. If you decide this isn't what you want after you've heard me out I will respect your decision...I will understand." His jaw tightens as he leaves my room, shutting the door softly behind him.

I let out an agonised groan as I bring my hands in front of me. Both of my arms are completely black. I stumble into the bathroom, I rip the dress from my body as I twist the handle to hot water. Steam fills the bathroom in seconds. I don't hesitate as I step under the boiling spray.

I muffle my screams with my hands, my mind turns white as I curl into a ball at the bottom of the shower.

I'm losing control, and there's only so much my heart can take before I break completely.

CHAPTER 19

I stare off into the distance from where I lean against the cobblestone courtyard wall, I swirl the glass of sparkling galaxy wine around vaguely. I feel as if I'm underwater, the music and chatter of all the creatures are dull and distant. I'd dressed quickly after a scolding shower, only getting out once the darkness had completely receded. I'd lagged behind everyone on the walk here, lost in my thoughts. Still lost in my thoughts.

My emotions are chaotic and my heart is breaking. I can't control my magic in this state but I can't control when my heart breaks. I puff out a breath and take a sip of the wine, blinking into the present. I look around slowly from my darkened spot. Faeries are the most common species I see, aside from goblins and small pixies flittering about.

A large black cauldron sits in the middle of the courtyard, refilling to the brim magically as a soft mist wafts over its thickened edges and dispels once it hits the ground. Almost everyone here is drunk, even the queen has softened slightly. She sits atop her throne and two golden faeries guard her as they keep an eye on the restless crowd.

My father talks with Hemlock and Odin, occasionally casting his eyes to where I stand. He'd tried to talk to me once

I'd left the room back at the manor, but I'd kindly refused and said I'd tell him my problems later on.

Helena sits on a large unfolded green leaf with Kay, the two girls talk in hushed tones as they sip from their glasses. I'd lost sight of Eleazar once I'd arrived. I tell myself I only look for him to make sure he's okay.

I can't bring myself to think about the situation between us. Would it be better in the long run if I tell him I don't want him now, so that when my time comes to step up and show them my fallen magic he won't feel blindsided?

Would it be easier to keep him close in hopes he'll understand why I hadn't told him sooner? Can I show him I'm not evil?

I stare down into my glass.

"You sure know how to make a mess of things," I murmur to myself, watching as the purple liquid swirls on its own in my glass. Everything had been going so well and now it is an absolute disaster.

"You've resorted to talking to yourself now?" A deep, male voice breaks me from my trance. I glance up to see Eleazar approaching me, a full cup in hand. My heart stutters in my chest as my stomach coils with anxiety.

"I find I prefer my own company," I mutter. He stands in front of me, slightly closer than necessary. His long copper hair hangs around him, curling slightly at the ends. He wears a loose white shirt, the V of the neck drops deliciously low.

I curse myself for finding him so ravishing. His golden eyes find mine again.

"I can assure you there are others out there that value your company as well," he takes a sip of his drink, eyes looking down his narrow nose at me.

"Can't forget Ash now, can I?" I look away from him and sip from my glass, the liquid tastes of blackberries and is extremely sweet. It wouldn't take me much to get drunk off of it, and that is dangerous for my loose mouth.

"I can name a few others." He straightens, "how are you enjoying the night?"

"I can't complain." I sigh and look back to him, "why are you here talking to me?"

A muscle in his jaw feathers, "Because I want to talk to you. I know I told you I'd give you tonight to think about what you want, but I kept finding my eyes trailing to you."

"So you thought you'd just come over and assume I want your company?"

"Do you?"

I'm silent, staring at him in defiance. He stares down at me with the same fire.

"I'm impatient for you to hear me out." His nostrils flare as he takes a step towards me, I plant my feet. My hands shakes, the liquid threatens to spill out of my cup as I tip my head back to look up at him.

"What's there to hear? You love Helena. I've heard enough," I snap. My bottom lip trembles as my heart aches in my chest. I refuse to cry here in front of everyone, I refuse to give him those tears again.

"Am, I've known her long before you were even thought of. She is one of my best friends and a warrior I can rely on when I need someone to back me up. I trust her and she's never done anything to show me otherwise. I care about her, just as much as I care about Hemlock and Odin. We're a family," he says softly, eyes flickering over my face.

"It's better if we end this here," I whisper. My heart explodes in my chest, this is not what it wants but I need to protect him. From me. This is for the better.

"Give me a good enough reason to walk away from you," he growls, reaching out to cup my cheek with his free scarred hand. I avoid leaning into his warm touch, wanting nothing more than to embrace him.

"I will be your undoing."

"You've already undone me Amaryllis. That night we shared in the river...I meant every word I said to you."

This is hard, far too hard.

"I'm trying to make this easy for you," I search his eyes, "we aren't going to end well. We're chaotic and we burn in each other's flames."

"We're passionate. You want me as much as I want you Am, just admit it to yourself. I can't walk away from you, not after everything we've gone through. Not after you've let me in and I've let you in." He presses his forehead to mine, I reach my free hand up and press it gently against his chest. God he feels like home. A warm shower after a cold day. The first rays of sunlight caressing the earth at dawn.

"Why can't you just trust me when I tell you it won't end well?" I beg, fisting my hand in his shirt, "you are the wolf and I am the lamb."

"You promised to tell me what you're keeping hidden once this was all over. I need to know if it's going to put you in harm's way."

"Eleazar there is so much you don't know."

"Well tell me!" He raises his head, looking down at me. His frustration is evident on his features and...his hurt. I am hurting him. I shrivel in on myself. I don't want to hurt him, that isn't what I was trying to do with this. I'm trying to protect him.

"You'll hate me." Tears glisten in my eyes as I stare at him through the watery haze. His eyes soften, his thumb brushes my cheek.

"I could never hate you Amaryllis. Far from it."

"Why are you so persistent? Why are you still hanging

around?" I'm defeated as I stand in front of him, my heart is in tatters and my sanity and control over my magic isn't much better.

"Because I care about you, more than anything. I'm sorry I've hurt you and that you had to hear what I'd said to Helena but I hope you understand the friendship I have with her is completely platonic. But you Ama..." he trails off, brushing a stray tear away as it rolls down my cheek, "You make me burn. You ignite me and you don't flinch from my flames. I don't scare you like I do with the others."

I sniffle, "What do you want from me?"

"I want you and whatever you will give to me. I told you to trust me and you still can, I'd never betray that trust or do anything to harm you. I am truly sorry for how I've been behaving once we arrived. I was hesitant for the conversation with your father." He sighs, a phantom kiss dots my forehead.

"What did he say?" I relent, wanting to know if father approved of this. Whatever this is turning out to be.

"He was hesitant to approve of it, you're his daughter and I'm his best friend and warrior. You and I both live very different lives and he's extremely protective of you. Once I explained how I feel and how deep it runs he relented. He's cautious but he's given me his blessing to court you."

My father had approved of Eleazar pining after me. I glance away from Eleazar to find my father with his violet eyes on us, he nods slightly as a ghost of a smile brushes his lips. I look back to Eleazar. He looks down at me with his eyes blazing, full of hope.

I've never doubted that I wanted this, from the moment I met him I had the distinct feeling our fates would be intertwined.

"Will you allow me to prove myself to you Amaryllis? Will you allow me to show you that I will protect you and earn your trust back?" he whispers, capturing me. Everyone around us fades to dullness, in this moment there is only him and me.

"We still have other problems to talk about." I say weakly, "You're not offering yourself up for this magical creature. I don't care what you say, there has to be another way."

"The only way to retract fallen magic is for someone with that magic to do it," he says softly, sadly.

Do I tell him now? Do I wait? I can't risk telling him now, if someone else figures it out I'll be a dead woman before I can try to heal this creature.

"Maybe...maybe I can help once we get there. I might be able to find another solution." I uncurl my fist in his shirt and gently stroke his chest. He shivers into my touch, his breath fans my face; all I can smell is the sweet acidic scent of wine.

"If anyone is able to solve this problem, it's going to be you." He reaches up, his fingers trace my nose and continue down to my cheek. His feather light touch caresses my jaw before he cups the back of my neck.

The look in his eyes...it's hungry.

"We should enjoy the rest of the night. We have a big journey to trek tomorrow." I sigh as I lean back into his hand. His thumb idly strokes the hair at the base of my neck as he continues to stare down at me. My heart races in my chest being this close to him, this vulnerable.

"Stay with me?"

A whisper. A silent plea.

I nod once, giving him a strained smile. He relaxes, planting a kiss on my forehead before straightening. He lets me go and I immediately miss his warmth, his touch. Everything around us comes back into full swing, more faeries dance around the cauldron; their lips stained purple from the wine as they sing and chant.

"Care to dance?" Eleazar asks before finishing off his wine. I shake my head, staring out at the crowd.

"I'm afraid I have two left feet." I look up at him. "Sorry. I'd just make a fool out of us both."

"Come on," he places his glass on the ground before taking my free hand. He tugs me towards the thickening crowd of dancers. I throw back the last of my wine before sitting the glass on the ground. He grins as he walks backwards into the dances.

My smile is genuine as he pulls me to him, his large hands rest on my lower back and hold me flush to him. I rest my hands at the base of his neck, running my fingers through his hair. We sway like a leaf in a soft breeze, the others dance around us.

"Tell me a secret," I whisper. He arches an eyebrow as he looks down at me.

"A secret?"

"Yes, a secret. Something no one else knows." The music is a frantic heart beat around us, but right here in this moment I only have Eleazar. His lips twist a few times before he relents, he squeezes me briefly.

"I will give you a secret if you give me one." His eyes flare as the music and life around us falls to silence. I gasp in shock at the sudden change and look around, everyone still dances and the music still throbs. We're in a bubble of silence. "I don't want anyone else to know your secrets, or my own." He draws my eyes back to him.

"Okay, fine. A secret for a secret. Can be big or small, but has to be a secret," I say. I desperately want to know how he came to have the scars on his hands, but that's something he will tell me when he's comfortable. I can't force that from him.

"Okay...when I was ten I'd been visiting Oakwood with my mother and father, something about needing to the see the

Queen. I'd only been young so I'd left them at the base of the throne and I'd gone exploring." He begins, his thumbs rub a lazy patterns into the thin material of my dress.

"It's hard to see you as a little kid," I admit, smiling softly. He chuckles, shaking his head.

"I was mischievous, always finding trouble. That day I'd decided to explore the castle grounds and I'd found a secret passage way that led me right to the kitchens. I'd found their stash of hazelnut chocolate, the small golden balls were sitting in a large basket for the taking at the back of the pantry." He grins, eyes twinkling. I smile back. My heart warms seeing him so relaxed, even if it is for a moment.

"I'd gorged myself on them and left four at the bottom of the basket. My parents found me passed out in the corner, chocolate covered hands and my mouth was smeared with it. I'd even managed to get it in my hair, they had to carry me home that day. They figured I'd eaten two hundred and ninety six." His chest rumbles as he's momentarily lost in his memory.

"I can see it too, I'm surprised you didn't stash the last four in your pockets." His eyes focus back to me, the happiness is dimmed slightly by a deep sadness. A sadness I doubt he lets any other person see.

"I would have if I had been conscious. It was a long time ago but it's always been one of my fondest memories my parents gave me." His jaw twitches as he clenches his teeth, I frown slightly.

"It's okay, thank you for sharing it with me." I rise to the tips of my toes and bring my lips to his own. A fire sparks between us as my lips meet his, pulling him back to the present, back to me. It takes him a moment before he responds to my touch, his tongue trails over my bottom lip before I meet it with my own.

The kiss Salis had given me when he tasted my soul could never compare to fire I feel when Eleazar touches me. Nothing could compare to this.

He pulls back, resting his forehead on mine. We both breathe heavily and my knees threaten to give out on me. He makes me weak in a way I never thought possible.

"Come, I'm sure there's still chocolate." Eleazar takes my hand and I walk close beside him, intertwining our fingers together. The bubble of silence around us evaporates as we head towards a propped open wooden door that is nestled at the back of the courtyard. I feel eyes on us as we walk along, his long legs eat the ground as we grow closer.

We duck into the passage. Although he mentioned chocolate, I wouldn't mind if we finished what we started. I want to kiss him again, feel his hands all over me. It entices a shiver out of me, imagining his skin against mine. He chuckles in the dark as we head deeper into the passage.

"If you keep that up it won't be chocolate I'll be eating." He growls into the darkness, his deep gravel tone has me walking on weak legs. He pulls us to a stop, a small pop echoes in the silence before he pulls me through another small door. The air is stale as he closes the door behind us. The passageway is barely wide enough for both of us to fit comfortably.

He pulls me forward as we begin to descend, the dirt is firm beneath my feet. I cough into my shoulder from the stale air that's now mingled with dust.

"Almost there." He moves faster and I imagine his shoulders scraping against the walls around us. He lets my hand go momentarily. I stand there and wait, focusing on the rough outline of his shoulders in the darkness. He pushes the door forwards and yellow light floods into the passage as he pulls himself out. He reaches for me, helping me straighten before he closes the secret door. We stand at the back of a pantry, the white wooden shelves spill with all sorts of vegetables and herbs.

"There's so much." I whisper in awe as I look up, the shelves go to the ceiling. It's huge.

"There's a fair few mouths to feed." He takes my hand and leads us behind a row of shelves. The pantry smells of sweet bread and herbs, it makes my mouth water. Eleazar stops as we reach the end of the pantry, I peer around him and look at the six wooden half barrels that are screwed to the wall. I see golden, orange, red, purple, blue and green balls in each of them.

"Is that all chocolate?" I say. He moves forward, grabbing a handful of the golden ones. He smiles over his shoulder at me before moving to the side. He sits down on the pile of empty hessian bags, propping himself up against the wall and watches me.

I move forward and grab one of each, wanting to taste all of them. I take a seat beside him, tucking the skirts of my dress in between my legs as I look at the chocolate. I pop the red one in my mouth. It explodes with a distinct cherry flavour, I scrunch my nose up at the onslaught and do my best not to spit it out.

Eleazar laughs beside me, his shoulder bumps into mine. I narrow my eyes at him.

"The look on your face..." he shakes his head, licking his lips, "I should have warned you that they're strong."

I manage to swallow it down, wishing I had a drink to chase away the taste. "Apparently I'm not a fan of cherry."

It causes him to laugh again, the sound fills my ears and I relax. My darkness is quiet, not begging me to steal his soul. I pop the blue one into my mouth, liking the blueberry flavour that accompanies it. The green is next, distinctly apple. The purple is blackcurrant and the orange has a vague hint of citrus. I save the hazelnut one for last.

Eleazar pops another in his mouth as he watches me with childish delight.

"I saved the best for last," I say before popping it in my mouth. The hazelnut is warm and pleasant and I sigh as I chew happily. I lean my head on his shoulder, stomach content with all of the wine and chocolate I'd consumed.

"What did you think?" he asks.

"I really liked them. Hazelnut probably wins, but the purple one comes close." I stifle a yawn as I stretch my legs out besides Eleazar's.

"I thought you would. Aright, it's your turn for a secret."

I think over what I could tell him and settle for something more intimate that may show him just how deep my feelings are beginning to run for him and when they started. My cheeks heat as I find the courage to tell him.

"My secret...it was the day Odin came to help me study and you joined us," I begin, as I trail my fingers over his thigh and trace invisible patterns as I go along.

"What about it?" he asks.

"When you'd dropped my crown of water down and it almost spilt on my maps and I got angry and drew the blade on you..." I flush, "when I had the blade pressed to your throat and leaned in I had wondered in that moment if you had wanted to kiss me. I wondered what it would feel like to be kissed by you."

"Is it what you imagined?" he murmurs, I look up at him to find him already looking down at me. I grin lazily, the blush still heavy in my cheeks.

"It's even better."

He leans down and kisses me, he tastes of hazelnut and wine and I greedily feed myself off his lips. I turn feverishly as my body begins to burn, his large hands clasp my hips as he brings me around to the front. I straddle him, pressing my chest against his own as I deepen the kiss.

His hands scorch my skin as they trail from my waist and head upwards, his thumb caressing the underside of my breasts as they ache for his touch. I grind my hips into him, feeling his hard planes moving against my soft ones.

It elicits a deep groan from his chest, my hands run down his chest as I desperately claw at his shirt, wanting nothing between us. He breaks the kiss for a moment as he leans forward, pulling the shirt over his head. I almost drool at his defined tan chest, his golden eyes burn brightly as he looks up at me, bringing a hand to my cheek.

"Is this okay?" he asks, voice rough and breathless. His eyes mirror my own, full of desire and longing.

"This is perfect." I lean down to kiss him again, he stops me gently. I begin to frown.

"I won't take it any further, even though I want to. I want to claim you in every way I can...but this is enough for now." He whispers, stroking my cheek. The rejection stings and has me drawing backwards.

"Amaryllis. I want you, but I'm not going to take you in the back of a pantry like we're young lovers. For your first time...I want to make it something you will cherish for the rest of your years. I want to explore every inch of your skin and more. It's hard enough to restrain myself now...please don't think I don't want this because *gods* I do." He brings me back to him, holding me in place. His need for me is more than evident as it pushes against me, straining against the confines of his pants.

I hate to admit it but he's right, I relent and nestle closer to him.

"Fine. I'll take whatever you're willing to give me and then some, but I won't push it further," I whisper, resting my forehead on his. He grins wolfishly, his fingers tighten against my waist as he tugs me down. I shiver with need, my hips desperate to move against his own but his hands keep me in place.

"Why are you stopping me?" I dig my fingers into his shoulders as I wiggle against his hold. He tips his head back and begins to pepper kisses along my throat, down to the hollow in my collar bones. My eyes flutter shut at his gentle touch.

"I like to see you squirm for me," he whispers against my skin before letting my hips take full rein. Our lips crash together in passion as my hands roam his chest and his back, my hips are feverish against his own. Knowing we won't go further than this has me desperate for release as pleasure begins to build in every cell I possess.

We lose ourselves in each other's touch, in each kiss we share. I'm addicted to him and the feelings he entices from me, from the fire that burns brightly whenever our skin touches. We're a tangle of limbs and I want nothing more than to rip my dress off, but I respect his wishes.

He shows me every single pleasure point in my body and has me moaning into the silence of the pantry, he is the earth and I am the sun that orbits him. Each touch and kiss is a secret we now share together, this moment in the pantry will be a memory I'll cherish. A memory that will bring me light in my darkest moment.

I push the darkness away, giving myself over to Eleazar's burning bright light.

CHAPTER
20

I pack my bag as droplets of water slide down my neck. I'd showered as soon as I'd woken and thrown on the shirt Eleazar had given me, along with my tight leather pants and boots. I only pack lightly, a few changes of clothes and my small blade. My temples throb slightly from the wine I'd consumed the night before, Eleazar and I had lost track of time in the pantry and once we'd emerged almost everyone was drunk. It felt only right to fit in with them, a choice I am dearly regretting this morning.

I pull my bag on over my shoulders and leave the room, shutting the door behind me. I walk into the kitchen, heading straight for the pot of coffee. I listen for any noise, everyone else is just beginning to stir. A dull glow begins to light the room, reminding me of the day we have ahead of us. I go through the cupboards, finding the jar of honey and a mug. I drop a small amount of honey in before pouring the coffee.

I take the steaming mug and head out to the front of the house, wanting to watch the sunrise. I sit on the top step, sipping as I look over the rolling green mountains. The five large rabbits mill about, picking at the lush grass. It's incredibly peaceful this early, the green grass illuminates gold as the sun rises over the peak of the distant mountains. The fresh, cool air makes my wet hair feel icy but I pay it no mind.

Footfalls sound behind me, I look over my shoulder to see my father there; a mug of steaming coffee in his hands as well. He'd dressed like usual, a deep green tunic over a white shirt with matching pants as well as his deep blue cloak clasped at his throat. I shuffle over on the stairs, he takes the seat; his thigh and shoulder press against my own.

"Morning," I say, looking over at him. He smiles, the skin creasing at the corners of his eyes. It almost draws the attention away from the shadows gathering under his eyes.

"How are you feeling this morning?"

"Is like death an acceptable answer?" I groan, looking back out to the mountains. Truthfully I'd been almost excited for the journey to the Covnos mountains, but now that I'm closer to having to betray everyone—I couldn't want to escape something more.

"I could have warned you about the wine." Father chuckles, shaking his head. I smile weakly, resting my head on his shoulder. His warmth seeps into me, a comfort and security. Emotions tidal wave, threatening to have me erupting into tears.

"I'm sorry. For running away, for coming here. I'm sorry I've made it hard for you," I whisper, blinking back the few gathering tears. Father puts an arm around me, pulling me to his side.

"You have nothing to apologise for petal. I always wanted to protect you from all of this because I know how cruel my world can be. You have an innocent heart Amaryllis but you take after your mother in more ways than I can tell you. She'd be incredibly proud of how brave you've been. I am sorry that my need to protect you over clouded what you may need and want. I wish I could send you home because it's going to be dangerous but I'm also glad you're here. I love you Ama, more than anything." He kisses the top of my head, squeezing me gently.

Guilt gnaws at me, wanting to tell him all of the secrets I'm holding close to my chest. My father wouldn't toss me away or think I'm evil. I wipe my now wet cheeks, sniffling.

"I love you too. I just wanted to be closer to you," I murmur as I bring the mug of coffee to my lips.

"After we deal with this we'll return home briefly and then I was thinking both you and I and your mother can go on a small holiday for a few weeks."

"I'd really love that." Now I'm definitely crying, thinking of the bright future he's offering me with him and mother. My love for them runs so deeply through me, my family mean everything to me.

"Hey, don't cry. It's going to be okay. Eleazar is strong, he might be off for a while but he will come back." Father murmurs, the dread in his voice doesn't go unnoticed. He believes Eleazar will be okay but it's not a given. Nothing is a given in this world.

"I know he's strong but I worry. I can't help it. What if he isn't okay? What if he doesn't come back?" I whisper, blinking through my watery gaze. The sun has crested the mountains now, its warmth covering both Father and I.

"I've known Eleazar my entire life and I can promise you it's going to take more than this to take him down," Father assures me, slightly more confident. I force the crack in my heart to close, not wanting to spend the entire journey crying.

"Do you...do you really approve of Eleazar and I?" I ask, looking up at him. He sighs as he looks down at me, brushing the hair from my face. He studies me, black waves fall down his face and shelter his brows.

"I do. I can't say I was blindsided by his proposal to me.

Your mother was nagging me at home about the two of you and I see...I see the way he looks at you."

My breathing stops, "What way does he look at me?"

"He looks at you the same way I look at your mother," Father says softly, kissing my forehead lightly. I find my breath again, recovering from the shock. Father looks at mother with nothing but undying love in his eyes. Eleazar...does he love me? Has it been long enough to love someone? I know I've fallen for him and deep down know that warm feeling whenever I see him or think of him is *love,* but is it different for him?

"Don't panic, he'd protect you with his life. He's an honourable man."

"I know just how honourable he is," I grumble, cheeks heating as I remember our secret reprieve in the pantry from the night before. Father laughs, shaking his head.

"That is always something a father likes to hear."

I manage to grin up at him.

"What's so funny?" Hemlock asks. He stands behind us on the porch. I look over my shoulder at him and smile, his blonde hair is still messy from sleep but he's dressed for the day that we face. He smiles lazily down at me as he stretches his arms above his head and yawns. Father stands and takes my empty cup from my hands.

"We'd just been talking about the honour of a man." Father chuckles as he heads into the house. Hemlock walks down the steps and stops at the base of the stairs as he looks over at the rabbits, he puts two fingers to his mouth and whistles. Their large ears perk up as they bound over to him.

"There's only five?" I ask as I walk down the steps to where he stands.

"You'll be doubling with someone," he assures me, running his hand down the face of the closest rabbit. I reach out and burry my fingers into their soft fur. "You can always double with me." He smirks, waggling his brows.

"She'll be doubling with me," Eleazar grunts. I look past Hemlock to see him standing at the top of the stairs staring down at us. His eyes narrow slightly at the short distance between Hemlock and I. I burst into laughter, shaking my head.

"Are you always this grumpy in the mornings?" I ask, challenging him. He prowls down the stairs, his eyes not leaving mine. Hemlock laughs as he steps back, hands up in feign of innocence.

"I thought you assumed I was grumpy all the time," he says roughly, stopping in front of me. He breaks into a lazy smile, a dimple forming in his cheek. I raise my head in defiance but smile up at him.

"Are you lucky enough to double with me?" I lick my lips, watching as his eyes trail my tongue. My thoughts spiral to last night, the way we'd kissed. The forbidden areas my hands and his had roamed—I'd even managed to get him shirtless and he is a sight for sore eyes. His eyes darken as he swallows thickly, knowing exactly where my thoughts have taken me.

"I think I'm lucky enough." Hemlock stirs, grinning devilishly at the both of us. I burst out laughing again as he dances out of Eleazar's fist that is determined to connect with his face. Hemlock runs around the rabbit, laughing madly as Eleazar stands there; almost like an angry mother bear protecting her cub. I come up behind him and wrap my arms around his waist, he tenses for a moment before relaxing into my grip. He rests his hands over mine. I press my cheek against his back, breathing him in. He wears his pants like a second skin, his deep brown boots lace up to his calves. He'd tucked in his white shirt, his black cloak is missing along with his weapons.

"Are all faerie males this broody?" I ask, closing my eyes as I breath him in.

"They sure are. More fun you have to look forward to," Eleazar murmurs, rubbing his thumbs over my hands. I grin.

"Eleazar is one of the worst," Hemlock chimes before his footsteps retreat, no doubt inside where he's protected from Eleazar. It makes me chuckle again. Eleazar unclasps my arms and turns to face me. His hands come down around my waist, pulling me into the hard planes of his chest. My chest is flush against his own, causing my breathing to pick up.

"I like when you wear my shirt," he murmurs as he kisses the top of my nose, I smile lazily back up at him. I reach up and toy with his soft hair, running my fingers through the long lengths.

"I like you when you wear no shirt," I say as I look down to where my fingers have snagged on a knot. He laughs.

"Trust me when I say I like when you wear no shirt as well," he leans down and runs his nose along my cheek. I tilt my head to the side as he presses a kiss to my throat. I groan and pull myself against him. "If you keep making noises like that we won't be leaving for this trip." His voice is rough and deep in his throat. My toes curl in my boots.

"Ugh," a female snorts. I look through Eleazar's curtain of hair to see Helena scowling our way. I step slightly back, my cheeks flush. Eleazar turns and looks towards her.

"Good to see you still have a foul attitude," he says.

"Good to see you still have horrible taste in women." She smiles as she turns and stalks towards her rabbit. Hemlock, Odin and father walk out of the manor before Eleazar can reply. My heart deflates. I try to step out of his grip, looking away from him. His hands tighten on me.

"Don't let her get to you," he whispers.

"I'll work on it," I murmur, still unable to meet his gaze.

"Alright, let's go," Father says.

Eleazar takes my hand and leads us to a rabbit, I place my hands on its side as he grabs my waist and hoists me up. I swing my leg over and settle on its back. Its soft fur makes me feel like I'm sitting atop a plush mattress. Helena, Odin and Father mount their rabbits while Eleazar grabs his cloak, weapons and travel bag from Hemlock. He straps his weapons to his back before clasping his cloak around his shoulders.

He comes to my side, "Hold your bag in front of you."

I do as he says, twisting my bag to my front. He mounts swiftly, settling in behind me. He wraps both arms around my waist as he moves closer until my back is flush with his front, even his legs mould against my own.

"Are we ready?" Father asks, his rabbit shakes it head as its ears perk. I look over my shoulder towards the Covnos mountains and the growing black cloud that shrouds their sharpened peaks. Blue lightning breaks through the darkness.

The rabbits are spelled, suddenly all bounding through the bright green grass towards the mountains. I lean back into Eleazar, holding my hands over his own. Father takes the lead with Odin just behind him. Eleazar and I ride in the middle while Hemlock and Helena take up the rear.

Dread begins to unfold in my chest as I keep my eyes on the blue streaks in the dark clouds. As if they sense me watching, more blue streaks break through, dancing.

As if they know a fallen is coming.

CHAPTER 21

We ride through the day, only stopping every hour for five minutes so the rabbits can have a nibble and some water. It doesn't take long for their soft fur to be slick with sweat from the hounding sun and continuous running. I don't complain, enjoying the closeness of Eleazar and the warmth that seeps into my back. His hand had drifted under the hem of my shirt at one point, his fingers had trailed the skin just above the waist of my pants.

I was afraid someone would hear my gasp and small moan, which he quickly silenced with his other hand. His hand had left my shirt after a few more moments and then I had showed him just how much I could tease as well, especially when I arched back into him and felt his need for me.

He'd almost fallen off the rabbit and I'd burst out laughing.

The rabbits come to a stop at the entrance of a large, grand forest that towers over us. The long, dark brown trunks groan in the breeze as their canopy of olive green leaves dance with the wind. I watch as the sun begins to sink below the mountains, casting the land in a deep orange and pink hue.

Eleazar slides from the rabbit behind me.

"Alright we'll set up camp here for the night. There's a stream that's safe to bathe in just five minutes away." Father says as he slides off his rabbit. Everyone else follows his lead, I'm grateful when Eleazar's large hands reach for me. I lean on his shoulders as he helps me climb down. I scrunch my nose up at him playfully.

"You definitely need a bath," I say, leaning away. He doesn't smell awful, his natural musk is extremely strong and it's making it hard for me to think straight. He smells amazing. My comment causes him to laugh while he pulls me closer, large hands splaying against my lower back.

"Care to join?" he grins, eyes shining.

"Not the first time you've seen me in nothing," I whisper as I lean up and kiss him on the cheek. I step out of his arms and stretch, readjusting my bag. Father leads the rabbits over to the trees and makes quick work of giving them carrots and grains for dinner. Hemlock and Helena head into the forest. Odin finds a patch of grass for all of us to sit on. He sets his bag down and looks towards where I stand.

"They're going to find wood for the fire, Eleazar can take you down to the stream if you'd like," Odin says, voice quiet. His brown eyes flicker over my shoulder before he grabs a worn leather book from his bag and turns away from me.

"Come." Eleazar takes my hand and leads us along the tree line, away from the camp for the night. I let him lead me. My eyes drift from him and to the forest to my right, the shadows are black. Darker than any normal shadow that would be cast from the dying light. It seems like the shadows are alive, looking out at us as if we're the next meal.

"Eleazar is this forest...enchanted or something?" I whisper, intently looking at each dark part I can find. I may not feel the magic radiating from it, but I'm more aware now that I'm looking for traces of it.

"Everything in Faerie is magic but this forest had...it had a lot of fallen magic wielders perish in it." He says the last part softly, squeezing my hand briefly. I almost trip over my own feet.

"Why do you say that?" I ask, walking faster until I'm beside him on his left side; away from the forest. Away from the prying eyes of the ghosts that haunt the shadows.

"When I hunted them down to kill them their trail lead me to this forest. It didn't take me long to realise they'd been hiding here. I...I used my magic to send thorned vines up through the ground to capture them. There was fifty-six in total hiding in the forest." His voice sounds far away as he recalls a memory I'm afraid to hear him share. I stay silent, squeezing his hand in comfort.

"I had to offer something of myself in turn to kill them all. I offered my hands. As each fallen was killed a thorn would cut deep on my hand, enough to leave a scar. There are fifty-six scars over both hands. It took me a few months to recover from the toll it took on me and my magic, but I came back."

"I'm sorry," I whisper, unable to find other words. I look down at our clasped hands, the scars are a light contrast against his tanned skin.

"There's no need for you to apologise. Helena was there to help me through it, this is before we realised we'd be better as friends." He shakes his head before looking down to me. His golden eyes are raw with emotion, a soft glow in the darkness that has begun to envelope us.

"I'm glad she was there for you." I smile up at him before resting my head against his shoulder. "Are we nearly there?"

"Almost, just through here." Eleazar guides us into the forest down a well-worn path. As we walk along, the moss underneath our boots begins to glow bright blue with each step we take, leaving an ocean path behind us.

"That is so pretty," I whisper, staring down to watch the moss explode bright blue underneath my foot.

"Wait until you see the stream." Eleazar urges us forward before taking a left. The moss opens up as the forest stops. In front of us is a large stream, running from my left down to my right and disappearing into the forest. There is no dirt or rocks, only moss. Eleazar lets go of my hand as he runs his feet over the moss, it illuminates bright blue with each sweep of his foot. I place my bag down next to the trunk of a tree and strip my cloak off before pulling my boots off. Eleazar stops once most of the moss clearing before the water is lit, it glows and illuminates the area around us.

"This is quiet romantic." I blow him a kiss as he walks over to me, he drops his bag and weapons before sliding his arms around my waist and bringing his lips down to mine. I don't resist as I wrap my arms around his neck, reaching up on the tips of my toes to deepen the kiss.

His hands slip under my shirt and explore my back, causing me to shiver.

"Would you like to bathe?" he asks, breaking the kiss. I'm breathless, aching with need and the feel of his hands on me.

"As long as you join me," I murmur. I step out of his grip and tug my shirt over my head, I let it fall to the ground at my feet before I slowly begin to unlace the front of my pants. My bare chest heats as Eleazar's eyes trail from my face and down to my hardened peaks, his eyes trail lower to where my hands have nearly finished the lace to my pants.

"You make it extremely hard to behave myself," he says roughly, pulling a hand through his long hair. I pull my pants and underwear off, standing naked before him. I resist the urge to cover myself, feeling far more exposed than ever. I gather my courage. He unclasps his cloak.

I want this. I want Eleazar. Even a wicked thing like myself can *want* love. A wicked thing like myself *deserves* love, even though it will be a fleeting feeling.

"I don't want to behave anymore." I take a step forward, he stares down at me. I take another and grab the hem of his shirt, rubbing the soft material through the tips of my fingers.

"Amaryllis..." he trails off as he helps me with his shirt, it falls to the ground forgotten. I let my eyes roam over his tanned chest, tracing the curves of his muscles and scars. I find them beautiful, a scar is a story to tell and his body is a book I want to read for the rest of my life.

"I want this, I want *you*." I lower my hands and gently untie the lace to his pants. My hands shake slightly with nerves, my inexperience obvious. He stares down at me with awe and hunger, his hands overtake my own as he pulls his pants and undergarments off. I keep my eyes on his as he steps out of them and wraps his arms around my waist.

"Are you sure I'm what you want?" He brings a hand up and cups my cheek, rubbing his thumb over the soft skin. I lick my lips, coiled with anticipation.

"I have never been more sure of something in my life." I'm breathless as I'm lost in his eyes. His eyes flick down to my lips.

"I don't want you to regret this," he murmurs, kissing my forehead.

"I could never regret giving you this...you're my first, and I wouldn't want to share this with any other man," I whisper as I kiss his cheek. I slowly drag my hands down his bare chest. He's so warm it chases away the night's biting breeze. It chases away all my doubts and fears, there is nothing in this moment but him and I and the love I can feel between us.

"Now isn't the best time to be talking of other men while your naked body is pressed against mine." He growls, nipping my bottom lip. I grin up at him as my cheeks heat.

"Someone sounds possessive." I slip out of his arms and wink at him, I take slow steps backwards before the stream. His golden eyes swirl with desire as he stands there, eyes tracking each movement. My every breath. My chest is flush as the heat rises up my throat and to my cheeks. Warm water laps at my ankles as I reach the water, its welcome against the chill in the air.

Eleazar takes a step forward, causing my eyes to trail from his face and over his chest. I look lower, breath guttering out of me when I see how much he truly desires me. I don't know if I'm going to be able to *fit* all of him. He is sculpted by the gods.

"See something you like?" he purrs. Each deep note of his voice sends warmth through me and southwards. I squeeze my thighs together to relieve some of the pressure that's building.

"Yes." My voice is a soft caress in the wind, strands of my black hair tickle my cheeks and throat as I continue to take another step; the water laps at my calves. Eleazar takes another step forward.

"Look at the water." He looks down at my feet so I do the same, the moss in the water has lit up in bright violet foot-steps. It reminds me of my father's eyes, of my own eyes. I look back up to find him arms-length away.

"Beautiful," he whispers.

"Join me." I reach out for his hand, intertwining my fingers with his own. He walks with purpose into the water as I walk backwards. We reach the deeper part of the stream as the water laps at my waist. The violet glow of the water illuminates us, casting away the shadows it held moments ago. I step in to Eleazar, reaching up and wrapping my arms around his neck.

His arms snake around my waist, pulling me tightly to him. My chest is flush against his own while the length of him is nestled between our stomachs. He groans softly, so soft I almost miss it. The deep sound has me squirming against him, causing him to throb against me.

"You...you are naughty," he says, bringing his lips down to

pepper kisses against my jaw and underside of my ear and down my throat. I tilt my neck and allow him more access, hands tightening in the hair at the back of his head.

"Are you sure you want to do this?" he murmurs against my skin, grazing his sharp canines against my erratic heart beat that pulses in my neck. Nothing exists outside of this moment, there's no daunting mission we must complete, no fallen magic in my veins. Only Eleazar and I.

"I'm sure. Just be gentle with me, you're quite..." I pause for a moment, cheeks on fire, "large."

He chuckles, his chest rumbling against my own. I rub my chest into his, gasping at the pleasure that comes from the hardened peaks rubbing against his smooth skin. I never could have imagined something so small could elicit pleasure.

"I will be gentle. I'll try not to hurt you, but it will sting." He pulls back from my neck, concern overcoming the desire in his eyes as he searches my face. I look up at him, blinking through the haze of my own desire.

"I trust you Eleazar." I kiss the tip of his nose, purposefully rubbing my body against his own as I stand on the tips of my toes and back down again. He groans as a hand comes up and cups one of my cheeks, his thumb strokes over my wet bottom lip.

"I trust you as well Amaryllis."

He lets me go and grabs my hand as I begin to protest. "I'm not going to take you in the water. Give me a moment." He leads us out of the water and drops my hand, striding over to grab his cloak and my own. I watch as the muscles in his back ripple and look lower...my god *his ass*.

He lays out both of our cloaks out, overlapping the other. An area large enough for both of us to lie on. My heat beat picks up in my chest as he turns and walks back over to me. I'm nervous but I have never wanted anything more.

He takes my hand and leads me over to the cloaks, he helps me lay down before laying down beside me. He rests on one elbow as he looks down at me, I reach up and tuck the loose copper hair behind his pointed ear. I gently run my fingers down his thick throat and over his chest before finally resting my hand on his arm.

"Are you sur—"

"If you ask me one more time if I want this and if I'm sure I might just scream," I growl, rolling onto my side to face him. I grip his chin in my hand firmly, staring into his golden eyes. "I. Want. You."

"If you're screaming I can assure you it won't be in frustration." He smirks, a spark of amusement lights up his eyes.

"Then what are you waiting for?" I lick my lips, running my tongue slowly against my bottom lip. He smiles, dimples in both cheeks. A genuine smile. He doesn't waste another moment as his lips meet my own, they're soft and gentle. I lay back down, guiding his face as I move. I thread my fingers through his hair as I kiss him, taste him. He groans low in his throat as one calloused palm runs against the curve of my breast, dipping with the curve of my hip and resting on my thigh.

I open my mouth as his tongue dances with my own, each touch and kiss is more urgent than the last. My hands leave his hair as I grip his shoulders, tugging him on top of me. He breaks away from the kiss as he slowly gets on top of me. I open my legs for him to rest between, each elbow is braced against the side of my face as he looks down at me.

I wrap my legs around his waist, rubbing against him; causing him to growl.

"I want to take my time with you," his voice is thick with need, heating my blood. I run my hands down his chest and trail lower, I gently take him in one hand. I can barely wrap my fingers around him.

"There will be plenty of moments when we can explore each other's bodies. Right now I *need* you Eleazar. I need you," I whisper, staring into his eyes. He's conflicted for a moment before relenting, shaking his head slightly although he smiles.

"I'm sorry if I hurt you." He kisses my forehead before reaching down between us, his hand guides my own as he rests against my entrance. I'm wet with anticipation as my breathing hitches. This is it.

Ever so slowly he pushes against me, sliding with both of our desires. He watches me with concern as he inches against the barrier. I hiss as something breaks and tense against the pain. He stops. I move my hand from his and cup his face.

"Take some deep breaths." He kisses my forehead, each cheek and nose. I shut my eyes and do as he says, the throbbing pain subsides and becomes bearable. I open my eyes again and smile softly before leaning up and meeting his lips.

He moves inch by inch inside of me until we're joined. He rests like that for a moment and lets me adjust. I groan against his mouth at the fullness, wrapping my legs tightly around his waist. It jolts him against me, causing him to tense.

"You're not hurting me," I whisper against his lips, nipping and kissing them.

"We'll go slow." He captures my lips with his own, his tongue dancing with mine as he slowly pulls out of me before sliding back in. Each slow thrust has me moaning with pain and pleasure, the pleasure overcomes the pain as we find a steady pace.

Eleazar breaks the kiss and lowers his head to my left breast, his tongue slides over the hardened peak. I gasp as I move against him harder, more urgent. Fire ignites my veins as his mouth continues to pull every small noise out of me, until I'm throwing my head back and pleading for more.

He swiftly sits back on his heels, pulling me with him. I wrap my arms around his neck as I slide back down onto him, the new angle is deeper and causes him to groan as he thrusts against me. His calloused hands run down my back and rest on my ass.

I kiss him more urgently as warmth begins to pool lower, the spark of pleasure feels like an inferno between us and I need it to be released.

"Please," I whisper, unsure what I'm exactly begging for.

"I love you, Amaryllis." His voice is thick and my heart clenches in my chest. I rock against him with force until we're both at the edge. His golden eyes are ablaze as he catches my eyes.

"I love you, Eleazar." I say between each breath.

He grinds his hips against my own and hits the fire inside of me. I clench around him and open my mouth to scream my release, his lips capture my own and steal the sound as he thrusts faster and harder than before. He rides me though my own release before his hips stutter and still. He throbs inside of me.

I collapse against him and nestle my face into the crook of his neck. My whole body aches in a pleasant way. One of his hands runs down my back, tracing invisible patterns as we sit there and regain our breathing.

"Are you okay? Are you hurt?" he asks, rubbing his cheek against my own.

"I'm okay. Better than okay." I sit up and wince. He helps me slowly dismount and sits back, cradling me to his chest. I ache more than I'm willing to tell him, wouldn't want to concern him more and boost his ego at the same time.

"I hope that was okay for your first." He kisses the top of my head.

"That was...that was amazing Eleazar. We should have been doing this sooner." I smirk as I lean back to look up at him, sweat coats both of our bodies. Cooper strands stick to his throat and sides of his face.

"You're a little heathen under that innocent mask aren't you?" he grins.

"You're the one that fell for it." I steal a kiss from him before climbing out of his arms. My legs shake with the effort but he's standing by my side a moment later, both hands resting on my hips. I lean against his back and sigh, happy.

I am happy.

It almost chases away the dark secret I harbour. Almost.

"Come on, let's bathe. I'm ready to eat and sleep and get some cuddles," I murmur. He kisses my neck once more before scooping me up in his arms. I squeal as he carries me into the stream, he helps me stand before cupping water and letting it fall down my chest. I watch in awe as he washes me, gentle and loving.

I do the same once he's done, admiring him and selfishly indulging on his bareness. I lock this moment away in my most treasured memories. Tonight has changed everything between us, something we'll definitely need to define sooner rather than later.

Once we're finished bathing we dry quickly before getting dressed into a fresh pair of clothes. I wrap my cloak around my shoulders as I pick up my bag. Eleazar has re-strapped his weapons to his back, his cloak conceals them nicely. He intertwines our fingers as he begins to lead us back through the forest and out to the path.

We walk in silence along the tree line, the flicker of flame catches my eyes as the campsite comes into sight. I yawn and fight the exhaustion.

"Did I wear you out?" Eleazar murmurs, kissing the back of my hand.

"It'd take more than that to wear me out. I could go for round two easily." I waggle my brows at him when he looks down, most likely to see if I'm serious or not. He laughs, the smile stretches his cheeks. It makes him look younger.

"I love your laugh, I wish you laughed more often," I say, squeezing his hand.

He doesn't say anything back but I see the warmth in his gaze. It's enough for me.

We reach the camp to find my father and Hemlock looking over a map. Helena pointedly ignores us from where she sits beside them while Odin peers up from the book he's got his nose stuck in. An idea lights up in my mind, on the journey I might be able to coerce information about fallen magic out of Odin. He'd most likely know the depths better than anyone else here.

The sun had set not long ago and I'm glad we hadn't been missing for too long. My cheeks heat as I look away from Odin and take my seat near the fire. I prop my bag behind me and lean against it, holding my hands in front of me for warmth. Eleazar grabs two bowls from near the fire before sitting beside me, his thigh rests against my own.

"Thanks." I take the bowl from him and heap a mouthful of the soup, it's warm and hearty. Perfect dinner to regain my strength.

"Well I'm going to go bathe now," Helena declares as she stands. Her eyes linger on Eleazar before her jaw tightens. She gathers her bag before walking past us and down the path. Odin sighs before turning back to his book.

"Did you like the moss?" Hemlock asks, drawing my attention to where he and father sit near me. Father smiles, eyes flickering between Eleazar and I.

"It's amazing, I've never seen anything like that before." I smile at him before taking another mouthful of soup. Odin murmurs something under his breath, causing Hemlock to burst with laughter as my father turns red from the base of his throat to the tips of his ears. Eleazar growls as he stares daggers at him. I huff out a breath as I lean against Eleazar, he pulls me between his legs. I lean into his back and nestle in, my eyes grow heavy from the comfort.

"Are all faerie males this grumpy?" I ask.

Hemlock grins, "He's the worst."

"I am not," Eleazar retorts.

"Oh my god stop," I groan. Eleazar grunts in response before going back to his bowl of soup. I shake my head before finishing my bowl. I sit it off to the side before nestling back into Eleazar, I end up laying on my side between his legs with my head on his lap. He runs his hand through my hair as the men talk with one another. The caress is gentle and thoughtful, my eyes flutter shut as I relax.

Not only has Eleazar given me hope, he has also given me happiness.

True happiness.

CHAPTER 22

I stir from my sleep, blinking into the soft morning sun as it breaks the hills and spills over the land. I yawn as I look over my shoulder to the weight that's wrapped around me. Eleazar sleeps peacefully, his legs are shaped in the curve of my own while one of his arms is draped over my waist. His copper hair spills over his bag. I look forward again to see the sleeping forms of Hemlock and my father. I crane my neck to find Helena and Odin's sleeping areas empty. I gently pull Eleazar's arm off of my waist and wiggle away from him, not wanting to wake him.

I need to relieve my bladder urgently.

The fire is nothing more than a small pile of charcoal, long burned out. The rabbits are nearby, nibbling at the ground. I look over the open expanse of the open field we'd ridden from and find no sight of the two missing from the camp. Something nags at the back of my mind but I push it away before giving it thought. I turn and face the forest which is far more welcoming in the light than it is in the darkness.

Although I swear I see black shadows moving, hiding and reappearing. It makes me shiver.

I gather my courage and slowly begin to walk into the forest, following a worn path. Every few moments I look over my shoulder to make sure I can still see the camp. The last thing I want to be is lost in a magical forest full of ghosts that are wanting someone to haunt.

A cool breeze passes over me, stirring my knotted hair from last night's sleep. I gently tug at the knots as I continue to look around the forest, Odin and Helena always could have gone to the stream to bathe...together? No that doesn't sound right, not with the way Helena still seems transfixed on Eleazar, not that I can blame her.

The path in front of my veers sharply to the left, the trees are more dense here and the shadows are everywhere I look. I stop and look over my shoulder, still seeing the camp vaguely. I shake myself and begin to walk back towards the camp. I'd been foolish looking for them, they're grown adults and know what they're doing.

I keep my steps as silent as I can still, not wanting to alert anything that may be in the forest around me. An eerie feeling falls over me, dread curls in my lower abdomen as I look over my shoulder. It feels as if a million eyes are watching me.

I'm a few feet from the camp when I come to an abrupt stop. I inhale in a sharp breath as spirits appear before me. One moment they hadn't been there and then the next, when I'd blinked, they're everywhere. All of their lifeless eyes are on me.

My lungs burn with the need to breathe but fear overrides any good sense that I have. A female spirit strides forward, she's littered in thick scars that wind up her bare arms and legs. Eleazar's vines and thorns. She stops in front of me, transparent if I don't focus on her wholly.

She brings a finger up to her lips, "*Shhh.*" Her voice is a phantom breeze.

She stays standing in front of me while others begin to gather around me, the spirits herd me closer to safety but suddenly pull me into the darkness of a shadow. It stirs with life as I'm held in place by their phantom hands. I look over my shoulder to see the outlines of the spirits and darkness. I knew the shadows were alive.

I finally take another breath, unable to hold it any longer. The female who had told me to be quiet stands to my side, silently watching the path we'd been standing on only moments ago. I raise an eyebrow in question, although I'm full of fear...I'm curious. Why are they doing this? Is my magic calling to them?

She points towards the path with a scarred finger, I follow her line of sight and continue to listen in silence. Moments pass and I begin to grow restless. Suddenly, footsteps approach from in the forest. My ears perk at the sudden noise, it seems so loud after being quiet for so long.

Helena and Odin appear on the path, coming from the thickness of the forest. Helena's wiping her hands on her pants while Odin looks placidly around the forest. His eyes go straight over where we stand.

Is this...is this what the spirit wants to show me?

"I have a bad feeling about her Odin, I don't know how to explain it but my skin *crawls* with warning whenever she's near." Helena says in a hushed voice, standing beside him. He sighs and tucks his hands into the pockets of his pants.

"I know your instincts have never been wrong before but I've spoken with the girl more times than you have and in the human world. She seems fine to me."

"My instincts have never been wrong. Don't you think it's funny that she has no magic? All magical creatures are born with sacred magic unless they have old magic or fallen magic. We both know old magic is only in the ancestral beasts," Helena insists. They begin walking slowly back towards the camp.

"Are you sure your emotions aren't the reason for this

pestering?" Odin asks smoothly, looking sideways at her. Helena scowls at him, "I'm just saying. You and Eleazar have been best friends for centuries and were together for a long period of time. I know you're hurting more than you let on."

"Of course I'm hurting. I love him." She growls in frustration, "I still care about him which is why I'm so worried he's with her. He doesn't even realise how much of a threat she is!" She throws her hands in the air.

"Say you're right and she does have fallen magic, Eleazar is under oath to the queen to slaughter any creature who has fallen magic. If she shows fallen magic he will have no choice but to hunt her, even if he doesn't want to."

My blood goes cold in my veins, I look to the female beside me and she watches me with sadness and pity in her depthless gaze. The spirits around me moan and groan, causing Helena and Odin to look at their surroundings.

"You'll wake the spirits if you continue talking about these things," Odin says, looking back to her.

"I'm going to protect him when push comes to shove. I know she has fallen magic, I just need to convince him that she has it as well. Do you think she is a fallen wielder?" Helena whispers in a hushed tone. Odin's mouth twists as he thinks while he stares down at her.

"I don't know what I think. I believe it's strange she hasn't shown any sign of magic but she also doesn't seem corrupt to me. She isn't turning evil. If the fallen magic was eating her soul she'd definitely be showing obvious signs by now." Odin begins to walk forward, leaving her behind, "I suggest you don't mention these theories to Eleazar, I doubt he would take it lightly."

She hurries to catch up with him, protesting in a whispered tone I can't hear as they break the tree line and reach the camp.

I shake with fear, if Helena has evidence or catches me slipping she won't hesitate to turn me in or take the blade to me herself. I look to the female that had wanted me to listen. She stares at the space Odin and Helena had disappeared through with longing.

"I'm going to die, aren't I?" I whisper.

"*I'm unsure. She is one you must watch. She conspires against you.*" Her velvet soft voice barely reaches my ears.

"Is that why you showed me this?"

She looks to me and smiles softly "*Yes. I also wanted to meet the last fallen who walks this earth...you lay in bed with the hunter.*"

I blush furiously at her words, clearly spirits see everything.

"Yes...I do. I know it isn't going to end happily ever after, but I don't believe we all deserve the happy endings." I whisper, looking to the spirits around me. "I'm truly sorry this is the fate that was dealt to you. I've met with Salis multiple times and I don't think there is a shred of light in him."

"*Ah Salis. The soul eater.*" She gestures around us, "*We are the spirits the hunter slayed. We are trapped in this forest by the enchantment Salis has placed over it. We relive our deaths each day at random moments, this was his punishment. Do not trust that god.*"

"Is there any way to break the enchantment?" I ask. She shakes her head sadly, shoulders slumping in defeat. No wonder they groan and moan all day, it's in despair. "and Eleazar...I didn't intend to fall for him like I have. We both travelled here together and I'd only just discovered my magic. I hid it from them all."

"*You heard the female. He is oath bound. Whenever he is made aware of a fallen he must hunt them down and rid the earth of them. There are fallen around you right now who weren't corrupt or rotting. We'd been living with this magic for years but with the rumours and lies spread by others we were all deemed a danger to be put down."* She reaches out and caresses my cheek, her phantom touch is freezing, *"How strong is love if it cannot break an oath? How strong is an oath if it is so easily broken by the declaration of love?"*

"I don't know what you're saying."

"You will learn of your fate soon enough. We will grant you and your companions safe passage through this forest for you and only you. Be safe Amaryllis and keep your eyes open." The spirits begin to herd me out of the pocket of the shadow we'd been hiding in. I can hear everyone at the camp talking, Eleazar's deep growl has my ears perking. They'd be wondering where I am, no doubt causing Helena to conspire more.

"Thank you. If I can find a way to break this enchantment and free your souls I will do it. For the right price I know Salis won't resist," I say softly as I begin to walk back towards the path. The spirits walk side by side with me, their presence a comfort now.

"Goodbye Amaryllis." I reach the path and turn to say goodbye to find them all gone. I'm utterly alone as I stand on the path. My bladder clenches, I quickly hurry behind a bush and relieve myself. I sigh with content as I finish and dry myself. I walk back to the path and towards the camp. I push all terrifying thoughts from my head as I emerge from the forest, all eyes snap towards me.

Eleazar rushes forward, eyes full of concern. Helena snarls before turning away from me. Father and Hemlock look at me with relief. Odin is silent. I gather my courage.

"What? I had to relieve myself," I say sheepishly, feeling my cheeks heat. Father and Hemlock relax, Eleazar sighs as he reaches me. He plants a firm kiss to my forehead before tucking strands of my hair behind my ears.

"I thought you'd run off," he murmurs, standing close to me. I roll my eyes and smile as I brush past him.

"Please, we both know I don't run," I sweetly sing over my shoulder as I go back to my bag. Eleazar chuckles behind me as he follows. He'd already strapped his weapons on and readied his cloak and bag. I hurry to clip my cloak around my shoulders and grab my bag. I position it to my front before turning back to him.

"Are we riding the rabbits through the forest?" I ask.

"Yes, we'll be riding them to Covnos. It's still a small journey away, our next stop will be at the base of the mountains. We'll need to be more alert once we reach them, they're full of serpents." Hemlock says as he gathers his bags. Father whistles sharply, one by one the rabbits bound towards us.

"Serpents..." I murmur, unsure what sort of creature they are. I recall the wendigo, remembering my close encounter when I'd first spent time with Eleazar. The terrifying creature had almost made a meal of me. Eleazar sees the concern on my face and takes my hand, threading our fingers together.

"No foolish plans this time," he whispers, tugging me toward the rabbits.

"If I hadn't have been foolish we'd most likely still be in that paddock," I hiss back, squeezing his hand. He throws me a look over his shoulder as we reach the rabbits, I narrow my eyes at him. We could argue about this for centuries if I allowed it.

Eleazar helps me mount our rabbit before mounting behind me. I wince as I position myself, not able to fully stop the throbbing between my thighs. The soft fur of the rabbit is definitely helpful, I can't imagine how painful it would be riding a horse.

"Are you okay?" Eleazar murmurs into my ear, his hot breath excites me. Now that I know exactly what pleasure he can bring me it's hard to think of innocent gestures as that;

innocent. He wraps his arms around my waist as I'm pressed firmly to his chest.

"Just aching," I whisper against his jaw as I tilt my face towards him. I kiss the rapid building pulse in his throat before facing forward again. A hand rests on my lower stomach while the other rests on my thigh, all innocent movements. All making my blood turn to liquid fire.

"I'm sorry I hurt you." He kisses the top of my head.

"I'm sure after a few more...times it won't hurt anymore," I say back as I thread my fingers through the rabbit's fur. If we keep talking on this topic I won't be able to make it to the mountains without dragging him behind some bushes and having my way with him.

The others have all mounted their rabbits and we all begin to bound down the path that leads through the forest. I look to the shadows and catch glimpses of the spirits that linger. Of the spirits that didn't deserve to die like they did, to be trapped in this forest to suffer for eternity.

Eleazar is tense behind me. We're riding at the back of the group so it gives me privacy to talk somewhat freely to him.

"Do you ever regret what you did here?" I whisper, holding a hand over the one that sits against my stomach.

"I do. We all have our ghosts that haunt us," he murmurs back leaning his cheek against the side of my face.

"I guess you're right," I sigh. The rabbits take the turn in the path and we head deeper into the forest, the shadows and spirits follow us as we bound along. I decide to gather my courage and ask more questions about Eleazar and his past with the fallen.

"Eleazar..." I trail off.

He sighs against me, "You're going to ask a question I'm not going to like aren't you? I bet you even have that small frown on your face while you debate what to ask."

I smooth the frown off my face, gods damn he knows me far too well.

"Does that mean I can ask?"

"I suppose it does," he grunts. I grin, but it's quickly wiped from my face when I think of the questions I'm going to ask. Odin and Helena already suspect me to be fallen. Eleazar is my only chance of protection against them. I haven't had a chance to talk to my father but I feel Hemlock would back him up with whatever choices he makes.

"I overheard Helena and Odin talking, she mentioned you were oath bound to kill the fallen. I know you've told me before but I'm curious...as to what that entails."

He stills against me. "Is that were you'd run off to this morning?"

"No. I had to relieve my bladder." I scowl even though he can't see it.

"Yes I am oath bound."

"How does it work?"

He sighs, "Why do you want to know these things?"

"I'm simply curious. We've never really spoken about your past before." I keep my words soft as I gently stroke my fingers against the back of his hand. The guilt and betrayal are coming to the front of my mind and heart, knowing once I reveal what and *who* I truly am there may never be an Eleazar and I again. I will be lighting that bridge between us on fire and watching it disintegrate.

I never claimed to be a good person. Not all the princesses in the fairy tales are the image of innocence.

"That's because it's in my past and it's not a pleasant place I like to visit often. Yes I am still oath bound by the queen, when the fallen had first become a problem I swore to her that whenever a fallen made themselves known to me I would hunt them down and rid the earth of them. I have no control over the oath...it's extremely hard for me being here now when I know there's someone in the human world that is fallen. It's a constant tugging in my chest that demands my attention."

"Does that mean once we finish here you'll return to the human world to track the fallen?"

"Yes. Once this mission is complete I will be returning to Orrinshire to try and pick up the trail. The oath is relentless, it could take me months to track them down." He sounds...sad.

"Once you find them does the oath release its hold of you?" If it does, he won't have to kill me. He'll just have to find me and then I'd have to deal with the consequences.

"I wished it did Ama, but it doesn't. It binds me until the fallen magic isn't detectible, which means their soul has been claimed and their magic with it. It's almost maddening."

"Is there any way we could break the oath?" I ask, looking over my shoulder at him. He looks down at me with a calculating expression.

"Why do you ask me these questions, Amaryllis?" he says softly. I swallow the thickness in my throat.

"You wouldn't like my answer." I turn and face forward once more, afraid of what I may see on his face. Of what he may see on my own. His arm tightens around my waist as we continue the ride in silence. The spirits move along side of Eleazar and I, glancing at the hunter that ended their lives.

He is right, we all have ghosts that haunt us. His just seem to be more than my own.

CHAPTER 23

I should have known my luck would run out sooner rather than later. It started with the dark clouds rapidly expanding over the land and covering the blue sky above us. The next sign was the thunder that boomed across the land; strong enough to almost shake the ground. My heart is close to failing in my chest once we reach the thicket of another forest, the trees howl and the canopy of leaves shudder with each gale of wind that reaches us.

I hold Eleazar's hand, squeezing until my knuckles are white. The storm we'd had back at home had been a result of this one, I had the safety of the castle to protect me from the worst of it. Out here I have nothing but the shuddering forest that surrounds us.

"We need to get to cover before it hits!" Helena screams over the wind, her voice almost washes away on the breeze. Eleazar nods in agreement and spurs our rabbit to hop faster. Hemlock and Odin are at the front of the group while Father rides behind them with Helena. Eleazar and I take up the rear.

"If we don't reach the cave shelter the storm is going to be the least of our worries," Eleazar shouts in my ear, almost a whisper against the wind.

"Why?" I shout back, daring to look over my shoulder and up at him. His face is tight with concern as his eyes meet mine.

"These storms...they bring influence creatures we don't want to face." He holds me tightly to his chest, as if holding me will protect me from what's to come. I look forward, unable to stop the look of terror on my face at his words.

"This way!" Hemlock screams over his shoulder, gesturing to his left.

We reach the end of the forest, the air is thick with tension as we reach an open expanse of land. The yellow grass stalks whip back and forth as the thunder echoes over the land. I look up to see the familiar blue electricity streaks lighting up the now black clouds.

I watch in dismay as the clouds block out the light, shrouding the land as far as I can see in almost darkness. A blue streak of lightning breaks from the clouds and rockets towards the earth, hitting with such force that it sounds as if two boulders have collided.

Our rabbits begin to grow frantic as they hop across the land like foxes hunting a mouse, more bolts of blue lightning begin to hit the large towering mountains in front of us. Each connection is like whiplash, causing a scream to bubble in my throat.

I hate storms when I'm out in the elements.

Large cold drops of water begin to hit us, I'm too afraid to think rationally. I want to get to shelter, now and fast. I am terrified beyond my wit.

I brace myself as the downpour hits us full force, immediately drenching us and the rabbits. I can barely see the others hopping in front of us, my breathing begins to grow shorter and sharper as terror sets in. Eleazar is my only lifeline keeping me from completely giving myself over to the fear.

He swears behind me and holds me tightly, urging the

rabbit forward. He screams something over my shoulder to the others but it's drowned out by the rain and thunder.

A large clap of lightning illuminates the drowning earth and I see it.

See the cause of his scream.

My heart is left in the middle of the field as I accept that this might be the way we go.

A large, serpentine like creature is unfurling from the mountains to our right. Its sleek black scales shine with each drop of rain. It's the size of the manor Eleazar lives in and as thick as the rabbits we ride.

Its large diamond shape head swivels around before it finally spots us as we're once again thrown into darkness.

I do scream this time.

The mountains in front of us grow closer but my relief is short lived. As the clouds light up with each thunder crack, more serpentine creatures unravel from the tops of the mountains. They all are heading in one direction; towards us.

Odin is the first one to reach the base of the mountains, he disappears into them before Hemlock and Helena follow behind. Father rides in front of us, gesturing for us to follow. The path we enter is narrow, large broken trees are lodged high above us and almost create a shield from the torrential rain.

I don't dare look behind us as we follow the winding path, growing higher with each curve we take. I don't care where it leads us, as long as it's away from those creatures.

After what feels like an entire lifetime Eleazar brings the rabbit to a skidding stop. To our left Hemlock and Odin are both holding up a large fallen tree that's encased one side of the mountain path to reveal a hidden cave. The opening is large enough for the rabbits to squeeze in.

I slide from the rabbit and run towards the opening, biting my tongue to stop myself from screaming until I'm within safety. I skid to a stop at the entrance to see Eleazar still astride our rabbit looking over his shoulder. His face pales before setting with grim determination.

My heart stutters in my chest. *Don't play the hero, not now.*

"Come." Father says, grabbing my arms from behind.

"Eleazar!" I shout, struggling against my father's strong hold. Hemlock and Odin nod their heads once before they begin to lower the tree, blocking Eleazar and our terrified rabbit from sight. I fight and kick out against my father.

"Eleazar!" I scream his name over and over, begging for him to come back. Hot tears stream down my cheeks as he watches me, jaw tightening. He can't leave us. He can't sacrifice himself for this. I can't lose him now, not when I've only just found him.

He whispers three words to me before the tree completely blocks him from sight. Before we're thrown into complete and utter darkness. I collapse onto my knees, curling in on myself as I cry. It feels as if my heart has completely ripped itself into two. We'd only told each other once before that we loved the other...the '*I love you*' that just left his lips seems final. It seems like it's a goodbye.

"He'll come back. He's leading the serpents away from us," Odin says, his voice soft. The cave blocks out a majority of the thunder and crashing of rain, although the storm still rages on outside.

"What if he doesn't come back?" I sob, sitting up and wiping away the tears that still escape my eyes. I can't seem to stop crying, all I see is him leaving.

"He has something to return to," Father says, wrapping a sodden arm around my shoulders. He helps me stand before leading me deeper into the cave and away from the ice wind that bites at the entrance.

He sits me down against the wall before sliding down

beside me, his arm around my shoulder. I lean into him, we both shiver against each other. Moments later someone sits to my left, cuddling up to my side.

"It's freezing," Hemlock says. I relax slightly to know it's him on my other side. The other two sit down beside Father and Hemlock, both taking one side. The four rabbits hop over to us, shielding the front of us as they lay down and huddle together. I bury my feet under the wet coat of one, feeling its own shiver course through my legs.

"What are those creatures?" I whisper, teeth chattering. I need someone to distract me from the thought that Eleazar may never return.

"They're the serpents of the mountains. These mountains are large and vast, this is just the beginning of what we'll most likely face before we reach Covnos. Legend has it that they're protectors of the mountains, this storm...it makes them act out. Usually they're docile creatures who let us pass with ease, when a storm hits they're transformed into savage beasts," Father says, taking my hand in his own.

"Eleazar is out there in that weather. He's out there with those *savage beasts*." I feel my breathing begin to shorten again until I'm gasping for breath. I lean forward and let my head hang between my knees as two warm hands rub my back.

"It's okay. You're alright," Father murmurs.

"Eleazar knows the ins and outs of these mountains better than anyone here, he'll return to us once it's safe to do so," Hemlock assures me. It does little to help me relax.

"What if he returns and there's no one to hold the tree for him?" I ask, beginning to panic.

"He'll use a small kernel of magic to hold the tree aside for the rabbit before letting himself in. It's safest that we stay well away from the entrance and try and get warm. The storm should pass soon and the serpents will return to normal once it does," Father says while still rubbing my back. I nod a few times into the heavy silence.

"Okay," I whisper, sitting back up and leaning into my father's arms. I huddle into his side, feeling Hemlock cuddle into my back while we all huddle together in one large ball trying to replace our warmth.

Father runs his hands through my wet hair from where it rests on his chest. Hemlock's cheek rests against the back of my shoulder, the constant rise and fall of his chest helps me to relax. I let my eyes close in the darkness, letting the comfort of his breath and the feel of my father running his hand through my hair lull me into a fitful sleep.

I KNOW before I've opened my eyes that Eleazar still hasn't returned, a deep sense of urgency settles low in my stomach. Something isn't right and the longer I lay here and do nothing the worse it progresses. I open my eyes to a small fire in the middle of the cave, the rabbits are huddled together near the fire while Helena, Hemlock, Odin and my father sit on the other side. I sit up and yawn, rubbing the ache out of the back of my neck. Rain still pours down, the howling wind fills the silence and echoes around the cave.

I stand and walk over to the fire, standing just behind the others. I wrap my arms around my waist as I look into the small golden flames.

"He still hasn't returned," I murmur to no one in particular.

"He will. He always does," Helena says as she looks over her shoulder and up at me. I meet her stare that's full of venom.

"He is always there for everyone else when things go wrong, who is there for him? Who will come running when he gets himself in a situation he can't escape from?" I demand, clenching my hands to fists. Helena snarls.

"I've known Eleazar for triple your life span, so have the others. He has never once needed us to run after him."

"Just because he hasn't before doesn't mean he won't now! Something is wrong, I can feel it!" My voice begins to rise as I grow restless standing here once more. Helena stands threatening only for Hemlock to jump between us, placing his hands on her arms.

"She's right, Helena," Father says, looking up at us. "Just because he hasn't needed our help before doesn't mean he won't now. The storm is worse than the others we've come across. Once it settles more we'll head out in search for him."

"Amaryllis, would you like to go and see the crystal cavern?" Odin says softly, standing beside me. I hadn't even seen him stand or approach me.

"We should go and find Eleazar."

"We will once the storm settles. If we go out there now we might not be any help to him at all," Odin reassures, watching me with sad eyes. "I want to go out after him as much as you do, but until then the crystal caves might be a nice distraction while the storm passes."

I look away from him to the others before nodding stiffly. I turn away and follow as Odin begins to walk towards the darkness of the cave, heading deeper into the mountain. A moment later his palm flickers with light, illuminating the path and walls around us. I stay silent as I continue to follow him, keeping my eyes trained on his back. We're all still damp from the rain, my hair still hangs thickly around my face.

"He's in trouble, I can feel it," I whisper to Odin, walking closer behind him. I glance over my shoulder, unable to see the spark of light from the fire. I shiver and walk beside Odin instead. He glances down at me before looking forward, we begin to descend a rough rock stair case. I hold a hand out to the wall to steady myself as it grows steeper.

"We'll be in trouble if we leave now. These storms will do anything to keep us in these mountains with the serpentine and they can sense us once we're in the open," Odin says softly, his voice echoing around the large black cavern that now sits to our right.

"I think it's a risk we're going to have to take." Odin offers me his arm as we reach the end of the steps, it evens out to a deep blue smooth marble floor. The flame in his palm goes out and throws us into darkness. I squeeze his arm and blink rapidly.

"Give it a moment," he murmurs. We stand in silence. Just as I'm about to open my mouth to speak, the cave roof begins to glow a pastel green. I look up in awe and watch as the crystal covered roof above us begins to light up, the pastel green bleeds to a pastel blue. The cave walls are the next to light up, their pastel purple shimmers into existence and sets of the large mounds of crystal in front of us rise from dark blue water.

"Oh my..." I whisper, the entire cave in front of me is a rainbow of pastel colours.

"It only lights up in the darkness, hence why I had to put the flame out. It's truly beautiful." Odin looks up towards the roof. I let go of his arm and walk to the edge of the crystal lake, I crouch down and dip my fingers into the ice cold water.

"It's freezing." I wipe my hand on my pants as I stand, I look up and scramble backwards when I see the water beginning to ripple in the middle of a crystal mound circle. Odin grasps my arm and pulls me behind him, readying himself as we both stare intently at the now violently churning water.

"Stay behind me," Odin whispers, hands flexing at his

sides. I snort softly but continue to peer around him, wanting to see what sort of creature we're about to encounter.

The water cascades around a willowy figure as it emerges from the water, a bright white light shines suddenly before dulling. A woman stands in the middle of the crystal lake, the water churns around her legs. *Wait, it is her legs.* Her golden hair flows around her as if caught in a breeze as she turns those bright galaxy eyes towards us.

Odin freezes in front of me. I slip out from behind him, wanting to get a better view of her. The layers of silk are slick against her body, transparent against her milky white skin due to the water. She frowns, those golden eyebrows furrowing as she looks to me.

"A fallen child."

It's my turn to freeze. The breath leaves my lungs as she walks closer, the water aiding her each step. She towers over us, looking down once she nears the shore.

"I..." I'm lost for words. She blinks slowly, her eyes unnerving. Stars sparkle against the dark purple and black colour of her eyes. She isn't of this world.

"Although you are fallen, your heart is as pure as a sacred." Her voice is unlike anything I've ever heard, there's no sharp edges to her words. They flow smoothly like the water around her legs. I gulp, unable to look away from her.

"You're...you're Du'ur, the goddess of life." Odin finally finds his voice, coming to stand beside me. I can't meet his burning stare, shame heats my cheeks even though I'm unable to help what magic I was born with.

"Yes, I am Du'ur. Your copper haired male is in trouble." Her expression changes to worry as she bends down to come to our eye level. She looks between the two of us before blowing out a deep breath.

I watch in shock as the scenery around us begins to mist

over and change until all three of us are standing on a smooth piece of large mountain face, three serpents are attacking at a jagged crevice; too small for them to enter. Their hisses are furious as they relentlessly pound their large heads against the crack.

I run over and go through one of the serpents, skidding to a stop as I reach the crevice. I look down in dismay to see Eleazar lying at the bottom. He's battered and bruised, cuts litter his face as well as smeared blood. He grimaces as he looks up, holding his left arm close to his chest while his right hand holds the hilt of one of his sword tightly.

A serpent head bangs the crevice where I'm standing, I look down to see the rock beginning to splinter. The serpent sees it as well, it's large black tongue flick out before it continues its attack on the now spider-webbing crack.

"He is hurt and if you don't hurry...he will not make it," Du'ur says as the mist disappears and we're once again standing in the crystal cave. I'm already turning towards the entrance when Odin grabs my arm, pulling me to a stop.

"We have to go and help him," I say desperately, trying to pull my arm from his grip. He still looks to Du'ur.

"Is she to be trusted?" he asks, glancing down at me. I frown up at him before looking to the goddess. She watches me with sad eyes as she begins to sink lower into the lake, the black water hungrily begins to swallow her up.

"She is to be trusted more than most. Keep her secret safe. I will guide you to the copper haired hunter." She sinks underneath the water. I grab onto Odin's arm and break into a run, dragging him behind me as I clumsily do my best to run up the stairs. He huffs and lets go of my arm, lighting up his palms as we begin to run through the cave.

"Please...please don't tell the others." I manage to say between each breath.

"Du'ur said you're to be trusted so I will trust you. Does anyone else know?" he asks.

"No...I've given Eleazar hints but I don't have the heart to tell him." I shake my head, pushing my legs harder.

"That's why you insisted on coming to these mountains...if the creature has fallen magic and you do as well, you're going to try and save it," Odin confirms. I stay silent, letting him process the information however he sees fit.

"I didn't ask for this magic and I have only used it once before in self-defence. If I can use it for good then I can show the others that I'm not some evil monster to be killed," I murmur. We've almost reached the others so this conversation will need to cease.

"For your sake I will give you the benefit of the doubt." Odin pulls me to a stop, the flame of the fire the others had created is now visible. He leans in until his lips are grazing my ear. "This...this will break him. He is oath bound to hunt and kill the fallen. Either he's purposefully made himself ignorant against your hints to bide time for the two of you or he truthfully doesn't suspect you. I'm afraid this will not be a happy ending for you."

I lean back, wiping at the few tears that spill. I give him a sad smile, my heart breaking in my chest "I know it won't be a happy ending for me, but even monsters deserve to feel what happiness is; even if it's only for a fleeting moment. Now let's go and save him."

CHAPTER 24

"What do you mean you saw Du'ur?" Helena demands. I'm panting, leaning over to catch my breath. Odin has just told the others about our encounter with the goddess and how we must leave to save Eleazar now.

"I mean exactly that. She showed us a vision and Eleazar is trapped and injured with the serpents surrounding him. We must leave now." Odin moves to grab a weapon from his bag. Hemlock hesitates for a moment before launching into action beside him.

"Alright. It will be dangerous leaving in the heart of the storm but it seems we have no choice. Let's gather our weapons and leave," Father says, rummaging through his own bag. I rush to my worn bag, desperately looking for a weapon. I slide the small knife I find into my boot. Helena grabs her sword before mounting her rabbit.

I reach Odin as he leads his rabbit towards the entrance, the storm still rages on outside. He turns and looks at me in question.

"May I ride with you? Du'ur said she'd lead us, and I thought the both of us in front would be the best option," I say as I hold my chin high. His eyes sweep over me before he reaches out for me, I take his warm and smooth hand in my own as he helps me mount the rabbit. He settles behind me moments later, his chest pressing against my slick back.

"Eleazar is going to kill me if he knows I've been this close to you," Odin murmurs, the hint of amusement in his voice. I smirk over my shoulder up at him, admiring the angles of his face. All the fae males are devastatingly attractive, but none could ever capture my attention the way Eleazar has.

"Let's give him something to fight for then," I declare, facing back towards the tree that protects us. The others have mounted their rabbits and are now beside us, all braced for the storm and fight we're about to walk into. Hemlock uses his magic to move the tree aside, immediately rain and wind attack us. Odin spurs our rabbit into action, we leap around the tree and head down the rocky path.

Lightning cracks in the sky as the rain soaks us down to our bones. I keep one hand buried and holding onto the rabbits fur and the other holding Odin's arm around my waist.

Ahead of us the winding path forks, a large black crow swoops down above us and veers sharply down the right path. Odin doesn't hesitate to follow the large black flapping bird who doesn't seem to have any trouble flying in the elements. This is how I assume Du'ur is leading us to Eleazar.

I keep my senses open as we continue onwards, bounding over fallen branches and rock debris. The others have no trouble following behind us. The path begins to ascend, leading us deeper through two large towering mountains. I look up at their sharp peaks which sit close to the heavy, black and grey churning clouds.

Dread fills my stomach as Odin slows our rabbit down, the crow caws once as it lands; beak tapping at the ground. Our rabbit hops along nervously as the crow walks beside us, the narrow path opens up until we're on a large rock face. A blood trail catches my attention and I hastily slide from the rabbit, ignoring Odin's angry command.

I run alongside the blood trail with the crow now flying low beside me. I can't hear anything over the deafening rain as it beats down on the hard rock, I round the corner of the rock face to find the rabbit Eleazar had taken in a bloody heap. My throat closes up as I look over the disembowelled rabbit, I look to my right to see the large three serpents surrounding the crevice; they hadn't noticed me yet.

I steel my stomach against the stench of blood and hurry to hide behind the rabbit, I gesture Odin and the others over as they emerge from the same path. They rush over and we all crouch down, looking over the rabbit's side to survey the area.

We're on the edge of a cliff, a few metres ahead of the crevice the stone drops off; no doubt leading down to a fast and sudden death. The crow lands on top of the rabbit, looking down at me with those galaxy eyes Du'ur had.

"We need a distraction so two others can go and get Eleazar," Odin whispers. Hemlock nods in agreeance.

"Helena and I will retrieve Eleazar," Father says, looking to her. She nods before turning back towards the serpents, the agony on her face makes my heart twist painfully in my chest. She still loves him, regardless of what he says or feels for her.

"Amaryllis, you will stay here. You will not defy me on this," Father says sternly, turning those violet eyes onto me. I open my mouth to protest. "No. You can't fight and you have no magic, you're safest here. You can lead us back to the rabbits once we have Eleazar."

"Hemlock and Odin, do you think you can distract them long enough to get them away from the crack?" Father asks. Hemlock grins, cracking his knuckles.

"Sure can, this will be fun."

Odin nods once, looking to me with a question in his eyes, one he's unable to ask. Deep down I know he's wondering if I will use my fallen magic to get us out of this situation, but we both know I won't be able to reveal myself just yet. Not with Eleazar's life on the line.

"Let's go." Hemlock unsheathes his two daggers and leaps out from behind the rabbit, Odin untethers his long sword before following close behind. We all hide as their shouts of distraction are drowned out by the rain.

I wipe the droplets from my face as I steady my breathing, focusing on a small crack in the rock. I look up in time to see Odin sprinting past us, a large serpent snapping at his heels. Hemlock howls as he brings down his two daggers, slicing through the tail of the serpent after Odin.

A moment later a second serpent appears and sends Hemlock flying past Odin, hissing in fury as it curls in on itself. I look over my shoulder to find my father and Helena gone, I look up to see Du'ur in crow form, watching me.

"You know I'm not just going to sit here and watch, don't you?" I sigh, sitting up to see where the third serpent had gotten off too. I can't see anything, I scan the mountains around us to find it gone. Helena is lowering herself into the crevice with my father standing guard. I stand, pulling out the small knife I had stashed in my boot. Du'ur lands on my shoulder, her sharp claws digging into the soft flesh.

"I hope you have a plan," I tell her, turning to see Hemlock and Odin battling the two serpents. I gather my courage as I charge towards the closest one, a battle cry rattling from my throat as I throw myself at its large body; my small knife embeds through two large scales as slick red blood begins to spill freely. Du'ur screams as she flies at the serpents face, her crow form doubles until she's as large as a horse; clawing at the serpents eyes.

It swings its large, slick body around. I keep a strong hold on the handle of my knife, eventually it comes free as I fall to the ground. I roll to my feet, standing in front of Hemlock and Odin.

"I'm glad she's on our side," Hemlock whistles.

Du'ur shoots into the sky and the serpent I'd injured swivels its large head towards me as it forks out its black tongue. Blood streams from the gashes Du'ur has made on its face, blinding it in one eye. I search for Du'ur, finding her hovering at the edge of the cliff. I frown before I'm pushed to the side, one of the serpents strikes us.

Hemlock's blades groans against the weight of the serpent as Odin stabs and jabs between the scales of it. I'm quick on my feet as I jump onto its back, I run along and leap into the air towards the other one; blade extended in my hand.

I land hard against the serpent's neck, driving my blade in deeply. It tries to snap its large jaws at me, hundreds of razor sharp teeth glimmer. I swing my legs around its body, I look over my shoulder to see Du'ur still hovering at the cliff side. She caws out to me, flapping her wings with urgency. I pull my dagger from the flesh and slide down the serpent's back, rolling off its body and jumping onto my feet.

"Hey! You want an easy meal? I'm all yours!" I scream at the two serpents who had circled Odin and Hemlock. Their large heads swivel towards me, blinking in unison. Hemlock and Odin yell out in protest as they begin to rush towards me. I turn to see Eleazar clasped between my father and Helena's arms. They're almost at the dead rabbit, all heads turn towards me as I launch into a run.

I meet those golden eyes once before turning towards

Du'ur. She swoops down before flying up into the sky. As my feet pound against the stone I know what she's asking of me.

I look over my shoulder once more to find both serpents almost upon me, too focused on their next meal to realise we're all about to leap from the cliff side. I face forward and push myself, I swallow my fear as I reach the end of the cliff and push off against it with all my strength.

My stomach flies into my throat as I begin to plummet, the jagged rocks rise with quick succession. I scream as I fall, turning to see the two large serpents flailing in the air above me. I squeeze my eyes shut, ready to accept what is about to happen.

To my amazement and shock I land with a huff on a large, rain drenched feathered back. I roll onto my belly and hold onto the black feathers for dear life. Du'ur lets out a cry of glee as she banks sideways, away from the serpents plummeting to their certain death. As the shocks wears off I begin to laugh and cry, throwing my fist into the air against the storm. A silent show of defiance against the violent rain. Du'ur circles upwards, beating her large wings as we reach the edge of the cliff face. The others are surrounded by the last serpent who has its large body circled around them and the large dead rabbit.

It's larger than the other two, its eyes more calculating and full of intelligence. Du'ur lands, allowing me to climb down. I look to the others, having no idea what I'm supposed to do. The rain hasn't lessened and it's freezing, the cold soaking through my bones. Hemlock and Odin have their blades raised, Eleazar is still pressed between Helena and my father.

"They need a distraction," I murmur, looking up into the goddess's eyes. Her large head nods once before her form begins to grow small until she's the size of a small house cat. She flaps up and lands on my shoulder.

"Together. We'll distract it together," I nod to her as I pull out my dagger and ready it in my hands. I'm a good distraction for others, I've never been much better than that. I let out the loudest, most curdling scream I can. All heads turn towards me as I hurtle towards the large beast's body that's closest to me. Eleazar is screaming out, his eyes wild and frantic.

I throw my weight at the creature, stabbing furiously in between its scales. It screeches as its body unfurls from around the group, swinging me with it. Du'ur flies from my shoulder and begins to attack at the creatures eyes.

I hope that gods can't die.

I'm thrown from the serpent, landing hard and rolling against the stones. My blade flies from my hands as I groan, my wrist throbs painfully as I pull it to my chest. I manage to sit up, finding the serpent towering over me with Du'ur flying around its head.

I scramble to my feet and begin to run, heading up the face of the rock. I grab at the rocks as my feet threaten to slip and slide underneath me. I glance over my shoulder to find the snake giving chase, catching me faster than I had anticipated.

Hemlock and Odin have their weapons ready, a golden tether blazes from one side of the mountain to the other; a cord of metal of sorts that sections the serpent and I from the others. I slip, falling hard to the ground and begin to slide towards the serpent. I try to find anything to anchor myself to but the rain does nothing to help me.

I crash into the serpent, the breath leaves me as it begins to wrap its large body around me as we both slide down the slope of the rock face. I begin to scream as my body is squeezed painfully, my bones threaten to break under the pressure as my insides feel like they're turning to liquid.

My screams are cut off as my lungs contract, burning from the lack of oxygen, I look up to see the gaping jaws of the serpent lowering over me. Its razor sharp teeth gleam as its jaw unhinges, opening its mouth even wider to swallow me whole.

The flaming metal wire cuts clean through the serpents neck, beheading it. Red blood sprays from the open wound as the serpent unwinds from around me as it spasms. I gasp and choke for air, curling into a ball as I cough violently. Warm hands pull me into a warm body while another set of hands rub my back up and down.

"You're safe now you foolish girl," Odin murmurs, holding me to him.

"You were the distraction we needed, thank you for that," Hemlock says, rubbing my back. I cough and splutter, drawing in sweet lungful of glorious air. I have never been more grateful for air. Odin picks me up and cradles me against his chest. I raise my head to see the flaming metal go out and drop, the vine now shrivels up and dies.

"Magic," Hemlock shouts, winking at me as we head towards the path we'd entered on. Du'ur flies in the sky above us, swooping down every few moments to check on me. It's sweet, the gesture from a goddess.

A sad reminder I'm not one to carry her magic.

"You did good Ama, damn good," Odin says, looking down at me, his brown eyes full of respect and pride. I smile weakly at him, resting my head against his chest. Hemlock grins over his shoulder, winking.

"I couldn't sit there and do nothing."

"Thank god you didn't listen to your father, we'd be serpent dinner by now if you did." Hemlock chuckles, shaking his head. I smile and look forward, finding Eleazar on one of the rabbits with Helena behind him. Father rushes over to us, Odin lowers me to the ground as father crushes me to him. I moan in protest, my body aching from almost becoming a meal.

"My wrist hurts," I murmur. Father lets me go, only to take my hand in both of his. My wrist has turned a nice yellow brown.

"I think you've fractured it. It should heal over the next few hours." He kisses me on the forehead, gently holding me to him, "God, I want to yell at you for being reckless but I am so proud of you, Ama. So proud of you," he murmurs, looking down at me with shining eyes. I smile up at him, my energy waning.

"Let's go back to the cave," I say, looking over his shoulder to find Helena and Eleazar already bounding towards to path that takes us to the cave. I ride with father as we weave down the winding paths, I keep my eyes peeled as we ride through the rain and towards the cave. Eleazar is okay, he's going to be okay. We'd saved him.

As we reach the cave I slide from the rabbit, cradling my wrist to my chest as I rush in through the open tree branch. I find Eleazar lying down by a roaring fire, his shirt has been cut from his chest to expose multiple gashes. Helena kneels beside him, gently tending to his wounds.

Jealously cuts through me but the relief to see him alive and here with us overpowers it. He looks upwards, wincing as the movement moves his chest. Helena snaps at him to stay still, but he's not listening. His eyes are on me. I slowly walk over, the others come in with the rabbits and the tree is pulled once more against the cave opening. The enclosed space begins to fill with warmth.

I stop near Eleazar's head and sit down, gently resting his head in my lap. I cradle his face with both hands, ignoring the pain in my wrist as I begin to cry. My tears hit his cheeks and lips as I sob, my wet hair hangs around us.

"You never, ever make yourself a distraction again," he scolds; his voice rough. I laugh lightly through the tears and lean back, his golden eyes swirl with pain even though he manages a small smile that turns into a grimace as Helena begins to stich the deeper cuts closed.

"I'd do it all over again if it meant having you here to reprimand me over it," I say, my bottom lip quivers again.

"I never want to hear you say that again," he groans, eyes fluttering shut. I lean down and press a kiss to the tip of his nose, he extends his neck and claims my mouth with his own. His warm lips are gentle, tasting purely of him. I intertwine my tongue with his own before I pull back.

"You never, ever run off and try and to be the hero again," I say. "I need you too much for you to throw your life around so recklessly."

"I only did it so you and the others would be safe," he grunts, moaning in pain. I gently caress his cheek with my fingers, grinding my teeth against the pain in my wrist.

"You are so stubborn," I sniffle, shaking my head.

"It's what you love the most about me." His eyes search my own, a million words hang in the air between us but are not said. My heart bleeds with warmth in my chest, knowing wherever he is, I will be home. Where he goes, I will go.

"I'm only agreeing because you've been hurt," I murmur, looking up to watch as Helena continues to work silently on his cuts. "Thank you, for getting him out and tending to his wounds. I could not have done that."

She glares up at me before nodding once and continuing her work. I kiss Eleazar once more lightly before looking into the fire, I sit in silence as I continue to touch his face and run my fingers through his hair. I eventually end up resting my right, sore wrist against his shoulder when the pain becomes too much.

Odin watches me from the other side of the fire, pity is etched on his every feature. I smile sadly at him, nodding once.

My happiness may only be temporary and fleeting, but I am going to savour every moment of it. Eleazar reaches up and intertwines our fingers, drawing my attention back to him. Helena has finished cleaning his wounds and bandaging them. I help him sit up, watching as his back muscles ripple in the fire light.

I ignore the pulse between my thighs as I stand and grab his bag, pulling one of his shirts out. It's still wet, but being near the fire will help it dry faster. I gently help him pull it on. We wriggle backwards until the fire is a comfortable distance away, he props his bag and my own as pillows as he lies back down.

"Lay with me?" he asks, holding onto one of my hands as I kneel there.

"Of course," I whisper. I lie on my side, my back facing the outer cave. I made sure Eleazar was the one closest to the fire, I don't need its warmth as much as he does right now. I gently rest my head on his chest as I cuddle into his side, his arm wraps around my back and his large hand rests on my waist. I intertwine my free hand with his, looking up to meet his stare.

"I was so afraid I'd lost you when you leapt from that cliff," he whispers, rubbing his thumb against the back of my hand.

"You'll have to try harder to get rid of me," I say weakly. He shakes his head lightly.

"Nothing could ever make me want to get rid of you. I hope you know that it's going to be you and I now until our immortal days are over." He leans down and presses a kiss to my forehead before settling back.

"I couldn't ask for a better tomorrow," I whisper, blinking away the hot tears that are gathering in my eyes.

"Get some sleep my beautiful, brave and daring flower. I'm here now, it's okay. I love you Am," He murmurs, voice thickening with sleep. I let my eyes drift close as I breathe him in, warm and safe in his arms. The distant hounding storm only works in sleep's favour as I begin to sink into the darkness.

"I love you Eleazar, no matter what happens I will always love you." I murmur, letting sleep drag me into unconsciousness.

CHAPTER
25

W e emerge from the hidden cave to find the sky clear and blue, the only sign of the storm from the night before is the build-up of debris and the large puddles of water that litter the rock path. I ride with Odin on his rabbit, with one rabbit deceased and Eleazar injured he'd been tasked to ride with Hemlock. I'd overheard snippets of an argument between Eleazar and Helena when we'd been arranging riding partners.

She'd wanted him to ride with her while he wanted to ride with me and someone else double. Obviously that wasn't going to happen, even I wasn't that naive to think we'd have our own rabbit. He's still recovering and I had no control of the large beasts. I'd chosen to ride with Odin because I need to talk to him about what is to come.

I feel Eleazar's burning gaze on the side of my face as he mounts the rabbit with Hemlock's help. I look over and raise an eyebrow at him, he scowls and looks away. I grin before looking forward once more. Odin is more than a respectful riding partner, although his chest is pressing against my back his hands are resting on the fur of the rabbit in front of my legs. We're not touching unless necessary.

Father takes the lead with Hemlock and Eleazar following behind him. We're heading back into the mountains, taking the opposite path to the day before that will lead us through and out. Helena pauses beside us, looking to Odin.

"Why aren't you going?" she asks, refusing to look at me. He tenses behind me as he looks over at her. I recall their conversation from a few days earlier, she suspects me to be a fallen and had tried to convince Odin. Now that he knows I am, I'm afraid she might manage to get it out of him, it's clear she's still suspicious.

"I told Nyx that we'd take up the rear and follow." He gestures for her to move forward. She narrows her eyes at me before she bounds ahead, once she's out of hearing distance Odin relaxes. I sigh, shaking my head.

"I know that she suspects me to be fallen, I sort of overheard your conversation with her when we camped at the forest," I say weakly as we begin to bound forward, following the others.

"Mmm. I doubt she's going to do anything to expose you as she has no hard proof you're a fallen magic wielder, but she is more than determined to find some. That morning wasn't the first time she'd tried to convince me of it as well."

"I mean, she's right. More than right, she has good reason to be on her guard." I can't blame her, even though I wished she'd just let the matter rest. She's going to find out soon enough who and what I am.

"What's your plan?"

"I haven't really thought of it, I just assumed once we reached the creature I'd tell everyone to stand back and I'd just reach in and pull my magic forward and try and entice the fallen magic out of the creature. That's if it does have fallen magic corrupting it, if not I guess I won't be able to do anything and everyone will know what I truly am." I look over my shoulder at him, the wind whips at my hair that's pulled back into a low tight bun, "I won't harbour ill feelings towards you if you tell them what I am. I know...I know my people are bound to fall to darkness."

He looks down at me, brows creasing downwards, "Do you honestly think I'm going to tell them that you have fallen magic? After everything you've done?"

"Why wouldn't you? From everything I've been told, the fallen end up rotting and turning evil. I don't want that to happen to me and I know Eleazar is oath bound. I...I don't want to die but I'm afraid I have no choice in the matter and have come to accept it. Salis has come to me and taken claim of my soul, a claim I can't fight him against." I look forward, unable to meet his eyes.

"You've had two gods come to you, do you know how rare that is?" he murmurs in my ear.

"Rare, I'm assuming. You forget one of them is the god of death."

"*You* forget one of them is the goddess of life and she has taken a liking towards you. You were ready to sacrifice yourself yesterday to save us. You didn't hesitate to throw yourself off the cliff if it meant two of the serpents would perish with you."

"I told you I would do anything to save Eleazar, I'd do anything to help protect you all as well. I've grown to like you all, except for Helena, but I have good reason not to," I grumble. He chuckles against me, the rumble moves through his chest and into my own.

"I don't have any comment. Not many others like Helena, she's just who she is. I grew up with her so I know she isn't the hardened shell everyone else sees. She doesn't like you and I know it's only due to Eleazar being smitten with you."

"Yes well I can't help that. I didn't expect it either." I sigh and lean back into his chest, resting my head on his shoulder. I can see the others now riding ahead of us, Helena shoots us a look over her shoulder. "Where are we heading anyway?"

"We're in the mountains but just before we head to the caves where the creature is being kept we'll be stopping at a small village that resides half way. It's a bit of a journey to reach the caves as we wanted the creatures to be secure and away from hurting anyone else."

"What's the village like?" I ask, excitement sparking deep in my chest at the thought of exploring even more. I love the adventure. I love going to new villages and meeting new folk and seeing more. I love to travel, a new trait I've learnt about myself, among others.

Once I started this journey, I've found myself finding reasons to *like* who I am and who I'm becoming. Before, I was so sad and felt like I had no real purpose and I hated myself for it. Now I have purpose and that hate has wilted away to a small kernel.

"It's nice. The fae folk there are lovely. A little weird...but they show us respect and house us." We're almost behind Helena now, anything we say in a few moments will be for the taking if the others decide to listen. Which Eleazar will no doubt be doing, it's probably eating at him to know we've been talking and he can't hear what we're saying.

"Odin...thank you for listening to me and keeping my secret safe. I know it wouldn't be easy for you with the history my kind have. I am truly grateful, it's been a relief to talk to someone about it and confide in someone," I whisper, looking over my shoulder to meet his deep, murky chestnut eyes. He smiles down at me, shaking his head slightly.

"Your secret is safe with me Amaryllis, it's been an honour

to become a friend of yours. I wish...I wish I could change your outcome once Eleazar truly finds out. The oath will hold him in its grip tightly until your magic is erased from this earth." His eyes sadden, the emotion so strong in his gaze it makes my own eyes being to sting.

"Until then, I'm going to make the most of every moment. I'm not afraid to die anymore." I smile sadly, patting his leg. "It'll be okay. Don't be sad for me."

"It is far easier said than done."

"What's easier said than done?" Eleazar shouts, looking over Hemlock's shoulder towards us. I wipe at my cheeks and smile, meeting his golden blazing eyes. My chest tightens with warmth.

"Making you behave," Odin shouts back, warmth in his voice. Eleazar scowls, causing Hemlock to curse at him until he faces forwards once more. Helena glances towards us as we reach her side, her eyes narrow before she looks away.

We've reached a gulley in between the mountains, the path is four horses wide and small purple flowers and bright green weeds sprout from the cracks in the rock underneath us. I tip my head back, my eyes trail the large peaks of the mountains. I spot a serpent curled around one of the peaks, its large eyes watch us.

"Odin—" I begin to panic, pointing towards where it surveys us.

"It's fine. They're the guardians of the mountains, they only attack us when the godawful storm covers everything. Whatever is in the air with the storm, it gets into their heads and causes them to act out."

"Were you not listening when they explained it in the cave?" Helena asks pointedly. I look at her.

"Sorry, I was worried about Eleazar and not exactly focusing on anything else," I snap, tensing against Odin.

She scoffs, "Don't act like you're the only one who gives a shit about him."

I don't say anything else, my heart thunders in my chest and I'm still annoyed at her comment. If I wanted her opinion on *anything* I'd simply ask her. I don't understand why she has to go out of her way almost every time to make me feel stupid. It's infuriating.

Darkness churns low in my stomach; its eyes flutter open at the call of my annoyance and silent seething rage against the female that rides beside us. It begins to rise to a call I didn't know I was emitting, ready to do anything for its master.

"Amaryllis you must calm down *now*," Odin hisses, so close that his lips are pressed against the skin of my ear. I startle, looking at him. I hadn't realised. Panic sets in as I scramble to hide my magic once more, begging for it to return to its slumbering state.

I doubt sacred magic is like a wild beast inside of the others, one that has to be tamed and called upon. In my mind sacred magic is simply a part of who you are as a person, as if it is an extra limb. Fallen magic is like having a rabid wolf inside of you, trying to tame it with small treats which happen to be other magical creature's souls.

"I'm sorry I let my emotions get the best of me," I murmur, taking deep breaths in through my nose and out my mouth. The repetition helps calm my anger and tames the darkness, letting it return to a fitful slumber once more. When we reach the caves of Covnos I'm afraid I won't have much say in how it will act.

"I could sense *that*," he whispers before pulling his head away from my ear. I look up to see Eleazar watching us.

I mouth, *not what it looks like. Helena is being a bitch.*

His lips twist in discomfort before he mouths, *I'll talk to her.*

I don't know if that's going to help the situation I'm in but

I'm afraid I have no choice in the matter. I spend the rest of the small journey in silence, not wanting to risk my magic rising, no matter how small the chance might be. Helena is becoming a trigger for me, a trigger I can't stop.

The rock path dips down, opening up to a deep gulley like the one Elderview resides in. Small, weather worn cottages and stables are scattered throughout the gulley with wild thorn bushes growing along the edges against the rock wall; some even have deep red roses blooming.

Through the middle of the village is a wide sandy path, tall trees grow throughout the village and offer the only shade from the harrowing sun. I look past the village and spy a large lake, light reflects off the ripples in the dark blue water.

Our rabbits come to a stop once we finish hopping down the stone decent. A grey skinned fae emerges from one of the stables to our right, their deep moss green hair hangs limply around their narrow face as their white eyes assess us.

Others emerge, all of them having the grey skin in differing shades. They blend in with the deep grey of the stone mountain around us, which must be how they survive so well in the middle of the mountains. Each of them wear simple garments of clothing, covering the necessary parts of their body in deep brown material.

"Your majesty," the male that first emerges bends deep at his waist, the others who have emerged followed suit. My father climbs down from his rabbit and approaches the man, extending a hand for him.

"It's nice to return Maruki," Father says, clasping his hand before shaking twice. Maruki smiles, exposing sharpened teeth.

"You've always been good company. How long until you set off again?"

"We leave tomorrow morning. It should only take us a day

to reach Covnos if we continue to keep up the pace we're currently travelling at."

I lean into Odin, tilting my face towards his, "Do all of them have sharpened teeth?" I whisper, keeping my eyes on Maruki. His eyes snap towards me and I freeze, feeling utterly exposed under his gaze.

"You—"

Father interjects, "This is my daughter, Amaryllis. Heir to the throne. She has never ventured to Faerie before, I apologise for her manners. She's unused to seeing other fae."

I slide down from our rabbit, legs feeling weak as I approach Father and Maruki with as much courage I can muster. I pause just shy of Father and bow my head, clasping my hands behind my back.

"I am Amaryllis, it's lovely to meet you. I do apologise for my absurd comment." I straighten and meet his eyes. He raises a white brow and tilts his head to the side as he studies me. I stay still under his gaze as he makes his assumptions about me.

"I am Maruki, leader of the tribe Stoneweather. I forgive your comment but to answer it, yes. We all have sharpened teeth." He grins, exposing each sharpened edge. "It makes hunting extremely easy."

I hide my shock with an easy smile, "I could imagine you wouldn't have the need for cutlery either."

He laughs deeply, shaking his head. He's rather handsome when he laughs, the sharpened teeth add to his character. I hear the others dismount the rabbits and approach, I feel a strong presence surround me. I hide my smile with my hand as I pretend to scratch my cheek, knowing exactly who stands behind me.

Four of the tribe fae move around us and halter the rabbits, leading them to the stable Maruki emerged from when we first arrived. I watch as they leave, the rabbits would no doubt be relieved to be out of the sun and able to rest.

"Come, you all must be parched." Maruki makes a gesture with his hand before turning on his heel and striding down the open sandy pathway. The large towering trees shade most of the path, the coolness in each shadow is more than welcomed. My back is slick with sweat from being pressed against Odin's chest.

"What were you and Odin speaking of?" Eleazar asks, limping slightly beside me. I keep my pace beside him slow, allowing him to walk without needing to rush. Father now walks with Maruki and they converse in hushed tones, Odin, Hemlock and Helena walk ahead of Eleazar and I.

"We'd been talking about the serpents in the mountains and he'd been explaining how they're docile when the storm isn't present. Helena interrupted us with a snarky comment." I look straight ahead, not wanting to meet his eyes. I'm being deceptive, but to keep him safe I have to be for now.

"I'll have to speak with her again." He sighs, "I spoke with her at the manor about what we were becoming but she's certain on the idea that you'll betray me. I can't make her like you, but I can make it known I won't handle her disrespect towards you."

"You don't need to swoop in and save me from every bump in the road. I'm capable of taking care of myself. She's just a small thorn in my side, nothing I can't handle," I point out. More tribe members emerge from their cottages covered in plant life. All of them watch us with curiosity, I even spy a few children running about. We'd walked through nearly half the village, ahead of us a large circular wooden home comes into view with a thatched roof. Far larger than any other building in the village. This must be the leader's private quarters.

"I know you're more than capable of taking care of yourself, Amaryllis. You've proven that to me time and time again. It doesn't stop *me* from wanting to protect you though and it won't. If I can help lessen a burden on you I will do it in a heartbeat. Are you saying you wouldn't do the same for me?"

I look up at him and gasp, "Of course I'd do the same!"

"Exactly, try to understand where I'm coming from and why I want to help protect you. I'm not doing it to undermine you or get under your skin." His eyes soften as he laces his fingers through mine. I squeeze his hand gently in apology before looking forward. We'd come to a stop in front of the leader's home.

"You're all more than welcome to stay under my roof," he calls from where he stands on one of the wooden steps that leads up to a balcony which runs around the entire building. "There will be beds, food, water and the comfort of safety. You may explore the village as long as each of you are respectful to our people and land."

"Of course. We truly appreciate your hospitality," Father says, bowing his head. Maruki smiles and walks up the rest of the stairs and opens a twig door held together by green vines. We all follow him up, I help Eleazar with the stairs before shutting the door behind us as we enter. Immediately the air cools drastically, a relief to my reddening skin.

I look around in awe, the large open area is sectioned off with large green leaves that span half the size of a horse. Animal skins are draped across the open floors, ranging from white and black striped furs to deep browns. A large black metal cauldron adorns the middle of the room, cushions of mismatched colours are set up around it.

"The bedrooms are to your left, take your pick. We will have dinner here tonight. You're welcome to bathe in the lake whenever you feel. Please, enjoy." Maruki walks over to the cauldron and takes a seat on one of the deep maroon cushions knitted with bright yellow. I walk to the first section of leaves, pulling them back to reveal small hammocks made of vines and leaves. Eleazar grunts as he looks over my shoulder.

"Looks like we won't be sharing a bed tonight." I walk in and dump my bag on the ground beside my hammock. I look over at Eleazar and place my hands on my hips.

"Why not?" he demands, frowning at me.

"You're injured and I'm not risking being in such a confined space for sleeping. I don't want to hurt you and make it worse."

"After tonight I'll be fully recovered, you're worrying for no reason." He begins to walk into my room, determination on his face. I gently but firmly press my hands to his chest, looking up at him with a small smile.

"Trust me, I don't like it either but it's only one night. Take the room beside me and if you need me you can just call for me and I'll be there." He opens his mouth to protest so I jump in, "How about we bathe together later on?"

His golden eyes spark with desire, remembering how the last bath we took together went. I feel my cheeks begin to heat. "Are you sure that's a wise idea?" he smirks, taking a step closer to me.

My breath hitches as I look up into his eyes, "No but when have I ever been one for wise ideas?"

"There's my girl." He captures his lips with my own, his mouth is warm and attentive. I wrap my arms around his neck and stand on the tips of my toes, letting his tongue explore my mouth as deeply as he desires.

His large hands grab my lower back, the tips of his fingers dig into the curve of flesh at my waist causing heat to spread between my thighs. I could stay in this moment forever, indulging on the man before me. Giving him everything he's willing to take from me, it's intoxicating.

He nips at my bottom lip before trailing kisses along my

jaw and down my throat. He nuzzles my erratic pulse before running the tips of his canines over it. My mind goes blank at the spike of pleasure that erupts in each cell I possess.

I whimper in protest as he pulls back, his lips wet and eyes heavy with lust. He blinks through the haze, although my body is still plastered against his hardening one. It only entices me more as I wiggle my hips against him.

"Petal, if you keep that up *I will be taking* you here where everyone will hear your moans for me," he growls. His rough voice causes goose bumps to pebble my skin. I shiver in anticipation, liking the sounds of the idea...until I realise my father would be one of those hearing my moans. It sobers me up slightly.

"Fine, but you won't be getting away from me that easily later," I grumble, rubbing my thumbs against the back of his neck. He shakes his head and smirks, eyes full of light.

"Who said I would be getting away from you?" He kisses the tip of my nose and breathes me in. I rest my head on his chest, feeling his heart beating wildly against my cheek. I hold myself tightly to him, not wanting to let him go. He rubs a hand down my back as we stand there in a silent embrace.

"Am, I'm worried you're up to something," he murmurs into my hair. "I'm worried I won't be able to save you from whatever it is you're planning."

"Please don't concern yourself with my silly plans. I told you I would tell you what's bothering me after we've left the mountains and I will." I blink the hot tears away, not wanting him to see me cry. He'd be more than worried if I were to burst into tears. He sighs against me.

"I wish you could trust me. I promise to work harder for your trust." He kisses the top of my head, before gently rocking me side to side against him. *It's not you, it's me.* The words I can't speak. I can't assure him that it's not his fault. That I do trust him, but I am the problem. His words and the soft gesture break my heart even more, if this is how my heart is feeling – how will his heart feel when I finally reveal I am not the bright red rose everyone adores. I am the sharpened thorn hiding underneath the petals.

CHAPTER 26

I leave Maruki's residence against the protest of Eleazar, I'd demanded he stay and rest and that I would come to retrieve him once I'd finished exploring. He wasn't happy with the idea of me walking around a village I've never been to before by myself, but I assured him I'm a grown woman and can manage a small walk.

Sweat dribbles down my back as I walk along the large open sandy path, I observe the tribe people that continue with their duties. Most acknowledge me with genuine smiles that show their sharpened teeth, the small minority ignore me all together which doesn't bother me in the slightest.

I walk back towards the descent we'd arrived from, looking up towards the path that continues to climb before disappearing from view. I look over to the small wooden stables, watching as the large rabbits nibble happily at a large pile of golden straw.

"Hi," a small voice squeaks from behind me. I turn and look down to find a child no more than seven standing there. Her blue orb eyes shine as she looks up at me, a soft pink blush stains her grey cheeks as she twists her hands in front of her.

"Hi there, I'm Amaryllis. What's your name?" I crouch down, bringing myself to her level. Her white hair has been braided down the middle of her head, swinging down to her waist.

"I'm Anula. Daddy said that I shouldn't come near the guests but you're very pretty." She blushes again, looking down at the sand in front of her. I chuckle softly, my heart warming at her compliment.

"Well Anula it's lovely to meet you. Your daddy means well but you have nothing to fear from me. You're very pretty yourself," I say as I smile.

"What's magic tricks can you do?" she asks, beaming up at me with excitement. My smile falters, I don't want to disappoint her, but if I tell her anything and she tells her dad I might find myself in a situation I can't get out of.

"Hmm how about you show me around the village first and I'll let you sit on one of our rabbits?" I rise from where I stand, rubbing my hands against the back of my pants. Her small mouth twists as she debates before finally nodding.

"Okay! Can I sit on the rabbit first? They're far closer." She peers around my legs, her braid falling over her shoulder. I relent.

"Fine, come on." I turn and we walk the short distance to the rabbits. One of them looks up from the hay, its large green eyes blink once before it continues to eat. I gently pat its side, letting it know what my intention will be.

"Alright, you stand here and I'll help you on." I gesture for her to stand in front of me. She reaches upwards as I grab her small waist and heave her into the air. Anula swings her leg over the rabbit's side and buries her hands into the fur. She beams down at me.

"It's so soft!" she exclaims, swinging her legs back and forth. I smile but stay close, just in case the rabbit gets a scare. It continues to eat, unphased by the small weight on its back.

"They're great for travelling, very soft. I miss my horse though," I say, patting the large creature's side.

"What are horses like?"

"They're as big as these rabbits, but they've got four long legs that can run as fast as the wind. They come in all different colours and they're very friendly." She nods in thought, running a small hand through the deep brown fur.

"I've never left the village before," she admits, puffing out her bottom lip.

"I'm sure once you're old enough you'll be able to." I hear footsteps approaching us. I look over my shoulder as she looks up at the newcomer. A large male with an indifferent look on his face is approaching us. His broad chest ripples with muscle as his arms swing by his side. His blue orbed eyes are identical to Anula's.

Ah. This is her father.

"Hi daddy," she squeaks behind me. I brace myself as he comes to a stop in front of me, staring down.

"I told you not to talk to the guests," he grits out, eyes flashing as he looks over my shoulder at her.

"I just wanted to tell her she was pretty." She sulks.

His jaw tightens as he looks back at me, eyes sweeping me over "That doesn't mean you can just tell her."

"Why not?" she demands, voice rising. I have to hide the smile on my face, she's so alike her father it's uncanny. I turn around and look up at her.

"Ready to get down now?" I ask, my back itches as her father no doubt stares daggers at me. She nods and holds her hands out for me. I gently hold onto her as I pull her from the rabbit and place her on the ground. She pats the rabbit a few more times before skipping to her father's side.

"I've never seen you travel with this group before," the father says, drawing my attention back to him.

"This is my first time in Faerie actually," I admit, scratching at my arm "Nyx is my father, I'm sure you've met him."

"Yes, I've met him. The resemblance is striking." He crosses his arms over his chest.

"I've been told that a lot. I'm sorry for distracting your daughter, I was just exploring the village. Everything here is so new and intriguing for me."

He looks down at his daughter, lips twisting in thought before looking back towards me. "Would you like to come back to our residence for a cup of tea?"

"Oh please! Please Ama!" Anula squeals running forward and wrapping her small arms around my legs, I pat her head and smile softly up at her father.

"If it's no problem I'd love to."

"Come. It's a short walk to the other side." He gestures over his shoulder towards the opposite side of where we stand. I nod and fall into step beside him. As we walk, Anula skips in front of us, stopping every now and then to sniff the small purple flowers that blossom on the path.

"I'm Credin," her father says, breaking the silence between us.

"I'm Amaryllis. It's nice to meet you. Thank you for the invite." I glance up at him, surprised at his height. He'd have to be a warrior of some sort for the tribe, maybe a hunter? He seems far too aware to just be a general tribe person.

"My daughter's taking a liking to you. Just a word of warn-ing, my mother resides in my home." He looks at me, his eyes intense.

"Ah, okay. Is there something wrong with that?" I query, raising an eyebrow. He straightens and looks ahead, eyes focusing on his daughter.

"She's the village seer. I'm sure she'll want to speak with you, she loves enticing the newcomers into a reading."

I nod my head a few times, ignoring the warning that churns low in my stomach. A seer, like my mother. Will she be able to tell I'm of darkness? If she does, will she let the entire village know? I'm about to find out as we come to a stop outside of a hut. Anula moves the wooden door out of the way and smiles as she runs inside.

"After you." Credin moves to the side to let me through. I smile in thanks before walking inside. I weave between the herbs that hang from the ceiling, enjoying the overwhelming smells of herbs and spices. It smells like magic.

The hut is made of twig walls as I head towards Anula's voice. I turn into a small living room. Furs have been spread over the ground, while an elderly fae woman sits in the middle of the room. Her white fuzzy hair is pulled back from her face which is lined with years and years of living. Her light grey eyes look up as I enter the room, her frail hands still on the cup she holds as steam curls over the rim.

"Hello," I say, waving half-heartedly unsure of what I'm expected to do. Anula skips over to me and takes my hand, dragging me down to sit in front of her grandmother.

"How do you like your tea?" Credin asks, head popping in through the opening.

"Just black please." He nods before disappearing. Anula kisses her grandmother's sagging cheek before she runs out of the room to follow her father. I stay silent as I sit in front of the old woman, feeling on display like a piece of art.

"How did you find yourself in the situation you're in?" she clicks her tongue, shaking her head. Her long nose hangs slightly at the end. She's rather skinny and very ancient looking, as if a small breeze might just turn her to dust.

"Sorry ma'am I'm not sure what you mean?" My heart begins to race in my chest anyway, having a fair idea of what she might mean. She takes a sip of her tea.

"I've been around a very, very long time child. You haven't even skimmed the surface of the start of my life. I'm no fool. I was here for the magic divides."

"The magic divides?" I frown.

"Old. Sacred. Fallen. I was here for the separation of all three. You...you walk a very dangerous and dark path." She sits her cup down in front of her, my hands shake in my lap. This is it, she's going to tell Credin once he returns that I'm fallen and I'm going to be dragged outside and killed.

"Don't look so worried. The history books forgot to mention that there were a few faeries who could fight the fallen darkness from corrupting their heart." She reaches in between the folds of her cloak and retrieves a crystal ball with a black snake base holding the sphere.

"I-I'm not—"

"Aht. Don't lie to me girl, I'm too old for games. Your secret is safe with me." She sits the sphere between us, rubbing a hand over the top of it. I sit in silence, unsure of what to say.

"I've met many fallen who have been wonderful people and lived full lives. It is a shame that their soul is forsaken to the Underworld, nothing in life is fair. We live to die, and what we make of the in-between defines us." I look down at the crystal ball as the contents inside of it begin to churn and turn cloudy.

"I'm not evil," I whisper, knowing true to my heart that there isn't a seed of evil in me.

"I know. You have the heart of a sacred but the magic of a fallen. You're courageous and risk your life for those you love, even if it means receiving nothing in return. Your mother I've met, she's a strong woman and a seer like myself."

"Yes...I've always known mother is a seer but I've been sheltered my entire life from everything. This is my first time visiting Faerie. I had no idea about magic until a few months ago." I look up to see Credin enter, a steaming mug in his hand.

"Here. I hope it's fine to your liking. I'll leave you with mother." I take the cup from him gratefully; glad to have something in my hand.

"Thank you, I'm sure." He smiles before leaving the room, calling out for Anula. I take a sip of the tea and focus back on the woman. She smiles, her cheeks creasing.

"You do know why your mother made sure to keep you under her thumb, don't you?"

I lower my cup, "No."

"She's a seer my dear. She knew the magic you possessed far before you did."

The entire world around me goes still. Mother...*mother knew?* I try to think back to the conversations we shared before I'd journeyed here but come up empty handed. How could she keep something like this from me?

"She did it to protect you. We will do anything for our children, even if it means they hate us for it."

"I don't hate her," I protest, frown deepening.

"Of course you don't, but there are others out there that aren't so lucky for their child's love." She taps the crystal ball, "look into it and tell me what you see."

I lean closer, watching as the churning smoke begins to clear. I see a large open field for a split second, the image morphs into the flutter of red material before morphing into blue electricity streaking a dark sky. I watch as the image turns to black, so black it's as if it is alive.

"What do you see?" she asks gently. I swallow, mouth dry.

"I saw a field, red material, blue electricity and darkness."

"There is a deep betrayal coming, death and reincarnation. I can't say who or what but you're strong enough to answer the call that is being put out for you, the gods are watching." She grabs the crystal ball and tucks it back into the folds of her cloaks. She looks up at me, suddenly appearing to me as myself.

"Look at the strong woman you are, search deep in yourself and find the things you love about who you are. That make you worthy of being loved. Your inner strength is going to be needed on that field as darkness descends." She shivers and returns to her frail form, picking up her cup of tea once more.

"Death?" I'm breathless, my mind whirling.

"Yes. Death. You shouldn't be afraid of it."

"But someone...someone *dies!*" I exclaim, feeling my heart constrict. She reaches out and pats a soft hand to my cheek, a wave of calm washes over me.

"We all die one day dear, when it's our time the gods will call us home. Now go, you have a rather broody copper haired male waiting for your return." She leans back, taking my cup in her hand and pouring the contents into her own. I sit in shock for a few moments before getting to my feet.

"Thank you for your time and warning," I say, voice shaking. She nods and begins to hum, dismissing me. I leave the small hut, unable to find Anula or Credin anywhere. I rush out into the street and run through the streets for the residence where I'll find Eleazar. The sun has lowered in the sky, the air has cooled as night approaches.

I find Eleazar standing on the balcony watching the street in front of him as I emerge from bushes to the side. I sag in relief, he turns to the sound of my footsteps and relaxes. He has a bag in his hand. No doubt carrying both of our clothes.

"I began to think you'd run off."

I smirk at him as he walks down the steps, we walk around the residence and begin to head towards the large lake that sits in front of us. I lace my hand with his own, leaning my head on his shoulder. His limp is barely there now.

"You wouldn't let me run off," I scoff. He chuckles, squeezing my hand.

"You're right. I wouldn't. How was your adventure?"

"It was..." I refrain from telling him of my visit with the seer, not wanting to recount the events of what is to come. "It was good. I met a small girl and we chatted while I showed her the rabbits."

"Always attracting stragglers aren't you?" Eleazar jokes, kissing the top of my head.

"I'm a straggler to the people here," I laugh, cheeks heating. Other tribal fae walk back from the lake, their skin glistening with droplets of water against the dying light. They smile politely as we walk pass them.

"Where will we bathe?" I question, raking my eyes over the lake. To my left there's a cluster of a small forest around the edge. I point towards it, heart beginning to race at the reminder of what happened the last time we'd bathed together. I shiver in anticipation.

"Cold?" Eleazar questions, leading us towards the trees.

"I'm shivering for an entirely different reason and the weather has nothing to do with it." I look up to see his eyes ablaze, his tongue trails his bottom lip; causing all warmth in my body to pool between my thighs. I tug him along faster as we reach the trees, once we're out of range for prying eyes Eleazar grabs me and roughly pulls me to his hard chest. I melt against him as I readily meet each hungry kiss, I trail my hands through his hair as I rise on the tips of my toes.

He pulls back, panting with wet lips, "I want to take my time with you but I'm afraid I won't be able to resist."

"That's more than fine with me." I pull my shirt over my head, letting it fall somewhere to the ground around me. His eyes dip to my chest as he lets out a growl. The sound pebbles my skin with anticipation as he pulls his shirt over his head. He drops the bag of our things before he begins to unlace his pants.

We'd reached the side of the lake, wide trees protect us from the outside world. In this moment it's only him and I and the fire between us. I unlace my shoes and pull them off before removing my pants. I stand bare in front of him, chest heaving with the need for him.

A moment later he stands naked before me, more than eager to see me. He prowls towards me, I back up until my back presses against the rough bark of a wide tree. Eleazar traps me to the tree, I arch my back, rubbing my chest against his own as he grabs my hands and holds them above my head.

"You are mine." He growls, nipping at the peak of my left breast. I lose my breath.

"Say it." He nips at the other peak, causing my eyes to flutter shut. His body is warm and hard against my own, more than ready to join with me. I rock my hips against him, feeling that pleasure beginning to build.

"I'm yours," I manage to say, proud that I'm able to form a coherent sentence with the way his mouth is assaulting my breasts in the most enticing way. One of his hands trails down the length of my arm before tracing the underside of my right breast, he gently squeezes before trailing his hand down the curve of my hip and dipping between my thighs.

His lips claim my own as his fingers begin their soft, slow torturous assault. I move against his hand, trapping his hardening length between his stomach and the crevice of my thigh and his hand. He groans into my mouth as his fingers work faster, blindly dragging me to that edge.

I kiss him more viciously, claiming his lips as I run on nothing but urgency for release. He pulls his hand away, I whimper in protest—which turns into a moan of pleasure as he pushes into me. His hips move slowly against my own as I adjust to his size once more. He presses his chest against my own; trapping me to the tree. I wrap my arms around his neck as my legs wrap around his waist. My hair falls over my left shoulder as I suck at his neck.

"If you keep doing that I'm not going to last long." He pants, his hips begin to pulse into me faster. The friction between our joining bodies has me chasing my high.

"I'm close," I whimper, nails digging into his back as I lean my head back against the tree. His tongue intertwines with my own as his thrusts turn urgent and hard, pounding into me with enough force to shake the tree I'm pinned against.

My body explodes with euphoria as I throw my head back and gasp with pleasure, my toes curl as my body tightens around him. Eleazar groans his own release as his hips slam into mine and stutter. He rests his head on my shoulder as we pant, both enjoying the bliss while it lasts.

"Is it always going to be that amazing?" I sigh happily, running a hand through his hair. He holds me to him as he pulls us from the tree. Sweat coats his chest and my own, running down the sides of his forehead. The sun has almost thrown us into complete darkness now.

"I'm sure it can be even better." He chuckles as he walks us into the water, he slips out of me as he lowers me into the water. I sink into the water, enjoying the pleasant throb. He sinks down in front of me, gently cupping water and letting it flow between his fingers and over my chest.

"I might just explode if it is," I say, half serious. He grins before stealing a kiss from me.

"I'd explode right alongside you. You do wonders for my ego, flower."

I laugh, splashing him. He splashes me back until we're both splashing each other. I laugh as he swoops me into his arms. I gently hit his chest, careful not to hit anywhere that may hurt. He smiles down at me, kissing the tip of my nose before walking us out of the water.

We dry quickly and dress just as fast and grab our discarded clothes, the sun sinks and throws us into darkness. Eleazar takes our bag and my hand in his own as he leads us out of the small forest. I stay close to his side, admiring the view of the village lantern as we approach.

The walk is spent in comfortable silence, simply just enjoying the company of one another. My heart is little more than a puddle in my chest, the smallest gestures from him have me falling head over heels all over again. We enter the residence to find the cauldron boiling with dinner, the herby aroma causes my stomach to growl. The others sit around the cauldron, looking up as we enter. Eleazar dumps the bag into his room before coming back to my side. We sit between Odin and my father and are handed two brown bowls. I ignore Helena's glare.

"We're just discussing our plan of action," Odin says. I hear the underlying message to his words.

"Once we arrive at the caves we'll let the rabbits wander. We enter the cave and prepare for any form of attack that might come. Eleazar will be breaking away from the group and assessing whether it is corrupted with fallen magic," Father says softly beside me. Maruki begins to spoon the soup into our extended bowls. I fill my mouth with soup, stopping myself from protesting. Odin watches me warily, eyes flashing with warning.

"We'll do our best to extract the magic, but if it fails Eleazar will kill the creature. As the death is being performed we will be guarding him. When he comes back we'll have to use our magic to bind him to unconsciousness as we make the journey back to the manor." Father looks to me, eyes soft. I look down at my crossed legs, Eleazar rests a large scarred hand on my thigh and brushes his fingers back and forth.

"Once we return to the manor Ama and I will be returning to the human world, but you three will stay with him until his essence is restored. Is that clear?" Father asks, voice firm.

"You know the chance of his essence returning to normal is quiet slim. Are you all ready to wait to find out?" Maruki says calmly.

"We'd do anything for one another," Helena remarks, staring at him. He shrugs, twirling his spoon in his bowl.

"I'm just making sure you're all aware."

"Of course we are," she whispers, glancing towards Eleazar.

"Won't be the first time babysitting him anyway," Hemlock jokes. Odin chuckles. The mood is dampened, Maruki is right. The chance is very thin. It makes my determination to succeed even stronger.

"Oh please don't act like you do it often," Eleazar protests lightly, squeezing my thigh. I finish a few mouthfuls of soup before sitting the bowl down. I lean over to my father and press a kiss to his cheek.

"I'm going to get some sleep. I love you," I murmur. I need to be alone otherwise I'm going to ruin the careful plan I have in place. Father wraps one arm around my shoulder and kisses my forehead.

"I love you too Ama, get some sleep. Tomorrow is going to be a big day." He leans back, his violet eyes full of concern. I smile tight-lipped at him and nod before rising to my feet. Eleazar looks up, ready to stand and follow me. I lean down and press a kiss to his cheek, I rest my mouth against his ear. "I'm going to sleep. You've worn me out. I'll see you in the morning. I love you. So much."

"I love you too," he murmurs back, kissing my cheek. I run

a hand through his hair, my eyes meet Odin's and I nod slightly. He gives me a sad smile before turning back to his bowl of soup. I leave the conversation and slip into my room, my heart is heavy in my chest as I slide into my hammock and lie on my back.

Tomorrow my entire life is going to change, for the better or worse. I must be strong enough to face either outcome.

CHAPTER 27

I clasp my cloak around my throat. Once it's secured I tuck the white shirt Eleazar gave me into the waistband of my black pants, my hands flutter over my outfit as nerves take a hold of me. It's more than nerves, there's a low burning acidic taste crawling up the back of my throat each time I think of what I must do. A deep unsettling feeling has settled in my bones and although it feels wrong, I must go through with my plan.

I walk out of my small room, holding the straps of my backpack tightly. I find the others waiting with the silver haired leader at the back of his residence, our rabbits wait patiently for me as well. Maruki smiles with his sharp teeth as I approach, I smile through the dread that I can't ignore. He doesn't notice my internal struggle as I join them.

"It's been lovely having you all stay and keep good company. You're all more than welcome to return on the journey home and stay a night once more." He clasps my father's hand. Father smiles at him, his black raven hair curves around his pointed ears and compliments his high cheekbones. As I watch him I have to wonder...does he know I'm fallen? Surely mother wouldn't have kept it from him. If she has, has she doomed us both?

"Of course. I'm afraid the journey home will be fast and fleeting as it will be a matter of importance." Father steps back, glancing over at me with a strained smile. I notice the tension is palpable in everyone.

"Ah that's a shame but alas, safe travels and I wish you all the best success in your mission." Maruki shakes each of our hands, his warm hand lingers clasped with mine for a heartbeat too long as his white eyes study me. Eleazar clears his throat, a warning. Maruki winks before letting my hand go and stepping away.

"Odin, can I ride with you?" I ask, closing the distance between us. I tip my head back to look up at him, his nostrils flare slightly before he glances over to Eleazar. His deep brown hair curls in combed waves at the base of his throat.

"Come along then." He sighs, walking over to the rabbit we ride. I take a step to follow when a hand wraps around my arm. I look up to see Eleazar staring down at me, eyes searching.

"Why are you riding with him?" he asks, voice low.

"I must talk with him." I place my hand around his that is wrapped around my arm. My heart begins to thunder in my chest, this will be our last moment as *us*. After we mount our rabbits, we will be over. The thought is enough to bring tears to my eyes as my heart wrenches violently in my chest.

"I was hoping we'd ride together." He steps closer, his scent wraps itself around me. He smells of *us*.

"On the way home?" I offer, eyes pleading, "I just need to speak with him. I promise I'll tell you everything after. I'm not being unfaithful to you and I have no ill intentions with Odin. He's become a friend to me and I don't have that many to begin with. I love you Eleazar, more than anything in this entire universe. My heart will always, *always* be yours."

He frowns down at me, clasping my cheeks in both hands.

"You sound like you're saying goodbye. I'll come out of this Am, I will always come back to you."

I close the distance between our lips, kissing him with apologies I will never get a chance to tell him. A million *I love you's* that I will never get to say. I pull away and smile, biting my cheek to stop the tears from falling as I look into the depths of his golden fire eyes.

"I love you too Ama, it'll always be you for me." He kisses me briefly once more before letting go of my face, taking all the warmth and happiness and good with him. "I trust you."

"Come on, we need to leave!" Helena barks, breaking us from our trance. I blush before moving past Eleazar and rushing to Odin's side. He helps me mount the rabbit before sliding on behind me. I hold my bag to my chest as I try and slow my breathing, Odin's chest against my back is a comfort.

"Are you okay?" he whispers.

I nod once but keep my eyes trained on Eleazar as he mounts the rabbit with Helena, sliding in behind her. I have no room to be jealous anymore, she will be the one to pick up the pieces of him I am going to shatter.

"Let's go! Keep pace but call if you need a break. Covnos caves here we come!" Father calls before launching his rabbit into motion. He begins to bound around the large sparkling lake, the other rabbits take control and begin to hop after him.

I watch as the mountains around us begin to expand once more, opening up to overgrown green and deep golden grass fields. The stony grey mountain walls only seem to make the plant life more vibrant. Odin keeps us at the back of the group, Helena and Eleazar are the closest to us.

Mother had a vision while we'd been here and the seer I'd been to had shown me the crystal ball images that were extremely similar. The blue electricity, the battle field of souls.

Some sort of deep red material. Is there any hope in changing the fate of what's to come?

"What is the plan?" Odin whispers into my ear, keeping his head bent low. I gather the last scraps of my courage.

"Once we arrive and head to the infected creature...I'm going to reveal what I am and what I'm planning to do. I don't expect you to take my side. Actually I'd rather you didn't. It could put you in more danger."

He's silent for a moment, "Ama, I didn't come this far to throw you to the wolves. You're making a huge sacrifice, the least I can do is protect you while you make it."

"If I begin to change, let the oath take control of Eleazar and let him finish me." My hands tighten on my bag as my heart begins to race again, my palms sweat profusely.

"You know I'm going to do everything in my power to get you out of that cave once your plan is finished. I'm not just going to leave you for dead, you're no monster."

"But I am. I'm betraying everyone here and I would have betrayed you if the goddess hadn't said that I was fallen. I may not be a monster with fangs and glowing eyes, but I am just as deadly as one," I murmur, shaking my head. No matter what he tries to tell me I won't believe it. I know what I'm doing and I'm ready to face the consequences.

"You're very stubborn." He finally relents, sitting back. I sigh with relief, although I wish he wasn't a part of this plan I'm glad he is. I wouldn't be nearly as strong on my own, I'm not foolish enough to believe I'm invincible.

We stay in silence for the rest of the ride, I find my eyes trained on Eleazar the entire time. His shoulders are tense and he seems full of worry, I would almost even say anger. Helena continues to sneak glances at me, snarling if she catches me staring right back at her.

I wish I could tell her she's right, but I also wish I could shove my fist into her face.

"Look," Odin says, pointing towards the path ahead of us. The rabbits slow down as we reach a break in the mountains, to our right a large waterfall rages and flows. A thin layer of mist in the air clings to the strands of my hair and eyelashes, covering my face.

There's a large, fallen tree covering the gap between the two mountains; the path well-worn down over the many years of travellers crossing. My stomach bottoms out when I peer over the side of the rabbit as we slowly bound across one by one. The drop is so far down that there's a cloud of mist that covers the bottom.

Aside from the fear of falling to my death, I can appreciate the beauty that grows on the other side of the mountain path once we arrive safely on the solid ground. Bright purple and pink flowers bloom from green vines that have large black thorns. Moss has grown over the stone walls as we begin to wind down a path that's covered in undergrowth.

Ahead of us the path opens up, the debris path becomes soft grass as a large field takes my breath away. I lean into Odin, this is the same field I saw in the crystal ball. The mountains tower over the field as the sun breaks through the thickening clouds, lighting the grass up in green and golden hues.

In front of us is a large, towering cave opening that is larger than a house. A thick, flourishing forest grows around the cave sides, running down the side of the cave. I lose my breath as a large creature lumbers out of the forest, standing as tall as one of the trees. Its white fur flows like water in the breeze as its paws take slow steps. It looks towards us, its long white ears hang down around its head. Bright blue eyes blink slowly as our rabbits begin to come closer. It tilts its head to the side, a pink tongue falls from its mouth as it licks its muzzle.

"Is that..." I ask, unable to take my eyes from the beautiful creature.

"That's the bulburoos." Odin chuckles, admiration in his voice.

The bulburoos's large tail swishes around it, stirring the tree canopy. An air of innocence and light hangs in the air around the creature. It sniffs a few times, the whiskers on its noise twitching. Without another glance it turns and lumbers back into the forest, the trees creak and sway as it moves, before growing still once more.

"It's so beautiful." I say, eyes searching the shadows of the forest it has disappeared into.

"They are. Their cubs are even cuter." Odin steers our rabbit to the right until we're riding right for the dark, gaping mouth of the cave. Dread and fear hit me with the force of a horse, stealing my breath.

"That's where we're holding the infected one," Odin murmurs as we all come to a stop outside of the mouth. The others slide from their rabbits but I stay seated, stealing one more moment of normality. I reluctantly slide off and rearrange my backpack onto my back, I watch as Odin tucks his deep green shirt into the waistband of his dark brown pants; I catch sight of a deep red handkerchief for a second before it's gone.

"We all know the plan. Be ready. Eleazar, we will be right here with you," Father assures, coming to stand in front of him. They hug, patting the other on the back. Helena watches, her face guarded but eyes full of worry. Hemlock joins the hug, shaking his head.

"I've got your back," Odin whispers. We walk over to the others, Eleazar takes my hand and leads us up over the moss covered black stones of the cave. I keep my steps steady as I intertwine our fingers, I want this moment to pause so I can just admire him one last time.

The light is sucked from the cave, my eyes adjust the best they can as we continue to head deeper into the darkness. Moisture fills the air until it feels like a second skin, the black stones begin to smooth out until we're walking on even ground. A thin glow of light grows brighter as we draw closer, Eleazar stops me short and keeps me behind his back. I peer around his shoulder to find lanterns nailed into the smooth cave walls, illuminating the bulburoos who is trapped here.

My heart sinks as it swings its head towards the sudden noise, black eyes stare back at us. Its white fur is dull, its tail hangs on the stone floor as it watches us all filter into the space. The field keeping it contained glimmers with magic, holding strong now that we're all here.

"It looks terrible," I murmur, bottom lip wobbling. The bulburoos I'd seen moments ago was full of life and this...this poor thing couldn't meet death sooner. I step away from Eleazar and begin to walk towards the creature who now stares at me. I feel my magic stir in my chest. I stop and just stare at it. Odin comes up beside me, looking at the creature as well. I narrowly avoid the urge to vomit, sick with anxiety. I turn towards where the others stand, Odin unsheathes his sword and stands in a fighting stance. Hemlock, Eleazar and my father frown as Helena watches us; so many emotions flash across her face. Confusion, realisation and fury. She snarls, unclasping her own sword.

"What are you doing Odin? You both need to come over here," Father says, taking a step up to stand beside Eleazar. My heart is bleeding in my chest.

Breaking.

"I knew it," Helena states, her voice holding an air of promised death. *"Odin what the hell are you doing on her side?"*

"I have my reasons," he simply says.

"What's going on?" Eleazar demands, frown deepening as confusion and anger take hold of him.

Thunder echoes throughout the cave as a storm begins to take hold of the field outside. I take a steady breath even though tears stream down my cheeks. Now isn't the time to cry but I'm unable to stop them.

I hold my hands up, palms facing them as my delicate pale fingers begin to grow black until the darkness is bleeding down my arms and under my shirt, I keep my eyes on those golden ones as my magic comes forward "My name is Amaryllis and I am the last fallen to walk this earth."

CHAPTER 28

My heart completely dissolves in my chest as Eleazar seems to shut down. His golden eyes flare, almost glowing in the darkness of the cave as his jaw tightens. I feel the connection between us strain and snap, causing a fresh burst of tears to escape me. I can practically here his thoughts, *traitor.* Odin jumps in front of me, shoulders tense as I furiously wipe at my cheeks.

"I knew it! She's a fallen!" Helena yells in rage.

"Please, I can explain!" I press my hand to Odin's shoulder. He steps beside me but keeps his eyes and blade focused on Eleazar. I know the oath will take hold of him at any moment now, I am on time I do not have.

"I don't need an explanation. You're a monster. You're nothing but darkness and evil, all fallen are." Helena seethes, coming to stand beside Eleazar. Hemlock is pale, but makes no move to join the three in front of him. Father is watching me with sad eyes, tears streak his cheeks. Understanding flashes in his eyes.

"I'm not a monster." My voice is weak, afraid.

"I knew you were a fallen wielder from the night we all went to the feast. There was something wrong with the air around you and once I grew suspicious it was so obvious. You were in the forest hiding when I tried convincing Odin to look closer at you. I never had hard evidence or proof to bring to the others."

"Do you think I asked for this?" I yell at her, my pain contorting to anger. "Do you honestly believe I wanted to be born like *this?*"

"I don't think evil can have a say," she growls.

I look to my father and Hemlock, "I am so, so sorry. From the bottom of my heart I know that I have betrayed you. I had to hide what...what I am from all of you. It was for the better. I had one purpose of coming here and I knew the sacrifice I had to make."

"Ama..." Father trails off, eyes trailing down to my stained hands. I can feel the darkness now covering my throat, stopping just at my jaw. I must look like a monster to them. I shake my head, unable to face the words he might say.

I look to Eleazar and my lungs refuse to draw breath, silent tears streak down his hardened face as he watches me.

"Eleazar...there are no words that can undo the pain I've caused you. I am so sorry for betraying your trust and hiding this part of myself from you. I wish it didn't have to be this way. I knew from the start that we were running on borrowed time, but I don't regret one second of it."

"You deceived me." His voice is low, sounding a million miles away from his body.

"Yes," I whisper, nodding slightly.

"I trusted you. I opened up to you and showed you my scars and my heart. I gave it to you freely and willingly and you didn't even have the decency to tell me you're fallen?" His eyes burn with hurt. My mouth is dry and my *soul* shrieks in pain.

"How could I?" I croak a sad laugh, "You are the hunter and I am the hunted. I couldn't tell you I was the one thing you were bound to kill. I couldn't show you my magic because you would have cut me down before I could try and do something good with it."

"Even now I fight the oath that binds me to killing *you*." He snarls, taking a slight step forward. Odin points his sword at him in warning. "Even now while my heart shatters in my chest, I am fighting the only primal urge I currently have. To kill you."

"You can't fight it forever. I knew there would be consequences." I wrap my arms around my chest, the pain begins to leave and I fill with emptiness. It's even worse than the pain. Feeling nothing at all, it's more than painful. It's devastating.

"You betrayed me," he says again, as if not believing it. "You betrayed me."

Those three words break something in my soul, I bite my bottom lip until I taste blood. I look towards the cave floor as tears hang on my eyelashes. "I love you."

"*Don't you dare.*" He snarls, voice full of fury. I look up again. He stares at me with nothing but hurt and anger and indifference. "Everything you've said to me has been a lie. Everything we've done and shared has been nothing more than your plan all along. You used me."

"Everything I feel for you is real. Everything we share is real!" I exclaim. I begin to panic. He can't think that.

"Nothing between us is real. It never was. You're right, I am the hunter and *you* are the hunted." He raises his sword once more, the air around him threatens to explode like a bomb and leave everyone in ruins. "I have an oath to fulfil."

"I came here to try and retract the fallen magic from the creature. You told me only someone who wields fallen magic may remove it. I wanted to save the creature and save *you* Eleazar. The risk you're willing to take isn't worth it." I turn away from them. Odin covers my back as I study the creature.

It stands closer, its face is pressed against the invisible shield. I press a stained hand to the barrier.

"Once I retract the magic from the bulburoos I will allow you to honour your oath Eleazar, I won't fight you." Tears run down my throat and dampen my shirt, "I knew it would come to this. I wasn't a fool Eleazar. I never planned to fall in love with you."

"Ama—" Father begins to protest.

"Nyx, she is *fallen*. You know just how dangerous they are," Helena says, her voice as sharp as a blade.

"She is my *daughter* and she is not dangerous," my father growls in protest, magic surges through the cavern. "I'm not going to let her offer herself up to be slaughtered. My daughter is not a monster and she is far from evil."

"She's thrown herself into danger to protect us more than once," Hemlock says, voice hesitant.

"Because she *knew* that she's evil! It's all a ploy to try and trick us!" Helena protests, voice growing louder. I look over my shoulder and meet Eleazar's eyes around Odin's body, it takes me a moment to place the look that's overtaken his face.

He looks as if he doesn't even know me.

I suppose he never did.

"I have Ama's back. I will fight anyone who tries to attack her while she tries to get the magic from the creature. I will protect her." Odin declares. Thunder booms throughout the cave as heavy rain begins to fall. "She deserves the right to show us that her magic isn't like the other fallen. She deserves the chance to prove it to herself."

I close my eyes and clear my mind, it's extremely difficult but as I count my breaths the world begins to drown out as the echo of rain and thunder calm my nerves. It helps calm my fear and doubt until I am left with nothing but confidence in my ability.

I call the fallen magic forwards as I open my eyes, black mist emerges from my hands and thickens as it breaks through the barrier that is holding the bulburoos. My magic is hungry, diving straight through the bulburoos's mouth. I fall to my knees as my magic dives deeper into the creature, my vision goes black as I brace my hands on the cold stone floor.

I open my eyes again to blinding golden light, I blink rapidly with burning eyes through the light and find my darkness. It spreads through the light like poison, coming to a large black growing density. It connects.

I try my best to pull the density out of the light and towards me, into me. Anywhere to get it out of this creature. It fights against me, making my own magic erratic and uncontrollable. I begin to lose my hold on the darkness, it slips through my fingers like water.

I try again and again to take control once more, but no matter how hard I fight I get nowhere. The darkness is a creature of its own and I have no sway over my magic. It is not something that can be controlled. The creature begins to grow hysterical; painful and angry screeches threaten to blow my eardrums. I blink once more through the light as I lose control of the darkness altogether. I look up to find the creature swinging its large head towards me as the barrier keeping it contained dissolves, it connects with my side and I'm thrown across the cave and into the stone wall.

My entire body explodes with pain as every bone seems to shatter from impact. I fall into a heap on the floor, blood trickles from my split lip as I gasp for air. Each breath in I take burns my lungs.

A deafening roar of pure rage overtakes the cave as the creature charges for me, jaws open and lips pulled back in a feral snarl.

The roar doesn't come from the creature, it comes from the

copper haired fae male that is launching in the air with his sword raised. His golden eyes burn brightly as his pure golden magic mists from his body and wraps around the silver blade of his sword.

There's nothing I can do as Eleazar lands on the creature's back and buries the blade into their thick neck. The magic seizes them, gold and black tendrils begin to wrap around both of them as they're frozen together.

The binds tighten and tighten before they explode, shimmering to the earth as Eleazar and the creature spasm. His golden essence leaves his body as he falls from the creature and to the stone floor, he doesn't move. His golden essence dives into the creature, it falls to the ground and breathes out its life force. Both gold and black essence float over them for a moment before it mists towards the ceiling.

A warm hand grabs me by the arm and drags me up, I gasp in pain as Odin wraps an arm around my waist and begins to run for the cave entrance. I can't control my magic as it flows from me freely, black vines snake the ground in front of us as I manage to place one foot in front of the other.

"We need to get on a rabbit and get out of here. They'll stay with Eleazar, he'll wake in a few moments and the first thing he'll do is come for you. With his essence out of balance and the oath to fulfil, coming for you is the only thing he will be able to do." Odin shouts as the sound of lightning and rain grow louder as we reach the entrance of the cave. Footsteps speed rapidly closer, Odin throws me forward as he turns in time to meet Helena's blade. I stumble down the moss covered stones and reach the grass. Rain soaks me as I look up to see blue electricity erupt through the darkness. A loud crack draws my attention as blue bolts of lightning connect with the earth.

The storm only grows worse as I move forward, I gasp each breath as I try my best to move my feet. I head for the open field, unsure where I'm meant to run to or where to go. I can't reach the forest in time and the rabbits have fled. A female shriek has me stopping and turning. I've only walked a short distance, Odin runs towards me as Helena presses her hands to a deep gash on her thigh.

"Come on!" Odin shouts, grabbing my arm once more. I look from Helena to see copper hair flailing in the wind. The auburn strands dance rapidly around the hardened angles of the male's face as he emerges from the darkness of the cave, blood stained sword in his right hand.

Never ending black eyes meet mine. His once golden eyes are now gone, replaced by darkness. The Eleazar I know is gone and now I am facing the hunter. Odin pulls me after him, desperately trying to give me a chance.

"I can't win this," I yell. My words scratch my throat as I pull Odin to a stop. I stumble backwards as I turn to see Eleazar stalking towards us with slow precision. Odin tries to get in between us but is launched by an invisible force to the side, thrown too far away to protect me as Eleazar reaches me.

Danger. Danger. Danger.

My magic screams inside of me, rising to try and protect its host. I can't fight against it so I let it take control, moving freely from my body as it pleases. I am exhausted, my magic is eating away at any energy and life I have.

I move to the side, just escaping Eleazar's blade as he swings it down. The air of the sword brushes against my bare arm.

"Eleazar it's me!" I yell as I twirl towards him but trip over my foot as he swings again, I don't escape in time. The sword slices cleanly through my left slide, blind pain overtakes me as a scream rips from my throat. I look down at the blood that flows freely down my side.

I numbly press my hand to the wound and pull it away, staring at the deep red blood covering my hand. My blood.

Before he can take another swing, the earth groans as white ghostly spirits begin to claw their way out of the ground, there are hundreds of them emerging on the field as the storm rages on. The closest spirits rush forward and their energy throws Eleazar backwards, enough for me to take a single step backwards. My knees wobble as I feel myself beginning to weaken.

My energy is leaving me faster than ever, leaving behind a deep and heavy urge to close my eyes and sleep. I press both hands to my side, gagging as I feel some sort of organ threatening to slip out of the deep cut.

"I will find you if you escape. Through heaven and hell, earth and space, I vow I will scour this earth and find *you*," Eleazar declares, his words cement and bind him to me. Thin golden threads glow brightly between us before snapping. I cough and spit blood out onto the ground. Father screams behind Eleazar. I risk a glance to see that Hemlock, father and Helena are surrounded by fallen spirits. Unable to move from where they stand. Father fights viciously, his violet eyes flaring each time he tries and fails to use his magic. I look to Eleazar once more as he reaches me, the spirits unable to stop him this time from the oath that binds him to killing the fallen.

I brace myself for the killing blow, keeping my eyes on his. *I'm sorry. I forgive you. I love you. I will find you in our next life and each one we have together after that.*

A warm, lean frame throws me backwards. A strong wind wraps around my back and legs and stops me from collapsing as I stand, only to see Eleazar's blade being driven down into Odin. His deep maroon handkerchief flutters to the ground. He raises his own blade to meet Eleazar's.

He isn't fast enough.

A raw agonising scream rips from my throat as the blood stained blade embeds into the soft skin between Odin's shoulder and throat. Odin gurgles in shock as Eleazar rips the blade from him. His black eyes look at Odin, tilting his head in an animalistic way.

Odin collapses to the ground, blood pools around his head and shoulders as the deep gash that tethers his head to his shoulders pulses with every beat of his heart.

Blood spills from his mouth as he coughs, his dark hair sticks to his forehead as he tilts his paling face towards me. The edges of my vision begin to darken and I know the shadows have come to whisk me away.

Odin's sacrifice has given me the few seconds I needed to escape with my life.

I look to Eleazar to see one of his black eyes flare golden. He looks down with me as Odin bleeds out, shock covers his features.

"Go."

Odin's last word rattles around in my brain, tethering me to this life as his chest stills and those deep brown eyes dull. Tears flow as darkness begins to envelope me, I'm screaming with agony as Odin's still face is gone and I'm wrapped in the warmth of darkness. I let myself fall into it, not caring if it takes me to the Underworld or beyond.

Go.

CHAPTER
29

I gasp in a shaky breath as my screams come to a stop and the darkness unwraps me. I fall to the ground, the impact has the wound at my side reopening. I groan in agony as I press both hands to my side, I roll onto my back and take laboured breaths. Warm sunlight bears down on me, not even its warmth can chase awake the cold grip that death has on me.

I look to the side to find a small, overgrown cottage. Deep green vines with lilac flowers wrap around the wooden structure, puncturing through the small glass window with black thorns. A small garden runs along the front of the cottage, overgrown with weeds and wild flowers. I have no idea where I am. I roll my head to the other side to find a small, thin forest covering the area around me. Peaks of mountains roll as far as I can see. Wherever I've been spat out, it's on the top of a smooth mountain. No one will find my body up here.

I cough, my chest rattles with the effort as blood splatters my chin and lips. I'm dying.

Odin is gone. Eleazar is hunting me, even though I'm most likely going to be gone before he finds me. I've betrayed everyone and I failed to save the bulburoos. I failed Odin, Eleazar, Hemlock and my father.

My betrayal has cost me everything and I've failed.

"Well, that was a spectacular show indeed," Salis purrs, his voice coming from across the clearing. I tilt my head to the side to see him emerge from the forest and walk towards me. His eyes are hungry as he looks over my broken figure.

"Go to hell," I whisper. A coughing fit takes control of me again, ending in a groan as my body aches.

"Only if you come with me, dear Amaryllis." He stops a few feet from me, his lips peel back in a snarl as he looks to the other side of the clearing. "What are *you* doing here?" he growls low.

"I cannot let you take this girl," Du'ur says, her voice sounds full of life and light. Such a change to the darkness that twines with each word Salis speaks.

"You don't have a say," Salis threatens, "she is *mine*. The magic in her essence is *mine*. You have no right or say in taking her from me."

I find the energy to turn my head towards Du'ur, she looks as stunning as she did in that crystal cave. Her golden hair flows like liquid fire around her heart shaped face, those unnerving galaxy eyes flicker towards me before looking back to Salis. A small, brown kitten squirms in her arms. The tips of its ears are black, as is its tail and two front paws. Tiny meows reach my ears as it claws at her arm.

"If you haven't noticed dear, she is almost crossing the line of death. She has only half of your magic that she was born with. I'm sure you can feel it already seeping back into you," Du'ur says calmly as she begins to stroke the restless kitten.

"I am entitled to *all* of my magic."

"Yes, you've made that well known. She is dying, Salis and I do not wish to see her perish. Can't you see the purpose she has? Can't you feel the earth around us crying at the loss of her?" Du'ur demands. Salis scowls, darkness begins to rapidly spin around his legs.

"I do not care of the purpose you claim she has. It is you against I and we both know there is no room for life in death."

"Ah Salis, forever the greedy bastard aren't you?" A new voice chuckles, it's sweet like honey. A female with golden skin and deep green hair emerges from behind Du'ur. Her multi-coloured eyes of blue and purple find mine, "Oh honey."

"Ma'an, forever a displeasure to see you," Salis grits. She shrugs her thin shoulders, blue and purple eyes flicker to him as she smiles sweetly. The grass at her feet begins to grow and gently caress her calves and soak in the golden glow of her skin. The goddess of day.

"I wouldn't be here if it wasn't for Du'ur. She has reason to believe the girl must live. Who am I to argue with the goddess of life?" She walks over to me, crouching down near my head. Her shadow covers my face as she peers down at me. She clicks her tongue as her large doe eyes search mine. "She has fight in her. Any other faerie would have become one with the earth already."

"Comforting," I murmur. My lungs struggle to draw in breathe, I'm losing my grasp on reality faster than this goddess believes. She smiles down at me before rising.

"It is two against one. You may not take her."

"You both have little choice. She comes with me today. The two of you alone cannot replenish her magic." Salis harnesses his darkness like a weapon as black vines burst from the ground and encase my wrists and ankles. I don't struggle against their hold on me.

"I'm assuming seeing me won't please you?" Another female emerges from behind Du'ur. Ma'an walks over to them and takes her place beside them. The new female has stars in her eyes, her skin is a map of constellations in the night sky.

"Nula." Salis begins to chuckle. "All three goddesses here to best me. Why is this one soul so important to you all?"

"Every soul is important to me. I will not let you take hers."

"Her soul is mine to take!" Salis yells, dark clouds begin to gather in the sky above us. Large, fat droplets of water begin to lazily hit my skin.

"With the other two goddesses of sacred magic here with me, I declare that the soul of Amaryllis Morgan is not yours to take. I will use our combined sacred magic to bind her to this world and use a small essence of my own life to keep her here." Du'ur begins to walk towards me, the other two goddesses also follow suit. Du'ur passes the kitten to Nula, who clicks her tongue at the small thing.

"This...this is unheard of!" Salis comes closer, rage billows off of him in waves.

"She will be the first to have fallen and sacred magic," Du'ur murmurs, crouching beside me. With one sweep of her hand the dark vines unwrap themselves from me and swim back to Salis.

"I am not leaving without out something. Her soul is rightfully mine to take."

An idea strikes me, I try and fail to swallow through the dryness in my mouth "Once a month on a full moon, from the sun set to sun rise, you may take me to the Underworld," I manage to whisper. Salis snaps his attention towards me and his jaw tightens. "I know how much you like to bargain."

Another death rattle shakes my lungs. I'm so cold.

"For twelve hours of each month you'll willingly come with me to the Underworld?" Salis licks his lips.

"Yes."

"Amaryllis you do not know what you are offering him," Du'ur murmurs, resting her warm palm on my sweat slickened forehead.

"It's okay. I know." I feel the urge to cough again, Du'ur rests her other hand on my chest and the itch disappears. It's a short-lived release.

"Save your words. I do not like this, but if it is the only way for Salis to accept my request, then so be it." She looks towards him. "Do you accept?"

"Yes. I accept." He chuckles darkly, "I will see you soon, Amaryllis. We are going to have centuries of fun. You will be mine."

The darkness lingering in the clearing disappears as light and life surround me. Nula and Ma'an approach, both looking down at me. Nula's black, cropped straight hair spills over her shoulder as she leans towards me.

"It's been so long since we've done this," she says, reaching down to press two fingers to my forehead. Du'ur presses both of her hands on my chest while Ma'an presses her hands onto my thighs. Life vibrates from each of them, warm and welcoming.

"This will not hurt," Du'ur murmurs. My eyes flutter closed as my body finally gives in to the darkness. Warmth begins to spill from my forehead, chest and legs. It moves like honey through my vacant body, golden tendrils of sacred magic scatter throughout and bind to the remaining fallen magic that swims in my veins.

I lose track of time as I lay there in the darkness with my body beginning to burn with life. Still my heart does not beat in my chest, still my soul floats in the empty vessel.

"Now, I will give you life," Du'ur whispers. Her soft, cold lips press to my own as she blows a deep breath into me. My lungs expand with life as Du'ur pulls away, I take a gasping breath of my own as my eyes open. My heart begins to beat in my chest once more and the pain of my wounds comes back to me in full force.

"Recovery will be hard, but you will live," Nula comments, taking her fingers from my head. Ma'an lets go of my legs as Du'ur still lingers by my side. I meet her galaxy eyes to find worry lining them.

"This has never happened before. I am unsure of how your magic will react. You live with sacred and fallen magic and the essence of a goddess."

"Why did you do this for me?" I whisper. She gives me a sad smile and gently pats my cheek.

"How could I not? You have a heart of gold. I could not let that foul god take you to the underworld forevermore. You deserve a better life than that." Du'ur stands tall and takes the kitten from Nula.

Nula crouches down and with the help of Ma'an I'm able to sit. I look down at my side to find the wound sealed with a silver scar that has pink, purple and blue sparkles throughout it. I look to Du'ur in question.

"I have sealed your wound. It is still unhealed, but you will not die from it." She smiles down at me radiantly.

"Thank you." I brace myself, gathering the courage to stand when she gently places the small kitten at my feet. It yowls as it scampers over my legs and onto my chest. It paws at my shoulders as it buries its face into my neck. I bring a hand up and cover it, gently rubbing my fingers against its soft fur.

"He wasn't ready to leave you just yet. You will need a protector in this world." Du'ur gestures to the kitten.

"What are you saying?" I ask, hope flaring in my chest.

"Odin will be your protector, although he now lives in a different form."

I begin to cry again. I pull the kitten away from my neck and hold it in front of my face. Intelligent, chestnut brown eyes meet mine. "I am so sorry, Odin." I cradle him to my chest, rocking back and forth. He's still here, although not how I wish he was.

"He forgives you, as he forgives Eleazar. This cottage is yours to live in. I returned you to the human realm and you'll be pleased to know Elderview is only a four-day journey away when you wish to return to your mother and father to explain." Du'ur clasps her hands behind her back. "It has everything you need to survive. There is running water not far from here."

"I don't deserve this." I look up at her, wiping the tears from my cheeks. The sun shines from behind her, her golden hair creates a halo around her figure. She truly is the most gorgeous goddess.

"Yes, you do. You have survived every hardship this life has thrown at you no matter how unfair it has been. It will never be easy being who you are, but there is no one else in this world you should wish to be. Take pride in knowing you faced the odds and conquered them. The time for healing is now and tomorrow, tomorrow is a new day. Become the woman you are meant to be Amaryllis, do more than survive. Live."

The three goddesses disappear into thin air without another word. I look down at Odin, trying to process what has happened. I am alive. I have survived with the help of three generous goddesses. I may have bargained with Salis, but I am here.

"I suppose we should see what the cottage is like." I wince as I stand, holding Odin in my arms. I look over the rolling mountains, their deep green peaks are covered with the life of new spring blooming.

Warm tears streak my face as I limp towards the cottage. I hold Odin in one hand and gently pull away the green vines that encase the wooden door. I push it inwards and duck inside. It's only small, a kitchen sits to my left with a thick layer of dust covering the surface of a round wooden table and kitchen cabinet that runs against the wall. I continue down the hall and push open the door to my right, a large bed takes up most of the room. The dark blue blanket has no trace of dust, as does no other part of the bedroom, a last parting gift from the goddess. I continue down the hall and enter the last wide room, a brick fireplace sits at the back of the room. Two chairs have been pushed against the far wall with other small trinkets.

I place Odin down and walk back into the kitchen, I supress a cough as I rummage through the cabinet under the silver sink. I find a dusting brush before rising. Odin sits on the table, his small tail curls around his paws as he looks up at me.

"I'm glad you decided to come back for me. You are a friend I don't deserve." I reach out and scratch behind his ears, he purrs loudly. "I promise your sacrifice will be worth it. Welcome home, Odin." I leave Odin and push open the kitchen window, a cool breeze stirs my hair as I look out over the rolling mountains of my home.

I will honour your words Du'ur. I will live and my life will be one worthy of having. Today I will heal but tomorrow? Tomorrow I will learn to live.

EPILOGUE

six months later

"Rosemary, thyme, sage," I say out loud as I cut the herbs from their branch in the small garden outside my cottage. Odin curls his tail around my legs before he trots over to the edge of the garden. My chest heats with warmth as I send a small breeze towards him, picking up a leaf on the way. It's been six months since I collapsed in the dirt with my dying breath. Six months I've spent recovering and turning this cottage into my home, as well as Odin's. We've found a silent way to communicate and he's helped me tremendously with my sacred magic.

The leaf hits the back of his head; he twirls around and narrows his eyes at me before bounding over to me. I laugh as he jumps up at me, I hold him with one hand and my small wooden basket full of herbs with the other. He's large for a cat, reaching my knees when he stands beside me.

"Silly kitty," I coo, holding him tightly to me. One ear flattens against his head, but he paws at my cheek gently. I roll my eyes at him as I walk through the propped open door. My heart has healed from a majority of the heartbreak I suffered, but when its nighttime and I am alone with nothing but my thoughts I can feel the deep crevice that may never heal.

A deep crevice I created between me and El—

I can't even think his name without the pain flaring like a brand-new heartbreak. I can only hope he has moved on from the pain I've caused. Odin meows in my arms and I sit him down, he trots into the living room with his tail raised as I follow behind.

I walk into the room and sit the basket beside the burning hearth, a black cauldron hangs from a metal beam I'd created. The water boils and bubbles, the hint of lavender hangs in the air. I'd refurnished the living room, hanging up trinkets from Elderview and throwing down a new rug I'd picked up from Elk. I'd returned home twice and was able to talk to my mother and father, we'd all cried together as I told them everything.

They still love me regardless of what magic I have.

I'd made the journey to Elk after leaving Elderview but only stayed for the day. Father had been kind enough to bring Ash home and I was more than overwhelmed when I was able to ride him. Father insisted I take him back to the cottage with me, so now he plucks at the grass outside the cottage. Soon I'd have to get father up here to help me build a small stable for him in the cooler and hotter months. I know Odin doesn't mind the company of another animal.

"Today we'll make three potions for protection and three for healing. I'm sure Elk is running low on them," I murmur to Odin. I kneel down on the carpet and begin to rummage through my basket of herbs. I've begun to make the journey to small towns with my trusty cat as my protector and my noble steed as my feet. I take small potions and charms enchanted with sacred magic.

I begin to hum as I pluck out the herbs I need for the

protection potion. I hold the herbs in one hand before untying my apron from my waist. I lay it down to my side and lay the herbs on top of it. I brush my hair back over my shoulders, the length now reaches my waist. I look more like mother than ever these days. I adjust the thin straps of my pale blue dress when Odin hisses to my left. My humming cuts off as I look over to see him puffed out twice his size and snarling towards the door.

"What on earth..." I stand and turn to find *him* standing in the doorway to my cottage. His copper hair catches on a cool breeze. It'd been cut across his chest. His large frame takes up the entire doorway. My brain refuses to form coherent thoughts as my eyes trail over his muscular form, from his brown worn boots to the two sword handles that emerge over his shoulders. We're both silent, barely breathing as we take in one another.

"I told you I'd find you," he says calmly. A statement.

"Are you here to fulfil your oath?" I swallow against my throat thickening. My heart is a wild bird in my chest, seeing him here and having him so close is exposing every wound I've nursed for the last six months.

"No."

I look at him surprised, I frown slightly as I slide my hands into the pockets of my dress. "What are you here for then?"

"You deceived me. You betrayed me," he states, voice thickening with emotion as his chest rises with each heavy breath. "You left me."

"I couldn't exactly stay, could I? Yes, I did. I can't return and change the choices I chose. I chose them for a reason." Odin yowls in warning when Eleazar takes another step forward, I lean down and brush my hand against his back. "Hush, Odin."

"What did you just say?"

I look up to see Eleazar staring at the cat. "After...after I left,

I emerged here. Du'ur and Salis appeared, I struck a deal with Salis in order to live with sacred and fallen magic. Salis left and Du'ur, Ma'an and Nula healed me. She gave me this kitten." I scratch behind Odin's ear. "she told me he wasn't ready to leave me alone and that I needed a protector. It's still Odin, he's just in a different form."

Eleazar is silent, so silent I can hear the bubbling of the boiling water in the cauldron behind me. I clasp my hands in front of me, he continues to stare at Odin's cat form. Odin's ears perk as he slowly trots over to Eleazar, butting his head against his thigh as he purrs.

"He forgives you," I say quietly, watching as Eleazar reaches down and scoops Odin up in his arms. He has a silent tear streaming down his cheek as Odin paws at his face.

"You're a better man than I," he murmurs to Odin before gently putting him back on the ground. Odin bounds back over to me, taking a seat at my feet as he stares up at Eleazar. I've come to love him and enjoy his company. He is my little protector indeed.

"What deal did you strike with Salis?" Eleazar asks, crossing his arms over his chest.

"Every full moon, from sundown to sun set he will retrieve me and take me to the Underworld. I've been six times. It's quite boring but keeps him happy that I'm fulfilling my promise."

"I don't like it."

I smirk softly, "You don't like any choice I make."

"Can you blame me?" He arches an eyebrow, still watching me with those guarded eyes.

"No, I don't. It's been a pleasure to see you again Eleazar but what is your purpose of being here? I don't want your harsh words or regrets if you're not here to kill me."

"Have you noticed I haven't done that yet?" he asks. I purse my lips in thought.

"I don't know what you're hoping for me to say."

"I can't fulfil the oath because there is *no oath to fulfil.*"

I let his words wash over me and blink slowly, that means... that means he isn't oath bound anymore. Somehow, he's managed to escape the oath and the ties to it. My heart rises in my chest with hope as I look up at him, really look at him.

"What do you mean by that?" I find my voice, not letting complete hope strangle me just yet.

"It means I worked tirelessly to get out of the oath, with your father's help and sway he was able to convince the queen that there is no use for me anymore. There hasn't been a fallen for centuries...until you. Amaryllis, you cannot help what power you were born with, and I have no doubt in my mind that you could never be evil. Faerie kind have a skewered image for the fallen, but I will always know your heart."

He takes a step forward and another, slowly closing the distance between us. He easily covers the distance from the doorway to where I stand in the living room, his vibrant golden eyes devour me. "I have many regrets in this lifetime...loving you will *never* be one of them. Where you go, I go. My heart is yours Amaryllis, it has been from the moment I laid eyes on you."

"But...how can you forgive me for what I did? I lied to you, betrayed you?" I frown, not wanting to give myself false hope. This could be a cruel joke, a way to get back at me for what I've done. He shakes his head and closes the distance between us in two large strides. His calloused hands take my cheeks gently as he tips my face towards his. His golden eyes swirl, flames I'd let devour me.

"I wouldn't be here now if I hadn't come to terms with what you've done. It took me a few months to return to myself, my essence returned and is full once more. I understood why you deceived me and kept your secrets as much as I don't like to admit it. You didn't have a choice. I wouldn't have been able to stop myself from following through with the oath. You were protecting yourself as well as protecting me." His thumbs caress my cheeks as silent tears begin to streak my face.

"I don't deserve you."

"It is I that doesn't deserve you. If you will give me the chance I would like to try again and show you that I'm a man worthy of your love. I know we will face hurdles but together we are a force to be reckoned with. All we have is now and I would hate to spend a moment longer without you by my side."

"Eleazar—"

He brings his lips to my own, his mouth soft and warm and tasting exactly like I remember it. Exactly how I envisioned on many lonely nights. "Please. Please say yes," he whispers against my lips. Odin meows, rubbing his large head against my calf before winding his body around Eleazar's leg, butting his head as he twirls around us both.

I crack a small smile, "I guess we have Odin's approval."

My heart thunders in my chest as I wind my arms around his waist, pulling his hard body to the soft crevices of my own. I look up into his eyes and know that there isn't anything more I want in this life than the man that stands in front of me and the future he's offering. Our love has conquered the odds, gone the extra mile and has prevailed.

"Yes. Where you go, I go. I love you Eleazar. I haven't stopped."

He sweeps his arms around me as his lips take control of my own again, I hold onto him for dear life as I kiss him back, each kiss an apology words will never be enough for. He seems to understand as he kisses me back just as fiercely. He breaks from the kiss and smiles down at me, "I love you too, my little flower."

I smile back up at him as my heart explodes with light.

I realise for six months I have just been surviving.

But tomorrow? Tomorrow I will begin to *live.*

ACKNOWLEDGMENTS

Here we are yet again, at the end of yet another book. Another story. Another life that came to me suddenly and demanded their story to be told. Originally, I never planned to write another book in the Enchanted Series, but I knew I had to tell Ama's story.

I'd like to say a huge thank you to the book community on Instagram, the constant support and encouragement helps writes more than they realise! Every author has doubts about their work and sharing an intimate part of themselves like this, so knowing there's people out there who are excited for this piece of you is more than enough to keep going and giving.

Tara Routley, thank you for once again taking this manuscript and polishing it to perfection! I'm so glad you enjoy following along with these stories and pour your heart into them as much as I do. Without you, this script would still be sitting forgotten in my folder.

A huge shout out to my amazing Beta Readers, Courtney, Melisa, Kelli. Angel, Natalie, bookdragonstbr, maberreads, phoebejane93, my_last_writes, Jodie, Samantha, Clare, Trinh, Laura. Without you wonderful people I'd still be rolling in self doubt about this book! I loved your feedback and the passion you also had for Ama's story!

Thanks to everyone in my close knit life for supporting me and allowing me to escape from reality to create tales, this wouldn't be possible if I never had a moment to spare for myself.

And finally, a huge thank you to my readers. You're truly the icing on the cake, if you've come this far and have read my other books, I am so grateful for you. No words can describe the love I have for my original readers and my new ones. Well, I best be onto my next book now! Keep an eye out 😉

About the Author

Shana J. Caldwell is an Australian self-published author, who is either knee deep in reading or crouched over her laptop with her trusty cat, Luna, as her writing companion. When she's not writing she's got her nose stuck between the pages of a book or can be found with a coffee in hand.

Visit her website:
https://shanacaldwell03.wixsite.com/website

Follow Shana on:

facebook.com/shanajcaldwell
twitter.com/ShanaJCaldwell1
instagram.com/shanajcaldwellbooks

BOOKS BY SHANA J. CALDWELL

Immortal Awakening series

Immortal Awakening

Immortal Suffering

Immortal Reckoning

Enchanted Series

Enchantment of Darkness

Enchantment of Thorns